...ise for

Good-Time Boys

I was completely charmed by Sonny and the little we learn about his brothers and am thrilled to report that the other books in this series are just as enchanting so be sure that you pick up the whole series. Believe me, they're definitely worth it. ~ *Romance Junkies*

Ms. Lynne has continued her action packed series and this book is no exception. From the very start, the reader is pulled into the story with real-to-life characters and a plot line... ~ *Fallen Angels Reviews*

This book has lots of great scenes which not only had me anticipating the next book in this series – Twin Temptations. ~ *Romance Junkies*

Ms. Lynne has written a very loving and thought-provoking story that is captivating from the start. ~ *Fallen Angels Reviews*

Carol Lynne proves that literary gay sex does not have to be rough to be exciting, and that love is a universal turn-on. ~ *Author, Lisabet Sarai*

GOOD-TIME BOYS

Sonny's Salvation

Garron's Gift

Rawley's Redemption

Twin Temptations

CAROL LYNNE

SONNY'S
SALVATION

Dedication

To the amazing Drew Hunt, and my friends, Brynn, Lacey and Bronwyn.

Chapter One

Sonny Good hung up the phone cussing a blue streak. His older brother, and town Sheriff, raised his eyebrows as he walked into the kitchen. "What's got you so fired up this morning?" Rawley Good took a mug out of the cabinet and poured a strong cup of coffee.

"That new guy next door's bull got into our pasture last night. Shelby thinks he might have bred some of my Angus." Sonny sat back down at the kitchen table and took another gulp of his coffee, the burn going down his throat just what he needed. "I tell ya. That city boy doesn't deserve a ranch. Why Jack decided to sell it to him and not me is beyond me. I bet the guy's never even seen a cow before last week."

Rawley chuckled. "Jack always had a reason for everything he ever did. I bet we'll figure it out eventually. Didn't you say Jack told you he met the city fella when he went to Chicago for the cattle convention? Maybe he saw somethin' in him that made Jack think he'd make a good rancher. It's only been a week. Cut the poor guy some slack. Maybe if you tried helping him instead of always criticising he'd turn into a damn fine rancher." Rawley rocked back in his chair, tipping it back onto two legs. Sonny gave him the look. Their momma would have killed Rawley for doing that had she still been there.

Taking his empty cup to the sink, Sonny ran water over it and set it in the dish drainer. "No, I think I'll just ride the city fella out. Let him screw up so bad he's forced to sell the ranch to me." He took his battered straw cowboy hat off the hook by the door and adjusted it on his head. "Will you be home for supper?"

Setting his chair on all four legs, Rawley shook his head. "I've got a date with Meg. I probably won't be home at all. I'll just pack an extra uniform in the cruiser."

Sonny started to turn around and stopped. "When are you gonna just admit you're gay and stop stringing that poor girl along? It's been almost two years, if it hasn't happened by now, it's not gonna."

Rawley shook his head as he put his cup on the dish drainer. "I'm not gay. Three gay Goods are enough. I've had my share of fights with some of the people in this town. I'm not interested in another. Besides, how long do you think it would take this town to run off a gay Sheriff? And for the record, Meg and I are perfectly happy." Rawley took his Sheriff's Stetson off the peg by the door. "Now I've told you my personal business, don't bring it up again." Rawley shoved past Sonny and walked to the brown and tan sheriff's SUV.

Shaking his head, Sonny strode towards the barn hollering for his ranch hand. "Shelby. Let's get that fence fixed."

* * * *

It was close on seven-thirty when Sonny quit for the day. His back felt tender as he slipped off his T-shirt. Summers in

Nebraska were damn hot and this year was no exception. As much as he wanted to sit in front of the television in the air conditioned house and drink a beer, his stomach told him he also needed food.

Walking into the house, Sonny stripped off the rest of his clothes on the way to the bathroom. He figured he would take a quick cold shower and head in to the Dead Zone for a beer and a bite to eat.

Standing under the cool spray, Sonny soaped his hands and ran them over his body. He was the first to admit he wasn't a big tough cowboy like folks saw in the movies. He stood only five foot nine and weighed no more than one hundred eighty pounds. His muscles though, those he was plenty proud of. Not buffed up like some crazy weight lifter but they looked good on his smaller than average frame.

Running his hand down, Sonny quickly relieved himself of the day's tension. After coming, he cleaned up again and turned off the shower. He needed to get laid and stop taking care of it himself, he decided as he put on a fresh pair of jeans and a tight black T-shirt.

Grabbing his keys off the dresser and putting on his black-dress cowboy hat, Sonny headed into town. His stomach growled as he pulled into the Dead Zone's parking lot. It looked pretty empty, but then it was only Tuesday. The Zone was normally packed on a Friday and Saturday once everyone's work was done for the week. Although for Sonny, work was never done. He'd come back home when his daddy died and took over the ranch for his momma. She'd been happy to hand over the duties and went to live with her sister in Florida. He knew one of his brothers could've taken over, but Rawley was the town's sheriff and his twin baby brothers ran their own feedlot. So Sonny quit his job with the FBI and returned to Summerville.

Opening the heavy bar door, he tried to adjust his eyes to the dim lighting inside. He walked towards his usual table in the back and took a seat. Lilly came right over.

"Hi, gorgeous. You want the usual?" Lilly cracked her gum and winked at him. He'd known Lilly since she was a girl in pigtails. She was only twenty-one now, and he didn't understand what her momma was thinking letting a beauty like her work in a rowdy cowboy bar.

"Yeah. Give me the usual." Sonny finally looked around. "Seems kinda dead in here tonight." Sonny adjusted his black dress Stetson. This was one place that taking it off wasn't necessary.

Lilly nodded her head. "Yeah, that's why I'm taking off as soon as I get your order. The new bartender, Garron, will bring it over. I'll make sure I get your beer first though." With another wink, Lilly walked up to the bar and talked to the bartender. Gary? Garron. That was it.

Sonny looked at the hulking man behind the bar, definitely his type. Shoulder length dark brown hair held back in some sort of ponytail. He was big, at least six three with shoulders wider than a barn. He looked a little rough too. That was also how Sonny liked them. If he wanted sweetness and walks in the moonlight he'd be dating a woman. No, Sonny liked his sex hard and fast. Men just didn't require all the other. Sure a quick snuggle before he got up and went home was fine, but he didn't want anyone hanging on to him all the time. When he'd worked for the FBI in Dallas he'd had his share of rough looking biker dudes like this one. They were, by far, his favourite. They never wanted any ties from him. Sex on a regular basis and they were good to go.

Lilly brought him out of his musings by setting his beer in front of him. "I'll catch you later. How are Ranger and Ryker by the way? I haven't seen them in here lately."

Sonny smiled at Lilly. Everyone in town knew she'd had a crush on his twin brothers for years. "Good, the feedlot is going gang busters right now. You should stop in sometime and say hi." Sonny was an evil man and he knew it, his brothers had spent the last four years skirting poor Lilly.

"I might have to do that. See ya later." Lilly took off her dingy apron as she walked towards the bar. She went behind it and picked up her purse saying something to the delicious bartender and pointing towards Sonny. She waved as she walked out the door.

Taking a good swallow of his beer, Sonny continued to watch the bartender. He could see a tribal tattoo of some kind on the back of the guy's neck. It reached around his sides like talons. Fuck that was hot. Sonny wondered if he had any more hidden on his body. From this distance he could tell he had one on each arm plus the one on his neck. What the hell was a biker dude doing in Summerville? Right now Sonny didn't care. As long as he had this nice piece of muscled man to look at, he'd be coming into the Zone more often.

Sonny almost swallowed his tongue as the perfect specimen of manhood came walking towards him with his rib dinner. His eyes were black as coal, framed with long black lashes. Sonny swept his eyes quickly down the long length of the man. Mmm…legs that wouldn't quit ended in a much bigger than average bulge in his low-rise jeans. The tight yellow Dead Zone T-shirt accentuated his sun bronzed skin to perfection. Yum.

His meal was set in front of Sonny bringing him out of his lustful haze. "Rib platter, right?"

Looking up into the face of the God, Sonny nodded and cleared his throat. "Yeah. Could I trouble you for another beer before you leave?"

"No trouble at all." Garron walked back to the bar.

Sonny watched that perfect ass move across the room. He slid his hand down under the table and tried to adjust his steel hard shaft. When Mr. Perfect brought his beer, Sonny smiled. "Looks like I'm your only customer. Care to sit a spell and have a drink with me?" Sonny picked up a sloppy barbequed rib and started eating as he waited for Garron's answer.

Garron watched Sonny eat for a couple seconds then nodded. "I think you could damn near talk me into anything. I'll go get a drink."

When Garron came back, he turned the spindled chair around backward and straddled it. Sonny almost groaned but managed to look unaffected as he licked the sauce off his fingers. He wiped his hand on the napkin and stuck it out. "I'm Rutger Good but that was my dad's name too, so folks just call me Sonny."

Garron stuck out his big hand and enveloped Sonny's. "Good to meet you. I'm Garron. Most folks just look at me funny and don't call me anything."

The heat from Garron's hand travelled up Sonny's arm and straight to his already aching erection. When Sonny tried to release him, Garron held on. "Can I be honest with you?"

Sonny swallowed and nodded. "Sure."

"Lilly told me that you might be looking for a bed warmer and I'd like to apply for the position, or positions." He winked and released Sonny's hand.

Barely managing not to swallow his tongue, Sonny took a gulp of beer. "Why'd Lilly tell you something like that?"

Shrugging his shoulders, Garron watched Sonny pick up another rib. Sonny felt Garron's eyes on him as he ate his dinner with gusto. When Sonny started to lick his fingers, Garron grabbed Sonny's hand in mid-air. He brought the hand to his mouth and slowly sucked the sauce off his fingers.

Eyes rolling to the back of his head, Sonny moaned. "Ah fuck. Why'd ya have to go and do that?" Sonny opened his eyes and looked at Garron. "Consider the position filled. What time do you get off?"

Garron stood and looked around at the empty bar. He pulled Sonny up from his chair and lead him towards the bathroom. As soon as the door was shut and locked, Garron slammed Sonny up against the wall. "I'm getting off in about three minutes." He started unfastening Sonny's jeans. "You?"

"Hell yeah." Sonny reached for those sexy low-risers. He was surprised when he pulled up Garron's T-shirt and was greeted by a cock head sticking out the waistband. "Damn that's sexy. Could get kinda dangerous though. You shouldn't be flashing that pretty thing around to just anyone in this town. Could get a fella in a hell of a lot of trouble."

Garron thrust into Sonny's hand as he lowered Sonny's zipper. "You're the first to make Goliath take notice. And he's mighty glad you did." Garron wrapped his hand around Sonny's bigger than average cock and began stroking it. Sonny returned the favour and kissed him. It wasn't gentle or sweet, but a claiming kiss, all tongue and teeth.

Oh shit, this man felt good. When Garron insinuated his long leg between Sonny's, he broke the kiss and flung his head back, hitting the wall behind him with a solid thump. "Oh fuck that's good. Been too long." Sonny rode Garron's thigh like the cowboy he was. "Gonna come, man." Sonny had the presence of mind to lift Garron's T-shirt higher so his seed wouldn't ruin it. His cock erupted with spurt after spurt of his pearly essence.

Garron looked down as his hand milked Sonny's cock. The sight of Sonny's seed seemed to send Garron over the edge.

As his stomach muscles clenched and his cock continued to shoot, Garron leaned in to him and took another deep kiss. "Beautiful." He attacked Sonny's mouth again. "You're fuckin' beautiful, man." He pulled away and wet some paper towels. Cleaning them both up Garron looked into his eyes. "I'm off work in about three hours. You wanna stay or do you wanna meet me somewhere?"

Sonny stuffed his still half-hard cock into his jeans. "Why don't you come by the ranch and let yourself in. I'll be naked and waiting in the first bedroom at the top of the stairs." He ran his hand down the front of Garron's jeans.

"Sounds good to me. Just give me some directions and I'll be there as soon as I can." Garron thrust his hips against Sonny.

"Go down Fisher road about seven miles. It's the Flying G." Sonny leaned in and kissed Garron one more time.

"Cool. That's right next door to my brother's place. I won't have far to go to get clean clothes in the morning." Garron unlocked the restroom door and started to walk out.

Sonny stopped him with a hand on the door. "You're Jeb Greeley's brother?"

Garron nodded. "Yeah. Why?"

Sonny felt the heat rise in his face. "Because that no good son-of-a-bitch bought that ranch out from under me. He doesn't know a damn thing about ranching. He even let his Hereford bull get in with my Black Angus."

Garron narrowed his eyes at Sonny. "I'm not the one to tell the tale, but I'll say up front that Jeb didn't buy that ranch out from under you. The rest you'll have to discuss with him. I'm his brother, not his keeper." Garron put his hands on either side of Sonny's face and tilted it up to meet his eyes. "Is this gonna be a problem?"

Breaking eye contact, Sonny shrugged. "Don't know. Need some time to think about it." He looked back up at Garron. "You have a problem with that?"

Garron leaned down and swiped his tongue across Sonny's lips. "No problem here, cowboy. You're too damn pretty to just throw away because you have a problem with my brother. When you work it out in that finer-than-fuck head of yours, come see me." Garron picked Sonny up and physically moved him out of his way. Before setting him back on his feet, Garron kissed him, slow and deep. He opened the door and looked back at him. "Don't think too long. I want a piece of that ass and I'm not gonna be able to think of anything else until I get it."

Chapter Two

Friday afternoon, Sonny was in his office doing some bookkeeping when his brother Ranger came in. "Hey bro. How's it going?" He flopped down on the red leather couch and put his feet up on the coffee table.

Grunting, Sonny motioned towards Ranger's feet. "Get your feet off the table, boy. Were you raised in a barn?"

"Well, yes, actually, I believe I was. As were we all. But I guess that answers my question." Ranger took his booted feet off the table and stood. "Rawley came by the lot today and said you've been in a foul mood. What's up?"

"Nothing's up. Just trying to figure out how I'm gonna expand this ranch enough to make some more money." Sonny got up and fixed a glass of scotch and water.

Ranger walked towards the bar. "I thought the ranch made good money? What's happened?" Ranger fixed his own drink, whiskey straight up.

"The ranch is doing well enough, but what's the point of me giving up my career if I can't better it?" Sonny tossed back his drink in two gulps and set the glass down.

Ranger narrowed his eyes. "You shouldn't have quit your job and come back to run the ranch if you didn't want to. We could've figured something out."

Running his fingers through his midnight black curls, Sonny sighed. "It's not the ranch. I love this place as much as any of us. And it's not quitting my job. I'm just lonely, I guess." Sonny went back to his desk and sat down. "In Dallas I didn't have trouble meeting men, but in Summerville it's next to impossible."

"I thought you were looking towards that new bartender down at the Zone? That's what Lilly said. Thanks for sending her to the feed lot by the way. You're a real peach. It took us over two hours to get rid of her."

"Why did Lilly tell you that?" Sonny shook his head and waved his hand. "Well I guess it doesn't matter anyway. I liked him yeah, but he's Jeb Greeley's brother. I just can't do it. No matter how much I think about all that hair and those tattoos. I can't bed my biggest enemy's brother."

"Enemy hell. You've never even introduced yourself to the man. How can he be your enemy?" Ranger fixed Sonny another drink and passed it over.

Taking the drink, Sonny looked out the window. "I'll tell you how, because I thought I'd always had a special relationship with Jack. He was like an uncle to all of us. I talked to him about his land for years. I practically begged him to let me buy it when he found out he had cancer. He just kept putting me off, and now I know why. He was a greedy sonofabitch. That's the only thing I've been able to come up with."

Ranger took the empty glass from Sonny and walked towards the door. "You and I know that Jack Anderson didn't do anything out of greed. If he sold that land to Jeb Greeley he must've had a damn good reason. Stop feeling sorry for yourself and get over it." Before he disappeared out the door he looked back at Sonny. "Seems to me if you like that fella at the Zone it shouldn't matter who his brother is, or are you just after another piece of ass?"

* * * *

Sonny sat in his blue truck outside the bar. Damn his brother. Between Ranger and the three scotch and waters he'd guzzled down, Sonny was contemplating the unthinkable. He thought of Garron and immediately went hard. Dammit, not now. Willing his erection to subside he thought about all the lonely nights he'd spent since taking over the ranch three years earlier. At thirty-two, he was still a relatively young man. Why shouldn't he continue to sew his wild oats?

With his cock at semi-rest he locked up his truck and went inside. The music and smoke hit him in the face as soon as he opened the door. Nothing like the Zone on a Friday night, he thought. They had a little country band playing in the corner and the dance floor looked filled to capacity.

When he didn't spot an empty table, he looked towards the bar. Garron was talking to one of the cowboys, but his dark brown eyes were trained on Sonny. Sonny nodded and found an empty stool at the end of the bar next to the wall. He watched as Garron filled another tray for Lilly and turned towards him.

Garron wiped the bar down in front of Sonny and smiled. "Good to see you again. What can I get you?"

Almost blurting out what he really wanted, Sonny said, "You can get me a beer, for now." Sonny held Garron's eyes for another couple of seconds.

With a slight lift to the corner of his mouth, Garron went to the cooler. Sonny was impressed that he remembered what brand he drank. He slid it across the bar but refused Sonny's money. "It's on me." He winked bold as you please and went to fill another drink order.

Sonny looked around to see if anyone else had noticed the wink and caught a smiling Lilly looking right at him. Sonny rolled his eyes and shook his head. Damn. It wasn't as if the whole town didn't already know about the gay Goods, but he was used to discreet encounters. Sonny had a feeling that an affair with Garron would be anything but discreet.

Taking a long pull of his beer, Sonny looked around the bar. Same old faces he'd grown up with. He watched as Delbert Short got turned down for a dance by Betty Jameson. Sonny chuckled to himself. He and his brothers had gotten into so much trouble when they were younger. The whole town called them the Good-Time boys because they'd always done exactly what they wanted and suffered the consequences later. He remembered getting Delbert into trouble with his father when he'd made the mistake of going out one night with the Good-Time boys. Delbert hadn't hung around any of them since. Of course it could also have something to do with their sexual preferences, but that was Delbert's problem.

A hand on his arm brought his head back around. Garron was leaning over the bar looking him in the eye. "You gonna stay and wait for me tonight?"

Sonny looked at him for a long time before nodding his head slowly. "Reckon I can do that. I'll have to call Shelby though and tell him to start chores without me in the morning. I've a feeling it might just be a late night." He surprised himself by winking at Garron.

Garron licked his lips. "I get a short break in about forty-five minutes. Not long enough to fuck you, but long enough to get off. Interested?"

"Hell yeah." Sonny pushed up the brim of his hat. "Just tell me where."

Garron actually reached across the bar and tweaked Sonny's nipple through his T-shirt. "The storage room."

Sonny rubbed his nipple as he watched Garron's fine ass retreating. He felt a body pressed against his side and turned his head. "What the hell do you want?"

"I just wanted to tell you how cute you two are. It gives me goose bumps just watching you guys flirt with each other."

"Yeah well don't go spreadin' that around. It's hard enough to be gay in this town without the townspeople thinking we're being too open about it."

Lilly bumped her hip against Sonny. "Well for what it's worth, I think it's hot."

Chuckling, Sonny turned back towards the bar and picked up his beer. He finished the remainder in one swallow then held it up for Garron to see. Garron fished another out of the cooler and brought it over.

Leaning with his forearms on the smooth surface of the mahogany bar, Sonny was mesmerised by the display of muscles trapped under the tight yellow T-shirt. He leaned towards Garron subtly. "I wanna kiss you."

Raising one brow, Garron leaned further forward. His lips came close enough to Sonny that a mere hair wouldn't have been able to pass between them. "Then kiss me."

Sonny thought about the table of red-necks in the corner. Even though most of the town seemed to except him, there were still a few that liked to cause trouble. He and his brothers had been in several big brawls over the years. For the most part, the trouble seemed to die down, but Sonny was afraid it was merely simmering under the surface. He looked back at Lionel and his table of lap-dogs.

To hell with the consequences, Sonny opened his mouth just a bit and thrust his tongue into Garron's mouth for a short but deeply sensuous kiss. They broke apart when they heard a few choice words shouted from around the bar. Seemed they had an audience. Sonny looked into Garron's eyes and winked. He turned around and yelled at the people in the bar he'd grown up with. "Oh right, like you guys have never kissed anyone in public before. Just because my date happens to have a hairier chest than yours is no reason to cause a scene."

That broke the tension and got the whole bar to laughing. Sonny turned back to Garron and rolled his eyes. "Rednecks. You gotta love 'em."

Garron shook his head. "Oh shit. I've a feeling you're gonna get me all kinds of trouble." He winked and went back to work.

* * * *

Once everyone had finally left and they'd cleaned up, Sonny went out to sit in his truck. He waited for Garron to lock up and get on his big black Harley. He felt the rumble in his chest when Garron started the bike. He watched as Garron rode his bike across the parking lot towards his truck. His long legs looked even longer astride that damn thing.

Sonny pushed the power button and his window slid down. "I'll follow you. No sense in you eating my dust the whole way."

Garron nodded and roared off. Sonny put the truck in gear and gave chase. He wished he didn't have to drive his truck home. He could just picture himself on the back of that bike, legs wrapped around Garron as the loud machine took them to heaven. He thought about their earlier rendezvous in the storeroom. You gotta love a man that carried current HIV papers in his wallet. Sonny had never even heard of such a thing, but evidently Garron was serious. He'd gone the day after meeting Sonny and been tested.

Fifteen minutes later they pulled up in front of Sonny's ranch house. It was still a good looking house despite being more than a hundred years old. Each generation made sure they'd left their mark. Sonny had already refurbished the kitchen and bathrooms. He was hoping to make enough profit in the coming season to add on to the deck and maybe install a hot tub.

He stood on the porch as Garron walked towards him. "Come on in. It's not much, but its home." He opened the door and led the way to the kitchen. Opening the fridge, he pulled out two beers and handed one to Garron.

Sonny took Garron's hand and led him up the stairs to his bedroom.

* * * *

Taking a drink of his beer, Garron surveyed the room. He was surprised to see how tidy the room was. He never thought of a cowboy as being particularly neat. "Like to clean do you?"

Sonny took off his hat and placed it on the peg just inside his bedroom door. "I wasn't always this way. It comes from being in the army for four years."

"No shit. I just got out of the marines five years ago." Garron took Sonny's beer from him and set both of them down on the bedside table. He pulled Sonny into his arms and kissed him.

Sonny rimmed Garron's lips with his tongue. "What'd you do after the marines?" He rubbed his hands over Garron's ass.

"I went to work for the Chicago Police Department." Garron looked down at himself. "As you can tell I worked vice until Jeb asked me to come out here for a while."

"No offence, man, but why'd you quit a job with the Chicago PD to come to Nebraska and be a bartender?" Sonny kissed him again before Garron could answer.

"Mmm that's nice." Garron held him even tighter. "I came because Jeb asked me to. We're not only brothers but the only family each of us have. I'd do anything for him." He pulled Sonny's T-shirt off over his head. "More. I need to see more." He went to work on the zipper of Sonny's Wranglers as Sonny toed off his boots.

When Sonny stood before him completely nude Garron stared in awe. "Damn you're fucking perfect. You have women hands down in the pretty department and men in the body department. How is it that you're not attached? Because man I have to tell you. I'm thinking of keeping you tied up in my house for the rest of our lives."

Sonny blushed and looked towards the floor. "If you think I'm pretty please don't go near any of my brothers. I'm the runt of the family."

Garron tipped Sonny's chin back up to meet his eyes. "You're not a runt. You're perfect. I've never in all my life seen eyes the color of yours. What do you even call that shade of blue, or are they purple?" Garron ran his fingertip around each of Sonny's eyes. He fanned the long black lashes on both the top and bottom.

"Momma always called them amethyst. They run in my dad's family. My brothers have them too." Sonny pulled Garron's shirt up. "Let's get you naked. I wanna feel your skin."

When Garron stood before him as naked as the day he was born, Sonny's eyes grew big as saucers. "You look even better than in my fantasies." Sonny ran his tongue around the two tattoos on Garron's arms. One a tribal design, the other was a piece of barbed wire. Sonny moved from the arm tattoos to Garron's chest. He watched as Sonny looked at his dark brown nipples before leaning forward and sucking one into his mouth. He bit down gently, just enough for Garron to feel it. "So hot."

Garron pulled him to the bed. "I need you. Now." They hastily threw off the covers and sprawled on the bed in a tangle of arms and legs.

Sonny ran his hand down Garron's six pack, and stopped at his closely shorn pubic patch. "So how do you manage to keep this cock contained in those itty bitty jeans you wear?" He ran his hand up and down the length of Garron's shaft.

Thrusting into Sonny's touch, Garron shrugged. "I just pack it in. It's not normally a problem unless I see you come in the door. I thought the damn thing was gonna rip through my fly tonight when I spotted you." Garron ran his hand down Sonny's back, then smoothed a finger along Sonny's crack and applied some pressure to his tightly puckered hole.

Sonny thrust back against his finger. "Yeah. Need it." He sat up and reached for the lube in his bedside drawer. He held the tube up. "You wanna get me ready or you wanna watch?"

Licking his lips at the bobbing cock in front of him, Garron shook his head and reached for the lube. "As much as I enjoy watching that fine body of yours, I need to feel you." Garron squirted a dollop of lube on his fingers and pulled Sonny back down on the bed. He positioned Sonny on his hands and knees and looked at his puckered prize. "Sorry, but I've got to have a quick taste." He ran his tongue up Sonny's crease and tongued his hole.

Sonny leaned down on his shoulders and used his hands to spread his butt cheeks. "Feels so good."

"Mmm hmm." Garron continued to lick and kiss the hole, feeling it relax. Withdrawing his tongue he pushed first one then two fingers inside the tight heat of Sonny's body. "Can't wait anymore. Need you." Once Sonny relaxed, Garron slipped another finger inside. He felt around and found Sonny's prostate gland. Pegging the smooth button with his finger, Garron stroked over it again and again. As Sonny writhed in ecstasy Garron used his other hand to slick up his cock. He grabbed the tube of lube and squirted a generous glob on the end of his shaft.

Positioning himself, Garron removed his fingers and replaced them with the head of his cock. He slowly rocked back and forth until the head and about a third of his length was inside.

Grabbing the sheets in a fisted hand, Sonny moaned. "Oh shit."

Garron ran his hand down Sonny's back trying to relax him again. "It's okay. I won't hurt you. Just bear down on my cock. Let me in." He continued to smooth his hand over Sonny's back until he could feel the muscles relaxing. Garron picked up the lube and applied even more as he continued to rock in and out. Eventually he was buried to the base of his cock, his heavy balls brushing against Sonny's soft skin. Garron stopped moving and savoured the feel of Sonny's body. He felt his chest tighten as he looked down. They looked perfect joined together. Shit, had he ever felt this way? What the hell was wrong with him?

Sonny looked back at him. "So good. 'M ready now." He braced himself back up on his hands and pushed back.

Taking the move for what it was, Garron began to slide his cock in and out of Sonny's hole. As Sonny slowly stretched to accommodate him, Garron picked up his pace. Soon he was driving hard and deep inside Sonny. "Oh God. Not gonna last much longer." Garron reached around and fisted Sonny's dripping shaft. He gave a few tugs and Sonny's heat exploded over his hand and onto the sheets. The smell of release and the grip Sonny's ass had on his cock sent him over the edge with a howl.

Garron was so loud he swore the windows shook. He collapsed on top of Sonny just as the bedroom door came bursting open. The light was flipped on and a naked Rawley stood in the doorway, still half asleep. "What? What's going on?"

Garron's head snapped up as Sonny started laughing. "It's okay, bro. Just havin' a little fun."

Rawley seemed to finally realise he was naked and quickly lowered a hand to hide his still asleep cock. "Fuck, Sonny. You guy's scared the shit out of me."

Garron repositioned them so he was spooned behind Sonny. He reached around and covered Sonny's cock with his hand as he continued to talk to his brother. "Sorry, I figured you were staying in town with Meg. Thought we were alone." Sonny looked down at the way Garron was protectively covering his cock. He looked up at Rawley and smiled. "We'll be quiet from now on. I promise. You can go back to bed now."

Rawley looked at the two of them and nodded. "See you both at breakfast." He started to close the door and stopped. "Hope this puts you in a better mood, Sonny. I was just fixing to go live with Ryker and Ranger." He shut the door and Garron could hear him laughing as he walked down the hall.

"Smart ass." Sonny turned in Garron's arms and kissed him. "Sorry about that. He's the big bad sheriff in town and protection comes naturally to him, even if he's naked." He looked into Garron's eyes. "Don't even think about going for my brother. He's got a girlfriend and he refuses to admit he's gay."

Garron smiled and kissed him again. "He's not my type. Too big, I like my lover's small enough to fit in my arms. Like you." He kissed Sonny's nose. "But my brother, now that's another story. Rawley is exactly his type. Jeb likes the big tough ones."

Snuggling in against Garron, Sonny sighed. "Okay you passed the test with Rawley. That only leaves Ranger and Ryker. They're both way hotter than me."

"Not even possible." Garron drew circles on Sonny's back with his fingers. "My heart is set on you. And I will accept no substitutes."

Nipping Garron's jaw, Sonny pushed his half-hard cock against Garron's. "Good, because I'm keeping you for myself." He ran his fingers through Garron's hair.

Moving his hands down to Sonny's twin globes, Garron squeezed. "I like that idea." He kissed the top of Sonny's head. "Sleep now, cowboy. We'll do another round before breakfast."

* * * *

Garron had Sonny backed against the counter dry humping him when Rawley walked in. Rolling his eyes he went over to take the burning bacon off the stove. "Nice breakfast."

Sonny and Garron broke apart. "Damn. That's all the bacon we had too." He looked at Garron's swollen lips. "But I gotta say it was worth it." He motioned towards Rawley. "I'd like you to meet Garron Greeley. This is my brother, Rawley."

Chuckling Rawley stuck out his hand. "I would have shaken your hand last night but it seemed to be occupied by my brother's cock."

"Watch it." Sonny stepped aside so Garron could shake Rawley's hand.

"Nice to meet you. Sonny tells me you're the town sheriff. I don't suppose you have any openings in your department? I just left the Chicago PD and I'd much rather be a cop than a bartender."

Rawley rubbed his jaw. His large hands were about the same size as Garron's, Sonny noticed. "Sorry, I don't need any help right now, but I'm thinking maybe Lincoln does. I could make a couple of calls for you. If you don't mind making the hour long drive everyday. I think my brother would kill me if I sent you off to live in another city."

Nodding his head, Garron pulled Sonny into his arms. "I worked vice in Chicago so I could get by with the hair and tattoos, but I'm not sure if a town the size of Lincoln would have a need for a cop that looked like me."

"Don't know until I ask." Rawley looked around the kitchen. "So what the hell are we gonna have for breakfast?"

Chapter Three

A month later, Sonny was sitting inside the air conditioned tractor cab singing to the radio thinking about Garron. They'd both had a couple of small altercations with Lionel and his crew, but nothing too bad, yet. Sonny could feel it coming though. It wouldn't surprise him if the town started picking sides any day now.

Feeling a low vibration in his chest, Sonny looked around. He smiled when he saw Garron's Harley coming across the freshly mowed hay field. "That crazy jackass is going to kill himself," he laughed as he turned off the tractor. Deciding the cab was a little too small for both of them, Sonny climbed down and waited for Garron to reach him.

The roar and rumble of the bike vibrated Sonny's chest as he pulled up beside him. Sonny eyed the beautiful machine. God he loved to ride behind Garron on that thing. Turning off the engine, Garron smiled at him. "Thinking about the ride we took the other evening?"

"Hell yes." Sonny reached down and readjusted his quickly filling cock. "Did you risk your neck to come out here and get me for another one?"

Laughing, Garron pulled him into his arms. "I came to tell you I got the job in Lincoln. Looks like I'll be sticking around."

Sonny leaned in and kissed him. "You'd better be sticking around." He ran his hands over the fancy dress shirt Garron was wearing. "Nice shirt, by the way. Of course it looks all wrong on the motorcycle." Sonny started unbuttoning Garron as he kissed his way down his chest.

With a hand to the back of his head, Garron directed him towards a nipple. Sonny greedily latched on and moaned. Garron gasped, "Nice. Tell me you and Rawley will come over tonight for dinner to celebrate."

Sonny pulled off his nipple and looked at him. "You mean with Jeb?"

"Yep. If we're going to be together, you two need to talk. Maybe what he has to say will change your mind about him."

Looking at the man he was quickly falling in love with, Sonny couldn't refuse. "Okay, but if he starts any shit, I'll finish it."

Garron looked at him and smiled. "You do that, Cowboy. But right now, why don't you finish me?"

Happily, Sonny began unfastening Garron's dress slacks. Easing the zipper down over his rigid shaft, Sonny sighed. "Yum and I haven't even had lunch yet." Swirling his tongue around the crown, Sonny began stroking Garron. Receiving a grunt from the man he loved, he took the head into his mouth. Sonny felt the ridges under his tongue as he used his tongue to press against the sensitive underside of Garron's crown. Feeling his own cock aching, he reached down and opened his own fly. Cock in hand, Sonny resumed eating his lunch.

"Oh God, yes." Garron panted as he ran his fingers through Sonny's curls.

Looking up to meet Garron's eyes, Sonny took him as deep into his throat as he could and moaned. He knew the vibrations surrounding his cock would set Garron off and he was right. Two strokes later, Sonny was rewarded with Garron's salty sweet essence jetting down his throat. After licking him clean, Sonny stood and kissed Garron.

"You're so good to me," Garron said between kisses as he reached down and began applying pressure to Sonny's cock.

Rocking into Garron's hand, Sonny took the next kiss as deep as possible without actually giving Garron a tonsillectomy. Feeling his balls draw up tight, Sonny ground against Garron's hand and unloaded. He felt the ripples of pleasure work their way from his cock up through his stomach muscles, and out through his mouth, as he broke the kiss and shouted Garron's name to the hay-field.

Sonny collapsed against Garron, who was still sitting sideways on the motorcycle seat. "Nice," he rumbled against Garron's neck.

After several more minutes of kissing and petting, Sonny pulled a bandana out of his back pocket and cleaned them both. He kissed his way up Garron's chest as he rebuttoned his dress shirt, and stood back to look at him. "Damn you're hot."

Garron started his motorcycle and leaned in for one more kiss. "You be done about seven?"

"Yeah, why don't you give Rawley a call for me and ask him to meet me there." Sonny took one last swipe across Garron's chest, tweaking his nipple in the process.

"Later," Garron said with a wink before he rode off across the field.

Shaking his head, Sonny climbed back into the tractor. "How the hell did I manage to go and fall in love?"

* * * *

Trying to tame his wayward black curls, Sonny couldn't believe he was nervous. "For fuck's sake, man, it's not your first date. What the hell is your problem?" He looked at his deep purple polo shirt and wondered if he should change. He'd never worn the thing, but his momma had got it for him for Christmas. She said it brought out the purple in his eyes. He thought it sounded stupid at the time, so why had he put it on now? It wasn't like he needed to impress Jeb or Rawley, and Garron already liked him. But did he love him?

Finally figuring out the cause of his nerves, Sonny gave up on his hair and put his good dress boots on. Grabbing his keys off the dresser, he went down the stairs and out the front door. Climbing into his truck, he took a deep breath. "You can do this. You can go over and play nice with the jerk that bought the land you wanted."

Driving down the ranch road, Sonny hoped to hell his brother was already there.

Pulling behind Rawley's Sheriff's vehicle, Sonny blew out a breath of air. "Thank God." He looked in the mirror and rearranged his windblown curls as someone knocked on his window. Startled, Sonny jumped a little and spun around. He narrowed his eyes at Garron and opened the door. "Trying to give me a heart attack?"

Garron pressed him up against the truck with his long body. "Damn you look good tonight. Usually the only time I see you without a hat is when you're in bed." Garron played with Sonny's curls. "So pretty," he whispered against Sonny's mouth, just before kissing him.

Forgetting himself, Sonny put his arms around Garron's neck and wrapped his legs around his hips, grinding his hardened cock against Garron's. A throat clearing broke the two apart. Embarrassed, Sonny let his legs slide to the ground. A gorgeous blond man stood next to Rawley. Nice first impression asshole, he thought to himself.

Garron started laughing and smacked him on the ass. "Don't worry, Jeb isn't a prude." He led Sonny over to the porch. "Meet my brother, Jeb."

Sonny reached out and shook Jeb's hand. "I guess you've already figured out who I am."

"Nice to finally meet the man my brother can't stop talking about. Come on in, dinner's almost ready." Jeb turned and walked into the house, followed closely by Rawley.

Turning to Garron, Sonny grinned. "Did you see the way my brother was looking at your brother's ass?" He shook his head and laughed. "He's so gay."

"Shh, don't tell him that. Let him figure it out for himself." Garron took Sonny's hand and led him into the house.

Jeb and Rawley were already sitting at the kitchen table with beers in their hands, when they walked in. Sonny took the seat across from Jeb as Garron handed him a beer. "So can I ask you something before we begin the small talk? I know I'm going to come off like an ass, but I gotta know. Why did Jack sell you this ranch instead of me?"

"Sonny!" Rawley yelled. "Show some manners, boy. You don't just come into a man's house and ask him something like that."

"It's all right," Jeb said. He rubbed his jaw and took another drink of his beer. "Jack Anderson was my father. I didn't even know he existed until about three months before he died. Seems he had an affair with my mother." Jeb looked over at Garron. "She was married to Garron's dad," he shook his head, "my dad at the time."

"And Jack didn't know about you?" Sonny couldn't keep from asking.

"He knew, but my mom asked him not to interfere. It would have ruined an entire family. So Jack kept his mouth shut until he found out he was dying. He came to Chicago and we met and talked for a couple of days. He told me about the ranch, and he told me about you and your brothers living next door."

Sonny felt the fight go out of him. Here sat a man who had only known his real father for a couple of days, and he'd been mad that Jack hadn't sold him the ranch. He felt like a Grade A bastard. "I'm sorry."

"Its fine, Jack told me how much you meant to him. He said it was up to me whether to tell you the truth or not." Jeb looked at Garron. "And my big brother has been on my case about telling you the story."

"Well I'm sorry I've been an ass. If you need any help or advice I hope you'll give me a call." Sonny reached under the table and took Garron's hand. Garron squeezed back and Sonny knew everything would be okay.

* * * *

After dinner, Garron took Sonny on a motorcycle ride. As they flew down the narrow country roads, Sonny held on tight. God he loved this. Feeling the wind in his hair as he snuggled against the man he loved. He leaned forward and kissed the tattoo on the back of Garron's neck. "I love you," he whispered against his skin. He knew Garron couldn't hear him, but it felt good just saying it out loud.

Taking an old farm road, Garron bounced them both along ruts until they came to a dead-end. He turned off the bike and pulled Sonny across his lap. "Did you say something back there?"

Looking into Garron's dark brown eyes, Sonny felt like shouting it from the rooftops. "I said I love you."

Closing his eyes, Garron took a deep breath before crushing Sonny's body in his arms. "I love you, too. I have for a while, but I didn't know if I could say it."

"Well I hope you know what this means." Sonny began unfastening Garron's jeans.

"What does it mean, Cowboy?" Garron shrugged out of his T-shirt and threw it on the ground.

"It means you'd better be prepared to be the centre of town gossip, because I'm gonna want you to move in with me. And I can think of at least a couple of people who might have a problem with that." Sonny took Garron's cock in his hand and lowered his head.

Leaning back on the bike, Garron groaned, "Bring 'em on."

GARRON'S GIFT

Dedication

Once again, to my dedicated,
often patient, beta reader, Drew Hunt.
I honestly couldn't do this series without you.

Chapter One

Garron was leaving the police station when his cell phone rang. Looking at the display he smiled. "Hey, hot stuff."

"They shot him," Sonny yelled into the phone.

Garron's stomach bottomed out as he stopped in his tracks. "Shot who?"

"Buford, someone killed him."

Quickly searching his memory, Garron came up blank. "I'm sorry, cowboy, but I don't know a Buford."

"He's my goddamn prize-winning Blank Angus bull."

"Shit, I'm sorry. Did you call Rawley?" Garron hurried to his black Harley and climbed on.

"Yeah, he was going to stop and get Jeb and head this way. How long before you get here?"

"I can make it in about fifty minutes. Will you still be there?"

"Yeah, it'll take a while I'm sure. We're just passed the pond on Jeb's side of the fence."

"All right, I'm leaving now. Love you."

"Love you, need you here."

Sonny hung up and Garron looked at the phone a moment before slipping it back into his pocket. Starting his bike, he roared out of the parking lot towards home. Funny how the Flying G had become home after only a month, of course a lot of it could be because his heart lived there. Garron decided to take the interstate to shave off a few minutes. Usually he took the back roads, but he had a feeling Sonny needed him as soon as he could get there.

Riding down the road, he thought about the phone call. He knew Sonny was supposed to go into town to pick up some new fencing material. Garron wondered if something had happened. Lionel Hibbs used every chance he got to run the two of them down to the rest of the town. At first it was just little comments here and there, but it had moved into shouts of vulgarity as soon as Lionel spotted one or both of them in town.

Garron had to quit bartending two weeks early because Lionel made such a scene every time he came into the Dead Zone, Jim, the owner, thought it was best. Sonny tried to act like the name calling didn't bother him, but Garron knew it did. Sonny'd grown up in Summerville, and for him to suddenly shy away from going into town was a sure sign.

The closer he got to the ranch the faster he went. Something had to have sparked this sudden change in Lionel's behaviour. Killing ranch animals was a big step from bigoted words shouted across the street.

Garron parked his bike by the shed and drove the four-wheeler to Sonny. Topping the slight rise in the landscape, Garron spotted Sonny, Jeb, Rawley and another man surrounding what he guessed was Buford. Slowing down, he stopped just inside the broken fence. Rawley looked up and walked over.

"Glad you finally made it. My brother's going off the deep end." Rawley rubbed at the back of his neck. Garron could tell there was something else Rawley wanted to tell him.

"What?" Garron asked as he started towards the broken barbed wire fence.

"Sonny and Lionel got into a fight this afternoon in town. I think Lionel ended up with a broken nose, but Sonny came away with a black eye." Rawley said as he followed Garron over to the fence.

Turning back towards Sonny, Garron pointed to the broken wire. "You look at this, it's obviously been cut. I'm gonna go check on Sonny." He walked towards the man he loved, fire heating his veins. How dare Lionel touch Sonny. He had half a mind to go into town and find that bastard right now. The only thing stopping him was the look on Sonny's face when Garron neared. Opening his arms, Sonny immediately walked into them. "You okay?" He looked down into Sonny's bruised face.

"No, but I'm better now." Sonny looked over at Buford. "He just killed him, for no good reason."

Rubbing his hands up and down Sonny's back, Garron looked over at Jeb. "The fence has been cut."

Jeb nodded, "I figured as much." Jeb pointed towards the older man. "This is our vet, Dr. Mac Whitcomb. Mac, this is my brother Garron."

The two men shook hands. Although his hair was totally grey, Mac didn't look much over forty-five. He looked Mac in the eyes. "Can you tell how long ago this happened?"

Scratching his jaw, Mac looked back at the dead bull. "Hard to say with this heat, but my guess would be only a couple of hours."

Looking back down at Sonny, Garron kissed his forehead. "What time did you get in your fight?"

Garron noticed Sonny's jaws tensing. "About the same time, I reckon."

"How'd it happen?" Garron kept his arms wrapped around Sonny's waist.

"Well, I guess he must've seen me walk into the feed store from his office across the street. When I finished up and left, Lionel was waiting for me. He started saying some stuff that I didn't much care for, and then he pushed me." Sonny gave a slight grin. "That's when I showed him I may be small, but I can still throw a punch."

Garron looked around the group, "You guys thinking the same thing I am?"

Mac nodded, looking back at the bull. "Set up to give him an alibi. I tell you what, I never much cared for that man, but anyone who can order this done is sick."

"Yeah, I think we all agree on that one. The question is, can we find anything to legally link him to the crime," Rawley said, stepping into the circle. "It's so dry out here there aren't any footprints, but I'll continue to search." Rawley pointed towards the dead bull. "What are you gonna do with Buford?"

"Shelby's out in the east pasture digging a hole now. He'll come back with the tractor and pick him up when he's done."

Rawley ran his fingers through his short black hair and looked at Mac. "The bullet still in there?"

Mac looked down at the dead bull. "No exit wound, so yeah. You want me to try and get it out for ya?"

"If you can without damaging the bullet. I'll send it to the crime lab in Lincoln and get a ballistics report done on it. It's a long shot, but it's probably my only piece of evidence."

Garron looked at Rawley, "Did you get some pictures? I'm sure the insurance company will want them, along with the reports from you and Mac."

"Yeah, I got them. I have done this before ya know," Rawley said.

"Sorry, didn't mean that the way it sounded. I just wanted to make sure everything was being taken care of before I took Sonny home."

"Go on and take him, we'll finish up here."

Garron looked down at Sunny. "Where's the truck?"

"Shelby took it. I guess I'll be riding on the back of the four-wheeler." He winked, "What a shame."

Slapping Sonny on the ass, Garron waved goodbye to Mac, Jeb, and Rawley.

* * * *

By the time they reached the house, they were both horny as hell. Making their way into the kitchen, Garron attacked his lips. "Need you."

"Yeah," Sonny said, pulling on Garron's clothes. He managed to get Garron's T-shirt up and over his head, before starting on his fly. As soon as he had him unbuckled and unzipped, Sonny was on his knees. He swiped his tongue across the head of Garron's cock and moaned at the flavour of pre-come. "Love your taste," he said just before taking the crown into his mouth.

Pulling the soft denim down, Sonny ran his hands over the firm globes of Garron's ass. He felt the taut muscles under his hands as Garron began to thrust. Sonny became lost in the passionate act, slipping his finger between Garron's cheeks to press against his hole. He'd yet to make love to this ass. Because of their size difference, Sonny had naturally taken the bottom's role in their relationship, which, up until this moment, had always suited them both. Right now, however,

Sonny wanted inside Garron with a need he'd never experienced before.

Sonny pulled off Garron's cock and looked up at him. "I want you."

Garron must have realised what Sonny was asking because he nodded his head, and pulled Sonny up into his arms. "It'll be easier in the bedroom." Garron pulled up his Levi's and led Sonny up the stairs.

As they quickly undressed, Sonny felt a moment of nervousness attack him. He couldn't understand it. He'd fucked plenty of men before, why this sudden fear that he wouldn't be good enough?

When they were both naked, wrapped in each others arms in the centre of the bed, it dawned on him. For the first time in his life, he'd be making love to another man, and Garron's opinion of him mattered. Breaking their kiss, Sonny looked into Garron's dark brown eyes. "You okay with this?"

Garron smiled and lifted his legs against his chest, presenting Sonny with the most beautiful hole he'd ever seen. "I love you," Garron said. "I've been waiting for you to take the initiative."

Sonny realised it didn't matter if he performed perfectly. The fact that he could express his love for Garron by loving him did. Reaching over to the table for the lube, Sonny tried to slow his breathing. He knew he needed to calm down and go slow. No telling how long it had been for Garron and the way he felt, he wouldn't last long.

Slicking his fingers, Sonny gave Garron a deep kiss while slowly slipping one finger inside his rosette. Breaking the lip lock, he smiled at the man he loved. "You've got a birthday coming up in a couple of weeks."

Moaning, Garron wiggled his ass. "Don't remind me."

"I was thinking about a party. Nothing fancy, just renting the back room at the Zone. Couple of friends, good food," Sonny winked, "maybe a little dancing?"

Garron stilled and looked into Sonny's eyes. "You serious?"

Sonny nodded and inserted another finger. "Of course I'm serious. And if we happened to say a few words of commitment to each other with all our friends and family around, well all's the better."

"Are you asking me to marry you?" Garron panted as Sonny pegged his prostate gland.

"I know we can't actually get married, but it would be close enough in my book." He looked deep into Garron's eyes. "Think about it?"

"I don't need to. The answer is yes." Garron wiggled around a little more. "Now, make love to me."

Sonny withdrew his fingers and applied a large dollop of lube to his swollen shaft. Crawling between Garron's spread thighs, he positioned himself at the relaxed entrance. "I love you," he said as he slowly invaded Garron's body.

When he was in to the root, Sonny closed his eyes and rested his head on Garron's chest. "Oh fuck, this wasn't a good idea."

He felt Garron tense around his cock. "You don't like it?"

Moving his head from side to side, he kissed Garron's chest. "Just the opposite. I may never want to bottom again."

Chuckling, Garron swatted him on the ass. "Well don't get too used to it, but I'm up for an equal partnership. But only if you move before I go insane."

Taking a playful nip of Garron's neck, Sonny began to thrust in and out. The louder Garron moaned, the faster Sonny's hips moved, until he was pounding hard and fast inside the hot hole. Yeah, he could get used to a lifetime of this. He watched Garron's face as sweat began dripping off himself, and onto Garron's chest and stomach. "Love you," he growled.

With one hand wrapped around it, Garron's cock erupted in stream after stream of pearly white seed. The involuntary contractions as Garron came, set Sonny off. He thrust in one last time and pumped his lover full of his essence. Collapsing on top of Garron, Sonny's body shook with the intensity of his orgasm.

He was sweaty, hungry, sleepy and totally sated. What more could a man ask for? Sonny smiled as Garron's legs wrapped around him. Evidently he wasn't the only one who didn't want to end the moment. "Do we need to buy rings?" Garron asked as he rubbed Sonny's back.

Sonny hadn't thought of rings, but the more he did, the more he liked the image of Garron with a gold band on his finger. He tilted his head up to look at Garron. "Can you wear one on the job?"

"Yeah, most of the time. I might have to take it off for something special, but that's no different than the other cops in vice."

"Then, yes, rings for two." They settled back in and drifted off to sleep for a short nap.

* * * *

Sitting down for a late supper, Sonny looked across the table at Rawley. "I'm throwing a big party in two weeks for Garron's thirty-sixth birthday." He took a bite of his hamburger before continuing. "We thought we'd say some commitment vows at the same time." He took another bite and waited for the explosion that was sure to come.

"What did you just say?" Rawley asked, setting down his glass of iced tea.

"I said Garron and I are exchanging vows." Sonny looked his brother in the eye, daring him to disagree.

"You really think that's a wise move? You've got a dead bull and a black eye. What do you think will happen if word gets out about this latest development?"

Sonny pushed his plate back and leaned on the table. "I grew up in this town and I think most people accept me. If a small pocket of bigots choose to hate me because of who I love, fuck 'em."

Rawley looked at a quiet Garron. "And you? Are you ready for this?"

Garron looked from Rawley to Sonny. "Seems to me, Sonny has the most to lose in this decision and if he's willing to have me despite all that, I'm jumping at the chance."

Standing up, Rawley walked towards the door, leaving his dinner on the table. "You're both crazy." Putting on his hat, he was just about to leave when Sonny spoke up.

"At least we're true to our feelings. You can only hide behind that badge for so long. It sure as hell isn't going to be much comfort when you're old."

Rawley didn't even turn around as he walked out the door and to his SUV. Sonny looked at a wide-eyed Garron. "What? It's the truth. There's so much heat generated between Rawley and Jeb it's a wonder the room doesn't catch fire when they're both in it."

"Maybe so," Garron said, and reached out to take Sonny's hand, "but it's not for you to say. Maybe if you backed off, he'd stop fighting it so hard." Garron pulled Sonny up out of his chair and onto his lap.

"It's just hard to see him so unhappy." Sonny knew he shouldn't have said those things to Rawley, but it was too late to take them back. He rested his head against Garron's and kissed him. "I'm an ass."

"No, cowboy, you're not. You just need to let your brother learn who he really is on his own." Sonny moaned as Garron began rubbing his cock through the denim. "Let's say we hurry and get these dishes done and head back upstairs?"

Looking at the table, Sonny wasn't surprised to find most of the food still on everyone's plates. "Too bad we don't have a house dog. We could just set the plates on the floor."

Laughing, Garron stood and set Sonny on his feet. "Come on, the quicker we get it done, the faster we get upstairs." He stacked the plates and carried them to the sink. Turning around, Garron winked at him. "And this time, I'm in the driver's seat."

Chapter Two

Before work the next morning, Garron stopped by his brother Jeb's place. He drove under the old ranch sign, which reminded him of something. He needed to talk to Jeb about renaming the place, The Tall A, no longer fit. Parking his motorcycle, Garron took the porch steps two at a time. He opened the front door and hollered for Jeb. When he didn't receive an answer, he walked back outside and looked towards the barn. Surely if he was around he'd have come out when he heard Garron's bike pull up.

Shaking his head, Garron headed towards the barn. "Jeb?" He reached the red behemoth and stuck his head inside, "Jeb?" he repeated.

"Just a minute," his brother called back.

Garron followed the voice towards the tack room. Jeb was sitting on a stool talking on his cell phone. He could tell by the goofy look on Jeb's face that he must be talking to Rawley.

"Okay. Yeah I'll call you if I see anything. Bye, Rawley." Jeb disconnected and stuffed his phone back in his pocket. "Hey, big brother."

Grinning, Garron pointed towards Jeb's pocket. "How's your crush?"

"Knock it off. Rawley just called to say he was hauling Lionel in for questioning. He sent the bullet off for a ballistics check, but Rawley said it usually takes a while. He wants me to keep a look out for any trouble." Jeb crossed his arms and looked at Garron. "So what brings you by?"

"Just stopped by to tell you I'm getting married, or committed. I'm not really sure what to call it, but it's happening on my birthday. Sonny's gonna rent the back room at the Zone and I wanted to ask if you'd stand up with me." Garron felt his face heat, which kind of pissed him off. There was absolutely no reason he should feel embarrassed about getting married, so why was he blushing? He looked up at Jeb and waited for the comment he knew was coming.

Instead of the lecture Rawley had given them, Jeb flew into his arms. "I'm so happy for you." He kissed Garron on the cheek before releasing him. "Of course I think you two are nuttier than Aunt May's fruit cake, but hey, who am I to criticise."

"You think I'm nutty for getting married?" Garron was totally thrown off balance by first, the unexpected hug, and then the whole fruit cake thing.

"No, I think if the two of you want to get married you should run off to Hawaii and take me with you." Jeb stopped grinning and touched Garron's shoulder. "You know it's going to stir the town up."

"Not the town, just Lionel and his lap dogs." He looked his brother in the eye. "I love him. Sonny wants this and I'll do anything for him."

Jeb looked at him for a few seconds before nodding. "Well, then we'll make sure you're both surrounded by people who care for you."

"Thanks, brother." Garron mussed Jeb's curly blond hair, just like he'd done since they were kids.

Jeb swatted Garron's hand away. "You'd better get to Lincoln before you miss out on a big-time drug deal or something, Mr. Vice Cop."

Garron smiled and waved on his way out. He climbed on his Harley feeling better than he had in a long while. He couldn't believe Sonny Good was finally going to be the one to make an honest man out of him.

* * * *

Rawley ran a frustrated hand through his thick black hair as he turned off the ignition. It had been a hell of an afternoon, and it was bound to get worse. Looking up at the R & R Feedlot sign, he knew it was time for the brothers to talk. Things were coming to a head in town and he needed his brothers to lie low for a while, not that they'd listen to him, but he needed to try.

Ranger and Ryker had always had a strange relationship. It was like an unbreakable bond had formed between the two of them in their mother's womb. They were like those twins Rawley had seen on TV. Having their own language was just one of their many quirks.

Even as kids, they refused to sleep apart. No matter how many times their mother and father had tried to separate them, they always woke up in the same bed. As children, it had been one thing, but as they grew into adults, their father had finally put his foot down. The twins had done the only thing they thought they could and moved out as soon as they turned eighteen. Lucky for them, they'd both worked at the feedlot all through high school and when Old Man Zook decided to retire, he sold the business to the twins. By that time, they'd made up with their dad and he agreed to co-sign a loan for them. That had been almost seven years ago.

Getting out of his Sheriff's SUV, Rawley headed towards the small building that housed their offices. In the relatively short time they'd owned the place, business had more than doubled. It seemed when it came to fattening cows, no one in the county much cared what Ryker and Ranger's relationship was. To their credit though, they never flaunted anything in front of people. Most gossips in town only surmised that the two of them were lovers. Not one person had ever seen proof, though. The brothers didn't so much as hold hands in public.

Rawley had heard of a woman sharing their bed a time or two, but to the women's credit they never mentioned their time with the Good twins. Opening the door, the little bell alerted anyone within hearing distance of his arrival. He knew better than to go looking for the two of them, so he took a seat in the small reception area. Looking down at the cracked harvest gold vinyl chairs, Rawley shook his head.

"What?" Ryker said coming into the room, followed closely by Ranger.

"I think ya'll have made enough money to replace these thirty-year-old chairs." Rawley picked at the cracked material.

"Why should we do that? It's mostly cattle ranchers that come in. If we fancied up the place they might think we're making too much money off 'em." Ryker looked back at Ranger and winked. "Of course we are, but they don't need to know that."

"Yeah, well don't ever invite them to your house then." Rawley thought of the large stone and timber house the twins had built a couple of years earlier on the edge of the family's ranch land. Surrounded by trees, the house was a dream and Rawley had always felt a little bit jealous.

Ranger sat down in one of the chairs beside Rawley. "No chance of that. Our home is our sanctuary. No business takes place there, ever." Ranger looked from Ryker to Rawley, "So what's brought you here today? Sonny already called to tell us about the bull and the party." He narrowed his eyes a bit, "Or is there something else?"

Heaving an audible sigh, Rawley rubbed his neck. "I had Lionel in for questioning. I know he's responsible and he knows I know, but I've got nothing on him. I sent the bullet off for testing, but that could take a while. It's just so damn frustrating. How am I supposed to protect Sonny if he's bound and determined to let the whole town know he's getting married? Does he think people won't find out?"

Biting his lower lip, Ryker shrugged. "Maybe he doesn't care who finds out. If you loved someone enough to spend the rest of your life with them, would you? I have a feeling when you eventually fall in love, you'll be willing to sacrifice anything to be with them. You just haven't fallen yet."

"I love Meg. We've been together over two years," Rawley said, trying to defend himself.

Reaching over to him, Ranger gripped Rawley's shoulder. "You're not in love with Meg. I'm not saying you don't love her, but it'll never be enough for you."

Shoulders tensing, Rawley stood and looked at his two brothers. "I'm not discussing Meg anymore. The two of you are just like Sonny."

He turned to leave and Ryker touched his arm. "We do have something in common with Sonny. We all love you and want you to be happy."

"I'll be happier once the three of you get the hell out of my love life." Rawley looked at Ryker and then Ranger. Shaking his head, he walked towards the door. "Keep an ear open for any trouble. My guess is this thing with Lionel is just heating up. And the two of you'll be next. Keep whatever's going on between you out of town."

Ranger stood beside Ryker and narrowed his eyes. "I appreciate you worrying about us, big brother, but don't come into our business and tell us how to lead our lives. We refused to take it from dad, and we sure as hell won't take it from you."

Looking back over his shoulder, Rawley nodded. "Fair enough, then just stay the hell out of my love life and be careful."

Rawley walked out the door and climbed back into his sheriff's vehicle. After buckling up, he scrubbed his hands over his face. He was so tired of trying to defend himself with his brothers. Since he'd been a boy, all he'd ever wanted was to be a policeman. Rawley had surpassed that dream when he'd been appointed sheriff. No way in hell would he jeopardise that for some crazy fantasy of love.

* * * *

Garron pulled into the ranch yard, feeling like a drowned rat. An unexpected summer rain shower had drenched him most of the way home. Climbing off his bike, he was pleased to see Sonny sitting in his favourite chair on the porch. He grinned as Sonny held up a dry towel and a cold beer.

"Thought you might need both of these when you got home," Sonny said, as Garron climbed the porch steps.

"Good thinking, but what I really need is a kiss." He covered Sonny's lips with his own, teasing them apart. Delving his tongue inside, Garron moaned at the taste of cold beer and Sonny. "You're always what I need first."

Sonny winked and stood. "I can live with that. Get yourself dried off and meet me in the kitchen. I've spent all afternoon on dinner because of the rain, and as much as I'd like to follow you upstairs, I want my dinner hot." Sonny gave him another quick kiss. "You're always hot, so I know I'll get my desert after dinner."

Laughing, Garron smacked his ass as he walked by. "Is Rawley coming home or can I eat in my underwear?"

Sonny stopped in his tracks. "Screw Rawley, I'll call and tell him to find his own dinner." Sonny licked his lips and looked down at Garron's crotch. "Go take a shower and come down wearing the sexy underwear I bought you last week."

Garron rolled his eyes. "You were serious about those? I thought they were like a gag gift. I don't know if they'll even fit."

Looking him up and down, Sonny moaned. "Oh they'll fit, perfectly."

* * * *

Sonny had just finished the salad, when Garron walked into the room. He almost swallowed his tongue at the gorgeous man standing in the doorway. "Holy fuck."

Setting the salad on the table, Sonny walked over to get a closer look at the white satin thong Garron was barely wearing. As he circled around his lover to get a good look at his ass, Garron covered his butt with his hands. "Stop it. You make me feel like a cheap piece of meat."

Groaning, Sonny pushed himself against Garron's back. "My meat," Sonny said, as he wrapped his arms around

Garron. Nipping his shoulder, Sonny worked his hands down Garron's muscular chest to rest on the satin covered package. The material was so soft against his rough and callused hands Sonny felt the cloth snag under his touch. "Damn hands," he muttered to himself.

Covering Sonny's hands with his own, Garron pressed them against his erection. "I love your hands, this underwear? I'm not so sure about."

Licking his way around Garron's neck, Sonny sighed. "You could always take them off?"

"And eat naked? No thanks. Let's just get dinner over with so we can get upstairs." Garron pulled Sonny towards the kitchen table. "Smells good."

Looking at the large pan of lasagne on the table, Sonny suddenly wasn't hungry. "We can reheat it later?"

Garron shook his head, "Nope. You got me into this silly outfit and I deserve a big piece of that lasagne."

Knowing he wouldn't win, Sonny broke away and took a seat. By the time he'd mixed the dressing into the salad, Garron already had a huge section of the pan on his plate. "Hungry?" Sonny asked, eyeing the huge portion of food.

"Starving," Garron replied with a wink.

They settled in to eat, but after only one small piece, Sonny was full. He looked over at Garron who didn't appear to be any where near finished. Thrumming his fingers on the table, he watched Garron devour the lasagne.

He thought he'd die before he got upstairs with this sexy man. That gave him an idea. Wiping his mouth, Sonny set his napkin on the table and slid down to the floor. The view from under the table was even better.

As Sonny crawled towards Garron, he watched as Garron's legs separated and his cock began to fill. Moving in between

Garron's thighs, Sonny pressed his face against the material and inhaled deeply. "Mmm, nice."

He began licking and mouthing Garron's hard-on through the satin, pleased when the fabric quickly became transparent. "You're breathtaking in white satin." He pulled the thong to the side and Garron's bound erection sprang free. Smiling, Sonny immediately took the leaking head into his mouth.

"Fuck, cowboy," Garron moaned, as he reached under the table and threaded his fingers through Sonny's hair.

Sonny knew what Garron was after, so he decided to play nice and give it to him. Relaxing his throat, Sonny opened wide and took as much of Garron as he could. Just when he'd thought he couldn't go any further, Garron thrust deeper into his mouth.

"Yes. Oh, shit," Garron cried out, as he started fucking Sonny's mouth.

With his jaw still relaxed, Sonny let Garron have his way and he was soon rewarded for his efforts. The taste of Garron's seed exploded in his mouth and down his throat, setting off his own cock. He shivered at the wet sticky feel as his own come saturated his underwear and jeans.

Garron slumped down further in the chair, just as the back door opened. Sonny pulled off Garron's cock and looked at the shiny brown cowboy boots that belonged to Rawley.

"Where's Sonny?" Rawley's deep voice commanded.

Rolling his eyes, Sonny spoke from under the table. "I thought I left a message for you to find your own dinner tonight."

Rawley said nothing for several seconds. "Um, I didn't think you were serious about that. I'll uh, go up to my room for a while." Rawley must have finally noticed that Garron was naked from the waist up. "Sorry, man," Rawley said, as he made his way out of the kitchen.

As soon as his brother was gone, Sonny erupted in a fit of laughter. He heard Garron's chair scrape across the scarred wooden floor and look down at him. "I don't know what the hell you think is so funny. I'm gonna burn this underwear."

Crawling out from under the table, Sonny knelt beside Garron. "Life is never going to be boring with my family around."

Chapter Three

Garron watched Sonny pace back and forth in front of the Dead Zone wearing his new three-piece suit. Checking his watch once again, he looked at Garron. "Where the hell is he?" he questioned for the tenth time. "I talked to him earlier and he said he'd be here."

Garron reached out a hand and stopped Sonny in his tracks. "Why don't we just try calling him?" He pulled out his cell phone and handed it to Sonny. The preacher from Sonny's church had agreed to perform the ceremony as long as Garron and Sonny wrote their own vows and didn't mention the words holy or marriage. Garron would have told him to shove it up his ass, but Sonny had belonged to Reverend James' church since he was a child, so he'd readily agreed.

Looking at the phone Garron held out, Sonny sighed and took it. He punched in some numbers and held the phone to his ear. Garron thought he was cute like this, all dressed up and nervous just like a groom should be.

Jeb came out of The Zone and waved to get Garron's attention. Leaving Sonny to his call, Garron walked over to his brother. "Something wrong?" Jeb asked.

"Who knows? Sonny's calling Reverend James right now. How're things going in there?" Garron inquired sticking his hands in his pockets.

"Everyone's trying to be patient, but I'm thinking maybe we need to let them eat if it's going to be a while."

Garron heard Sonny end the call and turned towards him. "What did he say?"

As if in a daze, Sonny walked over and handed Garron his phone back. He just stood there looking at the building, which started to worry Garron. "Cowboy? What did the Reverend say?"

"He's not coming. Seems it's not only Lionel and his friends that don't want this to happen. Charles, Lionel's father, doesn't think it's proper for Reverend James to preside over the ceremony either. He threatened to worship elsewhere if the Reverend performed the ceremony and since his money helps keep the church going, Reverend James feels he has no choice." Sonny looked into Garron's eyes. "What are we going to do?"

"Get married," Garron replied, with a quick kiss. "We asked the Reverend here more as a formality anyway. We aren't legally getting married, so we can just hold our ceremony and say our vows without him. In the eyes of our friends and family we'll still be committed to each other."

Sonny took a deep breath and closed his eyes. When he finally opened them, Garron could detect a little more moisture in his lover's beautiful amethyst eyes, but he nodded and smiled. "Okay, well let's get married then."

Pulling Sonny into his arms, Garron kissed him, totally oblivious to Jeb. Delving his tongue into Sonny's hot depths,

Garron groaned. "Let's do this. The sooner we're finished, the sooner our wedding night happens."

* * * *

Holding hands, the twosome walked to the centre of the dance floor. Sonny had asked Meg and a few of her friends to help him with the decorations. They'd decided on wildflowers and dark purple accents. Sonny was pleased with the way it had turned out. He was even more pleased by the man standing in front of him. Garron had been right. They didn't need Reverend James to preside over their ceremony, they only needed each other.

Sonny smiled as he turned towards Garron. He couldn't believe how yummy Garron looked in his black suit and white dress shirt. Hell, he'd even offered to get a haircut for the occasion, but Sonny had put his foot down. He loved the feel of Garron's long silky hair caressing his naked body when they made love.

He could tell Garron was nervous as he watched his Adam's apple bob every time he swallowed. Deciding to put him at ease, Sonny smiled and whispered, "I'll go first."

Sonny received a grateful nod from Garron as he gripped Sonny's hands even tighter.

Clearing his throat, Sonny looked up into Garron's eyes. "Several months ago I walked into this very bar and spotted the sexiest man I'd ever seen. Little did I know that man would change my life forever. You've become my entire world, Garron, and I can't imagine a single day without you in my life. Today I commit my life to loving you, to learning from you and to picking up the socks you refuse to see on the bedroom floor." Sonny waited a few seconds while their loved ones laughed. He spent the time looking into Garron's dark brown watery eyes. "My gift to you on this special day, is the gift of my heart. You'll forever hold it in the palm of your hand." After finishing, Garron leaned forward and kissed him.

Now Sonny waited for Garron to speak. He'd seen him sitting at the kitchen table on more than one occasion over the past week working on his vows. Sonny had also watched as Garron discarded page after page into the trashcan.

Looking down at him, Garron began. "I've spent a lot of time trying to figure out what to say today. Sadly though, I never managed to come up with anything that sounded half as lovely as what you just said. How do you tell someone in a couple lines how much they mean to you? How the air seems to leave the room when their not in it, or how the simple act of going off to work leaves them feeling empty and alone? I'm not the kind of man who can write poetry or pros. I'm just a man who loves you more than he loves his own life. I'm proud to become your husband today, cowboy, and I promise to try and pick up my own dirty socks." He winked at Sonny.

Sonny's throat felt so thick with emotion that he knew he was about to breakdown in a room full of people. Pulling Garron's head down, Sonny kissed him, long and deep. They broke the kiss, and Sonny whispered against Garron's lips. "That was better than poetry and pros. I love you."

"I love you, too, more than you'll ever know." Garron kissed him again before turning towards Jeb and holding out his hand as Sonny turned to Rawley. Lifting the simple gold band, Garron kissed it, before slipping it on Sonny's finger. Sonny felt a single tear slip down his cheek at the action.

Taking a deep breath, he blinked several times to dispel any more tears before kissing the ring and sliding it on Garron's much larger finger. They'd had the bands engraved with words close to their heart, 'Until death do us part'.

After settling the ring, Garron pulled Sonny into his arms for a proper wedding kiss. The crowd erupted in applause and well wishes. Sonny couldn't believe Garron was finally his.

* * * *

Immediately following the ceremony, Garron was pulled aside by Evelyn Good. "I'd like a word with you, young man." Evelyn said as she led him to a table in the corner.

Evelyn had flown in that afternoon and other than a quick introduction, Garron hadn't spoken to her. Mrs. Good stood only about five feet five inches tall, but she commanded her sons like a drill sergeant. He pulled out her chair and then seated himself. Chancing a glance at the rowdy crowd laughing, drinking and eating. "What would you like to talk to me about, ma'am?"

The grey-haired woman narrowed her eyes. "My Sonny tells me you're a policeman in Lincoln." She looked him up and down. "They let you wear your hair that long? I've never seen a policeman with tattoos either. Are you lying to my boy?"

Garron was caught off guard. He didn't know whether to be offended or tickled. "Yes, ma'am, I'm a detective with the vice squad in Lincoln. Before coming to Summerville, I worked vice in Chicago." Garron smoothed his ponytail over his shoulder. "This is part of my uniform, I guess you could say. I need to blend in to my environment." He grinned at the concerned mama bear. "Besides, I couldn't cut it now, your son loves it."

Evelyn smiled and patted his hand. "That sounds like my Sonny. You'll need to watch that boy. He can be a real handful," she said with a grin.

Garron almost choked on that last statement. Oh, if only she knew what a handful of Sonny was really like. "I'll watch him. He'll never get far from me."

Nodding once, Evelyn stood and smoothed down her lavender skirt. "Welcome to the family, young man."

"Thank you, ma'am," Garron said, standing next to his chair. As he watched Evelyn blend back into the crowd, he finally exhaled. He assumed he'd passed whatever test Mrs. Good had given. He felt an arm wrap around his waist from behind, and smiled.

"Momma checking you out?" Sonny asked petting Garron's ponytail.

"Something like that." Garron turned and wrapped his arms around his new husband. "Is it time to cut the cake and dance?"

"Yes on both accounts. I wanted to do the dollar dance, but Rawley said it wouldn't be appropriate. I don't know why. Lord knows I've done my share of dancing with brides at these things, forking over money left and right." He stuck out his bottom lip in a mock pout and Garron chuckled.

"I'll make you a deal. You dance only with me and I'll give you a hundred crumpled dollar bills tomorrow." He leaned down and whispered against Sonny's lips. "Deal?"

"Mmm hmm," Sonny moaned as the two of them kissed. A shout from Ryker broke them apart. The natives were getting restless, it seemed. Taking Garron by the hand, Sonny walked them over to the cake table.

Garron slowed and pointed towards the head table. "Should I grab my suit jacket?"

"Naw, I had the photographer take plenty of pictures with us all fancied up, time for a few casual ones, I think."

Garron smiled at the two grooms sitting on top of the cake surrounded by wildflower blossoms. Meg, who owned a pottery shop in town, had designed them. "Meg even got the size difference right."

Sonny stood a little taller and looked up at Garron. "Really? Because I thought she made me a little short. I do like the tattoos she painted on your guy though."

He didn't have the heart to tell Sonny that there was indeed that much height difference between the two of them. Instead he picked up the cake knife and looked at the engraved silver handle. "You're mom bring this?"

"Yep, it's been passed down from generation to generation in our family. Pretty, isn't it?"

The knife forgotten, Garron leaned down and kissed Sonny. "Gorgeous," he whispered as he broke the kiss to a chorus of cat calls. Blushing, Garron looked at Sonny. "Okay, cowboy, how do we cut this thing?"

Taking the knife from him, Sonny held it in his hand before placing Garron's over the top of it. "We'll just cut a small wedge out of the bottom tier, and then we feed it to each other." Sonny shrugged, "Its tradition."

Even though Garron knew he'd feel like an idiot, being fed a piece of cake, no way would he have denied Sonny the experience. He kissed Sonny's forehead and then looked down at their hands. "Let's do it."

After getting a mangled piece of cake cut and on a plate, Sonny took a small chunk and lifted it to Garron's lips. Taking a deep breath, Garron opened his mouth and accepted the token. It was worth everything to see the smile spread across Sonny's face. When it was his turn, Garron held the cake to Sonny's lips and was surprised when Sonny opened wide and took both the offering and Garron's fingers into his mouth. Sonny twirled his tongue around Garron's fingers and gave them a light suck. "Behave," Garron growled as he felt his cock fill.

Releasing his fingers, Sonny grinned. "Thank you," he whispered.

"Let's dance," Garron said as he took Sonny's hand. They walked around the clusters of guests towards the centre of the room for their first dance as a committed couple. As Garron took his groom in his arms, he couldn't believe how at peace he felt. Instead of letting his eyes stray around the private room, Garron only saw Sonny. God he loved this man. He felt totally complete for the first time in his life.

Feeling Sonny's erection pressing against him, Garron winked. "Not much longer and we can get started on that honeymoon." He gave Sonny a slow kiss. "I hope you're not too disappointed that we can't go on a real one right now, but as soon as I have vacation time, I plan on taking you somewhere tropical and secluded."

"Mmm, I like the sound of that," Sonny replied as the song ended. Sonny looked around at the crowd. "How 'bout we stay for another hour or so and then head home?"

Garron nodded, thinking about their ride home on his Harley. Nothing got Sonny hotter, faster, than riding on the back of his bike. He grinned as he thought of the wedding present he'd gotten his man. He hoped Sonny would like it.

They spent the next hour shaking hands and getting hugged by women wearing too much perfume. By the time they stepped out the door, they both smelled like women. The mere thought of which caused Garron to shiver. As they walked towards the Harley, Garron smiled at all the crate paper streamers attached to it. He waited for Sonny to notice his wedding present sitting on the seat and it didn't take long.

"Oh my God," Sonny said, as he picked up the custom painted white helmet. He traced his fingers over the air brushed Black Angus cattle on the side before turning it to read the Flying G painted on the back. Sonny looked over at him. "It's beautiful. It's the best gift anyone's ever given me."

Garron pulled him into his arms and kissed him. "I love you."

"I love you, too." He handed the helmet to Garron. "I think it's only right that you put it on me." Sonny took off his customary cowboy hat as Garron set the new helmet on his head and fastened the chin strap.

"Perfect," he whispered, kissing him once more. Garron heard Jeb and the Good brother's laughing in the background at their public display of affection. He turned towards the group of men. "Shut up."

They broke apart, and Sonny climbed onto the back of the bike, holding his cowboy hat out. "Hey, Rawley. Come get this hat."

Garron seated himself in front of Sonny as Rawley walked over. "The helmet looks good," Rawley said, accepting Sonny's black dress hat. "I'll be home in an hour." He grinned at Garron.

"Try Monday evening and not a second before, big brother." Sonny shot back at him.

Rawley pounded Sonny on the back. "Congratulations."

"Thanks," they both said at the same time.

Rawley stepped back and Garron started the loud bike.

Sonny leaned against him and wrapped his arms tightly around Garron's chest, already trying to work the buttons open on his dress shirt. Garron shook his head as he slowly pulled out of the parking lot.

Once on the main street, Garron started to give the motorcycle some gas when Sonny's head slammed into his back with such force Garron lost control of the bike. As if in slow motion, the bike tipped to the side, spilling both its passengers onto the pavement. Garron landed hard, knocking his head against the pavement as he felt the road tear some of the flesh from his arm. The first thing he did was to tear off his helmet and look for Sonny. Spotting him about ten feet away, Garron tried to crawl towards him. He started screaming hysterically when he saw the amount of blood covering Sonny's beautiful face. The closer he crawled to Sonny, the louder the voices running towards him got.

"Don't touch him," Rawley screamed as he tried to hold Garron back.

"Fuck you," Garron screamed as he fought to get closer to Sonny. His vision started to grow spotty as Jeb knelt down beside him to help hold him back.

"Garron, listen to me," Jeb said. "You can't touch Sonny or you may cause him more damage. Just wait until help arrives."

"I love him," Garron whispered as he drifted into darkness.

Chapter Four

The sound of sirens woke Garron. He tried to sit up, but was quickly pushed back down to the pavement. "Sit tight, brother. An ambulance is on the way."

Garron looked over towards Sonny. His eyes were still closed and he had several people kneeling beside him, but no one was doing anything. "Help him," he pleaded. "Don't let him die."

Jeb's hand smoothed over Garron's cheek. "He's been shot. Rawley called it in and St. Angeline's Hospital in Lincoln is sending their life-flight helicopter. They told us not to touch him."

Shaking his head slightly, Garron winced. "Shot?" He swallowed around the lump in his throat as he felt tears fall down the side of his face to pool in his ears. "Is he dead?"

"No, Rawley's monitoring his pulse until the chopper gets here. He figured that much touching would be okay and quite frankly, I think he needed something to concentrate on. Sonny's mom fainted as soon as she saw the blood. Meg and Mac already loaded her in their car and are on their way to the hospital."

Garron looked back up at Jeb. "I know I have a slight concussion and a bad case of road rash, but I think that's all that's wrong with me. Can you help me get closer to Sonny? I won't move him, I promise. I just need to be next to him." He sniffled as his nose started running.

Digging a handkerchief out of his back pocket, Jeb wiped Garron's eyes and then nose. "Come on, big brother," Jeb said, as he helped Garron over to Sonny. When Rawley started to object, Jeb held his hand up. "He won't try and move him, he's already promised. Come on, just let him hold Sonny's hand."

Rawley nodded and moved back enough for Garron. Hearing the ambulance pull up, Garron knew he'd only have a few moments. "Hey, cowboy," Garron said, squeezing Sonny's non-responsive hand. "I'm going to have to leave here in a minute, but I'll be with you soon." Garron heard the chopper overhead and Rawley left to tell them where to land. "Be strong for me because I can't live without you."

The EMT's loomed over Garron and started asking questions. Garron tried his best to answer everything, knowing the sooner he cooperated, the sooner he could go to Lincoln to be with Sonny. Before they picked him up to load him onto a gurney, Garron squeezed Sonny's hand once more. "You fight, you hear me. We've got too many years left for you to give up now. I love you," Garron whispered as they strapped him onto the gurney.

As they wheeled him towards the ambulance, Garron watched as the life-flight crew raced towards Sonny. The last thing he saw as they shut the ambulance doors was Sonny being carried towards the waiting helicopter. Jeb surprised him by knocking on the back window. "I'll follow the ambulance," he shouted through the glass.

* * * *

After enduring a CAT scan and thorough examination, the Summerville Medical Centre released Garron into Jeb's custody. They gave him strict instructions to follow-up with a doctor in Lincoln if he started feeling dizzy. Garron knew if it weren't for Sonny, the doctor would have never let him leave that night, but most of the people working the ER were also friends of his husbands.

With a heavily bandaged arm and killer headache, Garron sat in the passenger seat of Jeb's pickup. "Tell me again what Rawley said."

"Just that Sonny was still alive when he made it to the hospital. I guess they took him up to surgery before they even removed the helmet. The surgeon told Rawley it might take a while, but they wouldn't know until they got him in the operating room."

Hitting his fist against the dash, Garron looked at Jeb. "Can you please, just this once, drive over the speed limit?"

"What, and risk killing you for a second time tonight? I don't think so. I'm sure Sonny would rather have you arrive safely than ten minutes earlier."

"Just you wait, brother. Your time's coming, and then we'll see how calm you are." Garron settled in for the gruelling drive into Lincoln. He was surprised Jeb didn't say anything. When he glanced his way, Jeb seemed a million miles away, lost in his own thoughts.

Closing his eyes, Garron thought of Sonny. He'd never forget the look of love, awe and total devotion on his face while Garron recited his commitment vows. Had it really only been a couple of hours earlier? The day had been so perfect. Garron had never seen Sonny happier than when he toasted his friends and family for their love and support.

Jeb told Garron as soon as he finished with the CAT scan, that Rawley had called one of his deputies and told him to find Lionel Hibbs and bring him in for questioning. Rawley said that they weren't to let him leave until he finished with his brother and got there. Garron could imagine the kind of questioning Rawley intended. He may be the town's Sheriff, but he was Sonny's brother, first and foremost.

Jeb dropped Garron at the Emergency Room door, before going to park the truck. Garron ran inside and asked the lady at the information desk where he could find the Good family. He was told to go up to the second floor, surgical waiting room.

Garron nodded and looked towards the door, just as Jeb ran in. "Second floor," he said as they made their way to the stairs. Taking the steps two at a time, Garron's head felt like it would fall off by the time he reached the waiting room.

Ryker was the first to see him and rushed to his side. "How are you?"

"I'm fine, have you heard anything?" Garron winced as Ryker unexpectedly hugged him.

Pulling back, Ryker must have seen the look on Garron's face. "Oh shit, sorry. How's the arm?" Ryker asked, looking at Garron's heavily bandaged arm.

"Fine," Garron ground out. "Tell me how he is?"

Ryker motioned Garron over to the small room off to the side of the waiting area. Garron walked into the room, and nodded to everyone before turning back to Ryker. "Well?"

"The doctor's nurse has come in a couple of times in the last two hours to update us. According to her, the bullet was a twenty-two calibre, which is good. The helmet stopped the momentum enough that it didn't enter the brain. However, the impact caused an open depressed skull fracture. The surgeon is making sure none of the bone fragments entered the brain. After he's finished assessing Sonny, the nurse said the surgeon would almost certainly use a titanium mesh to cover the area, if the skull fragments turn out to be too small to repair."

Garron looked at Ryker while he analyzed all the information. "Did she say what his prognosis is?"

"No, she said the doctor would be able to tell us more once he finished. They do hold out a lot of hope because Sonny regained consciousness just before they took him into surgery." Ryker grinned, "The doctor was planning to cut the helmet off him, but Sonny begged him not to because it was a wedding gift from his husband."

Garron fell to the chair, and put his face in his hands as he finally broke down. Of all the things for Sonny to be worrying about it was just like him to think of that stupid helmet. He felt a hand on his back, rubbing soothing circles into his tense muscles. Wiping his eyes, he looked over and came face to face with Evelyn.

"Sonny's a fighter. You'll see."

Garron swallowed and gave her a nod. "I can't believe he risked injuring himself more by trying to save that stupid gift."

Evelyn took Garron's hand and squeezed. "Now you listen here, young man. That gift you gave him saved his life. According to the nurse, the helmet was removed without further injury to Sonny, so just leave it at that."

Looking into Evelyn's worried eyes, Garron longed for his own mother. His parent's had both refused to come down to Nebraska for such a sacrilegious event. Right now though, he wanted nothing more than to be safely tucked in his mother's arms.

Evelyn must have seen the need in Garron's face because she carefully wrapped him in a motherly hug. "He'll be fine. You need to believe that."

Garron nodded and wiped his eyes again. "I'm sorry. I knew having the ceremony in town was risky, Rawley tried to tell us both…"

"That's enough of that. It was a beautiful wedding, everything that my Sonny hoped for. You can't blame yourself for what happened." Evelyn kissed Garron's cheek and turned towards Rawley. "Speaking of which, why don't you go find out who did this?"

"I know who did it, Mom. He's sitting in an interrogation room as we speak, but I want to make sure Sonny's going to be okay before I go back to Summerville," Rawley said, never taking his eyes off the floor.

Garron happened to notice the look on Jeb's face. The need to comfort Rawley so strong Jeb's hands were shaking.

"You need to have a little more faith in your brother as well, young man. He's going to be fine, but the longer that man sits, the more alibis he's going to be able to come up with." Evelyn shook her finger at Rawley. "And you make sure you go by the book. I won't have this little weasel get off on some technicality."

Rawley sighed and looked at his mom. "Promise to call me as soon as you hear something?"

"You know we will," Ranger said.

Garron looked up at his brother. "Why don't you go with Rawley? I'll be fine."

Jeb looked at Garron for a few seconds and then turned to Rawley. "Would that be okay with you?"

"Yeah," Rawley said, as he bent to kiss his mother good-bye. "I'll be back as soon as I finish up with Lionel." He turned back to Jeb, "Come on, I think I'll let you drive if you don't mind?"

Jeb nodded and walked over to Garron. Running his hand over Garron's hair, Jeb leaned over and kissed the top of his head. "Love you."

"I know," Garron whispered.

* * * *

They rode the elevator down and walked out to the parking lot in silence. Rawley headed towards the Sheriff's SUV and Jeb stopped him with a hand on his arm. "Do we have to take that? I'd feel a lot better driving my own pickup."

Rawley stopped and looked at Jeb's hand. Of all the times he dreamed of Jeb finally touching him, this wasn't the scenario he'd fantasised about. "Yeah, we can take your truck."

Jeb pointed towards the opposite direction. "I'm parked over there."

Rawley nodded and they started towards the bright red dual-cab pickup. Rawley tried his best to concentrate on the truck and not the fine ass walking in front of him. Stop it, he told himself. This is the exact reason his brother was upstairs in surgery. Summerville was not the place for a man like himself. He'd tried his damdest to make his brothers understand that. Now they were suffering the reality of being gay in a small mid-western town.

Shaking his head to clear his thoughts, Rawley climbed into the passenger seat and fastened his safety belt.

Jeb got in and did the same, but before starting the truck he turned to Rawley. "You okay?"

Rawley just looked at Jeb. His curly blond hair reflected the street light above, creating a halo effect around his head, his warm brown eyes and long black lashes in sharp contrast to the fair hair and skin. If ever he were to fall, this was definitely the man it would be for. He wasn't sure what signal he gave, but the next thing he knew, Jeb had unfastened his seat belt and slid over into Rawley's open arms.

There mouths clashed together in a heated kiss that threatened to completely overwhelm him. He felt the ache of his cock as it pressed against the zipper of his dress slacks and he knew. God help him, but he'd already fallen. The sudden thought of spending his life with Jeb scared Rawley shitless. No, he refused to travel the path of his brothers, always being talked about, never truly safe. Nope, that kind of life wasn't for him. He loved his job, and his town and he couldn't see giving either of them up, even for Jeb.

Breaking the kiss, Rawley looked into Jeb's heavy lidded eyes. "I can't do this, I won't." He opened the truck door and fled before Jeb could utter a word. Jogging to his SUV, Rawley felt twisted to the point of nausea. He unlocked the door and sped out of the parking lot.

He had a job to do and nothing would keep him from it.

Chapter Five

Sitting beside Sonny's hospital bed, the doctors words replayed over and over in his head. Brain damage...would probably need months of therapy...seizures. Taking a deep breath, Garron reached out and touched Sonny's hand. They had him in a drug induced coma because Dr. Adams said it was best to let him heal a little before waking him. Although very little actual damage was done to the brain, Sonny had been left with a lesion and several contusions. Sadly enough, they just didn't know what they'd be faced with when Sonny woke up.

Everyone had tried to get Garron to take a break and go home for a while, but he just couldn't. Even though it was no longer his wedding night, he knew he couldn't face the house without Sonny. He'd called in and taken the day off work, but promised to be there in the morning. At least he'd be working in the same city with Sonny. He could come by in the morning, at lunch and then camp out in the evening. They'd need his income if Sonny wasn't able to work again. Although, he knew that the Good brothers and Shelby would take care of the ranch no matter what.

A nurse came in to check them both about every hour. She seemed like a nice woman, Mary, he thought her name was. Jeb had told her about Garron's concussion and asked her to keep an eye on him. Mary took the job seriously. Garron wasn't sure if it was because she felt sorry for him or because she thought Jeb was hot. Thinking of Jeb brought thoughts of Rawley to mind, and the phone call he'd gotten from Jeb the night of the shooting.

Garron wasn't sure what had gone on between Rawley and his brother, but Jeb clammed up as soon as Garron asked about their ride back to Summerville. Thinking of Rawley brought him to Lionel, which was never a good thing. His muscles tensed just thinking about that fucker. Rawley had questioned Lionel for all of an hour before he got a call from the mayor. Seemed Lionel's dad was pulling in favours. Mayor Channing demanded that Rawley let Lionel go unless he had solid proof against him. Poor Rawley was left with no choice but to turn him loose. He went to the judge to ask for a search warrant and the judge said he'd need a little more proof before issuing one. The Hibbs family were notorious for suing anyone who dared to cross them.

Rawley asked Garron to come back to Summerville and re-enact where the motorcycle was when he felt Sonny slam into him. Rawley had the trajectory angle from the surgeon but he needed to know approximately where Sonny and Garron had been on the street before determining which building the shot came from. That's the one thing they did know. According to Dr. Adams, the bullet had made a downward path. Garron told Rawley he'd go back to Summerville as soon as Sonny woke up, until then he wasn't leaving.

Dr. Adams had told Garron the previous night they planned to start weaning Sonny off some of the drugs that morning. Hopefully by evening he'd be a little more alert.

A hand to the side of his face made him spring out of the chair and turn around. Evelyn stood looking up at him. Damn, he was losing his touch. He hadn't even heard anyone come in. "Sorry, you startled me."

"Well it's no wonder you're jumpy. You haven't slept in two days." Evelyn walked over to Sonny and started straightening his bed. She brushed her knuckles across Sonny's cheek before turning back to Garron. "Why don't you go home and get a few hours of sleep? And while you're at it, go by the station and give Rawley the information he needs for his investigation."

Garron shook his head. "I can't leave him until I know he'll wake up."

Walking up to him, Evelyn put a hand on Garron's. "Don't you see Sonny will need you more once he's awake. Now's the right time to go, I'll sit with him." She held up her knitting bag. "I've plenty to keep me busy and I'll call you as soon as he starts waking."

Looking from Evelyn back to Sonny, Garron closed his eyes. He knew she was right, but it just didn't feel right to leave. "I don't think I'm safe to drive right now."

A smile spread across Evelyn's face. "That's why I made Ranger drive me. He's waiting just outside by the nurses' station."

He looked at her for several seconds before giving a short nod. Turning towards Sonny, Garron leaned over and kissed his cheek. Sonny had so many tubes running in and out of him, it was hard to find a spot of skin, but Garron had found the place on his cheek and kissed it often. "Love you," he whispered, "I'll be back in a couple of hours." Garron felt his eyes begin to burn and blinked rapidly. The Good family had seen him cry enough over the past few days.

Turning back towards Evelyn, Garron shrugged. "Promise me you'll call."

"You know I will."

With a glance back at Sonny, Garron walked out to the nurses' station. "You ready?"

"Yeah," Ranger said.

Getting into Ranger's truck, Garron put his head back and closed his eyes. Fuck he was tired. He felt the truck begin to move, but didn't open his eyes.

"Do you want me to take you home first or by the station?" Ranger asked.

Garron would rather go home, but knew the quicker he helped Rawley the faster they'd prove Lionel was behind the shooting. "What if I see Lionel in town? You know I'll try to kill the fucker."

After a few seconds, Garron heard Ranger talking on his cell phone. "Hey, I'm bringing Garron to town. Meet us at The Zone. We need to get this done before Lionel comes snooping around." Ranger ended the call. "Rawley will meet us there. It shouldn't take long. Why don't you nap a bit before we get there?"

"If I fall asleep, I'll be hard to wake up for at least a couple of hours. Better to get what needs to be done out of the way first." Garron forced his eyes open and looked at Ranger. "Can I have Shelby call you if he has any trouble at the ranch?"

"You don't even need to ask. Ryker and I know as much about cattle as Sonny does. We'll help Shelby out even if he doesn't ask."

"Thanks."

Ryker drummed his fingers on the steering wheel. "So what will you do if Sonny's bad when he wakes up?"

"What do you mean?"

Shifting uncomfortably, Ryker reached out and turned off the radio. "What if he's not the same?"

Garron knew there was a possibility that Sonny's personality would undergo a change, but he'd put off thinking about it. "Learn to love the new Sonny, I guess. I mean, he'll always be Sonny, but he might have a few more quirks to get used to. Hell, the man has enough now, what's a few more." Garron tried to smile, but new it looked more like a grimace. "I love him and no matter what, that won't change."

"I hope you're right, for both your sakes."

They settled into silence for the rest of the drive. Pulling into town, Garron felt his stomach knot as they neared The Zone. Rawley was already waiting for them in the parking lot and Garron took a deep breath. He'd tried like hell to forget the moment he felt Sonny's head slam against his back. Now he'd have to relive it in detail. "What happened to my Harley?"

"We took it to the dealership in Lincoln to have it repaired."

"Call and cancel the repairs. I'll never be able to look at that bike again. Eventually, maybe I'll get another, but I don't want that one."

"They might as well repair it, insurance will pay for it and then you can sell or trade it in," Ranger said, opening his door.

"Yeah, sorry, I'm not thinking too clearly right now."

"Understandable. Come on, let's get this over with." Ranger got out and slammed the door.

Taking another deep breath, Garron got out of the truck and headed towards Main Street. He didn't even look at Rawley and Ranger, just tried to picture the path his bike took that night. Closing his eyes, he pictured himself with

Sonny wrapped around him. Easing the buttons open on his shirt as he pulled out of the parking lot. He walked into the street totally oblivious to traffic. Luckily Rawley and Ranger were there to make sure nothing happened.

He was so deep in his memory of that night he swore he could smell the perfume that clung to their clothing. Garron walked to the point where he remembered Sonny's head slamming into him. God, he hadn't even known at the time it was the bullets impact that had done it. He knew he lost control of the bike within a second or two after impact, but he was having a hard time remembering where exactly in the road he was when he felt Sonny's helmet.

Opening his eyes, Garron looked around at his surroundings. He saw the scars left on the pavement from his bike and knew it would have been a second or two before that. He looked down at the road and shook his head. "I think it was right about here, but I can't swear to it in court." He looked at Rawley. "Does that help at all?"

Rawley nodded and shook the paint can in his hand. He walked over and sprayed a circle with day-glow orange. "I'm going to have someone from Lincoln come down who knows more than I do about trajectory. Hopefully, we'll be able to pinpoint which building Lionel was shooting from. The judge won't give me a warrant without some sort of information." Rawley looked at the building across the street. Rubbing his chin, he stood in the centre of the circle and held out his arm. "My guess is it came from there, but people will say I'm prejudice."

"Why," Garron asked.

"Because that building is owned by Charles Hibbs."

* * * *

Charles Hibbs watched the three men in the street from his second-floor window. When he saw Rawley point towards his building he shook his head. "Oh this won't do at all," he said out loud. He picked up the phone and called Lionel.

"Hello," Lionel said gruffly.

"Care to explain why Sheriff Good is standing in the middle of Main Street pointing towards my building?"

"Nope," Lionel replied.

"I'm getting damn tired of bailing you out every time you get yourself into a fix. Just make sure you and your boys get back over here tonight and clean up your mess. I can stall the Sheriff only so long before he comes knocking with a warrant."

"Will do," Lionel said and hung up.

Charles set the phone back in its cradle and ran his fingers over his bald head. "I wonder how much this is going to cost me."

* * * *

Stepping into the quiet house, Garron threw Sonny's keys onto the coffee table. He wandered to the kitchen and looked in the fridge. He hadn't eaten a decent meal in days, not since the reception. Thinking of the wedding, Garron closed the fridge door, no longer hungry.

He made his way to the bedroom and stripped out of his clothes, deciding sleep would come easier if he were clean. Garron quickly took a shower and shaved. After cleaning up, he felt a little better and climbed into bed. As soon as Garron laid his head on the pillow, he smelled Sonny. Grabbing Sonny's pillow, Garron held it to his face and inhaled deeply. "God I miss you, cowboy." He felt the tears come, but this time there was no one around to see him break down.

Squeezing the pillow tighter, Garron cried, whole body shaking, until he drifted off.

Someone shook him, and Garron managed to open his eyes. When he saw it was Jeb, he sat straight up. "What's happened?"

Jeb gave him a slight smile. "Sonny's starting to come around a little. I thought you'd like me to drive you to the hospital."

Garron swung his legs over the side of the bed and ran his fingers through his tangled hair. "Why didn't someone call?"

"They did, several times. You must have been too far gone, so Ryker phoned and asked me to come over and check on you." Jeb got up and went to the dresser. Pulling out a pair of jeans, underwear, socks and Garron's customary black T-shirt, he tossed them over. "Get dressed and I'll meet you in the truck."

Pulling on his clothes, Garron looked around. "I'll be a minute. I want to pack a bag for me and Sonny. I don't plan on coming back here for a while and I have work tomorrow."

Jeb started to say something, but snapped his mouth shut and nodded before leaving the room. Garron quickly dressed and brushed his hair, pulling it back at the nape. He found a duffle on the top shelf of the closet and started packing. He threw in a couple of changes of clothes for himself and one for Sonny to come home in. Next he rifled through Sonny's drawer and came up with a couple of pairs of pyjama bottoms. Getting his shaving kit, he threw that in too, before zipping the bag and heading downstairs.

Walking up to Jeb's truck, Garron gestured for him to roll down the window. "I know you need to bring Evelyn home, but I'll take Sonny's truck. I'll need a way to get back and forth to work."

"Sure you're okay to drive?"

"Yeah, I'm sure, but I don't plan on going the speed limit so I'll see ya there." Garron didn't wait for Jeb's answer. He threw the duffle in the passenger seat and took off in a cloud of dust. If Sonny was waking up he didn't want to miss a second of it.

The drive into Lincoln didn't take much time at all. Garron was damn glad he hadn't met up with any patrolmen because he pushed the needle past eighty most of the way. Grabbing the duffle, he locked the truck and ran towards the hospital entrance. Taking the elevator, Garron pushed the button for the fourth floor, and paced back and forth.

As soon as the doors opened, Garron was out and running towards Sonny. He stopped just outside the door and said a little prayer. Walking in the room, he saw Sonny's legs moving under the covers.

Evelyn noticed Garron and walked over as he set down the bag. "He's coming out of it, but he's restless. The doctor said it was perfectly normal, but we need to watch that he doesn't try and pull out any of his tubes."

Garron walked over and sat at the foot of the bed. He ran his hands over Sonny's legs, trying to calm him. "It's okay, cowboy. I'm here now. I'll take care of you." Garron continued to talk softly to Sonny until Jeb came into the room.

"How is he?" Jeb asked Evelyn.

"We don't know yet. Even when he wakes up, Dr. Adams said it may take a few days for him to be coherent enough to do any sort of testing."

"He's fine, he'll be back to his old self before you know it," Garron said, looking only at Sonny.

He saw Sonny's eyes open and watched as they seemed to roll around for a few seconds before the lids closed again. Garron never stopped rubbing and petting Sonny's legs, even after receiving a kiss from Evelyn. "I'm going home for the night, but call me if there's any change."

"Yes, ma'am," Garron said, looking at Evelyn briefly.

Evelyn kissed the top of his head again. "I think you've earned the right to call me mom."

Garron's throat constricted and he knew he couldn't talk without breaking down, so he gave her a simple nod. Jeb walked over and gave Garron a kiss on the forehead. "Call me if you need anything."

"Okay."

After the two of them left, Garron started talking to Sonny again. He didn't know how long he talked or how many times he thought Sonny was waking up, but never quite managed it. The next thing he knew a nurse put a glass of juice in his hand.

"Drink this. Your voice is starting to sound like sandpaper."

Garron looked at the elderly nurse and smiled. "Thank you." He drank the glass of apple juice in three swallows and handed it back. "How long will this take?"

"Hard to say, sweetie, every brain injury is different. You just keep doing what you're doing." The nurse patted Garron's back before tossing the plastic cup into the trashcan. She checked Sonny's IV and his urine output bag before leaving the room.

Clearing his throat, Garron went back to talking to Sonny.

Several hours later, Sonny's eyes opened again, but this time they stayed open, although they still looked a little swimmy. Garron stood and went to the head of the bed. "Cowboy? Can you hear me?"

Sonny's eyelids drooped down, but he gave a slight nod. "I love you, and I've been waiting for you to wake up. Your mom was here earlier, and your brothers have been here every day to check on you." Garron rattled on as Sonny continued to slowly blink, a blank look on his face. Garron finally realised he wasn't getting much response from him. "Sonny? Do you know who I am?"

Sonny's eyes, slid towards him, and he mouthed the word "no."

Chapter Six

Garron finished his reports and turned them in before leaving the police station. Damn he was tired, tired and grouchy as fuck. It had been two weeks since Sonny had first opened his eyes and he still didn't recognise him more than half the time. The doctor said it was normal to lose some short-term memory. That didn't sit well, knowing he was a short-term memory.

Driving back to the hospital, Garron wondered which Sonny he'd meet. It seemed like every time he walked into the room, Sonny was either screaming at someone or crying like a baby. He'd even had Garron taken out of the room on several occasions, claiming he didn't know who he was and was afraid Garron would try to hurt him. Garron had left the room, but not the hospital. The couch in the waiting room was starting to feel like home.

Two nights earlier, Sonny had become violent and actually punched one of his nurses who tried to adjust his catheter. He'd yelled for someone to call the police, insisting that the hospital staff was trying to kill him. It had taken a good deal of talking to get Sonny and the poor nurse calmed down.

Garron sure as hell wasn't looking forward to dealing with a scene like that again any time soon.

Walking through the door, Garron was surprised to see Sonny sitting in a chair eating his dinner. He turned when he heard Garron. "Where the fuck have you been? Everyone else has been in to see me except my own damn husband. You out cattin' around?"

Garron swallowed and sat on Sonny's made bed. "I was here at lunch, and breakfast, and last night, and every day since they brought you in."

"Bullshit, they would have told me if you'd been here." Sonny said, pushing his food tray away.

Sighing, Garron rubbed his eyes. He didn't know what to say to his lover anymore.

"Hey, love? Did you put the roast in the oven for supper?"

Garron looked at Sonny, "Yeah, it should be ready in about an hour."

"Good because I'm starving." Sonny held out his hand. "Come over here and give me some sugar."

Standing, Garron walked over to Sonny and knelt beside him. Leaning in, he kissed the lips he'd missed for so long. This was the closest he'd gotten to Sonny since he woke up and Garron didn't plan on wasting a second of it. He pushed his tongue deep into Sonny's mouth and moaned, feeling himself go hard.

Sonny broke the kiss and looked into his eyes. "Why won't you let me go home with you?" Garron saw the moisture pool in those pretty amethyst eyes.

"Oh, cowboy, I want nothing more than to have you home, but the doctor says you need to stay in here for a little while longer. At least until you get more of your strength back. I'll be here though, every day, just like I have been."

Running his hand down Garron's cheek, Sonny smiled. "I think we should plant some candy trees. I've always wanted some."

Garron closed his eyes, knowing Sonny was off again. "When you get home."

"Yeah, speaking of which, when will they let me leave?"

* * * *

Rawley shook the judge's hand, as he was handed the warrant to search the Hibb's building. It had taken almost three weeks and he doubted he'd find anything, but he had to try. Taking two of his deputies, Rawley walked into Charles' office and presented him with the piece of paper.

Crossing his hands behind his head, Charles leaned back in his chair. "Look all you want, Sheriff."

According to the criminologist from Lincoln, the shooter more than likely had been positioned on the roof of the building. When Rawley and his deputies walked out onto the roof, Rawley's heart fell. He looked over at Craig. "How many roofs have you ever seen that looked like this?"

Craig shook his head, "I don't know many houses that are kept this clean."

"Spread out and look anyway," Rawley informed his deputies. He started walking along the west side of the building that faced Main Street. It was obvious that the roof had not only been swept clean but scrubbed down as well. It was an obvious attempt to cover his tracks, but without evidence, Rawley couldn't prove Lionel had done it.

Knowing Sonny would be coming home soon, Rawley decided to step up his game and hope that Lionel would get so frustrated he'd let something slip. With new resolve, he motioned his deputies and left the building.

* * * *

Using a walker, Sonny made his way up the temporary ramp and into the house. He'd refused Garron's help so he followed close behind carrying the duffle. Evelyn was already there, having agreed to stay until Sonny was able to get around on his own. She opened the screen door and smiled. "There's my boy." She kissed Sonny's cheek as he passed.

"Mom," Sonny ground out.

Evelyn looked at Garron and he rolled his eyes. Sonny had bitched the entire ride home about something. He was either too hot or too cold, the radio was too loud or he couldn't hear it. This was Sonny's 'I'm-going-to-act-like-a-teenager mood'. God, Garron hated this particular one. He followed them into the house and took the bag to the laundry room.

Looking around it was obvious Evelyn had done a little cleaning. Not that the house had been messy, but now there was the distinct smell of lemon furniture polish. He also smelled dinner. "Something smells good," he said, walking into the kitchen. He knew enough not to hover around Sonny, so he left him in the living room.

Evelyn walked in and opened the stove. Getting a couple of pot holders out of the drawer, she withdrew a homemade beef pot pie. "I figured the two of you'd be hungry by the time you got here."

Garron's stomach growled at the smell of real food. He'd been living on nothing but cafeteria food and take-out for almost a month. "God, I think I love you." Garron kissed Evelyn on the cheek just as Sonny came into the kitchen.

"What the fuck is going on in here?"

"Oh you hush," Evelyn shook her finger at her son. "Garron was just thanking me for cooking dinner. Honestly Sonny, if you don't straighten up, Garron's going to set off for greener pastures."

Garron's head shot from Evelyn to Sonny. Sonny blinked a couple of times before turning around and shuffling out of the kitchen. Garron looked at Evelyn. "Why did you say that? There's no way I'd leave him."

"I know that, but maybe he needs to do a little thinking. I know a lot of his mood swings are because of his injuries, but I also believe a lot of them are because he's grumpy and frustrated. Those last two, he can control and he needs to start." She put her hands on Garron's cheeks. "You've been a saint so far, but how long do you think that can last before you get fed up? Nope, better for Sonny to adjust his attitude than to risk his relationship."

Garron sighed, "I hate myself sometimes for the way I feel. I know it's not his fault, but I miss my cowboy. I get tired of always being the strong one. I know the doctor said he'd continue to get better as the bruises healed, but it can't happen soon enough." He looked towards the door. "I'm gonna go find him and make sure he's okay."

Walking into the den they'd converted into a temporary bedroom, Garron found Sonny sitting on the bed. He sat down and held out his hand, knowing better than to just assume Sonny wanted to be touched.

After several very long seconds, Sonny placed his hand in Garron's. "You going to leave me?"

Pulling off his wedding band, Garron held it to Sonny's face. "What's that say on the inside?"

Sonny glanced into his eyes and then looked at the ring. "Until death do us part."

Garron nodded his head and slipped the ring back on his finger. "Are you dead?"

"No," Sonny mumbled.

"Enough said." Garron wrapped his arms around Sonny. "I love you, and I always will. There may be times when I get angry or frustrated, but the love part of our relationship is a given, it always will be. Do you remember what the doctor told you about getting better?"

"Yeah, he said it will come."

"Well, even if it doesn't I'm not planning on going anywhere. I'm a tough tick to shake." Garron captured Sonny's lips in a long slow kiss. "Come on, lets eat and then I'll take you on a ride around the ranch. I know how much you've missed it."

Sonny looked into Garron's eyes. The beautiful purple orbs filled with moisture. "I'm sorry. I don't want to be this way. I should have listened and had the ceremony here."

"Now don't go gettin' soft on me, cowboy. If the shooting hadn't happened in town it would have happened out here. Lionel and his friends are nothing but time bombs waiting to go off."

Garron kissed the tears on Sonny's face. He stood and pulled Sonny up. "Now, let's go eat that casserole before it gets cold."

* * * *

That night, as Garron helped Sonny into bed, he wondered if he should stay. Although Sonny had been in a decent mood most of the evening, Garron knew it could change in an instant. Sonny must have read his mind.

"You're sleeping with me, aren't you?"

"Is that what you want?" Garron asked, hoping for a night alone with his love.

"Yes, please," Sonny begged.

Garron undressed quickly and turned off the light before sliding between the sheets and pulling Sonny into his arms. "No acrobatics tonight."

Sonny smoothed his hand down Garron's chest to wrap around his cock. "I think we'd better get it while we can."

The feel of Sonny's hand on him had an immediate effect. Garron thrust into Sonny's grip. Shit, that felt good. Deciding to go with the flow, Garron reciprocated and reached for Sonny. "Been too long. I've missed you," Garron said, taking Sonny's mouth in a deep kiss.

"Yeah, I'm sorry about that," Sonny whispered against Garron's lips.

"No sorrys, not here, not ever." Garron felt Sonny's grip begin to weaken. Not wanting Sonny to feel bad about his current state of health, Garron rolled over on top of him and ground his cock against his lovers. "Yes, right there," he groaned as he felt his balls draw up. "Oh, gonna."

"Yeah, come for me," Sonny begged as his heat seeped between them.

God, Garron loved the smell of Sonny's seed. Latching on to Sonny's neck, Garron pumped jet after jet of come between them. Ears ringing, Garron collapsed to Sonny's side and pulled him into his arms. "Love you."

"Mmm, love you," Sonny yawned as he drifted off to sleep.

Garron knew he should get up and get a warm washcloth to clean them up, but he'd missed the smell of their combined essence so much he decided to leave it. He'd deal with the crusty mess in the morning, but right now, Sonny was in his arms.

Something woke him sometime later. He reached for Sonny and felt a cold empty bed. Springing up, Garron grabbed his jeans. Walking out of the den, Garron noticed the front door standing wide open. How the hell did Sonny manage to get up and out of the house without waking him?

He flipped on the outdoor lights and ran, barefooted into the ranch yard. "Sonny?" he yelled as he frantically searched the area. "Sonny," he yelled again.

He rounded the corner of the barn and saw a naked Sonny standing in the field behind the barn. Garron ran up to Sonny and wrapped his arms around him. "Damn, cowboy, you scared me to death. Why are you out here?"

"Just trying to remember where the chicken house is? I forgot to feed them earlier, but I don't remember where they are."

Garron could hear the frustration in Sonny's voice. He knew if he told Sonny they'd never had chickens it would either confuse him more or make him think Garron was lying to him. "I'm sorry. I forgot to tell you, I sold all the chickens. I hope you're not mad. It's just that we weren't here and the eggs were just going to waste. I'll get us some new ones this weekend, okay?"

Sonny looked at him for several seconds before nodding. "Yeah, it's okay. I never much liked them anyway. Is it time for you to go to work?"

"No, it's time for us to go back to bed. Sonny started to follow and it was then that Garron noticed Sonny didn't have his walker. He could tell by the way he was shuffling his feet that he was tired. "Hey, cowboy? I know you don't need it, but I sure do miss carrying you in my arms. Would you let me do that, please?"

"Okay," Sonny said. His voice still sounded a little far off.

Garron scooped Sonny up and walked towards the house. He'd been honest about one thing. He had missed the feeling of carrying Sonny. A naked Sonny was just icing on the cake.

Chapter Seven

Pulling up in front of the twin's house, Garron parked. The Good brothers had called a meeting, and he was glad to see Rawley was already here. It was the weekend and usually he'd be working with Sonny. Hell, he hadn't even gotten his morning snuggle, the meeting being called at such an ungodly hour. Garron opened the door. At least he should be home in time to get Sonny his lunch.

Evelyn had gone home a few days earlier on Garron's insistence. Sonny was using her as a crutch, and Garron believed until he started doing some things on his own, he'd never fully heal. It was hard to watch, but Garron knew it was the best thing for him.

Looking up at the house, Garron was impressed. He'd never been to Ranger and Ryker's sanctuary, as they called it. Set back in a grove of trees, the house wasn't even visible from the road. Garron doubted very many people had ever seen it. The twins were a very closed off pair, not antisocial, just private.

Climbing the steps, Garron marvelled at the deep porch that ran the length of the house. It was set up almost like an extra living room, with big comfortable looking outdoor furniture. Made sense he guessed, since the twins were both big men. Knocking on the door, he listened to the overhead ceiling fans as they stirred the thick, Nebraska morning air.

"Hey, glad you could make it," Ryker said, opening the door. He stepped back and Garron walked into the two story great room. Exposed beams crisscrossed overhead, accented by more fans.

"I hope this meeting is short," Garron said. "I don't want to leave Sonny for long. The weekends are kind of special to us." He followed Ryker into the kitchen where Ranger and Rawley were talking at the kitchen table.

"Coffee?" Ryker asked.

"Sure." Garron sat down.

"How's Sonny?" Rawley asked.

"Good, well, better. You know you can move back home. Sonny only wanted you out for that weekend." Garron's jaws tensed as he thought about his wedding night.

"You had enough company with mom there." Rawley said, sipping his coffee.

"You're not company, man, you're family. Have you been staying here?" He nodded at Ryker as he reached for his cup.

"Hell no," they all said in unison.

"I've been staying with Meg, but I haven't even been there much. I've been spending my off hours following Lionel. That's one of the things I wanted to talk to you all about." Rawley got up and poured himself another cup.

"I'm starting to catch some heat from the mayor. It seems Lionel doesn't like being followed. He complained to his daddy and his daddy climbed all over Mayor Channing." Sitting back down, Rawley looked around the table. "I've been told rather subtly to either stop following Lionel or Summerville would be looking for another Sheriff."

"That fucker," Ranger said, slamming his fist on the table. "What the hell does he expect you to do?"

"I don't know. I think the mayor wants me to drop the whole thing. He keeps telling me the city has spent money on this investigation and I've still come up empty." Rawley closed his eyes and shook his head. Garron noticed the lines of fatigue in his face, and wondered how much the investigation had cost him.

"I have the ballistics report on both bullets, but they don't do me any good without the actual guns to test. We know the bull was killed by a Browning Hunting Rifle and Sonny was shot with a simple twenty-two gauge rimfire, which almost everyone in the county owns. The roof of the Hibbs building was the location of the shooter, but that proved clean. Too clean." Rawley scrubbed his hands over his face. "I don't know what else to do. The judge won't give me warrants to look for the guns and I haven't heard a word around town. So I've been watching Lionel, hoping he'll break."

"What do you need from us?" Garron asked.

"I need someone on Lionel's ass twenty-four seven, and according to the mayor it can't be me."

Garron thought of spending even more time away from Sonny. With his long work days and the two hour commute, it sure wouldn't leave much time. "Sorry, man, but my time is kind of limited right now. I could do maybe two evenings a week and a half day on the weekend. Maybe it would help if we ask a few more people to help. I'm sure Jeb would be willing." Garron didn't miss the flex of Rawley's jaw at the mention of his brother.

"Craig would probably take a shift once or twice a week." Rawley looked over at the twins. "You two know anyone?"

"Well Shelby for sure, that's a given." Ranger looked at Ryker. The two of them seemed to have a conversation without words. Ranger finally nodded and looked at Rawley. "Why don't we hire a few outside guys to take up the slack? I don't think Garron should be involved for several reasons. First, Sonny will start to question why he's gone and with the way he's been, that might turn ugly. Second, Sonny really shouldn't be left alone. If Lionel knows Garron is following him, what's to stop him from calling one of his buddies and asking them to pay Sonny a visit? And third, I don't know that Garron can be that close to Lionel and not kill him."

"Yeah, we could probably all chip in and hire a few off duty cops or something from Lincoln." Rawley turned to Garron. "This could be dangerous. When you're dealing with someone like Lionel you never know. Jeb isn't trained for it, so I think it would be best to leave him out of this. Besides, it's not his fight."

"The hell it's not," Garron said, narrowing his eyes at Rawley. "He's gonna come asking why he wasn't asked to be involved, and I'm going to send him your way."

"Do what you have to," Rawley growled.

Garron looked at Rawley for several seconds. "I know this is frustrating for you, and I appreciate everything you're doing to try and get something on Lionel, but pushing people who care about you away isn't the answer."

Rawley drained his cup and looked at his watch. "I'm heading into town. Lionel should be awake by now." He looked at his brothers. "Can one of you relieve me at two o'clock? I'll go home and get a little sleep and be back for the night watch."

Ranger nodded, "We'll get on the phone and find some help."

"I'd appreciate it," Rawley said with a wave as he walked out.

After Rawley's SUV was heard pulling out of the gravel drive, Garron looked at the twins. "Let me make some calls. I worked with a couple of guys in Chicago on some undercover stuff and they're always looking for an excuse to get out of the city for a bit. I'm thinking one undercover and one tailing Lionel should work."

"There's a pretty nice little apartment over the offices at the feedlot. We've been thinking of renting it out anyway. Tell you're buddies they can stay there," Ryker said.

"Mind if I use your phone? I'd just as soon not have Sonny overhear me."

* * * *

Two hours later, Garron was finally headed home. He'd managed to hire Nate Gills, a friend of his and a damn fine surveillance man. Nate hadn't known anyone else that was looking for work, so Garron broke down and called an old marine buddy of his who put him in touch with Rio Adega. According to his friend, Ryan, Rio was the best at undercover work.

Shaking his head, Garron wondered how they'd gotten to the point of hiring outside men to catch one scrawny pansy-assed man. At least Nate wasn't presently on assignment, so he said he'd hop the first plane and be down by nightfall. Rio said he'd rather slip into town sometime within the next couple of days. If Ryan considered Rio the best, Garron would play by the man's rules.

Parking Sonny's truck, Garron hopped out and went straight to the barn, where Sonny had been spending most of his time. Sonny still wasn't able to get around like his old self, but he'd made great progress within the last couple weeks. Although he still had a few episodes of memory loss, his personality shifts had also settled down.

Whistling, Garron walked into the barn. "Hey, there's my cowboy." He walked up to Sonny and gave him a kiss. "Still shovelling shit, I see."

Sonny flashed him a smile. "If I could only teach the horses to use the can." Sonny set his pitchfork against the stall and leaned in for another kiss. "Where were you when I woke up?"

"I had a few things to do. Errands I've been putting off." He hated lying, but they'd all agreed to keep Sonny in the dark, for now. "I thought maybe after you're done with your morning chores, you'd feel like a picnic by the creek."

Teasing Garron's lips with his tongue, Sonny moaned. "Can we ride the horses?"

"Sorry, cowboy. The doctor said no riding for a while longer. I thought we'd just take the farm truck." He felt Sonny sigh more than heard it. "I'm sorry. You're well on your way to recovery. Let's not screw it up by getting ahead of ourselves."

"Okay." Sonny took another kiss. "By the time you make the food and grab a blanket, I should be finished. Shelby's already checked on the cattle this morning, so I gave him the rest of the day off."

As much as Garron wanted to strip Sonny down where he stood, the thought of skinny dipping sounded even better. "I'll go grab the food." He gave Sonny one more kiss and headed towards the house, suddenly feeling a whole lot better.

After grabbing some left-overs from the fridge, Garron hunted up an old quilt and a cooler of pop. Beer sounded damn good, but Sonny wasn't really supposed to have any. He looked down at the cooler and shrugged, getting back into the fridge for four bottles of beer. He didn't think two apiece would hurt.

Loading the truck, he called to Sonny. "Get a move on, daylights a wastin'."

"I'm coming," Sonny said as he made his way towards the truck.

"Not yet, but I have high hopes for the day," Garron said with a wink. He helped Sonny into the truck after giving him a quick kiss. Getting behind the wheel, he looked over. "Ya think we should take a couple of fishing poles?"

Sonny shrugged, "If you'd rather fish than get naked, by all means grab them."

"Forget fishing," Garron chuckled as he drove out onto the little farm road. "Talk to your mom since she left?"

"She called to say she'd made it home. I think she still isn't very happy with you for sending her away." Sonny picked at the rip in the thigh of his jeans.

"She's a mom. I didn't really expect her to like it, but I think it's for the best." Garron reached over and took Sonny's hand. "You feeling okay?" He noticed Sonny had gotten quiet.

"Yeah, I'm fine. A headache is all." He looked at Garron and grinned. "It's not bad enough to keep me from the creek though."

"Okay, just let me know if it starts getting worse and we can head back." Garron wanted a day out of the house with Sonny, but not at the expense of his suffering. He turned off the farm road and slowly made his way to the shaded area by the creek. He was glad to see some late season wildflowers were still sprinkled here and there in the field.

Garron got out of the truck and reached into the back, lifting the weed-eater out of the bed. He saw Sonny roll his eyes, and shrugged. "Hey, I'm still a city boy at heart. I don't mind picnicking, but I refuse to be surrounded by tall grass and weeds. I like to see the snakes and varmints coming."

Sliding out, Sonny laughed. "Are you telling me my big strong husband is afraid of snakes?"

"Shut up," Garron said as he started the weed-eater and began trimming a wide area of grass. He even trimmed a path down to the water, hey, if he was going to be accused of something anyway, he might as well go whole hog.

After spreading the blanket out, Garron went back for the cooler and basket. He was pleased to see Sonny already taking his boots and shirt off, by the time he got back to the blanket. "Looking good." He was too. The muscle tone Sonny had lost in the hospital was coming back nicely, and damn did his man look fine.

Unbuttoning the top of his Wranglers, Sonny laid back on the blanket. "Do I get some lovin' before we eat?"

"You know it," Garron said stripping out of his clothes. Naked, he crawled across the blanket and nibbled his way up Sonny's ever-present six-pack to his lips. "Love you," he said covering Sonny's lips.

"Mmm," Sonny moaned and pulled Garron's naked body closer. Garron felt the rough material of Sonny's jeans rub against his aching cock and damn near came. Breaking the kiss, he looked down at Sonny. "You feel up to riding me, cowboy?"

"Yee haw," Sonny said as he stripped off his Wranglers.

Garron reached for the picnic basket, and Sonny raised his brow. Garron held up the tube of lube. "What's a picnic without this?"

Settling between Sonny's spread thighs, Garron slicked his fingers. "Gonna make you feel so good," he said as he ran his hand across the tight rosette. Although they loved each other almost every night, this would be the first time they'd made love since the accident.

Garron didn't even get a finger inserted before Sonny suddenly sat straight up and wrinkled his nose. "Ooh, you smell that?"

Surprised, Garron looked up a split second before Sonny crashed back down on the blanket. Garron watched helpless as Sonny stared sightlessly up through the tree canopy. "Sonny?" Garron moved to kneel by Sonny's head. "Cowboy? Can you hear me?" Sonny's eyelids began to flutter and Garron knew he was having a seizure. The doctor had told him it could happen, but Sonny had been on medication to prevent it. He ran his hand over Sonny's tight as fuck abdomen until he slowly started coming around. The whole thing probably only lasted a couple of minutes, but it seemed like hours to Garron.

"What happened?" Sonny mumbled.

"You had a seizure. Did you take your medication when you got up this morning?" Garron asked as he started getting his jeans back on.

"I don't know," Sonny tried to sit up, but fell back and held his head.

Stuffing his feet into his boots, Garron wrapped the blanket around Sonny and picked him up. Sonny started squirming in his arms. "What're you doing? I don't want to leave."

"Too bad. We need to go home and get that medicine in you. We can try the picnic thing tomorrow if you feel like it." Garron carried Sonny to the truck and then went back for the rest of their stuff. Carrying the cooler and basket, he wondered if he should call the doctor. He'd read all the pamphlets the hospital had sent home with them and according to them, unless a seizure lasted more than five minutes or Sonny had another, he should be okay.

Getting in the truck, he was glad to see Sonny had fallen asleep. He'd have to figure out a way to remind Sonny to take his medication when he wasn't there. Leaning down, Garron kissed Sonny's cheek. "I love you."

Chapter Eight

The phone woke Sonny later that afternoon. He reached for it just as Garron's arm swung over him and snatched up the receiver. "Hello," Garron's voice rasped out, rough from their long nap.

Turning over, Sonny petted Garron's chest as he talked in short responses. Must be someone from work or maybe someone he didn't want to talk to because there wasn't a hint of friendliness in Garron's deep base voice. Oh shit, maybe it was Lionel. Sonny sat up, feeling the tension tightening his muscles. His head still rocked, but he was getting used to the ever present headaches. "Is it Lionel?" he whispered, wide eyed.

Garron shook his head and ended the call abruptly. Setting the phone back on its cradle, Garron pulled him back down onto the bed. "It wasn't him, but I need to go into town for a few minutes." Garron swirled his fingertips around Sonny's nipples.

"Why? Who was on the phone?"

"It's just business, cowboy," Garron said nibbling at Sonny's neck.

"What kind of business?" Sonny couldn't help but feel suspicious. Garron had been secretive lately and disappearing, like this morning.

Sighing, Garron stopped kissing him and looked into his eyes. "It's about Lionel, but I don't want to talk about it."

What the fuck? "You don't want to talk about it? Well screw that. I want some answers. What the hell is going on with Lionel? No one tells me anything any more. I don't even know how the case on him is going."

Taking a deep breath, Sonny watched Garron pull away as he swung his big muscled thighs over the edge of the bed and stood. He started putting on his jeans, totally avoiding Sonny's questions.

"Well, what? Am I not to be trusted with the truth anymore?"

He watched as Garron's face screwed up in a pinched look. Oh, he'd struck a nerve. That's exactly what was going on. Now he was pissed. Despite the pounding in his head, Sonny got up and grabbed a pair of Wranglers out of the drawer, he had no fucking idea what had happened to the jeans he'd worn earlier in the day. Pulling out a clean pair of socks and a white v-neck T-shirt, Sonny started getting dressed. "You don't want to talk, fine, I'm coming with you."

"No you're not. I need to do this alone. Please don't ask me for details because I can't give them to you. Trust me, please, just trust me."

God, he wanted to trust Garron, Lord knows he did, but something was definitely going on and he wanted the truth. Squaring his shoulders, Sonny narrowed his eyes at the gorgeous man in front of him. "You're not taking my truck without me, and that's final."

Garron rubbed his eyes and released another loud sigh before going to pick up the phone. Sonny listened in complete disbelief as Garron asked Jeb if he could borrow his truck. So that was it? Sonny turned and walked out of the bedroom and straight to the barn, snatching his keys out of his truck on the way. Sonofbitch, not only was Garron keeping things from him, he was using his brother to get around talking to him. Fucker.

Sonny picked up the grooming brush and went out to the pasture. Whistling, he was happy to see Lightning come racing towards him. Damn, that horse sure did like to be groomed. "Hey there boy," Sonny crooned to the Black and White Pinto Gelding. "How's my pretty baby been?"

When Lightning swung his head up in greeting he knocked it against Sonny's jaw, sending daggers of pain racing through his head. Dropping the brush, Sonny sat down in the grass and held his head. Never in his life had he thought he could live with this kind of pain on a daily basis. He just hoped to hell it got better because most days he felt like he'd rather be dead than endure another day.

He heard running footsteps seconds before Garron's arms wrapped around him. "You okay, what happened?"

Sonny tried to shrug off Garron's arms. The last thing he wanted right now was to be touched. Every nerve ending in his body was on high alert. "Don't touch me," he whispered. He heard a truck pull up in the yard and knew it was Jeb. "Just go, I don't need you."

Garron released him and stood. "I'll go, but I'm not leaving you here alone while you're like this." He walked off and Sonny could hear him talking to Jeb. "I'll be back in an hour or so," Garron yelled out as Sonny heard the truck travel back down the drive.

His head was starting to right itself finally, and he looked over to where Jeb was sitting on the porch step. Poor Jeb, being forced to baby-sit the crazy man.

Struggling to his feet, he dug the truck keys out of his pocket and walked towards Jeb. "I'm going to town."

Jeb, the sweet man that he was, looked at him wide-eyed. "I, uh, don't think that's a good idea. Garron said you've had a bad day."

"Yeah well it's not going to get any better until I find out what the hell is going on. Since your brother won't talk to me, I'll have to find out on my own." He looked at Jeb, seeing spots dance around his field of vision. "Unless of course, you'd like to tell me where Garron disappeared to this morning?"

"I don't know," Jeb said shaking his head. The wind ruffled Jeb's blond curls and damned if Sonny didn't believe him.

"Then he's keeping both of us in the dark." He held out the keys. "Either you drive me or I'll drive myself."

Looking down, Jeb seemed to be considering his options. He kicked the dirt a few times before grabbing the keys out of Sonny's hand. "You are so going to get me into trouble."

* * * *

Garron pulled up in front of The Zone, and rested his head on the steering wheel. Damn Rawley for getting him into this mess. He couldn't keep doing this. Hiding things from his husband just felt wrong, even if Rawley did think it was for the best. He was going to have to talk to Rawley about Sonny's suspicions. After the way he'd found him in the pasture, Garron knew the secrets were doing more harm than good.

Getting out, Garron walked towards the bar. Opening the door, he looked through the smoke haze and spotted Nate, sitting in the back corner. Nate smiled, and gave a little wave. That got a slight grin out of him. Nate was one of the few men he knew who could be so tough on the job while being just a tad too feminine at the same time.

Stopping by the bar to get a beer, Garron made his way to the table. Nate's sable brown hair was still impeccably styled in that just-got-out-of-bed look that he'd favoured last time Garron had seen him. Pulling out a chair, Garron sat down next to the much smaller man and patted him on the back. "How the hell have you been?"

Nate waved his hand slightly in the air like he was brushing away the smoke. "Peachy, although Chicago is boring without you." Nate stuck out his bottom lip.

Oh yeah, Nate's going to drive Lionel bat shit following him around. Garron smiled at his old friend. "I'm sure you're finding plenty of sugar daddies to keep you happy." Nate was famous in Chicago for attracting the richest men in town. Although, being as flighty as he was, he never stuck around long before he was on the hunt for the next eligible bachelor, and sometimes not so eligible.

"Boring, Chicago is filled with stuffy bores." Nate looked around the bar. "Although muscled farmers are having a direct affect on my slacks."

Garron laughed like he hadn't in ages. Nate always could lighten any situation with his own brand of charm. The thought of finicky Nate getting it on with any of the men in The Zone had tears rolling down his face. He knew he looked insane, but the more he laughed the harder it was to stop. Damn the tension must be really getting to him.

The next thing he knew, Jeb's hand was thrust in front of his face. "Give me my goddamn keys."

Surprised, Garron looked up at his brother. "What the hell are you doing here? I thought I told you to keep an eye on Sonny."

"Don't fucking say another word, just give me my keys." Garron passed the keys to Jeb, but grabbed his wrist. "What the hell is wrong with you?"

Pulling out of Garron's grasp, Jeb pointed towards Nate. "Don't think you can hide your little piece of candy from Sonny any more. He saw just like I did and took off." Jeb started to turn away and Garron grabbed him again.

"Wait, Goddammit, this is not what you think." That was all he got out before Jeb's fist slammed into his face. Garron's head snapped back, and he reached for his nose. By the time he dug his handkerchief out of his pocket, Jeb was already out the door. "Fuck," he said, looking over at Nate. "Do you have a rental car or something?"

Wide eyed, Nate nodded slowly. "In the parking lot."

"Come on," Garron started walking towards the door, holding his bleeding nose. Outside, he spotted Jeb's truck speeding down the street. Turning towards Nate, Garron held out his hand. "I'll drive you to the apartment at the feedlot and then call Rawley. He can brief you while I settle a little domestic dispute."

Buckling up, Nate shook his head. "Man, I'm sorry if I caused any problems at home."

"Not your fault," Garron said as he peeled out of the parking lot. "Sonny's brother, Rawley, thought it would be best if we kept this from him, and now it's back-fired right in my face. I'm gonna kill Rawley if Sonny has an accident on the way home." Garron shook his head, still unable to believe what had just happened. He knew exactly the way it would look to Sonny and the sad part was that he couldn't blame him. He'd been sneaking around, having secret meetings behind Sonny's back for several weeks now. Dammit, he should have known better than to keep it from his husband.

Pulling up to the feedlot office, Garron pointed upstairs. "That's the apartment up there," he dug in his pants for the key. "Here's the key. You'll have a roommate within the next couple of days, but no one knows exactly when. Ryker and Ranger, Sonny's twin brothers own the place. They said there was a separate entrance around back. I'll call Rawley and have him come over."

Nate nodded, getting out of the car. "Pop the trunk and I'll get my bags."

"Thanks for coming, Nate. Sorry everything's so fucked up right now."

"Don't apologise, just go make it better." Nate closed the door and pulled two large suitcases out of the trunk.

Garron shook his head, you can take the man out of Chicago, but you can't take the fashion hag out of the man. Nate waved and Garron took off towards home. Shit, at least he hoped it was still his home.

He pulled out his cell. "Hey, you son-of-a-bitch," he said when Rawley answered. "Sonny saw me meeting with Nate at The Zone. He's mad as fuck and I need to deal with it, so I need you to go fill Nate in on the situation. I just dropped him off at the feedlot. This is all your fucking fault. You had to keep people we both care about in the dark, well Sonny and Jeb both took off in their respective trucks like the hounds of hell were chasing them. If something happens to either of them, it'll be your fault."

Garron didn't wait for an answer. He was finished taking advice on Sonny from Rawley. He'd do things his way from now on and if Rawley didn't like it, well that was too fucking bad.

Chapter Nine

Garron's jaw dropped at the scene in front of him. His clothes lay strewn across the front yard, his duffle bag perched on top of his pile of books. "Fuck," Garron exclaimed. He just hoped he wasn't locked out of the house. Picking up handfuls of clothes as he went, Garron walked up the steps and put the pile on one of the rockers. Taking a deep breath, he tried the door and was pleased when the knob turned. He looked around the downstairs, but found no sign of Sonny.

Climbing the creaking steps, Garron made his way to the bedroom they'd started using again. Opening the door, he gingerly stuck his head in, "Cowboy?" He followed his head with the rest of his body, slipping into the room. Empty. Where the hell could he be? He saw that the master bathroom door was open and it too appeared empty.

Turning to leave, he heard a whimper coming from the walk-in closet. Bile rose in Garron's throat as he opened the door and looked down on a whimpering Sonny. He was rolled into the foetal position with his arms wrapped around his head, empty hangers all around him.

"Shut the door," Sonny screamed.

Garron knew when Sonny got one of his headaches, the light hurt his eyes. He quickly stepped inside and closed the door. Kneeling on the floor, Garron felt around for Sonny. There, he felt an arm. Mapping Sonny's body with his hands, Garron laid down beside him. "I'm so sorry, cowboy. I know you don't want to hear this right now, but it's probably my best shot at explaining while you can't run away."

Feeling Sonny's soaked T-shirt he decided to undress him. "I'm gonna help you out of your clothes first. Do you need a fan or a cold cloth?"

"No," Sonny mumbled.

Easing Sonny's clothes off, Garron took care not to move his head any more than absolutely necessary. The fact that Sonny was letting him do even that much was a testament to how bad he was hurting. Once naked, Garron positioned himself so Sonny was between his legs, leaning on his chest. Garron started massaging Sonny's neck and shoulders before working his way up to his head. The new growth of hair was only about an inch long, tickling his palm as he spread his fingers, being careful of the sensitive scar. Rubbing in a slow circular pattern, Garron whispered words of love as he tried to relieve his cowboy's pain.

When he felt Sonny's body begin to relax, he began explaining himself. "Listen to me, love. I have never, nor will I ever, cheat on you. The man you saw me with today is Nate Gills. He's sort of a private detective. Your brothers and I brought him in to help keep an eye on Lionel. I worked with him in Chicago and believe me, he's not my type."

"What's wrong with Lionel?" Sonny whispered so softly Garron barely heard.

"Rawley's meeting brick walls in his investigation. Seems the Reverend isn't the only person in town swayed by Charles Hibbs and his money. But Rawley has been tailing him every night. He asked me to meet him at the twin's house this morning to ask for our help in following him. I told him I could help some, but being here with you was more important to me. In the end, we decided to hire Nate and one other fella who'll be slipping into town to work undercover at the bar. Rawley's already cleared a job for him when he shows up."

Sonny reached up and stopped Garron's hands. "Why didn't you just tell me? Do you have any idea what it did to me to see you sitting there with that guy? I know I'm not the same man you fell in love with, and chances are I'll never be again. I'll always get these headaches, and I might have memory loss for some time. What happens when you get tired of taking care of me?"

Shifting Sonny again, Garron spread out beside him and covered Sonny's lips with his own. Garron tried to put all the love he felt into that one soft kiss, knowing Sonny couldn't handle anything too jarring. "I love you, don't you believe that yet?" He ran his hand down Sonny's chest to circle his soft cock. "This is nice, but it's not the reason I'm here." He ran his hand back up to cover Sonny's heart. "This is."

"You know you'll need to talk to Jeb. I think he was as hurt as I was. And I also want to help with Lionel."

Sighing, Garron rested his cheek on Sonny's chest. "Rawley doesn't want Jeb involved. He won't say it, but he's afraid something will happen to him. As far as helping with Lionel, that's a definite no-go. I'm not even going to help follow him because I think I might kill him if I get that close."

Garron chuckled and tweaked Sonny's nipple. "Besides, as homophobic as Lionel is, he's going to go nuts having Nate follow him around town."

"So this Nate's definitely gay then? I thought so when I saw him, but he's gorgeous and when you said he wasn't your type, I thought that meant he was into women."

"No, cowboy. Nate's not my type because even though I like my men small and lean, I like them to be real men. Nate's a little too flamboyant for me. Of course I think a lot of it's an act, but he'd never admit to it."

"Will you do me one more favour?"

"Anything you want, cowboy." Garron leaned up on his elbow.

"Find my medicine and get us a pillow and a blanket so we can take another nap. These headaches sap the energy right out of me."

Kissing his forehead, Garron got up. "I'll be right back."

* * * *

Garron bought two things in town the next day. An alarm clock, set to go off when it was time for Sonny to take his medicine, and a small pill vial to wear around his neck with his headache medicine in it. Sonny had explained to him that the headache the previous day had snuck up on him so fast he didn't have the faculties to go and find his pills. This way, Sonny would only have to reach as far as his chest for relief. Garron was quite proud of himself, as was Sonny when Garron presented it to him.

Sonny slipped the chain around his neck and then got wide-eyed and covered his mouth. "Oh my God, I don't believe I forgot. I never gave you your birthday or wedding presents."

"Yes you did, you gave me two wonderful gifts. The first when you became my husband and the second when you survived the shooting."

Sonny gave him a gentle punch in the arm. "Awe geeze, you're going to make me blush." He gave Garron a kiss and held up his finger. "Wait right there." Sonny disappeared into the house and Garron sat down in one of the rockers on the porch.

A few minutes later, Sonny came back through the door with a file folder in his hand. He extracted a piece of paper and handed it to Garron. "This is your birthday present. I had a guy in Lincoln draw it up for me and I was going to have it done after I found out if you liked it."

Garron looked at what appeared to be a tattoo design. The drawing was two interlocking G's with Angus bull heads on either side. The more he studied the picture the more he liked the design but he didn't quite understand it. "It's nice. Where are you gonna have it inked?"

Sonny rolled his eyes, and pointed towards the letters on the page. "See, it's a double G for Good and Greeley, and I thought I'd have it done on my upper back, between my shoulder blades."

Garron felt completely stupid for missing Sonny's meaning. "I think you'd look hot with a tattoo, but I think you need to get over your headaches some first. Those bitches hurt like hell. The last thing we need is to throw you into another seizure or migraine."

"Yeah, you're probably right." Sonny opened the folder and took out two more sheets of paper. "Here's your wedding presents," Sonny said, handing the sheets over proudly.

Garron took the papers and looked at the first one. It was the deed to the ranch, which Sonny had changed to add

Garron's name along side his as owner. The second was a drawing of a new ranch sign with the Double G logo cut out in it. Pulling Sonny down on his lap, Garron kissed him. "I love that you did this, but this is your family's land. You can't just give me half of it."

"Yes I can, and I did. I've already talked it over with my brothers. Besides, it's too late now, it's already done, and the new sign should be here in another month or so."

Looking around him Garron was filled with a sense of peace. He took a deep breath and inhaled the dust of his first real home since he'd left his mom's when he was seventeen. Sonny squirmed around on his lap, and Garron's cock began to fill. "Unless you feel up to doing something about the havoc you're creating in my jeans, I'd stop that."

Sonny squirmed some more and grinned. "I feel good today." He wrapped his arms around Garron's neck and straddled his thighs. "Carry me to bed, lover."

"That's what I needed to hear." Garron stood with Sonny still in his arms. "You're not expecting any visitors are you? Because once I get you in bed, that's where we're staying the rest of the day." God bless Sundays, Garron thought.

He was glad he'd gone over first thing that day to talk to Jeb. As predicted, Jeb was pissed at Rawley. Lord, he wouldn't want to be in that man's shoes right now. Jeb was a force to be reckoned with when angry.

"I haven't heard from anyone," Sonny said a little too softly.

Carrying Sonny through the house and up the stairs, Garron looked him in the eye. "What's wrong? I can tell by your voice that something is bothering you." He shouldered the unlatched door open and set Sonny on the side of the bed. He knelt at Sonny's feet and looked him in the eye, waiting for a response.

"I think I weird people out. Even my own brothers don't come around much anymore." Sonny toed off his boots and pulled his T-shirt over his head.

"Well," Garron said rubbing his jaw, "I think Rawley doesn't come around as much because he feels guilty. When he looks at you it's just a reminder that he still hasn't found a way to make Lionel pay for what he did. As far as Ryker and Ranger? Who the hell knows with those guys. They didn't come over much before you got shot. I think they survive in their own little world."

Sonny smiled, "Yeah, you're right about that, they always have." Sonny pulled Garron's shirt over his head and ran his hands down Garron's chest. "I'll have to talk to Rawley, but for now, get nekid and in this bed with me."

Standing, Garron quickly discarded his clothes before slipping between the sheets with his man. Pulling Sonny into his arms, Garron kissed him slow and deep, twining his tongue with Sonny's. "Love you."

"Love you right back," Sonny sighed against his lips as he started plucking and rubbing.

The two of them moved in a lazy dance of passion, mapping each other's body with hands and lips. Moving down Sonny's body, Garron licked a ring around his navel before dipping his tongue inside. Sonny giggled and swatted his head. "You know I'm ticklish there."

"Yep," Garron said, doing it again before moving south. He licked his way around Sonny's heavy sac, feeling the soft hairs brush his tongue, before sucking one ball inside. Sonny moaned and Garron grinned to himself. He'd missed those sounds. Releasing his sac, Garron travelled up the length of Sonny's erection, dotting the rigid, heavily veined cock with kisses. Reaching Sonny's weeping crown, Garron swiped his tongue across the slit and was rewarded with a groan and a good amount of pre-come. "So good," Garron said, as Sonny tapped him on the head with a tube of lube.

Looking up, Garron smiled and took the lube. "You wantin', cowboy?"

Spreading his legs even wider, Sonny nodded. "Please."

Slicking his fingers, Garron explored Sonny's poor neglected hole. After preparing the outside, Garron pressed a finger to the tight rosette and Sonny opened right up for him. It may have been a while, but Sonny's body remembered him, greedily taking one finger and begging for two. Obligingly, Garron pressed another finger into his lover.

"Yes, oh shit, yes," Sonny cried, pre-come dripping down the length of his cock.

Deciding they were both beyond ready, Garron sat up and applied a good amount of lube to his cock. Stretching out over the top of Sonny, he used one hand to guide himself to Sonny's entrance. Taking Sonny's mouth in a passionate kiss, Garron slowly pushed home. He felt the grip of Sonny's muscles around his cock and wondered how he'd gone without for so long. He meant what he'd said to Sonny earlier about love being about his heart and not just his dick, but this was a definite bonus.

Sonny began squirming under him, letting Garron know he was ready. Setting a slow rhythm, Garron made love to his man. Still afraid to jar his smaller frame, Garron rocked in and out with a slow, smooth rhythm. "You're mine, only you," he said between kisses.

"Yours," Sonny sighed, back bowing.

Picking up the pace the slightest amount, Garron wrapped his hand around Sonny's slick cock. Garron's balls started a steady slap against Sonny's ass. "Come for me, cowboy." He watched Sonny's face as he milked his cock to completion, Sonny crying out his name.

The look of total joy and love on Sonny's face had Garron tumbling over the edge to join him in dual ecstasy. Easing down beside Sonny, Garron felt his eyes begin to burn. The idea that in a split second he could have lost this wonderful man, had Garron thanking the heavens once more. Never would he take this love for granted, he vowed.

Chapter Ten

"You've reached the voice mail of Rawley Good, leave a message and I'll get back to you as soon as possible." Beep

"Rawley, you son-of-a-bitch, I've been trying to get you on the phone for three days. Who are you to decide what's best for me? In case you haven't noticed, Sonny's now a part of my family too. Not to mention the fact that my own brother was on the front of that motorcycle when Lionel took his shot. I've got just as much right to help you catch that bastard as anyone else. You know what I think, I..." Jeb swore as he was cut off.

Goddamit, he slammed the phone down. Rawley had him tied up in so many knots even a sailor would be stumped. Jeb relived their kiss, every waking minute of the day and in every dream at night.

Shaking his head, Jeb wandered outside. Taking a seat on the porch swing, he rocked back and forth. The longer he sat watching the sunset, the more ideas he came up with. He needed to prove to Rawley that he could take care of himself.

Maybe a good old fashioned bar fight was what was needed. Getting up, Jeb decided to pay a little visit to The Zone.

* * * *

Rawley listened to Jeb's message open mouthed. He didn't even know Jeb could get so riled up. He tried calling him back, but the answering machine at his ranch clicked on. "It's Rawley, give me a call."

He hung up and walked to the small stoop in front of Meg's bungalow. Knocking, he thought about Jeb. Shit, why did he tell him to call? The last thing he needed right now was to talk to him. He'd done a damn good job of avoiding his calls for days.

Meg opened the door and smiled. "Hey, Sheriff." She stepped back and let Rawley enter. He walked over and plopped down on the couch. "Rough day?" Meg asked, taking her chair beside the couch.

"Rough doesn't begin to describe my day. I spent all evening in Mayor Channing's office getting my ass chewed over this Lionel thing. Seems Lionel went to Daddy about the queer following him around town. Channing pretty much told me to put a stop to it or he'd have my job."

"Can he do that?"

"Yep, he's the mayor and my job's an appointed position, not an elected one. He pretty much owns my ass, well technically the City does, but we both know the council does anything he wants them to. Meanwhile I'm screwed." Rawley ran his hands through his thick black hair.

Getting up, Meg walked over to the couch and sat down. She wrapped her arms around Rawley and hugged him close. "You've been my best friend since I moved here, and I know how much this job means to you, but at some point, you have to take a stand. What this friend of Garron's is doing isn't illegal as long as he doesn't actually harass him, right?"

"Right. Nate's staying a good one hundred and fifty feet away from Lionel. He's damn good at annoying the crap out of him though. Which is exactly what I wanted."

"You need to tell Channing Nate isn't doing anything illegal, therefore, the Sheriff's Department has no say in what he does." Meg smoothed her hand down the side of Rawley's face.

Rawley looked into Meg's eyes for a long time before leaning forward and kissing her on the nose. "Why can't I be in love with you?"

"Because I have all the wrong parts," she said with a grin.

Nodding, Rawley sighed. "Jeb left another message on my phone. He's still pissed."

Taking a deep breath, Meg held Rawley's hands. "I've been fine these last couple of years helping you hide who you really are, but that was before you found someone to care about. Would it really be so bad?"

Rolling his eyes, Rawley nodded. "It would cost me my job."

"I don't really think that's legal besides, from the sounds of it, you're about to lose it anyway," she said giving him the look.

Oh, he knew that look. Meg was getting ready to lecture him on life and love, like she had any room to talk. She'd been a frightened domestic violence victim when she'd come to town. They'd managed to strike up a friendship when she'd reported her ex-husband for making threatening phone calls. When the men in town started sniffing around, Meg had gone to her only friend, Rawley. They'd struck a deal, keeping them both safe from prying busybodies, and so far it had worked like a charm. Now though, Rawley could tell something was on her mind.

"Just spit it out, Meggie."

"I think it's time we both grew up and moved on. You'll always be my best friend and you know that, but Mac asked me out, and well, I'd kinda like to go."

The fact that she was even considering opening herself up again brought a smile to Rawley's face. "Mac asked you out? What about me? The whole town thinks we're dating."

Meg laughed and swatted Rawley's chest. "I think we're not fooling as many people as we thought." She eyed him again. "It's time for you, too. You care for Jeb Greeley, I know you do. If the mayor fires you for seeing him, then sue his ass and live off the money. You can always get a job in Lincoln."

"But I always wanted to be the Sheriff of Summerville, not just a policeman in Lincoln." Rawley knew it sounded like he was pouting and he was. It just wasn't fair.

"This job has always been important to you because you really had nothing else in your life. I know that sounds harsh, but I think it's the truth." Meg tilted his chin up. "You have the chance to have that something else. Grab it. You can have a relationship and still be a cop. Yeah, you may no longer get to be the big honcho sheriff in town, but I have a feeling it won't matter to you as much as you think."

"What about Lionel and his friends? What if they decide to go after Jeb? Seeing Sonny shot down in front of me was almost more than I could handle, but what if it were Jeb?"

"That's something you need to discuss with him, not me. All I can tell you is that I would give my life for the right person. I'm betting Jeb feels the same way." Meg reached over and picked up the phone. She held it out to him and stood. "Call him, at least talk to the guy."

Taking the phone, Rawley watched Meggie walk into the kitchen. Pulling the slip of paper out of his billfold, Rawley called Jeb's cell phone.

"Yeah?"

"Hey, it's me. You got a minute to talk?" Rawley stood and paced around the tiny living room.

"Nope," Jeb slurred. "Just fixing to woop somebody's ass."

Rawley stopped in his tracks, his eyes narrowing. "Where the hell are you?"

Jeb gave a little chuckle, "I'm Zonin', man."

"Don't you move until I get there." Rawley stuck his head in the kitchen and waved goodbye to Meggie. "I'll call you," he mouthed. She nodded and smiled.

Going out to his SUV, Rawley still had the phone to his ear. He could still hear Jeb mumbling incoherently, "Man, you hurt me real bad. I'm gonna show you I know how to fight. Now I just need to find one."

"Listen to me," Rawley said in a harsh voice. "You don't need to get into a fight to prove anything to me. I'll be there in two minutes, stay put."

"I really liked you, did you know? I thought maybe you were the one for me," Jeb continued to slur. Rawley heard the phone clank around a little and then he heard only background noise.

"Jeb? Are you there? I'm out in the parking lot. Can you walk out by yourself?" With no reply coming, Rawley had little choice but to walk inside the bar. Looking around, he spotted Jeb face down on a table, the locals laughing at him. Feeling his anger heat his blood, Rawley stepped over and looked around. "You're laughing at him? What the hell kind of people are you?"

Shaking his head, Rawley reached down and picked Jeb's limp body off the table. "Come on, I'll get you home."

Carrying him more in a fireman's hold than a lover's, Rawley took Jeb out to the SUV. Settling him into the passenger seat, he buckled him up and hoped like hell, Jeb wouldn't puke.

Pulling out, Rawley looked over at the sleeping man. Damn, even drunker than a skunk, Jeb was still the hottest thing on two legs. His fingers itched to run their way across the long black lashes fanned down against Jeb's cheekbones. He didn't think he'd ever seen a natural blond with black lashes like that. Unable to help himself, Rawley reached over and ran his knuckles down Jeb's chiselled cheek.

Moaning, Jeb leaned his face into Rawley's touch and smiled in his sleep. What was he gonna do? He weighed his options all the way to the Tall A. Sitting in front of Jeb's house, he finally came to a decision. This time when he lifted Jeb he carried him like a lover, not a sack of potatoes.

He was a little surprised to find the house unlocked and vowed to talk to Jeb about it in the morning. Carrying the small lean body, Rawley made his way to the master bedroom. Laying him down on the bed, Rawley took Jeb's boots and shirt off. His cock immediately hardened at the sight of Jeb's sweet as sin body. Leaning over him, Rawley placed a kiss to Jeb's slack lips and sighed into his mouth as Jeb began to kiss him back.

Lowering his body, Rawley took the kiss deeper as he began to rub against Jeb's straining erection. Spreading his legs, Jeb's eyes opened and he stared heavy lidded into Rawley's. "Fuck me," he said against Rawley's lips.

That snapped Rawley out of his lust-filled haze. He stopped moving and kissed Jeb again before shaking his head. "I don't want to fuck you. I want to make love to you, but there are a few things I need to take care of first."

"Like?"

"Once I make love to you, I won't be able to lie to myself or the town again. I'll surely be fired and I need to take care of Lionel before that happens." He kissed his way along the side of Jeb's neck and up to his ear. "Tell me you'll wait for me?"

Jeb looked at him for several moments before nodding. "Stay with me tonight?" he slurred. "Just to hold me."

Rawley wrapped his arms around Jeb and buried his face in his blond curls. "I can do that." Stripping down to his underwear, he got them both under the covers. Jeb rested his head on Rawley's chest and it felt right. "Promise me no fights."

Jeb yawned and burrowed into his arms even deeper. "I won't go lookin' for any, that's as much as I'll promise."

"Fair enough." Rawley felt Jeb's breathing even out and in minutes he was snoring softly. Rawley couldn't get over how right Jeb felt sleeping in his arms. His cock was hard as a rock, but he knew Jeb would be worth the wait. Rolling his eyes, Rawley thought of Meggie and how right she'd been. Now he had another reason to tie up this investigation.

Chapter Eleven

Turning the chicken, Sonny looked over at Garron. "How's your friend doing with Lionel?"

Garron's shoulders stiffened momentarily like they always did when Lionel's name was mentioned. "He's having a ball. According to Nate, Torture is his middle name." Sonny watched as a smile spread across Garron's face at the thought of Lionel being followed by a very openly gay man. "The funniest part about it is that little shit has endeared himself to a lot of the townspeople. It's one of the reason's Nate's so good at his job." Garron went back to mashing the potatoes and Sonny felt the green eyed monster start to creep up his spine.

"They like him more than me?" Sonny asked, covering the frying chicken.

Garron turned off the mixer and pulled Sonny into his big arms. Sonny traced the tattoo on Garron's neck with his fingertip. "I know, you don't have to say it. I'm being stupid again."

"Never stupid, but you are a bit paranoid at times. You and I both know that most people in this town adore you. Why do you think Nate's fitting in so well? Folks around here have already accepted the gays. Believe me, they wouldn't have broadened their minds had it not been for you and your brothers." Garron bent down and kissed him.

Sonny ran his fingers through Garron's long hair and nodded. "I'm glad I have you to knock some sense into me sometimes. It's not that I don't like Nate, hell, I don't even know the man, but every time I see him I think of you two sitting in The Zone." Sonny felt Garron's shoulders tense once more. Standing on tip-toes he kissed him. "Here's me shutting up now."

Garron smiled and swatted his ass. "Let's finish this dinner and watch a movie."

"Mmm, you, me, The Rock, and some hot buttered popcorn. Sounds like a perfect evening." He licked up the side of Garron's jaw.

With narrowed eyes, Garron kissed him again. "I don't really like The Rock being in the same breath as the two of us. You and me eating hot buttered popcorn and watching The Rock."

"Jealous?" Sonny asked, batting his lashes.

Garron grunted and went back to making the potatoes.

* * * *

Leaning against the wall at the back of the bar, Nate watched Lionel and his buddies throw darts and guzzle whiskey. Knowing assholes and whiskey didn't mix, he eyed the brand new bouncer, again. He couldn't help it. Rio was the object of every one of his teenage fantasies, tall and dark with an accent that drove him wild. He'd yet to meet his new roommate, but had been briefed on what he looked like. Rio had slipped into town that afternoon and started work an hour later. Nate was beginning to wonder whether it was a good idea to share such a small space with this Latin heartthrob. He could so see himself walking around with a hard on for the rest of this job.

Lionel yelled something across the bar, breaking his musings. Looking right at him, Nate smiled and gave one of his infamous waves. He knew it drove people crazy, probably the reason he did it. People didn't think you were smart or able to take care of yourself when you were too feminine. Well, everyone but Garron. He did it to Garron because he knew it threw him off his game and Nate just liked to fuck with his head.

Turning around, Lionel said something to his buddies and they all laughed. Nate rolled his eyes, bigots were all the same. It didn't matter where they were from or what kind of accent they had, the words were always the same tired words gay men had heard for years. Popping his neck, Nate took another glance towards Rio. Sitting on a high stool just inside the door, he had his arms crossed in front of him, and boy oh boy what nice arms they were.

Feeling his cock start to also take notice, Nate tried to distract himself. All he needed was for Lionel to disappear while he went into the bathroom to jerk off. That would sit real well with the Good brothers. Besides, this thing with Lionel was starting to get personal for him. Thinking you could buy your way out of trouble reminded him too much of his own father. Nate would like nothing more than to bring Lionel and his dad down, like he'd done his own father. Thinking of Bruce Gills brought the customary upset stomach.

He was lost in the past, when a large shadow fell between him and Lionel. Nate looked up into the bulldog face of one of Lionel's cronies. "Care to dance," Nate said and batted his eye lashes.

The dog faced man, picked Nate up by his designer shirt collar and held him against the wall. "Stay away from Lionel. He don't like queer boys in this town."

Nate spotted Rio heading his way and Lionel trying to slip out the door. Knowing it was a ploy to distract him, Nate took matters into his own hands. A well placed jab of his thumb to a nerve ending in the bulldogs neck, had Nate on his feet in no time. He passed Rio at a run winking as he went by and out the door. Lionel was just getting into his expensive luxury car, when Nate pulled his rental one hundred and fifty feet behind him and flashed his lights as a courtesy to let Lionel know he was ready.

Giggling, Nate followed the smoke from Lionel's tires as he spun out of the parking lot and headed towards the other side of town. Nate knew this kind of defeated the purpose of following the bone head, but at least he knew Lionel wouldn't be doing anything illegal with a tail on his ass all night. He slowed as Lionel turned into the gated driveway of his father. Pulling up across the street, Nate parked the car and got out his binoculars. Seeing what he needed to, he set them in the seat and called Rawley.

"Hello," Rawley's voice sounded rough from sleep.

"Sorry to bother you, boss, but I just followed Lionel to his father's house and guess who else is here?"

"I'm not in the mood for twenty questions right now, Nate."

"Oh, right, well your favourite person Mayor Channing's car is also parked in front of the house and two others that I don't recognise."

Clearing his throat, Nate could hear Rawley whispering to someone before coming back on the line. "Do you have a camera with you?"

"Sure do, I got you covered. I'll download the pictures to your email account tonight."

"Talk to you tomorrow." Rawley fumbled with the phone before hanging it up.

Nate would swear he'd heard another male voice. Woo hoo hoo, things are not always what they seem in Summerville, Nebraska.

* * * *

The ringing cell phone woke Rawley. Extracting Jeb's head from his chest, Rawley bent over the side of the bed and grabbed his uniform pants off the floor. Unclipping the phone from his belt, he flipped it open. "Hello," he said as Jeb stirred beside him. Reaching out, Rawley brought Jeb back against his chest as he listened to Nate. He spoke in what he thought was a quiet voice, but suddenly Jeb sat up and looked at him.

"Is it Sonny? Has something else happened to him?"

Rawley covered the mouth piece, "No, baby, it's just Nate. Lay back down, I'll be done in a second." He quickly finished his call and set the phone on the side table. Cuddling back down under the covers, Rawley wrapped both arms around Jeb, and kissed the top of his head. Jeb was already back to sleep and Rawley knew he was only seconds away. He was amazed at how comfortable he was. He hadn't slept with anyone since he was away at college. Rawley grinned, he was damn near a virgin again he reckoned.

Yawning, Rawley fell asleep with a grin still on his face.

The next morning Rawley woke to the smell of coffee and an empty bed. Sitting up he swung his legs over the side and ran his fingers through his hair. Looking at the clock, he wasn't surprised it was early. Ranchers usually woke before the sun was up and he'd just spent the night with one. Rawley chuckled, thinking about the headache Jeb most certainly would have.

Getting into his clothes, Rawley walked into the bright sunny yellow kitchen. Jeb was making bacon and eggs and drinking a cup of coffee. He turned when Rawley cleared his throat.

"Morning," Jeb said, a tinge of pink shading his cheeks. "Sorry about last night. I never could hold my liquor."

Deciding to break the morning uneasiness, Rawley walked over and gave Jeb a quick kiss. "At least you didn't puke in my SUV."

Jeb blushed even darker, "Yeah, well there is that." He gestured towards the skillet, "Hope you like your eggs scrambled."

Running his hand up Jeb's back to land behind his neck, Rawley pulled him forward for another kiss. "Scrambled is great."

While Rawley sat down, Jeb filled a coffee cup for him and brought the food to the table.

Jeb turned the spoon towards Rawley, allowing him to take what he wanted. Growing up with three hungry brothers Rawley smiled at the manners Jeb exhibited without thought. Putting half the eggs and bacon on his plate, he reciprocated by waiting for Jeb before digging in. Taking a bite of the yellow fluffy eggs, Rawley moaned, "These are good."

"Thank you. They're fresh. I get them from Mr. Thompson down the road."

Rawley nodded his approval as he continued eating. Finishing up, he wiped his mouth and took a drink of coffee. "I noticed you have a computer. Do you mind if I check my email before I leave? I'm expecting some pictures from Nate."

Jeb's eyebrows rose. "What kind of pictures?"

Reaching across the table, Rawley covered Jeb's hand. "Not those kind. Nate followed Lionel to his dad's house last night. He spotted Mayor Channing's car and two others, but he didn't know who they belonged to. I told him to snap a few pictures and he said he'd email them."

"Mayor Channing? I wonder what sort of business he'd have with Charles that time of night." Jeb scratched his curly blond head in thought. "Oh, I'm sorry. Sure, you can use whatever you want." Jeb stood and started clearing the dishes.

Rawley stood and put his hand out to stop him. "You cooked, I'll clear."

"That's okay, you go do whatever you need to," Jeb said with a smile and a wink.

Walking around the table, Rawley took another kiss. "Mmm bacon kisses are my favourite."

"Had a lot of them have you?"

The smile disappearing from his face, Rawley looked into Jeb's eyes. "I've not been with anyone for almost eighteen years."

"Wow, and I thought I led a celibate life-style." Jeb looked at him for a few second and smiled. "That's good to know though. At least I won't have to fight any old lovers anytime soon."

Rawley shook his head. "You'll never have to fight an old lover. In the past, I've only had brief encounters that lasted at most a weekend. No one's cared for me like that."

Setting the dishes in the sink, Jeb turned back towards him. "I do."

"I know and I feel the same way about you." He walked towards the door and stopped. "I have a feeling I'll knock on your door one of these day's and never leave."

"No need to knock, the doors always open for you."

He knew Jeb was speaking metaphorically but it reminded him of the night before. "I wanted to talk to you about that. With everything that's going on, you need to lock your door at night and when you leave the house for any length of time."

"Yes, Sheriff Good," Jeb said with a smile.

Shaking his head, Rawley walked into the little den next to the kitchen and powered up the computer. Logging into his email account, he waded through the junk and found what he was looking for. Pulling up the pictures, he enlarged the screen to get a closer look at the cars. Smiling, he grabbed a pad and pen and wrote down the information he was after.

Feeling a hand on his shoulder, he looked up into Jeb's face as he squinted at the computer screen. "Get what you needed?"

Rawley tapped the picture. "Nate managed to take a picture of the cars, house number and license plates. He's good. I'm going to head into the station and run these plates. There might just be more going on here than we thought."

Chapter Twelve

Wearing a pair of ratty shorts, Ranger poured the charcoal into the grill. "So what's this meeting about?"

Taking another drink of his beer, Rawley looked out over the countryside. "Something's going on and I thought we could all put our heads together to figure it out. I invited Jeb to join us by the way."

Lighting the charcoal, Ranger turned and looked at Rawley, brow raised. "Something else you want to talk about?"

Shrugging, Rawley continued to avoid his brother's knowing look. "Not much to say, yet. There are feelings there on both sides, but this investigation needs to be taken care of before they're explored." He finally met Ranger's eyes. "You know I'm certain to lose my job when word gets out. I can't very well arrest Lionel if I'm an ex-Sheriff."

Closing the lid on the grill, Ranger walked across the big deck and wrapped Rawley in a hug. He didn't say a word for a long time and Rawley was damned grateful. He'd thought about Jeb all day, and he knew his heart was out there for everyone to see.

Breaking the contact, Ranger stepped back and grabbed his bottle of beer. "I think this town might be ready for a gay Sheriff, once you get the Hibbs' family taken care of. Summerville is one of the rare places in the world where people actually judge you more by the content of your character than who you're sleeping with."

"And I say hallelujah to that," Nate said walking out through the French doors. He continued passed until he reached the railing. Taking a deep breath, Nate spread his arms. "I love it here. I've lived my entire life in the city, had no idea what I was missing." He turned, tilting his head to the side. "Think there'd be any work around here for a gay private investigator?"

"You thinking of staying?" Rawley asked. Nate seemed like such a city boy.

"I'm telling you, man, I love this town. I don't feel this accepted even within Chicago's gay community. But there's the whole work thing to screw it up."

"Not really," Ranger said, finishing off his beer and reaching for another. "Lincoln's not that far away and it's a pretty good size city."

"Hmm, I'll have to give it some real thought." Nate walked over to the cooler and pulled out a wine cooler. "My new roomie didn't even bother showing up at the apartment after work," Nate said with a pout. "Probably hooked up with that waitress he was talking to all evening."

Ranger's eyes narrowed the slightest bit. "Which waitress?"

Nate rolled his eyes, "Well duh, there are only two and one of them has grandkids."

"And one of them is still a child," Ranger replied.

Nate looked shocked. "I don't know who you've been looking at, but I'm gay through and through and I can even tell you there's nothing childlike about that woman." He took a drink of his wine cooler.

Rawley watched as a twinkle appeared in Nate's eye. Oh shit, Nate was about to push Ranger. "She seems like a sweet one, too. Don't understand why someone hasn't scooped that lady up and carried her to the alter. Of course, with a body like that, I'm sure many have carried her to their bedroom."

"That's enough about Lilly," Ranger said a little too gruffly. "That girl's barely twenty-one."

"And...at what age did you lose your virginity?"

Without saying a word, Ranger stood and went into the house. Rawley looked over at Nate and shook his head. "You're mean."

"Yeah, I know, but sometimes the writing's on the wall and you just have to take the time to read it. I'm not a private investigator for nothing. I've got a good eye and an even better intuition."

Rawley heard the door open, and looked over to see Sonny, Garron and Jeb walk out. Sonny and Garron went immediately to the cooler and Jeb stood back, biting his lip a little. Rawley could tell Jeb wanted to touch him, but didn't know how Rawley would feel about finally being out to his brother. Knowing these next few minutes would change his life, he held out his hand. "Come here, baby."

Jeb looked at him and seemed to exhale. A grin tilted the corner of his mouth as he walked towards Rawley. Taking his hand, Jeb seemed surprised when Rawley pulled him down onto his lap. Jeb quickly looked from Rawley to Garron and Sonny.

Sonny seemed to study the scene in front of him before smiling and raising his bottle to Rawley. He turned to Garron and pulled him towards the house, "Let's go see if Ryker needs any help."

Garron nudged Nate on his way by. "Come on inside. I think you should get to know my cowboy." Nate nodded and followed.

Alone, Rawley pulled Jeb's head down for a kiss, sweeping his tongue in for a taste. "I missed you today."

"Really?" Jeb's face lit up.

Pulling him back against his chest, Rawley kissed the top of his head. "Really, truly."

The two of them sat just like that, not talking just being, wrapped in each other until the door opened and Ranger came out with a plate full of steaks. He looked at the two of them snuggled in the chair and smiled. "That's a good look for you, Rawley."

"I'm thinking you're probably right," Rawley replied, rubbing Jeb's side.

* * * *

Seated at the long dining table, Garron wiped his mouth and pushed his plate back. "So, can we talk about why we're all here, now?"

Rawley finished up and took a drink of his beer before answering. "I got the plate information back on the two other cars at Charles' house. One's a lawyer out of Omaha and the other a big developer from Lincoln." Rawley rubbed his jaw. "Now what do you suppose that meeting was about?"

"So you think Charles and Lionel are in some business venture with Channing?" Garron reached under the table to hold Sonny's hand. He knew the mention of Lionel still affected Sonny as much as it did him.

"Either they're going into business or money is changing hands to smooth the way. We all know Channing runs the council in Summerville. If you wanted to get something passed the council, Channing is the obvious way."

"Kickback?" Garron questioned.

"I don't know yet, but something's going on, and you don't meet with people at eleven o'clock at night if everything's on the up and up. Too bad we didn't put our undercover guy in the town bank."

Jeb cleared his throat. "You don't need someone inside the bank." Jeb looked at Garron.

Garron nodded back, knowing his brother was about to reveal a part of himself he didn't share with most people.

"None of you, besides Garron of course, know what I did before inheriting this ranch." Jeb started fiddling with his silverware until Rawley gently stilled his hands. Jeb looked up at Rawley and gave a half-smile. "I used to work as an accountant for a not so reputable employer. I did a lot of things I'm not proud of, until one day I woke up and decided I was better than that. I called the FBI and reported my own employer. After meeting with them, I continued to work for the company, gathering evidence. I was basically a stool pigeon."

Watching his brother, Garron wanted to reach across the table and take his hand. He knew how hard it was for him to disclose this information. Garron still remembered Jeb coming to him in tears, ashamed of what he'd been doing for the company. It was a testament to both Rawley and Sonny that he was willing to share it with them now.

"I worked with an agent that would probably help us find out what we need to know, but I'll have to talk with Rawley privately before I call him." He looked up at Rawley, who nodded and stood. Taking Jeb by the hand, Rawley led him into the living room.

After they'd gone, Garron looked around the table. "My brother trusts you not to spread this information outside this room."

Ryker held up a hand. "You don't even need to say it."

Sonny pushed back his chair and stood, gathering plates. "I'm going to start the dishes. You guys talk about your next move or whatever. I've had enough for the day."

Stilling Sonny with a hand on his back, Garron tried to read Sonny's mood. "You okay?"

"Yeah, just want to get the dishes done and go home." He smiled down at Garron.

Garron felt better, thinking Sonny was simply getting back to his old horn-dog self. "Okay, cowboy, you clean up and we'll finish plotting our revenge," he winked back.

As soon as Sonny left the room, Garron leaned on the table. "Seems we have two problems now. We still need to find evidence against Lionel and we need to know how Channing is involved in all of it." Garron looked at Nate. "Lionel might need to be pushed a little harder, are you up for that?"

Nate wiggled in his chair, rubbing his hands together. "You know it. Especially if I have that big hunk Rio around to help protect me."

Garron watched Ryker and Ranger both bristle at the mention of Rio's name. He wondered what that was about? Giving his head a shake, he continued, looking from Ranger to Ryker. "You think the two of you could subtly question the ranchers around the area? See if they've heard about any new developments going on around the county?"

"Sure, shouldn't be too hard. We usually swap shit when they come in to the lot," Ryker said.

He was interrupted when Sonny came back into the dining room with his hands on his hips. "I can't find any clean dishes to set the table with." He looked at Ranger. "Do you guys have paper plates you want to use for dinner?"

Everyone at the table looked from Sonny to Garron. Pushing his chair back, Garron walked over to Sonny and put his arm around him. "We just finished eating, cowboy. You went into the kitchen to wash the dishes."

Sonny looked at Garron. He seemed confused for a few seconds, before his face pinked. "Yeah, I'm sorry." He looked around the room before going back into the kitchen.

Turning back to the people at the table, Garron shrugged. "He still has memory lapses occasionally, but he's getting much better."

* * * *

By the time they got home and into bed, it was late. Rawley had reappeared after the small glitch with Sonny, and Jeb agreed to call the FBI agent he'd worked with in the past.

Sonny had been quiet the rest of the evening. Garron couldn't tell if it was the thing with the dishes or another headache. Snuggling up to Sonny's naked body, Garron ran his hand down his torso to brush across his cock. "You're awfully quiet."

Burrowing into Garron's neck, Sonny nodded. "I'm sorry if I embarrassed you tonight."

Pulling away just enough to tilt Sonny's head up, Garron kissed him. "You didn't. Those people are your friends and family. You had a slight memory lapse, so what."

"What if I always have them?" Garron could see the sheen of tears in Sonny's eyes.

"Then you do. I don't think you understand how close you came to dying. It's a miracle the only effects you still have are headaches and the occasional memory glitch." He kissed

Sonny, slow and deep. "Everyone around you understands that. You're harder on yourself than anyone else."

Sonny nodded and rested his head on Garron's chest. Running his fingers through Sonny's quickly growing hair, Garron was happily surprised when he felt Sonny's hand working its way around his chest. Sonny stopped to pluck at a nipple before latching on with his mouth. Garron felt his cock immediately go hard at the unbelievable sensation. "Feels good," he moaned and pulled Sonny on top of him.

Sucking harder, Sonny ground himself against Garron's cock. Knowing he'd have a nice bruise in the morning, Garron smiled and spread his legs. "You gonna make love to me tonight, cowboy?"

Releasing Garron's nipple, Sonny looked up and nodded. "It's been a while."

"Yeah it has, and I'm needin'." He spread further and wrapped his legs around Sonny's back. "You get me ready?"

Nodding enthusiastically, Sonny held out his hand for the lube. Retrieving it from the bedside table, Garron handed it over. Kneeling between Garron's spread thighs, Sonny rubbed Garron's stomach. "Turn over for me while I get you ready. You're not quite as flexible as me," Sonny chuckled.

"I just haven't had as much practice, Mr. Bottom." Garron turned over and slid his knees under him presenting himself to the man he loved. "Good enough?"

A wet tongue slid across his rosette. "Fantastic," Sonny cooed before placing a kiss to his opening.

God, it had been a while since Garron felt anything like this. Balancing on his shoulders he reached back and separated his cheeks, giving Sonny more room to work. "Ahhh," he groaned as Sonny scraped his teeth across the sensitive tissue. Garron felt his cock begin to throb, pre-come dripping onto the sheets below.

When he felt a hot tongue working its way into his body, Garron growled. "I'm gonna shoot if you don't stop."

Removing his tongue, Sonny slicked his fingers and slid one inside. "Come if you need to, but I intend on taking my time. It's not everyday I get you into this position."

Garron's body accepted the invasion like a starving man accepts a loaf of bread. "More," he moaned, looking behind him at Sonny. With a hand slowly stroking his own cock, Sonny looked damned sexy as he pushed another slick finger alongside the first. "Please," Garron begged as Sonny rubbed across his prostate.

Withdrawing his fingers, Sonny slapped Garron's ass playfully. "Turn back over."

Willing to do anything to relieve his torture, Garron flipped over and hooked his arms under his knees. Presenting himself once again, he licked his lips. "Now, cowboy."

Nodding, Sonny positioned himself at Garron's hole and slowly pushed in to the root. "Oh fuck," Garron yelled. The painful pleasure of having Sonny inside his body tipped Garron over the edge. He reached down and held his cock as pulse after pulse of come rocketed from his body. Shit, Sonny hadn't even started moving yet, and he was already finished.

Looking up at his cowboy, Garron blushed. "Sorry about that."

Lowering himself, Sonny kissed him. "Don't be sorry, it was hotter than hell." Sonny started moving in a slow rhythm, letting Garron get used to his size before picking up speed. Soon, Sonny was leaning back, sitting on his heels as he pistoned in and out of Garron's body at lightning speed.

Despite knowing he wouldn't be able to come again so soon, Garron enjoyed every deep thrust Sonny gave him. The look on Sonny's face was one of concentrated effort, the tip of his tongue sticking out the side of his mouth. Garron smiled, thinking his love looked cute.

Deciding to give him something else to think about, Garron reached down and lazily stroked his half-hard cock. Sonny's eyes zeroed in on the new scene and his pace picked up even more. He thrust into Garron hard. Sonny actually started moving Garron slowly up the bed on each thrust until Garron had to put a hand against the headboard. "Like that do you?"

"What do you think?" Sonny grunted, sweat running down his chiselled abdomen.

Releasing the hold on his cock, Garron slid his hand down to the point of contact, feeling Sonny's cock slide into him. The touch was all it took for Sonny to bury himself as deep as he could and stiffen. Garron swore he felt the jets of come like a power washer inside his body. "Fuuuccckkk," Sonny screamed as his body started vibrating with the strength of his release.

"Come here," Garron said pulling Sonny down on top of him. He ran his tongue across Sonny's lips and dipped inside. They ate at each others mouths like they had the first time in the restroom of The Zone. Never would Garron get his fill of this man. Before long, Sonny would be riding his horse. Back to the taciturn rancher he'd first met. Garron couldn't wait, but he also knew that Sonny would be forever changed by the shooting, just as he'd been. Sonny may show it in headaches and memory loss, but Garron knew it went deeper than that for both of them.

Despite everything, their love was stronger than it had ever been, and Garron vowed to make sure they lived every day to the fullest. He also vowed to make sure Lionel paid for what he'd done to his love.

* * * *

Fixing the latch on the corral gate, Jeb thought of Rawley. The last few nights spent sleeping in his arms had been the best of his life. Now if they could just get this investigation over so they could do something beside kiss and sleep. He was brought out of his thoughts by his ringing phone. Hoping it was Rawley, Jeb flipped it open and looked at the display. Not Rawley, but someone almost as good.

"Hey, James, how's that beautiful wife of yours?"

"Sore," his friend chuckled in his ear, "she gave birth to a baby girl about an hour ago. Congratulations, you've just become a Godfather."

"Oh, wow." Jeb walked towards the house. "I thought it wasn't supposed to happen for another couple of weeks?"

"Yeah, well you know women, always impatient," James joked. "Sophia's beautiful, man. She's already got her mother's curly black hair. No clue on the eye colour yet, but right now they're as blue as the ocean."

"How's Niki? Did she make it through the natural childbirth thing okay?" Jeb walked into the house and opened the fridge.

"Ha, she begged for an epidural about two hours in. Thank God."

"Well I'm opening a beer right now to toast the three of you. I'll make a trip up to Chicago this month to see my new Goddaughter. Will you be able to swing a Christening by then?"

"Oh I'm sure we can. You know Niki, when she sets her mind to something..." James stopped talking and Jeb heard someone else in the background. "Hey, man, let me call you back later, the nurse just brought Sophia back in."

"That's fine, you did good for a worthless fella like yourself."

"Gee thanks. See ya, buddy."

"Give the girls my love," Jeb said before hanging up. A Godfather, him, wow. Taking another drink of his beer, Jeb walked outside and sat on the porch swing. He couldn't believe how happy he felt.

The sound of a car coming up the road got his attention. He didn't recognise it, and was a little surprised when it pulled into his drive. As the small blue compact got closer, he saw Meg behind the wheel and Rawley in the passenger seat. The look on Rawley's face told him something was very wrong.

The car stopped and Rawley got out. He looked up and gave Jeb a little wave before going back towards the popped trunk. Shutting the trunk, Jeb watched as Rawley walked towards the porch with two big suitcases in his hand.

His chest tight, Jeb stood and walked to the steps. Rawley looked up at him and set his bags down. "I've been relieved of my duties as Summerville Sheriff. I no longer have a need to hide the way I feel about you. Care for a roommate?"

RAWLEY'S REDEMPTION

Dedication

Dedicated to my cowboy loving friend, DrewHunt.
Thanks again for all your hard work.

Chapter One

Standing at the bottom of the steps, Rawley looked up at the only person he'd ever been in love with. "I've been relieved of my duties as Summerville Sheriff. I no longer have a need to hide the way I feel about you. Care for a roommate?"

Jeb didn't say a word, but Rawley saw first the shocked look and then the brief smile. He simply held out his hand and waited for Rawley to join him. Turning around, Rawley waved good-bye to Meg, and picked up his bags. With a deep breath and a prayer on his lips, he walked up the steps to his future.

Taking his hand, Jeb led him into the living room and through to the master bedroom. "I'll clear some closet space out for you later." Jeb ran his hands up Rawley's chest and smiled. "Welcome home."

Letting out the breath he'd been holding, Rawley dropped the bags and wrapped his arms around Jeb's lean body. Leaning down, he whispered a kiss across Jeb's soft lips. "I love you."

"I know," Jeb said as he opened his mouth for Rawley's tongue.

The kiss was savage, both men tired of waiting. As Rawley continued to plunder Jeb's mouth, he began to pull his soon to be lover's clothes off. When he had Jeb shirtless, he broke the kiss and knelt before him. Lifting Jeb's foot, Rawley removed his boots before running his hands up Jeb's thighs to land on his fly. Burying his face in Jeb's crotch, he inhaled the scent of his man as Jeb ran his fingers through Rawley's short black hair.

Looking up, Rawley moved his hands to Jeb's button and slowly relieved him of his jeans and underwear. Pushing them down the leanly muscled thighs, Rawley's hands began to shake. "I can't believe I'm so nervous." Hiding his face against Jeb's closely cropped thatch of hair, Rawley inhaled again. Without looking up, he ran his tongue around the crown of Jeb's cock. "I've never done this before. I've had it done a time or two, but this will be my first time giving."

Jeb ran his hand over Rawley's cheek. "If you'd rather not, I'll understand."

"No. I can't believe how much I do, but I want to." Rawley held Jeb's generous shaft by the base and licked his way up and down its length. He felt each ridge and vein against his tongue as he heard Jeb begin to moan. Taking the heavy sac into his mouth, Rawley was amazed at how soft the skin was, no hair to get in the way.

As he took the head into his mouth, Jeb thrust forward. The generous erection hit the back of his throat and Rawley gagged slightly.

"Sorry," Jeb said.

Shaking his head, Rawley refused to release his hold on Jeb's cock long enough to answer him. He moved closer to the tip and sucked. He felt his cheeks hollow out as Jeb moaned. God, Jeb tasted good. Wrapping his hands around to rest on Jeb's sweet ass, Rawley ran his fingers through the crease. Finding Jeb's tight rosette he added a little pressure with his fingertip until it slid in.

"Shit," Jeb cried, shooting his essense down Rawley's throat.

Rawley drank it all and begged for more. He licked Jeb clean before leaning back on his heals. "Nap?"

Jeb shook his head and spread out in the centre of the bed. "Your turn now."

Oh, Rawley liked the sound of that. He quickly stripped off his jeans and T-shirt, it still felt weird not wearing the uniform, but Jeb was good at taking his mind off everything else. With the last of his clothes in a pile on the floor, Rawley stalked towards Jeb. Watching his fine as fuck man slowly stroking his spent cock, Rawley felt pre-come dripping down the length of his shaft. "You have any condoms?"

Jeb blushed and pointed towards the bedside drawer. Inside he found a new box of rubbers and a sealed bottle of lube. Rawley held the bottle up and whistled. "Wow, you bought the good stuff."

Pulling Rawley down beside him, Jeb began licking Rawley's chest. "I made a trip to Lincoln. There's a little shop there with all kinds of stuff."

Working on the seal, Rawley looked up and grinned. "Yeah, what kind of stuff?"

Jeb shrugged and finally took the bottle out of his hands. He opened it within seconds and handed it back to Rawley, spreading himself open. "You know, toys, costumes, stuff."

Before slicking his fingers, Rawley wanted a taste of his man. He'd seen this done, but had never thought he'd ever feel like doing it. Looking at Jeb, loving Jeb, changed everything. He set the bottle on the bed, and slowly licked his way down his lover's body. Positioning himself between Jeb's already spread thighs, Rawley ran his tongue up the crease of Jeb's ass. "Fuck, yeah," he moaned at the taste and smell of this man, his man. Centring his attention on the tight pucker of skin, Rawley kissed him, snaking his tongue out to taste. He suddenly had an overwhelming desire to claim Jeb and his body.

With a few more licks, Rawley reached for the lube. Dripping a few drops down the crevice, Rawley began preparing Jeb. He was surprised to see that Jeb stretched fairly easily. He felt his hackles begin to rise and looked up Jeb's body. "You been with someone recently?"

Putting his arm over his face, Jeb shook his head. "Just myself," he mumbled.

Rawley slipped in another finger and worked Jeb's hole for a few moments. "Hand me a glove." He sat back on his heals and continued to watch Jeb as he opened the box and gave him a condom. Tearing the package with his teeth, Rawley was sheathed in no time. Settling back between Jeb's legs, Rawley positioned his cock at Jeb's entrance. Before entering he had to know. "What do you mean, you've been with yourself. You mean jacking off?"

Jeb shook his head. He reached over and opened the drawer again. Reaching to the back, Jeb withdrew a rather large butt plug. He handed it to Rawley, still unable to look him in the eyes. Rawley looked at the toy and nodded before setting it down next to Jeb's hip. "Good to know," he said as he slowly worked his cock past the ring of muscles.

Arching his back, Jeb's ass sucked Rawley's cock right in. "Shit," Rawley groaned as sweat popped out on his forehead. With Jeb's ass squeezing his cock, he just hoped he'd make it all the way inside before shooting. Taking a deep breath,

Rawley pushed slowly in to the hilt. Closing his eyes, he rested his head on Jeb's shoulder. "Home," he whispered.

He felt Jeb run his fingers through his hair as he began to squirm underneath him. Rawley smiled, getting the hint. With a quick kiss, Rawley wrapped his arms around Jeb's thighs and spread him even further. He watched as he moved in and out of Jeb's body in a slow but hard rhythm. "See how pretty I look inside you?"

Jeb sat up on his elbows and looked down at their joined bodies. "Damn, that's hot." He grinned at Rawley as the pace quickened.

"I'm not gonna last long." He thrust even harder, his heavy balls slapping Jeb's ass on each thrust.

Jeb collapsed back down and Rawley watched the cords in his neck, pulse and stand out. Seemed he wasn't the only one. "Come for me, darlin'."

Reaching down, Jeb took hold of his renewed erection and stroked himself to Rawley's pounding rhythm. The sight of Jeb's cum spurting from his luscious cock was beautiful, tipping Rawley over the edge unexpectedly. His entire body shook at the force of his climax. "Baby," he howled to the ceiling.

Without losing contact, Rawley fell to Jeb's side, rolling Jeb with him. He felt his cock softening and knew they wouldn't be joined for much longer, but it's what he needed at that moment. "I love you."

Tracing his square jaw, Jeb smiled before leaning in for a kiss. "I love you."

* * * *

After a short nap, Rawley woke with Jeb still in his arms. For the first time in his life, he'd made a decision based on what he wanted and needed. Being the oldest of four brought with it an amazing amount of responsibility. Rawley had always been the Good boy's protector and leader. Now, he realised his brothers were grown and it was time he built his own life. He knew that life would forever involve this man. Speak of the devil, Jeb burrowed a little deeper against his chest and yawned.

"What time is it?"

Rawley turned over onto his back and looked at the clock. "Dinner time, almost five." He rolled back towards Jeb and felt something poke his hip. Lifting up, he held aloft the flesh coloured plug. "This definitely has possibilities."

Jeb blushed again and took the toy from Rawley. "I thought it looked about your size, but I can happily say that I underestimated you."

Just that fast, Rawley's cock hardened. He rubbed his erection against Jeb's hip and moaned. "We've got a lot to make up for."

"Uh huh," Jeb groaned as he turned his body to face Rawley. "Quick rub and then let's find something for supper."

Rawley nodded and slid his cock along side of Jeb's. "You're sure about this, right? About me staying here?"

"Not staying here, living here," Jeb panted as he put a little more force behind his movements. It wasn't long before the blossom of heat spread between the two of them, both crying out the others name.

Left sticky and sated, Rawley took Jeb's mouth in a passionate kiss. "Shower, then grub."

"You got it," Jeb said climbing off the bed and walking towards the bathroom.

Rawley watched that fine ass walk away. "Damn, this is way better than being a lonely Sheriff."

* * * *

After a dinner of left-over meatloaf sandwiches, they spooned together on the couch watching the news. Jeb hadn't asked Rawley what had gone wrong at work since he already knew most of it. He figured when Rawley was ready to talk he would, and Jeb wasn't the pushy sort.

They were into prime time TV when Rawley exhaled audibly. "I need to buy a truck or something in the morning."

"Okay," Jeb said, turning. "You want me to go with you?"

"If you can spare the time." Jeb could see the lost look in Rawley's eyes. As long as he'd dreamt of this day he was sorry that it had to come at such a professional cost.

Running his hand down the side of Rawley's strong face, Jeb kissed him. "For you? Always. I'll just need to tend to the livestock in the morning, but I'll drag you out in the fresh air to help."

"Deal," Rawley whispered against his lips before kissing him. When they broke the kiss Rawley looked into his eyes. "I'm getting my job back. Even if I have to investigate this thing on my own and prove Mayor Channing's in with Lionel and Charles."

Thinking about the town mayor's subterfuge heated Jeb's blood. "Why don't you go one better and take Channing's job." He hadn't realised he was serious until he saw the look on Rawley's face. "You're thinking about it aren't you?"

"I don't know, it's an idea I'll have to chew on for a while. Although clearing my name is my top priority aside from the investigation into Sonny's shooting."

Jeb felt his chest tighten. If he'd had visions of being Rawley's world he'd just been put in his place. "Okay," he said numbly.

"Hey, what's wrong?" Rawley pulled him closer and wrapped his leg over the top of Jeb's.

"Nothing, I guess I'm just getting a little tired." The words were barely out of his mouth before Rawley was carrying him. Well, he thought, at least he was important in the bedroom.

Chapter Two

After feeding the horses, Jeb took off on the four-wheeler to check the stock while Rawley made some phone calls. With everything that had gone on, he needed to get his brothers up to date, but first he needed to call Nate. Waiting for Nate's cell to pick up, Rawley started to worry. He'd just resigned himself to leaving a message when a deep voice answered.

"Nate's phone."

Rawley recognised the voice as Rio's. "Hey, it's Rawley. Is Nate around?"

"He's still asleep. He didn't drag his sorry ass in until about two hours ago. Can I help you with something?"

"I just wanted to see how everything's going with Lionel?" Rawley rested his booted feet on the desk, and leaned back in his chair.

"I'm sure he'd tell you things are going as expected."

Rawley noted some tension in the voice. "And how would you say it was going?"

Rio exhaled, "I think you're asking for trouble. Lionel's made it clear he doesn't like gays, and to have Nate and his fairy ways flitting all over town in Lionel's shadow is just asking for Nate to get hurt."

"Fairy ways? Excuse me, but I find that offensive." Rawley put his feet on the floor and stood.

"Well excuse me, but you haven't watched him in action lately. Since Garron told him to amp up the volume on his little act, Nate's out of control. He's giving us gay men a bad name and I for one am sick of it."

Rawley thought about what Rio said. No way was that six foot four, tough-as-nails man gay, was he? "Did Nate tell you about our change in plans? We haven't been getting anywhere in the investigation, so we thought if Nate pushed Lionel's buttons enough, maybe he'd screw up. I don't know if it'll work, but it's the only shot we have. I'm sure at some point, Lionel will seek some kind of restraining order against him. When that happens, you'll have to be our eyes and ears while Lionel is inside the bar. That'll probably be the only place that Nate can't go because of the distance specifications in the restraining order. I'll talk to him about toning it down some."

"Good. Something needs to be done before he gets killed."

Eyebrow shooting up, Rawley detected a hint of concern in the tough Latin man's voice. "You into him?"

"Hell no, I've already got someone back home. Doesn't mean I want to see the little shit hurt though."

Rawley smiled at the vehement response. Yep, little Nate was starting to get to the man despite his protests otherwise. "Can you have him call me when he wakes up?"

"I think you can do better than that. Why don't you come to The Dead Zone and see him in action for yourself? I'm tellin' ya, man, you're asking for a fuck load of trouble."

"All right, what time do they usually get there?" Rawley looked out the window, surprised to see Jeb back so soon.

Just watching Jeb climb off the fourwheeler had Rawley's jeans fitting too tight. Deciding he had too much work to do to be distracted, Rawley turned away from the window and sat back down.

"You still there?"

"Yeah, sorry, what did you say?"

"They've been getting there about eight."

"I'll be there." He hung up the phone and called his brothers, wondering how he was going to get out of the house without Jeb. No way would he take his lover into the lion's den.

* * * *

Waiting to sign the papers on his new pickup, Rawley turned to Jeb. "I thought we'd stop and get a bite to eat before heading back to Summerville."

"Okay," Jeb said, brushing his hand.

"I...um...need to stop by The Zone before I come home. Rio's a little concerned about Nate."

"Why would he be concerned with Nate? He's one of the toughest men I know. He's almost a legend in Chicago."

"Seems he's taking our change in plans to a whole new level and Rio's afraid Lionel's at the end of his rope."

Jeb smiled, "Yeah, I've seen that particular act a time or two."

Rawley narrowed his eyes, feeling his blood begin to heat. "What the hell is that supposed to mean? Did you have a relationship with him too? Wasn't your FBI friend, Caleb, enough?"

Jeb jerked back as if he'd been struck. "No, I didn't have anything going with Nate, but even if I had, it wouldn't be any of your damn business."

"The hell its not. You're mine."

Jeb groaned and ran his fingers through his blond curls. "Don't."

The sales manager chose that moment to come into the office. He looked from Jeb to Rawley. "Is there a problem?"

Jeb looked at Rawley for a few seconds before shaking his head. "No problem," he pointed towards the showroom, "I'm gonna wait outside."

Rawley watched his man leave with a tightening in his gut. He looked back to the manager and smiled. "Sorry, where were we?"

After the deal was complete and Rawley had the keys to his new maroon dual-cab pickup, he found Jeb sitting in his own truck. "You ready to follow me to the restaurant?"

"Why don't we just eat at The Zone?"

Taking a deep breath, Rawley leaned on the driver's door. "Listen, darlin'. I don't think it's a good idea for you to go with me. I don't need anymore fodder for the town gossips right now. Besides, I'll be working. You just go home and wait for me there."

He watched as Jeb's eyes dulled, his face suddenly sullen. "Fine, whatever," Jeb shook his head, "I'll see you at home." He started his truck and rolled up his window with Rawley still standing there.

Getting the hint, Rawley stepped back, and Jeb drove off. Shaking his head, Rawley closed his eyes, "Damn."

* * * *

Walking into The Zone, Rawley was already out of sorts. He'd much rather be home with Jeb instead of checking up on Nate. He gave a short nod to Rio as he sat at a table in the back. Lilly came over with a menu and a smile.

"Hi, Sheriff," she said, giving him a wink.

"So you've heard," Rawley said, looking at his menu.

"It's Summerville, of course I've heard, but you'll always be Sheriff Good to me." Looking around Lilly grinned. "I don't suppose you're meeting your brothers here?"

"No, just me. I'll take a burger and fries with a side of jalapeños, and a big beer." Rawley handed the menu back, noticing the disappointment on her face. He seemed to do nothing but disappoint people lately.

"I wanted to tell them they're fixing to get new neighbours," Lilly said, popping her gum.

"What do you mean? Jeb and Sonny are the twin's neighbours."

"Yeah, but the Douglas family just sold their farm to the north of ya'll."

"Who'd they sell to? I didn't even know it was on the market." He bet Sonny didn't either or he'd have snapped it up in a flash.

"Don't know," she shrugged. "I'll put your order up and bring that beer right over."

Lilly walked off and Rawley scanned the crowd. Hopefully, Lionel and his buddies wouldn't show until after he'd eaten. He contemplated calling Jeb, but figured he was better at smoothing things over in person. He knew he'd suck at a real relationship.

Lilly brought over his beer and Rawley took a long drink, the icy cold beverage feeling good on his parched throat. The place was fairly quiet when he'd first walked in but as he drank, more townspeople filtered through the door. He looked up at the bar and grinned to himself, ranch workers sitting next to bankers and lawyers, only in Smalltown, USA.

His food came seconds before Lionel and his crew stepped through the door. Taking a bite of his cheesburger, Rawley almost choked when Nate came in. He was wearing designer low-rise jeans with a silky powder blue shirt that showed his six-pack abdomen, with a shiny navel ring. "Oh fuck," Nate looked like sex personified to him, and he was sure, every other gay man in town, Rio included. No wonder Rio wanted the act stopped. If he had someone back in Texas, the last thing he needed was to share a small apartment with someone who looked like that.

He shook his head. Lionel had to be going absolutely fucking crazy with Nate following after him. Nate spotted him as he blew Lionel a kiss and walked over to his table. It wasn't a secret in town that he and his brothers had hired Nate, so there wasn't any reason they couldn't be seen talking, unlike Rio. All business with Rio was handled in secret. Rawley still didn't understand how he managed to slip to and from the apartment without anyone seeing him, but so far he had. They didn't think Lionel or anyone else in town had a clue Rio was their undercover guy.

"Hey, Nate." He wiped his hand on a napkin before holding it out.

Nate shook his hand before motioning to Lilly for a drink. "How's it going? Rio said you called?" Lilly brought over a club soda, shaking her head and giggling as she walked off.

"Yeah, Rio's concerned that you're asking for trouble with this step-up of your game. I gotta say, after seeing you walk through that door, I agree. When we discussed you trying to get Lionel off-kilter, I had no idea you'd become this...flamboyant."

Nate waved Rawley's concerns away. "Rio's a bear, totally uncivilized if you ask me. And that man," he pointed towards Lionel, big as you please, "is getting ready to crack. I can feel it."

"What do you mean?" Rawley took a drink of his beer and leaned forward.

"He's getting used to me following him, getting sloppy. He's been meeting with that contractor from Lincoln, a lot. He thinks because his daddy and the mayor took care of you, he's above the law." Nate took a sip of his soda as he watched Lionel.

"Well, I'm going to take over the day shift from now on. The sooner I can get Lionel, Charles and Mayor Channing nailed, the quicker I can get my job back. Our FBI guy will be in town tomorrow. You still okay with the evening shift? You know, if you need a night off, you can call one of my brothers or hell, we could just have Rio watch him. Lionel seems to spend most of his evenings here anyway. Until we find something out on him, our main goal is to keep Lionel away from Sonny, and no way in hell is he dumb enough to try anything with an obvious tail. So, evenings?"

"Yeah, I'm cool with evenings. As long as I get at least six hours of sleep, I'm good. Besides, it's not like I can get anything going in this town. Although I have been thinking about checking out some of the clubs in Lincoln. Living with that bear over there isn't easy."

Rawley just bet it wasn't. He could feel the sparks bouncing back and forth between them from where he sat. Rawley wondered just how taken Rio actually was. "Just be careful. If something doesn't feel right, get on the phone and one of us will be there within minutes to back you up."

"You do know that I have black belts in four different martial arts, right?"

"Black belts can't stop a bullet."

* * * *

The house was dark when he got home, so Rawley quietly let himself in and walked to the bedroom. It was only eleven, but he knew Jeb rose early. Stripping out of his clothes, Rawley slid between the sheets and spooned up to Jeb's back.

He felt Jeb stiffen, and knew he was awake. "I'm sorry," Rawley whispered, kissing Jeb's neck.

"Yeah, you seem to say that a lot lately," Jeb mumbled, pulling away just a little.

"I love you, it's just all new to me," he said.

"You keep saying it out loud and maybe someday you'll start to actually feel it."

"What the hell does that mean?" Rawley tried to turn Jeb over to face him, but Jeb pulled away.

"Nothing, I'm tired. I'll talk to you tomorrow." Jeb flipped over onto his stomach, pulling away even further.

Turning over onto his back, Rawley ran his hands through his hair. Damn, he was in deeper shit than he'd thought. He was too new to all of this to know how to dig himself out of the hole he'd gotten himself into.

Finally deciding he was going to have to swallow his pride and talk to someone, Rawley drifted off to sleep feeling cold and alone.

Chapter Three

Rawley woke the next morning to an empty bed. He reached over to Jeb's side and felt the cold sheets. Looking at the clock, he saw that it was only five-thirty. "Damn, darlin', how long you been up?" he wondered out loud.

After a quick shower, he dressed and walked into the kitchen. He was surprised to find Jeb hadn't even made coffee. Deciding a thermos full would be a good peace offering, Rawley set out to make a pot. As the black brew slowly dripped through the grounds, Rawley thought about the day before. He still wasn't sure what he'd done wrong other than not allowing Jeb to accompany him to The Zone. Looking up at the clock, he saw it was still too early to call Garron. His first choice would've been Sonny a couple of months ago, but with Sonny's head injury and subsequent headaches, he thought it best not to upset him.

Garron, on the other hand, would probably just try to kick his ass, but at least he'd tell Rawley how to make it up to Jeb. The most important thing was that he didn't lose his man. He loved Jeb with all his heart, and he refused to let his inexperience get in the way of their life together.

Filling the tall scarred thermos, Rawley went out the back door towards the barn. He knew Jeb found solace in his horses. Someday, Rawley hoped he would find it in him.

He found Jeb brushing Butterscotch, his Palomino mare. "Hey," Rawley said, leaning on the stall.

"Morning," Jeb replied without looking at him.

"Brought you some coffee," holding up the thermos.

"No thanks."

Sighing, Rawley set the thermos on the dirt and sawdust floor. He wiped a hand down his face and walked towards Jeb. "I don't know what I've done to piss you off, but I'm sorry. I know you're tired of me sayin' that, but it's true. I don't know how to do this. I told you, I've never been in a relationship."

Turning around, Jeb put his hand on his hip. "It's no wonder you haven't been in a relationship. You..." Jeb stopped and snapped his mouth shut. Rawley could see him trying to figure out what to say. "A relationship is more than fucking."

Something about the way he said it caused Rawley's hackles to rise. "You make it sound like it doesn't mean anything? Fucking? Seriously?"

Shrugging, Jeb put his grooming supplies away in the tack room. "When you love someone, you share your life with them, not just your bed."

"Now you're questioning my love for you? What the hell's going on? I screw up once, and this is how you treat me?" Rawley shook his head. "I'll call ya later."

* * * *

Rawley knocked on the front door of what used to be his home. Sonny opened the door half dressed. His lips were swollen. Rawley couldn't keep the smile off his face. "Morning, I take it Garron hasn't left for work yet."

Stepping back, Sonny grinned and shook his head. "He's in the kitchen. You hungry?"

Sonny turned and walked away.

Following, Rawley smelled frying bacon. "Mmm, smells good," Rawley said, taking a seat at the table.

Garron turned around and narrowed his eyes. "What? You haven't trained my brother to make breakfast for you yet?"

"Well, that's one of the things I came over to talk to you about." Rawley motioned towards the coffee pot and gave his brother a pleading look. Shaking his head, Sonny poured him a cup and set it on the table.

Bringing a pan of scrambled eggs and a plate of bacon over, Garron straddled his chair. "Talk," he said spooning eggs onto his plate.

Rawley glanced at Sonny before turning back to Garron. Evidently Garron knew what Rawley was thinking. "It's okay to talk about the investigation in front of Sonny. I had to learn the hard way about keeping secrets."

Rawley stopped and wondered if that could be Jeb's problem. Sonny loaded his plate and Rawley ate on automatic pilot. Was he keeping secrets? No, he didn't think he was. He told Jeb what was going on, but didn't want him involved. Why was it wrong that he wanted to keep his love safe? He felt a hand on his arm, and looked from his plate to Sonny.

"What's bothering you?" Sonny asked his face full of concern. Where was the cantankerous man who used to be his brother? Since the shooting, Sonny was different. They all knew it, although rarely spoke of it. He'd felt sorry for Garron and Sonny when it was first evident Sonny would probably never be the same. Looking into the concerned eyes that watched him so closely, Rawley realised this Sonny seemed to feel more than the old one had. Regardless of the seizures and headaches, his brother was still his brother, only better in some ways. He felt an overwhelming rush of love swell inside of him.

"I love you, brother," he whispered as he ruffled Sonny's short hair.

Tilting his head, Sonny grinned. "Well that's nice to know. Now, care to tell me what's wrong? Why you aren't at home eating breakfast?"

Closing his eyes, Rawley thought about earlier that morning. He knew he hadn't helped the situation by being snarly with Jeb. "I'm in the doghouse, and I honestly don't know why. I know it has something to do with meeting Nate last night. I told Jeb I didn't want him to go with me. But even before that, I don't know, I've felt him pulling away a little."

Garron broke into the conversation, having finished his breakfast. "Why didn't you want him to go with you?"

"A couple of reasons. I don't want to put him in harms way, and I don't think the town is ready to see me parading my new lover around."

Putting his face in his hands, Garron asked, "Did you tell him that?"

"Yeah, I thought honesty was important in a relationship." Shit, did he have that wrong, too? No way would he figure out this relationship stuff. He thought loving a guy would be easier than having to deal with a woman's swinging emotions.

Looking up from his hands, Garron winced. "Jeb tell you why he broke it off with Caleb?"

The thought of his man with someone else was like a punch in the gut. Rawley shook his head. "He just said things didn't work out."

"Well, I don't know the whole story, but I know Caleb refused to love him openly. His career with the bureau was too important for him to risk the retribution. It tore my brother apart to the point that when he inherited the ranch, he left Chicago without a backward glance."

"What are you saying? That because I won't show him off as my new lover to the entire town, I'm going to lose him?" Rawley pushed his still half-full plate away.

Garron started to answer, but Sonny cut him off. "Are you ashamed of him?"

Rawley thought about it for a moment. "No, I love him, but I don't want the same thing that happened to you…"

Fuck, did he just say that? He looked into Sonny's eyes. "I'm sorry."

Instead of answering, Sonny turned to Garron. "If you had it to do over again, would you have fallen in love with me, knowing what you know now about how things would go?"

Pulling Sonny out of his chair and onto his lap, Garron kissed him. Rawley watched in awe as Garron broke the kiss and looked into Sonny's eyes. "In a heartbeat. I wasn't alive until you loved me." They began kissing again, lost in their own world.

Rawley had heard enough, seen all he needed to. He quietly excused himself and walked out of the house without telling them about the Douglas farm being sold, no sense in spoiling their good mood.

* * * *

Jeb was hanging up the phone when Rawley walked into the kitchen. His throat felt thick as he tried to figure out what to say. Instead, he followed his heart and sunk to his knees in front of his love. "I'm afraid," he choked on a sob.

He felt Jeb's hand land on top of his head, and he couldn't control his tears. There had only been two occasions when he'd openly wept, at his father's funeral and the night Sonny was shot. Now, just the thought of losing this man was enough to crack his usual gruff exterior.

Hunkering down to Rawley's level, Jeb wrapped his arms around him. The sweet warmth of Jeb's embrace felt like home. "Shhh," Jeb whispered. "We'll work it out."

Rawley buried his face in Jeb's neck and held on. "I'm not ashamed of you. I saw Garron and Sonny shout their love for the whole town to see, and in a split second Lionel tried to take it all away. I didn't want that to be you. I love you so much and I don't know how to be a boyfriend." He pulled back and looked at Jeb. "I need you to teach me. I know how to love you, but it seems I need help with the rest."

Standing, Jeb held out his hand and looked down at Rawley. "Come on, we have some talking to do."

Taking Jeb's hand, Rawley got to his feet and followed him to the bedroom.

Once naked, and settled under the covers, Jeb rested his head on Rawley's chest. "You've made me feel cut off. You held me in your arms two nights ago, and told me the investigation and getting your job back were the most important things in your life. How was I supposed to feel about that? I've been so patient, waiting for you to wake up and realise that you love me. I finally get my wish, and then I learn that everything else still comes first."

"No," Rawley shook his head, and pulled Jeb up to eye level. "You're my constant, my heart. My entire life, I've done things because people expected it of me. I got my brother's out of trouble. I became a policeman so I could help others.

But you, you I want for me. I don't want to talk about the other side of my life when I'm with you because I just want to be lost in you, in this feeling." Rawley leaned in and gave Jeb a short but passionate kiss, dipping his tongue in for a taste of his man. "I'm sorry if I made you feel second best because nothing could be further from the truth."

Jeb kissed him again and settled back on Rawley's chest. "I love you."

Feeling the words run rampant through his body, Rawley exhaled. "Thank you."

Their moment of bliss was interrupted by the ringing phone. "That's probably Caleb. He said he'd call when he got into town. There are a couple of things I need to talk to you about. He called last night, but I didn't feel like discussing it when you got home."

"Should you answer it?" Rawley asked, reaching for the phone. At his nod, he picked it up and handed it to Jeb.

"Hello."

While Jeb spoke to Caleb, giving him directions to the ranch, Rawley thought about the investigation. He looked at the clock, he really should be following Lionel right now, but his relationship was more important than watching Lionel sit at his desk in front of the window in town.

Jeb reached over him and hung up the phone. "He'll be here in about an hour."

"Okay," he said cuddling back up with Jeb. "What did you want to tell me about him?"

"The FBI won't authorise him to search Channing's bank records."

"So why's he still coming?"

"To help, I think. He said if we managed to get in to the records on our own, he could look them over." He looked up at Rawley. "I don't know that it's legal though. We'd probably need a hacker?"

Rawley scrubbed at his face. "Maybe we're getting in over our heads. I mean, I may not hold the title, but I still believe in the law."

"What do you suggest we do then?"

Rawley rubbed Jeb's back as he thought. "Legally, is there any way we can find out if he's made any large purchases lately?"

"I'm not sure, but Caleb will know."

"Why's he coming to Summerville if he can dig around on the computer in his own home?"

"He said he could only spare a couple of days and he wanted to show me how to search the internet." Jeb shrugged, "He's still willing to help, I didn't want to cause waves."

"About...Caleb, do you still have feelings for him?"

"Sure, he was my lifeline during my months as a stool pigeon." He crawled back up Rawley's body and straddled his hips. "My feelings for Caleb were never as deep as what I feel for you. Don't worry, he had his chance."

Despite what Jeb said, Rawley knew he'd worry. He tilted his head to the side as Jeb began to nuzzle. "We have time if you're interested," Jeb said, sliding his lean body back and forth against Rawley's ever present erection.

Grinning, Rawley flipped Jeb so he was stretched out on top. "Since the day I met you, there's never been a second that I wasn't interested, it just took me a while to admit it."

Chapter Four

Getting dressed, Rawley looked at Jeb. "So, this Caleb, he as good-looking as me?"

Jeb zipped his jeans and walked over to Rawley for a quick kiss. "No one's hotter than you."

That made Rawley's chest puff up just a bit. "Good to hear. I'm going to stay a few minutes and meet him before heading over to babysit Lionel."

"I think it would be polite to offer Caleb a place to stay while he's in town. He took vacation time just to come help out."

Rawley looked at Jeb. He knew he could trust Jeb, but what about Caleb? "You sure that's a good idea given your past with him?"

"He knows I'm taken. I made that clear over the phone." Jeb broke away to gather his boots.

Sitting on the bed, he pulled one on and looked at Rawley. "If it'll make you uncomfortable just say so and I'll point him to the nearest motel, of course that means him travelling to Lincoln, but I'll do it."

Rawley took a deep breath and shook his head. "Okay, offer the man a room, but make sure he knows you're mine."

There was a knock on the door and Rawley took a few calming breaths. What the hell was he getting himself into? He held out his hand, and waited for Jeb.

Taking Rawley's hand, Jeb leaned in for a kiss. "I love you."

"Me too," Rawley said as the knock came again. "Let's get this intro over with so I can get to town."

Opening the front door, Rawley took in every inch of Caleb Spears. Perfectly styled blond hair and piercing blue eyes stared into his. Seemed he wasn't the only one doing some sizing up. Remembering Caleb was here to help, Rawley stuck out his hand. "You must be Caleb. I'm Rawley Good."

Caleb shook Rawley's hand in a firm grip. "Jeb's told me a lot about you. Mind if I come in?"

"Oh, sorry." Rawley stepped back and Caleb walked in. "Jeb's in the kitchen getting us something to drink. He figured you'd be thirsty after your drive from Lincoln."

Caleb didn't answer. He simply nodded and looked around the room. Rawley already didn't care for this conceited prick. Who the hell wore a three piece suit out to the country? He was relieved when Jeb came in, carrying a tray loaded with iced tea and cookies.

"Hey, Caleb," Jeb said, setting the tray on the coffee table. He walked over and gave Caleb a hug. Rawley felt a growl beginning to crawl its way up his throat. Jeb broke the embrace and turned to Rawley. "I take it the two of you met?"

"Yep," Rawley said.

Leading Rawley by the hand, Jeb sat on the sofa and motioned towards a chair. "Have a seat. Would you care for some cookies? I made them myself." Jeb offered the plate of cookies to Caleb.

Shaking his head, Caleb patted his stomach. "None for me. You know I don't eat junk food. The older I get the harder it is to keep the body in shape." He flashed his fake white smile and gave Jeb a condescending wink.

Oh fuck, Rawley already felt like smashing this fake sonofabitches face in. He saw the flash of disappointment across Jeb's face as he set the plate back on the tray. "I'd like a few," Rawley said.

He was rewarded with a big smile. "They're snickerdoodles, it's my grandma's recipe."

Rawley looked into Jeb's eyes as he took a big bite. "Oh damn, darlin', this is the best cookie I've had in ages." He leaned over and gave Jeb a kiss. "Thank you."

Jeb blushed, and turned towards Caleb. "We'd like to invite you to stay here in our spare room. There's really no reason for you to drive back and forth to Lincoln everyday."

Flashing that damned smile again, Caleb nodded. "I'd appreciate that."

Rawley couldn't stand any more. He gave Jeb one last kiss and stood. "I'm going to go check on Lionel. There's a meeting called for this evening over at Ranger and Ryker's. You want me to come back here and pick you up or would you rather just meet me?"

"I'll meet you," Jeb motioned towards Caleb. "I assume you want Caleb to come along?"

"Yeah, you can fill him in on what we're looking for, but he'll need to talk to Nate and Rio tonight." With a short nod to Caleb, he left.

* * * *

Thank God, Jeb thought, as he pulled up to the twin's house and spotted Rawley's new pickup. It had been a hell of an afternoon trying to dodge Caleb's roaming hands. He stuck with it though, determined to study the way he searched the different public databases. If he had his way, Caleb would soon be on a plane back to Chicago.

He couldn't figure out what he'd ever seen in the man. After meeting and falling in love with Rawley, Caleb seemed so artificial, and shallow. He'd had to remind the asswipe several times that he wasn't interested, but Caleb seemed to think Jeb was merely playing hard to get.

Getting out of his truck, he didn't wait for Caleb. He bounded up the stairs and into the house. The first person he saw was Rio, sprawled out on the couch sound asleep. Jeb followed the laughter and ended up out on the deck. He walked right into Rawley's arms and gave him a deep, tongue thrusting kiss.

Rawley seemed a little shocked and it showed on his face. "Hey, darlin', you miss me?"

"You have no idea," Jeb said, kissing him again. Breaking the kiss he looked around, "Where's Sonny and Garron?"

"They'll be here. Garron had to work, so they'll just be a little late. Sonny said to start without them if we couldn't wait." Rawley ran his hand up and down Jeb's back, the obvious attention having a direct affect on his cock.

He heard the door close and new Caleb was behind him. Trying to be a good host, Jeb let loose a quiet sigh and turned around. "Everyone, I'd like you to meet Agent Caleb Spears." Jeb went around the deck and introduced everyone. He couldn't help but see Caleb's wide-eyed look when he introduced Nate. Good, maybe he'd leave him alone for the rest of the night.

Rawley must have felt his tension because he turned and pulled Jeb into the empty kitchen. Wrapping Jeb in his big arms, Rawley kissed him. "What's wrong? You seem a little tense. Did something happen?"

Jeb knew he couldn't tell Rawley about Caleb coming on to him, at least not until he learned how to do the searches on his own. "I'm fine, just missed you."

Rawley looked out the window onto the deck. "Caleb seems to have taken a shine to Nate."

"What?" Rio's smooth, deep voice bellowed. "Who's Caleb?" he asked as he rubbed the sleep from his eyes.

"He's the FBI guy from Chicago we asked to come down and help us find out what Mayor Channing is hiding."

Rio grunted and went out to the deck. Jeb watched the big Latin manoeuvre over to sit on the railing about five feet from Nate. He crossed his massive arms and stared at Caleb. Jeb grinned. "What do you suppose that was all about?"

"Oh, I think you know the signs of denial well enough by now. Rio's mouth says he's not interested, but his body says differently." Rawley rubbed his hardening cock against Jeb. "Find out anything interesting working with Caleb?"

"Yeah, I found out I must have been completely insane to ever love that man," Jeb said as he rubbed back.

"Glad you've seen the light, darlin'. That guy's an ass."

"You know it. Although, I can't wait to see him get shut down by Nate."

"Do you think he will? Nate's been moaning about the lack of male companionship in Summerville. Caleb may just be the distraction he's been hoping for."

"Naw, Nate's far too smooth for the likes of Caleb. I told you before, Nate's almost a legend in Chicago. He can have almost any man he wants with a snap of his fingers. He's dated judges, politicians, rock stars and a few other well known millionaires. He never sticks around long though. I don't know what he's searching for, but he's not found it yet, and I doubt he'll give Caleb the time of day."

As they watched the scene out the window, Nate broke away and walked towards the house. "Quick, kiss me," Jeb said as he pulled Rawley's head down. The door opened and he heard Nate groan.

"Stop, you two or you're gonna make me cry."

Jeb released Rawley's lips and grinned at Nate. "What's wrong? Caleb getting a little too friendly?"

Nate's whole body shook as he made a funny face. "Creepy guy." Nate walked over to the fridge and started pulling out the food. "I told Ranger I'd get the steaks and finish up the salads. It's a hell of a lot less crowded in here." He flashed Rawley and Jeb a grin. "I still need to get home to change for my nightly date."

Jeb watched as Nate unwrapped the steaks and headed for the door. "Cover me, if Mr. Creepy gets too close, call in reinforcements."

"Oh I don't think you have to worry about that with your guard dog watching every move you make." Rawley motioned towards Rio.

A smile blossomed on Nate's face. "That big Latin hunk's watching me?"

"Every move," Jeb chuckled.

Unfastening the button on his low-rise jeans, Nate pulled them down another notch so his groin muscles were shown to perfection. "Let's see him notice this," he said with a wink as he opened the door.

Jeb and Rawley started laughing as all heads turned towards Nate, including Ranger and Ryker. Ranger turned back towards the grill and adjusted himself as Ryker punched him in the arm. Rawley squeezed Jeb's ass. "That man's a menace to society."

"Told ya," Jeb agreed.

Going back out to the deck, Rawley took a seat and brought Jeb down into his lap. Jeb watched as Nate handed off the platter, and dug in the cooler for a beer. He walked back into the house presumably to finish the salads. Sonny and Garron walked out and everyone greeted them enthusiastically.

"Sorry we're late. I had a lot of reports to fill out at the station before I left." Garron walked over and shook Caleb's hand, remembering him from the time Jeb had spent with him.

Sonny came over and pulled up a chair. "How's it going?"

"Good, I'm planning on taking a few head to the cattle auction in Greensburg if you're interested?"

"Yeah, I think so," Sonny said as Garron picked him up and took his seat, sitting Sonny in his lap. "I'll have to talk to Shelby, but I imagine we've got about ten head I'd like to part with."

Jeb was startled when Rio jumped down from the railing and stormed towards the kitchen. "Uh oh, where's Caleb?" He looked around and saw no sign of him.

"Shit," Rawley said as he hoisted Jeb up. "I'd better make sure Rio doesn't kill our FBI contact."

Walking into the kitchen, Jeb watched Rawley try to pull Rio off of Caleb. Rio's large brown hands appeared to be tightly wrapped around Caleb's fake-tanned throat.

"You mother-fucker," Rio was screaming in Caleb's face. "You leave your damn hands to yourself if you want to keep them."

"Calm down," Rawley said, using his official sheriff's voice. "Rio, goddammit, man, let him go."

Rio gave Caleb one last shove, and released him. "You stay the fuck away from Nate."

Jeb glanced over at Nate who was just glowing, despite the drop of blood where his lip had been split. His clothes were mussed and he had a feeling Caleb was responsible. What he couldn't figure out was why Nate would allow Caleb to get that close without taking him out. Nate was one bad dude, everyone knew that. He was surprised Caleb had even tried anything with him.

Rawley turned towards Caleb, "Why don't you go on back out to the deck. We'll eat and then have a short meeting before returning to the ranch." Rawley's eyes then swung towards Jeb. He saw the question in Rawley's eyes. Shit, he was gonna have to tell him about Caleb's come-ons that afternoon.

After Caleb straightened his hair and clothes, he went back outside. Rio turned to Nate, but didn't attempt to approach him. "You okay?"

Licking the drop of blood from his lip, Nate nodded. "He just surprised me. I won't let him get the jump on me like that again."

"You bet you won't because you don't need to be anywhere near that asshole." Rio's hands flexed at his side.

Jeb watched as Nate's spine stiffened. "Unless you're staking a claim, you've got no say in it." Nate crossed his arms and looked at a furious Rio.

"I'm already involved. I've told you that." Rio ran his fingers through his thick black hair. "Forget it." Rio turned towards Rawley. "I'm getting out of here. It's my night off, but I think I'll visit The Zone as a customer. You can give me a call later if there's anything I need to know." With one last look at Nate, Rio left.

Jeb grinned and rubbed his hands together. "Well this night is starting off well."

Chapter Five

Settling under the covers, Rawley pulled Jeb into his arms. "Despite everything, it turned out to be a pretty productive meeting."

"Yeah, I'll continue to learn more from Caleb tomorrow after my chores are done."

Rawley couldn't help feeling the tension in Jeb's back and shoulders. Rubbing them out, he wondered about Caleb. "You didn't have any trouble with him today did you?"

There it was again, that slight stiffening of the spine that he'd felt earlier. "I can handle him. I just need to learn as much as I can before sending him on his way."

Now it was Rawley's turn to feel tight as his blood heated. He tilted Jeb's chin up. "What happened?"

"I said I'd handle it. I'm a man, please don't forget that." Jeb burrowed back into Rawley's neck and began licking and kissing.

"Well hell, darlin'. I can't sit back and do nothing if he's bothering you. How am I supposed to sit across from the asshole at the breakfast table if he's trying to make a play for my man?"

"Because we need him for a couple more days, and he can make all the plays he wants. It won't get him anywhere."

"Is he still in love with you?" Rawley hated asking the question, but he needed to know what he was up against.

"Caleb never loved me. I'm just the one who left him, and his ego took a beating over it." Jeb started working his way down Rawley's body with his tongue. "Enough talking," he moaned, moments before he attached himself to Rawley's pebbled nipple.

The feel of Jeb's mouth forced all thoughts of Caleb to the back of his mind. Running his fingers through Jeb's curls, Rawley hauled him on top of him. "Feels good."

After sucking a bruise on his nipple, Jeb sat up, straddling Rawley's thighs. "I wanna ride you, Sheriff."

Hoo boy was Rawley ready for that. He reached over and pulled out the bottle of slick, his fingers brushing Jeb's plug in the back of the drawer. "Gonna get you a plug for you to wear while I'm gone during the day. Make you nice and ready for me when I get home."

Taking the bottle of lube from Rawley, Jeb started stretching himself, back bowing just showing off his fantastic body. "Don't know if I could function with something in me."

Grabbing the bottle, Rawley poured lube over his cock. Jeb rose up and slowly sunk down onto his length. "Oh hell yeah," Rawley groaned as Jeb impaled himself. "You seem to be functioning just fine."

Jeb moved up and down on Rawley's cock, enthusiastically. "Not the same thing," Jeb panted, "mind doesn't have to work riding you."

"You got that right." Rawley placed his hands on Jeb's lean hips and held him up so he could thrust in and out. He must have pegged Jeb's gland because his love cried out.

"Yes, more…"

Ready to oblige, Rawley quickened his pace until Jeb's body tightened around him. Screaming his name, Jeb painted Rawley's chest with his seed. "Oh fuck you smell good," Rawley ground out between clenched teeth as he buried himself in Jeb's ass and came.

Grinding down against Rawley, Jeb fell forward in a heap. "So good…" he mumbled against Rawley's chest.

Rawley pulled the sheet up over them without breaking contact, his dick still half-hard inside Jeb's hot body. "Love you, get some sleep." Jeb mumbled something he assumed was, "I love you," before drifting off to sleep.

Yeah, his man definitely needed a plug.

* * * *

Jeb woke up just before dawn to a phone call from Sonny. "Hey," he said rubbing the sleep from his eyes.

"Our cattle are loose and roaming the county road. Shelby's out of town so I'll need your help."

"Shit," Jeb replied, sitting straight up and swinging his legs over the side of the bed.

Rawley sat up, "What, what's going on?" Jeb reached out and took his hand, trying to calm him.

"See you in a bit," Sonny said before hanging up.

Jeb stood and bent over to place a kiss on Rawley's open mouth. "Someone's evidently cut the fences again. My cattle along with Sonny's are out roaming the street."

Walking towards the dresser, he dug out his clothes. Rawley was right behind him, digging through his own dresser. "You want to take the four-wheeler? I thought I'd take Buck." Jeb's buckskin gelding was the best suited for herding cattle without spooking them further.

"Doesn't matter to me, would it make it easier? I know how to ride ya know?"

"Yeah, yeah, I'm sorry. My heads going ninety to nothing right now. I'll saddle up Clyde for you." With one last quick kiss, Jeb strode out of the bedroom. He scribbled a quick note for Caleb and walked out the back door heading for the barn.

After saddling his horse, Jeb gathered a few items to patch the fence until he could fix it properly. Slinging the saddlebag over Buck's back, he was happy to see Rawley. "I didn't get a chance to saddle Clyde, but his tack's already hung on the stall."

Rawley nodded, "I'll catch up."

Jeb mounted and rode towards the road. His house sat approximately two miles from Sonny's, so Jeb didn't know where he'd find the cattle. As he rode, he scoured the area ahead, smiling when he saw the first bunch. "I've got you now my wayward friends." Riding up on the cattle, Jeb waved his arms and started yelling, trying to get them to turn around. As soon as that bunch got turned, another group headed his way.

He spotted Sonny and Garron in the distance trying to get the stubborn cattle back through the broken fence. With all the commotion and noise he didn't hear the first gunshot. He watched as the cow in front of him was thrown to the side, a red stain blossoming on her side. Realising what was happening, Jeb took off as several more shots were fired, not bothering to turn around to look for the shooter. He saw Garron riding at a fast clip towards him, worry etched on his face.

The first thing Jeb thought of when Garron finally reached him was Rawley. "Rawley's somewhere behind me, we need to see if he's okay."

"Stay here," Garron yelled at him. "The shots have stopped, but I'm not taking any chances with you."

Garron rode off as Jeb looked at the street behind him. His cattle were in chaos, several with injuries either from the gunshots or the panic. Pulling out his cell phone, he called Mac. He was just finishing the call when he saw Garron and Rawley riding towards him. Giving Buck the go ahead, Jeb rode towards them.

Once close enough, he hollered out, "You both okay?"

Rawley didn't say a word until he was beside him. He pulled Jeb over into his lap, his hands roaming Jeb's body, assessing his condition. "You shot?"

"No, you?"

Rawley shook his head and pulled him against his chest. "I was so scared he'd gotten you."

Jeb held tight to Rawley, afraid to let go. "Lionel?"

"Nope, one of his buddies, Kyle Locke. I think I shot him, though."

Jeb looked down to the ever-present holster at Rawley's hip. Thank God, he was in love with a lawman. "Is he dead? I didn't even see him shooting."

"No, he jumped in his car and took off. He was behind you, for how long, I don't know. I wouldn't be surprised if he's on his way to Lincoln to get medical attention, no way would he go into Summerville." Rawley ran his fingers through Jeb's curls, still holding tight. "I'll make a few phone calls."

"It would probably be better if I did the calling since I have jurisdiction in Lincoln," Garron said, riding up beside them. "You okay, baby brother?"

"Yeah, just scared me." He looked over at the cattle that'd begun to settle down. "I called Mac, several of my girls are hurt."

"Better the damn cattle than you," Rawley said giving him a kiss. "Let's get them back through the fence so I can take you home."

With one last kiss, Jeb was deposited back on his horse. It didn't appear that any of the cattle were too bad to walk, even those that had taken a bullet, so they slowly moved them back down the road. They met up with Sonny who was trying to separate the cattle.

As Jeb rode up he saw both fences had been cut at the property line. Shaking his head, he dismounted. He needed to keep the cattle that had already been herded in from coming back out. Grabbing his saddle bag, he looked over at Sonny, who was doing the same thing with his side. "The way this fence is cut, we're going to need some wire if we hope to contain them."

"Yeah, I put a call into Ranger and Ryker. They're on their way out with supplies." Sonny shoved one of Jeb's Herefords back from getting in with his Angus. "What happened?"

"Not really sure. I guess they figured if they cut the fences we'd come running. Strange thing is I don't think they were aiming for me."

"What are you saying?"

"I think they were just trying to scare us. Why, I don't know, but I have a feeling if he'd wanted me dead, I'd be on the ground back there." Jeb watched as Garron and Rawley rode towards them with the last of the cattle. "Rawley shot him. Garron's gonna call the police station in Lincoln and have them check out the hospitals."

After getting the last of the cattle sorted and into the pasture, they positioned themselves and the horses to block the exit until the twins showed up. As they made quick work of the fence, Garron borrowed Sonny's cell phone to call the police.

When Garron was finished with the call he looked over at Rawley. "I'm going to head to Lincoln. I'd like for Sonny to come over to your place until I get back this evening."

Rawley nodded, Sonny puffing up and turning red. "I. Do. Not. Need. A. Babysitter.," he ground out between clenched teeth.

Wrapping his arms around Sonny, Garron grinned. "Think with your head instead of your pride, cowboy. It makes sense for the two of you to watch each other's backs while Rawley and I are gone."

"What about my work, I have things I need to do." Sonny looked at Mac, who was busy assessing the injured cows. "Mac? Do we need to get these cows to your clinic?"

Mac stood from his squatting position. "A couple of them. I can treat the cuts here, but if I need to operate, that's best done in a sterile environment." Mac put his hands on his hips and looked at Jeb. "That is, if you want the bullets taken out?"

Jeb looked at the three Hereford's in question. It would be expensive to have them operated on, but he couldn't sell them at auction in the shape they were in. Rubbing his eyes, he sighed. "We'll get them loaded up. I'll have you fix the two heifers, but I'll take the steer to the butcher."

Mac nodded and began patching up the cattle injured in the chaos. Jeb turned towards Rawley. "If you can ride back to the ranch and bring the cattle trailer, I'll get them loaded and taken where they need to go."

Rawley wrapped his arms around Jeb. "I'm sorry."

"Yeah," Jeb said, leaning against his man.

* * * *

Getting two beers out of the fridge, Jeb passed one to Sonny. "Damn I'm tired." He walked to the living room and collapsed on the couch. "What time did Rawley and Garron say they'd be home?"

"They didn't," Sonny said, taking the chair beside the couch.

"Well there you are," Caleb said coming into the room. "After that hastily scrawled note, I was beginning to worry."

"No need." Jeb really wasn't in the mood for Caleb right now. "Find out anything?"

"Yes. Your Mayor Channing has a house he's recently purchased in Florida. He bought it with a cash transfer from a bank in the Bahamas." Caleb moved Jeb's feet and sat down.

"Where do you suppose a small-town Mayor would come up with that kind of money?" Jeb looked at Sonny and winked. "Is it enough to warrant an investigation?"

"I've talked to my boss, and though he wasn't happy about me digging around behind his back, he said he'd look into it." Caleb stretched his arm out on the back of the sofa, ruffling Jeb's hair with his fingers.

Quickly finishing his beer, Jeb stood and motioned towards Sonny's, "Need another?"

Narrowing his eyes at Caleb, it was plain that Sonny had witnessed Caleb's actions. "Yeah."

The two men were still eyeing each other when Jeb came back into the room. He was being rude not to offer Caleb one, but after the day he'd had he didn't give a fuck. Handing the fresh bottle over, Jeb sat in the old rocking chair. "What about Channing's bank accounts? You think your boss will be able to look at those?"

Caleb chuckled, "We're the FBI, we can get into damn near anything we want if we have a reason."

Rolling his eyes at the self important prick in front of him, Jeb was grateful when the phone rang. Walking into the kitchen for a little privacy, he picked it up. "Hello?"

"Hey, darlin', I'll be home in about an hour. Is Sonny still with you?"

"Yeah, Caleb found some stuff on Channing and called his boss. Looks like we might get to hand over the investigation to the Feds."

"That's good news. This thing with Lionel is all I can handle right now. Garron called, said the Lincoln police found his buddy at Mercy. Garron's hoping once they get him to the police station he'll do a little singing."

Jeb closed his eyes and thanked the heavens. "That's good. With everything that happened earlier, I think we should call Nate off Lionel. If he's desperate enough to have someone shoot at me in broad daylight, it's not safe for him to be trailing along after dark."

"I see what you're saying, but I'll need to talk to Nate about where he thinks this thing is going. I'll stop by on my way home if that's okay?"

"Sure, as long as you bring home dinner. I'm too damn tired to cook."

"I'll bring enough for all of us. I imagine Sonny's feeling the same way you are."

"I love you," Jeb said as he hung up the phone. Now he just had to get Caleb out of his house.

By the time he got back into the living room, Sonny was gone. "Where'd he go?"

Waving a hand in the air, Caleb looked bored. "Said something about taking care of the horses for you."

"Oh," Jeb was a little surprised. Although maybe Sonny just needed to get away from Caleb. "Rawley'll be home in an hour with dinner."

Caleb stood and walked towards him. Jeb took a step back and narrowed his eyes. "Don't even think of touching me."

"Now come on, sugar, don't you remember how good it was between us?" Caleb backed Jeb into the wall and pressed his body against him. It was easy to tell Caleb was getting off on this. Jeb tried to push him away.

"Get the hell off me," he struggled with the much bigger man.

Caleb ground his hard cock against Jeb. "Cooperate with me and I'll continue to help with your little investigation."

Unable to move the man, Jeb spit in Caleb's face. Rearing back, Caleb's fist slammed into the side of Jeb's face. "Fuck," Jeb yelled, feeling blood run down his cheek. He started kicking out, trying to connect with anything.

He heard the front door open and within seconds, Garron was on top of Caleb pounding his face. After several good blows, Jeb called him off. "Garron, he's not worth it, just get him the hell out of my house."

Jeb went to the spare bedroom and gathered Caleb's clothes. He knew he needed to get him out of the house before Rawley came home. Latching the suitcase, he carried it to the front door and threw it into the yard. Holding the door, he watched as Garron bent Caleb's arm behind his back and frog-marched him out of the house.

"What the fuck is this? How am I supposed to get to town?" Caleb stood in the yard with one hand covering his bleeding nose.

"I guess you start walking," Jeb said as he slammed the door. He turned to Garron, "Thanks, brother."

Garron looked at the small cut on Jeb's eye. "You're gonna have quite a shiner."

"Yeah, and one angry Sheriff."

Chapter Six

After applying a butterfly-bandage and an ice pack to his face, Jeb stretched out on the couch. "We need to call Caleb's boss. It would be just like him to try and talk him out of following up with an investigation on Channing."

"I'll take care of it," Garron said, facing him from his seat on the coffee table. "Has Caleb been harassing you since he's been here?"

"Some, but not like earlier. He had roamy hands, but he didn't put up a fight when I'd knock them back and remind him of Rawley."

Garron looked over at Sonny. "You have any trouble with him?" Jeb could see Garron slip into full mate protective mode.

"No," Sonny said with a grin.

Standing, Garron walked towards the kitchen. "I'm going to call the FBI headquarters in Chicago and see if I can get the name of Caleb's boss."

"It's George Bitterman," Jeb replied.

"Thanks, that'll make it easier."

After Garron left, Jeb looked over at Sonny. "What's wrong?"

"I shouldn't have left you alone with that ass." Sonny plopped down in the chair and took a drink of his beer.

"Don't sweat the small stuff. Caleb would've eventually found me alone and done the same thing." He yawned, wincing at the pain in his face. "I just want food and then bed. I feel like I could sleep a week."

"Rest your eyes, I think I'll go sit on the porch and keep a lookout for Rawley. He'll need a good dose of calm before he sees your cheek and eye."

The next thing Jeb heard was the sound of Rawley's voice bellowing on the porch. He listened as both Garron and Sonny tried to calm him down. Jeb braced himself as the door flew open. Rawley came in and knelt beside him.

Checking out his injury, Rawley's face went even redder. "I'll kill the sonofabitch." He started to stand, but Jeb reached out and pulled him back down.

"He's gone, let him go. We got what we needed, that's all that really matters." Jeb tried to sit up and winced at the pain banging its way through his head.

"Lay back down," Rawley's voice took on a concerned tone. He exhaled and closed his eyes. "You're going to give me a heart attack. First someone takes pot shots at you and now this." He pushed Jeb back down and kissed him. "I need you around, darlin'."

"Good, then please tell me you brought something home for dinner?"

"Yeah, I did, but I want a few more kisses first," Rawley said, seconds before his lips closed over Jeb's.

Moaning, Jeb tried to pull him closer, but Rawley broke the kiss and shook his head. "Let's eat and then I'll put you to bed."

"Spoilsport." Jeb stuck his tongue out, but ruined it with a grin.

* * * *

After dinner, Rawley put Jeb in bed, promising he'd be in soon, and went back to talk to Garron and Sonny. The two of them were curled up together on the couch kissing.

Taking a chair, Rawley cleared his throat. "What did Caleb's boss say when you talked to him?"

Garron broke the kiss and looked over at Rawley. "He said the ball was already rolling on the investigation. It wasn't until the contractor, Dick England's, name got brought into the equation that he really perked up. Seems the Lincoln office has had him under surveillance for a while now. Agent Bitterman didn't say why of course, but regardless it helps our case against Channing."

"And what about Kyle Locke? Did he sing after you transferred him to the police station?"

"They wouldn't let us move him yet, but I have a feeling he will. I went by Mac's office and picked up a bullet he dug out of one of the heifers. It was from a twenty-two rimfire. I think when we show him the evidence about the twenty-two being used in both Sonny's shooting and the shooting on Jeb, he'll sing. Even though we know Kyle didn't take that shot at Sonny, the evidence will show that he did. His only hope will be to give up Lionel."

"How long will it take?"

"Ballistics' are a little back-logged, but I'd say sometime within the next few days."

"Good, I'll breathe a little easier when we can call Nate off."

"I think we all feel the same way," Garron agreed.

"Yeah, especially Rio." Rawley tilted his head and looked at Garron. "You know much about Rio, like who this mystery lover of his is?"

"No mystery, Rio's been involved with my buddy Ryan since we both got out of the Marines. I know he's been working on and off down in Central and South America as a mercenary."

"They solid? Rio and Ryan? Because I'm definitely getting some heavy duty vibes from Nate and him."

"Rio would never cheat on Ryan. That I can guarantee." Garron stood and pulled a sleepy Sonny up. "I think we're gonna take off."

Walking them to the door, Rawley gave Sonny a hug and Garron a pat on the back. "Talk to you later. Thanks for being here with Jeb today."

"No thanks necessary," Garron said as he steered Sonny towards his truck.

Rawley shut the door and locked it. Thinking about the happenings earlier in the day, he went around the house and checked all the windows and doors. Better safe than sorry, he thought as he undressed.

Jeb was sound asleep when Rawley crawled in behind him. He knew his head was probably still hurting, so he tried not to wake him as he spooned up and wrapped his arms around his man. Just the thought of something happening to Jeb, tightened his chest. He'd had two close calls that day. Who knew what could have happened if Garron hadn't come in when Caleb was attacking Jeb. The thought of Caleb threatened to send Rawley out into the night to look for the asshole.

Taking a deep breath, he turned his mind away from Caleb to Kyle. Rawley was just damn glad he'd had his sidearm with him when that fucker started shooting. Kyle was lucky Rawley hadn't aimed for his head instead of his arm.

Jeb squirmed in his arms, apparently dreaming. Rawley drew him even closer against his chest and kissed his blond curls. "I love you, darlin'."

* * * *

Unlocking the apartment door, Nate yawned. Thank God Lionel had decided to call it an early night. He'd sat outside his house for a couple of hours after the lights had all gone off before giving up for the night. He just hadn't been getting enough sleep lately.

Stepping into the kitchen he tossed his keys on the counter and went through to the bathroom. Opening the door, he came face to face with a very naked, very large, Rio. "Sorry, I didn't know you were home yet."

Quickly wrapping a yellow towel around his toned waist, Rio nodded. "It was dead at The Zone so I got off early." He went to squeeze by Jeb, but the size of the bathroom caused Rio to rub against Nate.

Nate couldn't help the moan that escaped at the brush of Rio's hip against his rock hard cock. Rio stopped in the doorway and turned back. He looked at Nate for several moments, eyeing him up and down, before shaking his head and disappearing into their shared bedroom.

After a quick wank in the shower, Nate started to walk into the bedroom when he heard Rio's voice. "I know. It's just harder to be away this time, it's different." Nate knew he shouldn't be listening, but he couldn't help himself, just the sound of Rio's voice had his recently spent cock twitching. "You know I'd never do that, but it's hard. You're done with your assignment, why don't you come up for a few days?"

Shit, that was not what Nate wanted to hear. He thought he was finally breaking the big man down. "Because goddammit I asked you to." Nate heard Rio sigh, "Just fuckin' forget it."

He heard the phone slam down and retraced his steps to the bathroom, flushing the toilet, he waited a couple of seconds before emerging. He walked into the bedroom and looked at Rio sitting on his twin-size bed with his head in his hands. "Everything okay?" Nate asked as he dug clean underwear out of the little dresser.

When Rio didn't look up or reply, Nate shrugged his shoulders and dropped his towel. After getting his black boxer-briefs up he turned towards his bed and caught the look on Rio's face. Evidently the Latin lover had watched him get dressed and it appeared to have an effect on his own briefs.

Nate didn't let on he'd caught Rio staring. Instead, he made a show of pulling down the covers on his bed. He even pulled the sheet to the end of the bed. "God, it's been so hot lately. I've been meaning to mention the air-conditioning situation to Ranger and Ryker. I'd like to get a little window unit for the bedroom as well as the one we already have in the living room." Nate stretched out on his back, erection clearly visible for Rio's inspection.

Grunting, Rio stood up and grabbed his pillow. "You're right it's too damn hot in here. I'm gonna sack out on the couch." Rio put the pillow in front of his crotch and walked out of the room.

Sighing, Nate stripped off his underwear and took matters into his own hand, again.

* * * *

"Hello?" Garron spoke into his cell phone as he climbed into the truck after work the next day.

"Hey, buddy."

"Hey, Ryan, what's up?" Garron started the engine to get the air going.

"I was wondering how the investigation was going? Kinda worried about Rio."

"Why? He's working damn near every night at The Zone. As far as I know, no one in town besides us knows he's even in on the investigation."

"I'm not worried about the investigation, I'm worried about this guy you've got him staying with. He called me last night and said he was having a hard time. Even asked me to come up there for a couple days."

Garron leaned back against the head rest and closed his eyes. "I'm not gonna lie to ya, Ryan. There's definitely sparks there, but we both know Rio won't cheat on you."

"Who's this guy?"

"His name's Nate. He came down from Chicago. He's a private investigator that I worked with occasionally when I was on the force there." Garron picked at the oil change sticker on the windshield. "He's a good guy, but I'll be honest with you, if you like the type, he's hot as fuck."

"What type?"

"Small, lean, tough as hell even though he comes off as a little feminine, course I think most of that's an act. Geez, I don't know, like the complete opposite of you and Rio. I love ya, buddy, so I gotta be honest with you. If Rio was mine, I'd make a trip up to make sure he stayed that way."

"What are you telling me?"

"That there's a powder keg between the two of them, and I'd say it's set to blow at any time."

"I'll be there as soon as I can catch a flight. Can you tell me how to get to your place from Lincoln? Or should I go to the feedlot where Rio's staying?"

"Depends, if you're coming in tonight, you should come here because Rio's working and he'd be pissed if you blew his cover by going to The Dead Zone."

"I'll call him, and see where he wants me to meet him. Thanks for the heads-up, man."

"No problem. It'll be good to see you again." Garron hung up and pulled out of the lot. The gay population of Summerville was about to climb one more notch, he just hoped the small town was ready for it. His friend could be intimidating to the toughest Marine. He didn't think the friendly ranchers and farmers of the area had ever come across anyone like Ryan Blackfeather.

Chapter Seven

Ryan pulled his rented car into the parking lot. He looked around at the myriad of pickups and chuckled. "Just like home."

He'd called Rio earlier after getting his flight information and his man had given him directions to the feedlot, saying he'd meet him there when he called. Ryan couldn't help himself though. He knew from past conversations with Rio that Nate was at the bar every night, and he needed a peek at his competition. Knowing Rio was working the front door, Ryan took a guess and went around to the back of the building. Yep, just as he suspected, the door was propped open. He sidled into the bar and moved to the darkest part of the room.

Rio was easy to spot, sitting in all his massive glory on a stool by the front door. He was staring across the room, and Ryan followed his eyes straight to... "Oh fuck," he whispered. His own cock jerked at the site of the man leaning against the opposite wall. Nate was the same size as the men they'd shared a couple of times. Only this man was sexier than all the others put together.

Taking out his cell phone, he dialled Rio's number. Ryan watched as he unclipped the phone from his belt and looked at the caller ID. "Hey, you in town?"

"Yep, no wonder you were having such a hard time, Nate's breathtaking." Ryan watched as Rio's eyes scanned the bar.

Ryan felt the heat from his gaze from across the room. "I already asked to get off early. I'll meet you at the apartment in thirty minutes."

"Love you," Ryan said. He hung up and slipped the phone in his pocket. Taking one last look at Nate, Ryan shook his head and left through the back door. As soon as he was in his car, he adjusted his cock and sighed. "What the hell am I about to get into the middle of?"

He found the feedlot easy enough, so he grabbed his duffle out of the back seat and went to sit on the top step around back of the building. If he knew anything about Rio, it was that the man wouldn't be using the parking lot.

Waiting, Ryan's mind wandered to Nate. As hot as he was, he didn't look like the type to go for a one-night stand, and Ryan wasn't sure if he was willing to share Rio for the long haul. What if Nate and Rio really hit it off and decided they didn't need him around anymore?

Rio was the first person in his life to love him for who he was. He didn't see the colour of his skin, length of his hair or the myriad of tattoos scattered around his body. He saw only Ryan. Hell his own family had ostracised him when they found out he was gay. He'd been kicked off the reservation as soon as he'd come out, ending up in Texas.

That had actually been a damn good thing, he thought. If he hadn't been forced out, he wouldn't have met Rio and he probably would have ended up a drunk trying to pretend he was straight for the sake of his family. Now Rio and a handful of friends were his only family, and he wouldn't give any of them up without a fight.

"You're thinking too hard," Rio said, starting up the stairs.

Ryan stood and waited for Rio to join him. "Thinking about you," he whispered against Rio's lips as he pulled him against his body. The kiss went on for several moments, both men rubbing against the other. "Feel's good, missed you."

"Yeah, let's get inside and get naked."

* * * *

Stumbling in at dawn, Nate opened the fridge. He tipped the juice carton to his mouth and took a long swallow. He briefly thought about fixing a sandwich, but decided he was too damn tired to chew.

After a quick stop in the bathroom, Nate headed for bed, and was stopped by a pile of blankets and his pillow outside the door. He snatched the note off the pile and tried to focus his eyes in the dim light. "Sorry, but I've got company. Hope you don't mind sleeping on the couch. Rio."

"Well, damn," Nate sighed. He picked up a sheet and his pillow and walked to the sofa. Shucking his clothes, Nate threw down his pillow and stretched out, pulling a sheet over him. He was glad he was too damn tired to think about the implications of the note. Within minutes, he was sound asleep.

He heard someone rumbling around in the kitchen and opened his eyes. Clad only in a pair of low slung shorts, their houseguest was making a pot of coffee. Nate took the opportunity to ogle the strong back across the room. He could barely make out the bottom of a tattoo under that mane of long black hair. The tattooed arms were easy to study though. They all looked to be tribal symbols, but from the long hair and bronze skin, Nate figured they were Native American symbols. Regardless, they were hot, which surprised the hell out of him because he'd never been a tattoo kind of guy.

The professional-type men he'd always dated wouldn't be caught dead having a tattoo, so why did this man's turn him on? Scanning the length of the man, Nate spotted two more on his calves. He sat mesmerised by the play of bulging muscles in the guys back. Well if Rio was gonna cheat on his boyfriend Nate could definitely see why he'd chosen this man. It hurt though, he admitted to himself. The whole damn thing hurt.

The guy turned around and caught Nate looking. "Morning," he said. His voice was so deep Nate felt it vibrate his chest.

"Morning," Nate answered, taking in the tats on the man's sculpted chest and peeking up from his shorts. Nate swallowed and quickly made sure his hard cock was well covered by the sheet. "Where's Rio?"

"Still asleep, but I gotta have my coffee first thing in the morning. I'm sorry if I woke you." The guy came over and towered above Nate. He reached out his hand, "I'm Ryan Blackfeather, Rio's partner."

Taking a deep breath, Nate shook his hand. "Nate Gills." So this was Ryan. He was nothing like Nate had pictured. Ryan had always seemed like a name that went with a professional guy, someone mild-mannered. He'd heard that Garron had been in the Marine's with Rio's partner, but he just pictured a communications guy or something, not this warrior in front of him.

Nate heard a door open and Rio stepped into the room. He scratched his chest and looked from Nate to Ryan. "I guess the two of you have met."

"Yeah," Ryan said. "I think I woke him up making coffee."

"What time you get in?" Rio asked coming further into the room.

Looking at the kitchen wall clock, Nate shook his head. "Couple hours ago, I guess."

"Damn, I'm sorry. Let us grab a change of clothes and you can have the bedroom. We'll disappear for the day so you can get some sleep." Without waiting for a reply, Rio motioned for Ryan and they went into the bedroom and closed the door.

Nate heard them talking but he couldn't make out what they were saying. After several long minutes the door opened, both of them carrying a set of clothes. "It's all yours," Rio said.

Throwing back the sheet, Nate was just pissed enough he didn't care if the two men got a look at his morning wood. He watched as both sets of eyes went wide. Picking up his pillow and sheet, Nate squeezed past them. "Excuse me," he mumbled as his arm brushed Rio on his way through the door. He smiled to himself at Rio's quick intake of breath.

Yeah, Ryan may be here, but Nate knew he was still having an effect on Rio.

* * * *

Damn, another meeting. These Good brothers had more meetings than he'd ever heard of. Nate walked into the house, out of sorts. He hadn't slept much after Rio and Ryan had given up the bedroom. He heard voices for several hours before they finally left the house, but he still couldn't relax enough to drift off.

Rawley called him at about three and told him to come to Ranger and Ryker's place for dinner and a short meeting. He knew the reason they always met at the twin's house was because they couldn't be seen from the road, but he also got the feeling Ranger and Ryker would just prefer everyone left as soon as the meeting was finished.

Nate waved to Sonny as he passed through the kitchen on the way out to the deck. He needed a fucking beer. Getting into the cooler, Nate dug out a frosty bottle and downed it before closing the lid. Grabbing another, he shut the cooler, and walked over to the edge of the deck. Sitting up on the railing, Nate watched the brothers talking in a group around the grill.

He'd nodded as he came out, but other than that he didn't feel like being sociable. Nate didn't understand what was going on with himself, but he'd never felt this hollow ache in his chest. When Rio and Ryan stepped onto the deck holding hands, Nate felt his eyes begin to burn. Fuck, he so didn't want to be here.

It was made even worse when Rio broke away and walked towards him. "Hey," Rio said leaning against the railing. "You okay? You don't look good this evening."

"Thanks for the compliment, but I'm fine," Nate ground out as he took a long pull off his beer. He looked around and gestured to Rawley, "I need to find out what this meeting's about. I'm not hungry and I need to get on the job."

Of course Nate's stomach chose that particular moment to growl. Rio's eyebrows rose. "Sounds to me like you are." He pointed towards the beer. "Don't you think you should lay off the alcohol on an empty stomach? Especially if you plan on working tonight."

"What, all the sudden you care what happens to me?" He pushed off the rail and stood beside Rio. Nate saw Ryan looking over at them. "You'd better go take care of your man. I don't need your worry." Nate walked off in search of

Rawley. He needed to get the hell out of here before he broke down and begged Rio to love him. Shit, that wasn't right. He didn't need that big oaf's love, just his body for about the next hundred years.

Getting Rawley's attention, Nate motioned towards the house. He continued on through the kitchen to the great room. Too keyed up to sit, he took a swig of his beer and waited for Rawley.

"What's going on?" Rawley asked taking a seat.

"I want to get out of here and go do my job. Can you tell me what the meeting's about?" Nate started pacing around in front of the big picture window.

"Sure," Rawley said, studying him. "The ballistics came back, proving the same rifle was used to shoot Sonny and take the shots at Jeb. Kyle's lawyered up and it's just a matter of time before the DA gets the case together against him. We think once he hears the charges he'll tell us what we wanna know. Lionel tried to visit him in jail earlier, but Kyle turned him away. I thought maybe you should know because Lionel didn't take it too well."

"Okay, I'll keep on my toes tonight," Nate set down the beer. "If that's all, I'm gonna take off."

"Anything you'd like to talk about?" Rawley stood and picked up Nate's empty beer bottle.

"Nope, I just want to get this case over with so Rio can be on his way back to Texas or wherever the fuck he came from." He gave Rawley a short nod and strode out of the house.

When he was in his rental car, driving towards town, everything hit him at once. He pulled over to the side of the road and buried his face in his hands. "What the hell is wrong with me?" He wiped his eyes and looked at the road in front of him. He decided it was time to push Lionel a little harder. "Dammit, enough pussy footin' around." He put the car in gear and roared off towards his apartment. He needed to get dressed for his special date with Lionel.

* * * *

After leaving Ranger's, Garron invited them to the ranch. Sitting on the porch swaying back and forth in the swing, Rio looked out over the pastures dotted with cattle. "I miss home," he said absently.

"How is your little hobby farm?" Garron asked Ryan.

"It's going good. It's nice to have something to ground us when we get back from an assignment."

Sonny laughed, "Yeah, nothing more grounding than cleaning up horse shit."

Ryan chuckled and shook his head. "Naw, we hired a guy to work the ranch. We just get to enjoy it. Ride and fish," Ryan looked over at him, "ain't that right?"

"Yep," Rio replied, but his mind was on Nate. He and Ryan had spent a good part of the day talking about him. Rio had tried his best to convey his feelings without upsetting the good balance he and Ryan had. In the end, Ryan told him he just couldn't do it. As hot as Nate was it put their relationship in too much risk for them to all get involved in a threesome. He'd been pissed at first, thinking Ryan hadn't listened to a word he'd said, but it soon became clear that Ryan was scared.

"Rio?"

"Huh?" Rio looked up at Sonny.

"Would you like a beer?" Sonny held out a fresh bottle.

"Oh, yeah, sorry. You caught me daydreaming." Rio took the bottle and received a nudge to the ribs from Ryan. He knew Ryan hated it when he drank. Coming from his background, Ryan didn't let anything stronger than Coca-Cola pass his lips. He shrugged and opened his beer.

Sonny went back into the house, and Ryan cleared his throat. "How's he doing?"

Garron looked towards the front door. "Good for the most part. He still gets headaches, he's on seizure medication, and every once in a while he becomes forgetful, but compared to the way he was right after the shooting he's fantastic."

They heard the phone ring and seconds later Sonny came back out, phone in hand. "It's for you, it's Lilly."

"Lilly?" Garron took the phone. "Hey."

Ryan wrapped his arm around Rio and kissed his temple. "We okay?"

Rio turned his head and gave Ryan a kiss on the lips. "We're okay."

Garron hung up and looked at Rio. "Lilly said someone needs to get down to The Zone. Nate's drunk and putting on quite a show for Lionel. She said Lionel looked like he was about to blow a gasket."

"Shit," Rio said standing. He looked down at Ryan, "You want to go with me?"

"Well I sure as hell ain't letting you go alone." He stood and shook Garron's hand. "Thanks for the beer and the company. I'll call you tomorrow."

They headed towards the car and Ryan took the keys away from Rio. "I'll drive. You've had too much to drink."

"I'm not drunk."

"Maybe not, but I'm still not letting you drive." Rio blew out a breath and walked around to the passenger side.

"Just get me there. That man's gonna get himself killed." Rio put on his seat belt and stared straight ahead as Ryan took off.

Chapter Eight

As Ryan drove towards the bar, he kept glancing at Rio. It wasn't like his partner to get so worked up. Rio was usually calm in any situation. Ryan didn't think he'd even seen Rio strung this tight while in the jungles of South America being shot at. He just wondered how long he could put him off regarding Nate.

Ryan wasn't blind or a fool. Even if Rio had put his foot down at a one nighter with Nate, Ryan would have known he had feelings for the guy. At first, Ryan thought it was just a matter of screwing Nate and getting it out of Rio's system, but with Rio's vehement objection that Nate wasn't that kind of guy, all of Ryan's hopes fell.

He just didn't know if he could share the love of this man. He was very territorial when

it came to Rio. Several men had tried to woo him away from Ryan in the past, but Rio had always shot them down. Nate was different. There was absolutely no doubting that. He was honest with himself enough to admit Nate seemed like a nice guy and the fact that he was hotter than hell didn't slip his notice either.

"When we get there, we'll walk in casually. I occasionally show up for a drink on my nights off, so no one will become suspicious if I just happen to walk in. Being the bouncer, it would be natural for me to try and control a rowdy customer," Rio said, breaking into Ryan's thoughts.

"Wouldn't it be better if I went in and got him out? I mean, no one knows me. Why would you want to risk your cover?" He asked the question, but he was afraid he already knew the answer.

Rio didn't even bother answering the question, instead he looked straight ahead. "I'll get him out," he mumbled.

Pulling up, Ryan parked the car. "Okay, let's get this over with." He got out and walked beside Rio. He saw the hands at Rio's sides twitching and he knew he was preparing himself for a fight.

When they opened the door, the loud music assaulted him. Ryan tried to block it out as he followed Rio casually inside. He spotted Nate in an instant. It was hard not to as most eyes in the bar were on him. He was standing in the centre of the dance floor grinding his hips towards Lionel. With a scotch in one hand and his black silk-blend T-shirt pulled up high enough to expose not only his pierced navel, but his pierced nipples as well, Nate crooked his finger at Lionel.

"Come on lover, dance with me. I don't know why you keep pretending," Nate slurred. Lionel's buddies were trying their best to drag him out of the bar, but he was too busy looking at Nate with murder in his eyes.

In a split second, Lionel broke from his friends and advanced on Nate. Rio started pushing through the crowd towards Nate and all Ryan could do was watch as Lionel reared back his arm and let a punch fly. Nate's head snapped back and Ryan was surprised he was still standing. Instead of backing down, Nate smiled a knowing smile before leaping in the air and kicking Lionel in the chest. Unlike Nate, Lionel did go down.

Rio reached Nate as soon as his feet landed on the floor. Trying not to break his cover, Rio's voice took on the authority of a bouncer. "That's enough, break it up." He grabbed Nate by the arm and pulled him through the crowd. Nate tried to break away, but Ryan knew from experience how strong Rio was. Drunk or not, he was just happy Nate didn't use any of his martial arts moves on his man.

Looking back towards the dance floor, Ryan watched as Lionel was helped up. His face showed his obvious rage and embarrassment. "Oh fuck," he said. He knew there was about to be big trouble. Knowing they'd be followed to the parking lot, Ryan decided to save Rio's cover the only way he knew how. He stepped in front of Rio and looked him in the eye. "I'm sorry my lover got out of control. I'll take him home," he said in a voice loud enough for the patrons to hear.

Rio narrowed his eyes but released his grip on Nate's arm. "See that you keep him on a leash. We don't need that kind of trouble in here."

Ryan saw Rio swallow almost choking on his own words. He gave Rio a nod and whispered in Nate's ear. "If you care anything at all about protecting Rio's cover you'll come with me."

Nate looked at him and then at Rio. "Get me the hell out of here," Nate said as he pushed out of Ryan's grip and headed for the door.

Ryan followed him out and pointed towards his car. He managed to get Nate inside just as the doors opened and Lionel and his gang came out. "Buckle up."

He started the car and pulled out of the lot. Instead of heading to the feedlot, Ryan turned his car in the opposite direction. "Where the fuck are you going?" Nate asked.

"Back to the apartment, but I don't exactly want to leave a trail of breadcrumbs in my wake." Knowing Rio parked behind the feedlot's buildings, Ryan figured it must be pretty safe. He got them heading back towards the apartment and stashed the car as quick as he could. Deciding it would be safer to stay where they were until Rio showed up, Ryan rolled down the windows and turned off the engine.

"We'll wait here for Rio."

"How the hell is he supposed to get here? Didn't he come with you?" Nate slurred without looking at him.

"Yeah, but don't worry about Rio. He has his own way of getting things done." Ryan lifted an elastic band out of the ashtray and pulled his hair back into a loose ponytail. "Mind telling me what all that was about?"

"Not that I have to explain myself to you, but I was trying to get Lionel to make a move. Christ, I'm sick and tired of sitting back doing nothing. Besides making sure Lionel doesn't get near Sonny again, Garron brought me here to get Lionel off balance enough that he'd do something stupid. Well, it wasn't working. Lionel was getting used to me following him around like a puppy dog." Nate grinned, "I think I got his attention though."

Looking at Nate, Ryan wasn't sure if he wanted to punch or kiss him. Neither was an option, so he tilted Nate's face to inspect the bruise blossoming around his eye. "Nice shiner."

"Wouldn't be the first time. I know you and Rio planned to come in and save me, but I really didn't need your help."

"Yeah, and what would you have done when the entire bar decided to take you on? You have a death wish or something? You need to get your head back into the game. If you don't, you won't be around much longer. And although it would solve a few problems, I don't know how well Rio would take it."

That seemed to get Nate's attention. Nate let loose a bark of laughter. "Yeah right, Rio's gonna be concerned with me when he's got someone who looks like you in his bed. Give me a break."

"Haven't you looked in the mirror?" Deciding he'd said too much already, Ryan pushed his seat back to the reclining position and closed his eyes. "Just keep a look out."

* * * *

Hanging up the phone, Rawley walked out to the barn. "Jeb? You in here?"

"Back here," Jeb hollered.

Rawley walked back to the tack room. Jeb was sitting on a three-legged stool, reworking a bridle. "I didn't know you knew how to do that."

Jeb looked up from his work and grinned. "I don't really, but I thought it was time I learned. I looked it up on the internet. Seemed like an easy fix, but I'm finding out differently." Jeb set the bridle in his lap. "What's up?"

"I just got off the phone with Garron. Seems our boy Nate went a little nuts overnight and got into a fight with Lionel. Garron's expecting Lionel to file a civil restraining order against him."

"Damn." Jeb scratched his cheek below the cut. "What do we do now?"

Rawley shrugged and pulled Jeb into his arms. The bridle slapped against his boots as it landed in the dirt. "To be honest, I'm not sure. Nate told Garron he didn't care if Lionel filed the order, but it'll go on his record, possibly jeopardise his private detective's licence."

"Maybe we should just send him back to Chicago before anything else happens? Lionel isn't worth ruining Nate's future." Jeb kissed Rawley's chin.

"He won't go. He says he's done with Chicago. I think I'll call him off following Lionel though. Maybe we can get him to take a break and stay in Lincoln until this thing's wrapped up. Kyle's meeting with his attorney today to hear the list of charges against him. Cross your fingers we get lucky."

Rubbing his jean clad erection against Rawley, Jeb winked and knelt. "We finished talking?"

Rawley smiled down and nodded. "For now," he moaned as Jeb started mouthing his cock through the denim. Reaching down, Rawley unfastened himself before burying his hands in Jeb's mop of curls.

Pulling his cock free, Jeb ran his tongue up the underside of Rawley's erection before taking the crown into his mouth. "Yes," Rawley hissed. Jeb worked Rawley's length further into his mouth and sucked. Rawley couldn't stand it, he had to move. "Ready for me?"

Jeb mumbled his consent around Rawley's shaft as he backed off a little. Snapping his hips in a shallow rhythm Rawley rode Jeb's mouth for all he was worth. "So good..."

He heard a zipper lower, and knew Jeb was taking himself in hand. With his fingers gripping Jeb's curls and his balls slapping at Jeb's chin, Rawley buried himself as far as he dared and came with a cry to the rafters.

"Uggghhh..." Jeb moaned around Rawley's cock as he came with his own hand.

Looking down, Rawley whistled at the white patches scattered across Jeb's red T-shirt. "Damn, that's hot. Can I have that shirt?"

Jeb finished cleaning him up and looked down. "Shit. I soil more shirts around you than I ever thought possible." He stood and gave Rawley a tongue tangling kiss. "What would you want with a cum covered shirt?"

Pulling it over Jeb's head, Rawley reached down and cleaned Jeb's cock with it. "I'm gonna stick it in my truck so I can smell you when I start missing you during the day."

"Oh hell," Jeb looked down at his twitching cock. "You sure know how to sweet talk me." He gave Rawley another kiss, "Pick up my bridle and take me to bed."

Rawley was shocked. "You want the bridle in the bed with us?"

"No," Jeb's face went thoughtful. "Well, maybe. Oh hell, just bring it, we'll figure it out."

* * * *

They were just regaining their breath when the phone beside the bed rang. Reaching over, Rawley picked it up. "Hello?"

"Hey," Garron said. "Listen, Shelby just called and Sonny had another seizure in the barn. He said it wasn't a bad one, but Sonny's getting one of his headaches. I'm waiting for word on Kyle which should take another thirty minutes or so, but it'll be an hour and a half before I can get there. I was wondering if either you or Jeb would mind going over. Sometimes he gets sick and isn't able to get himself to the bathroom. It also helps if someone rubs his head."

"Sure, we'll both go. How're things going so far with Kyle?" Rawley sat up and reached for his pants.

"I haven't heard anything official, but I did get a smile and a nod from the officer in charge of the interrogation."

"That's good, maybe we'll take care of Lionel before he ever gets a chance to go before the judge with this restraining order against Nate."

"Let's hope. By the way, Sonny will probably be on the floor of the master bedroom closet. The darkness seems to help. Tell him I'll be home as soon as possible."

"Will do." Rawley hung up and turned to Jeb. "We need to get over to Sonny's. He's having one of his headaches and Garron's tied up in Lincoln."

Fastening his Wranglers, Jeb nodded. "I'll take the pot of stew I started this morning."

* * * *

Ten minutes later, they walked into the house and as expected, found Sonny in the closet. Rawley grabbed a pillow and blanket and stepped in before closing the door. Kneeling, he slipped the pillow under Sonny's head. "Did you take some of your medicine?"

"Yeah," Sonny mumbled. "Hasn't kicked in yet."

Sitting on the floor, Rawley began rubbing his brother's head. "You're hair's growing in nicely," he said in a soft voice.

It was too dark to see, but when Rawley moved his hands to rub at Sonny's temples he felt the tears sliding down Sonny's face. As much as it hurt him to witness his brother's pain, it was a good boost to his resolve. He'd begun to have doubts about his actions regarding Lionel. Not anymore. Getting justice was worth his job and everything else they'd all been through. One way or another, Lionel would pay for what he'd done to Sonny.

Chapter Nine

By the time Garron arrived home, Sonny was in bed. "How's he doing?" he asked as soon as he stepped through the door.

"Okay, he's finally asleep. I moved him to the bed and shut the curtains," Rawley said, from his place on the couch next to Jeb. "What did you find out?"

A huge smile broke across Garron's face. "That Kyle has a rather good singing voice. Let me grab a beer and I'll tell you all about it."

"Bring me one while you're at it," Rawley called out.

Garron pulled out two beers and nabbed an apple off the counter on his way back into the living room. Handing Rawley his beer, he took a long pull off his own and sat down in the chair. "Kyle claims Lionel paid him to shoot Jeb. He says he didn't have any knowledge of the shooting on Sonny until after it had happened. I guess Lionel did a bit of bragging to his buddies. Which is good, that gives the DA more witnesses to testify against him. Because Lincoln's in the same county as Summerville, the County Sheriff's Department is taking over the investigation. They don't have any proof that Kyle shot Jeb's bull, but they're getting a search warrant for his house. If they can find the shotgun he'll be charged with that too."

"So what about Lionel?" Rawley asked, leaning forward on the couch.

"He'll be arrested for conspiracy to commit murder for sure. I don't know what other charges he'll face. That's up to the DA. Kyle said Lionel paid him to shoot Jeb, but at the last minute he couldn't go through with it. Kyle said he shot the cows to scare Jeb." Garron finished off his beer and started eating his apple. "I'm gonna call everyone over and fill them in. Even if Lionel gets picked up today, there's nothing that says he won't be out on bond in a day or two. His daddy has enough money and county influence that he may be out on the street until his trial comes up."

Rawley stood and walked towards the kitchen, picking Garron's bottle up on the way. "Care for another?"

"Sure," he said, "While you're in there, why don't you call everyone and set up a meeting while I go check on Sonny?"

"Will do," Rawley replied.

Garron rose and walked upstairs to the bedroom. He opened the door quietly and crept inside. Sitting on the edge of the bed, he looked at his love. "I think we got him," he whispered to Sonny's sleeping form. Deciding to let him rest a little longer, Garron kissed his temple and slipped silently from the room.

* * * *

Rawley was sitting on the front porch trying to digest his dinner, when Ranger came out to join him. "Hey, have a seat."

Settling himself in one of Sonny's old rockers, Ranger looked at his brother. "So you gonna try and get your job back?"

"Yeah," Rawley replied. "I thought I'd give it another couple of days and go see Channing."

Ranger's eyebrows rose. "You gonna tell him we're on to his games?"

"Hell no. I'm gonna let him think I know nothing about his dealings." Rawley rubbed his forehead. "I just need my job back, brother. I know they haven't hired anyone to fill my position, so I'm hoping I can reason with him and the council."

"Give anymore thought about running for Mayor?" Ranger winked at him with a grin on his face.

"Sure, I've thought about it, but first things first. Right now, I need my job. After the FBI finishes with Channing, someone will need to dig into the council and clean house."

Ranger stood and stretched. "I think Ryker and I are going to head home."

"Why do you do that?" Rawley asked.

"What?"

"Distance yourselves. Have any of us ever made you feel like we don't approve of the two of you?"

Ranger shook his head and looked out towards the barn. "No one's ever understood us, so we just got used to not bothering with most folks."

"We're your family. I wouldn't exactly lump us in with 'most folks'."

Ranger shrugged, "Sometimes family can be the most critical of all. I'm going to get Ryker." Ranger disappeared back inside and Rawley was left to ponder his statement.

Had he been overly critical of them?

As he thought about it, he watched as Ranger and Ryker pulled out of Sonny's drive. They must have left through the back door. Rawley felt even worse knowing his brothers were avoiding him. Standing, he blew out a breath. "Fuck."

He stuck his head inside. "Jeb? You about ready to head out?"

"Yeah, hang on a sec and I'll clean up some of these pizza boxes first." Rawley waved to the rest of the group before going out to his truck to wait.

When Jeb climbed in, he scooted close to Rawley. "Something wrong?"

"Yeah, I think I have some changing to do," he replied as he pulled out of the ranch yard.

"Do these changes still involve being with me?" Jeb asked nervously.

Rawley slowed the truck and turned towards Jeb. "I'm afraid you're stuck with me." He gave him a quick peck on the lips. "No, this is about me and how I've evidently shamed my brothers to the point where they've pulled away."

Jeb nodded. "You're talking about Ranger and Ryker."

"Yep."

"Well in your defence, it's not exactly normal to be in love with your twin."

"You're right, it's not, but that shouldn't have anything to do with the fact that they're still my brothers. They fought my dad until they finally moved out of the house. I think that's where I got most of my animosity. Dad was so edgy and grouchy after they left. I think I blamed them for disrupting my home-life."

Rawley pulled up beside the porch and turned off the ignition. "How do I fix it? How do I undo years of making them feel less than they truly are?"

Jeb wrapped his arms around Rawley's neck and kissed him. "Just by treating them like you do anyone else, supporting them, telling them you love them. You can't undo anything overnight. But eventually they'll come to understand." Jeb kissed him again. "Now, how 'bout you come help me feed the horses so we have time to watch a movie before bed?"

Rawley grinned, Jeb always managed to make him feel better. He nodded and got out of the pickup. He knew he had some major making up to do with Ranger and Ryker. He just hoped they'd give him the chance.

* * * *

Instead of watching a movie, they decided to go for a horseback ride. While they were out, they rode the fence, looking for trouble spots. Jeb carried his saddlebag of tools just in case. The night was quickly approaching when they reached the back of Jeb's property. "What the hell?"

Rawley's head swung towards Jeb. "What?"

Jeb pointed across the fence. "It's gone. The entire farm's gone. I mean, I know you told me that Lilly said they'd sold it, but I didn't think the new owners would do this."

Looking at the levelled buildings that had once been the Douglas farm, Rawley was shocked. "What the fuck is going on? Did you ever hear who bought it?"

"Nope, it looks like they're fixing to build something besides another farm house though."

"Come on. I wanna make a few phone calls. Something smells fishy."

They rode back to the house at a much faster pace, keeping watch that the horses didn't step into any holes on the way. As soon as they reached the barn, Rawley dismounted. He started to unsaddle Clyde when Jeb stopped him with a hug. "I'll do it. You go make your calls."

Rawley kissed him. "Thanks."

* * * *

By the time Rawley finished on the phone and searched the internet, Jeb was asleep on the couch. After shutting off all the lights and locking the doors, Rawley picked Jeb up and carried him to bed.

Jeb woke as soon as Rawley lifted him. He snuggled his face in Rawley's neck and sighed. "Find what you needed?"

"Think so," he sat Jeb on the edge of the bed and undressed. Jeb already had his boots off, so his clothes came off in a matter of seconds. Sliding under the covers, Rawley pulled Jeb into his arms. "A corporation bought the Douglas place. I haven't found out who's behind the corporation, but I will. I have a feeling this is what we've been looking for. I'm going to call Agent Bitterman tomorrow and ask him some questions about Dick England, that contractor fella from Lincoln, and whether he's affiliated with Sundowner, Incorporated."

"Hmmm," Jeb mumbled as he snuggled further into Rawley's chest.

He felt his cock twitch and fill as Jeb began to kiss his way around his torso. "I figured you were too tired to play."

"Nope, had a little nap." Jeb kissed his way back up to Rawley's mouth. "Feel like making love to me?"

Rawley grinned and pulled him closer. "Always," he whispered against Jeb's lips. He felt Jeb's erection pressing against his own as they began to rub against each other. Rolling them over, Rawley attached himself to Jeb's neck and sucked a love bite. Their passion ignited and Rawley reached for the drawer.

Pulling out the lube, he slicked his fingers and began preparing Jeb's rosette as he continued his assault on Jeb's mouth. "Love you."

"Uh-huh...now," Jeb panted, bringing his thighs to his chest.

Rawley positioned his cock at Jeb's hole and looked into his chocolate brown eyes. Damn, how'd he get so lucky? Sinking into Jeb's heat, Rawley realised something. He shook his head to dispel the thoughts, but he knew he'd come back to them again.

When he was buried to the hilt, he put Jeb's legs over his shoulders and bent down to kiss him. He pulled out slowly before slamming back inside. Rawley grinned as Jeb went crazy. He knew this particular position pegged Jeb's prostate on every thrust. He enjoyed watching Jeb at the height of his ecstasy. His mouth opened and closed like he was trying to moan or say something, but his passion overloaded his brain and he was left speechless.

Rawley felt his balls tingle as they drew up close to his body. He knew he wouldn't last much longer and he needed to watch Jeb come. Bending over, Rawley kissed him again. "Do it for me."

Sweat dripped off his forehead onto Jeb's shoulder as he watched his lover reach for his cock. "Yes, that's it."

The sounds in the room were erotic as hell as Rawley pistoned his hips even faster, the distinct sound of flesh smacking together was erotic in itself. Jeb closed his eyes and Rawley watched the vein throb in his forehead signalling Jeb's climax.

Looking down, Rawley watched the head of Jeb's cock, coloured with a purple tinge at the tight fisted grip, erupt.

Several long streams of thick white seed splashed its way onto Jeb's chiselled torso.

Without warning, Rawley came. The explosion so intense he saw spots dance through his vision. Going boneless immediately, Rawley collapsed on top of Jeb, barely remembering to release Jeb's legs from his grip. He couldn't seem to catch his breath as his entire body felt like it was on fire.

Jeb scooted out from under him and turned him over. "Shit, are you okay?" He ran his hand up the side of Rawley's face, pushing his sweaty hair back. "Come on, talk to me."

Rawley opened his eyes and saw the panic etched on Jeb's face. He licked his lips. "I'm okay," he mumbled. "Never…never like that."

Jeb got out of bed and walked to the bathroom. Seconds later he returned with a glass of water. "Here, try and sit up enough to take a drink."

Feeling like a weak kitten, Rawley managed to get his head off the pillow enough to sip at the water. He nodded and Jeb placed the glass on the table. "Shit, don't ever do that to me again. You scared twenty years off my life, Sheriff."

Rawley pulled him back down into his arms. As soon as his breathing was under control, Rawley kissed Jeb's forehead. "I've never come so hard in my life. I felt like my soul was trying to escape through my cock to find its way into you."

"Well I thought you were having a damn heart attack." Jeb punched Rawley's ribs playfully.

"No, you're stuck with me for a good long time." Rawley and Jeb settled in and soon his man was asleep. Rawley thought back to that one instant when he understood his brothers. He knew he wouldn't stop thinking about it until he talked to Ranger. Looking over at the clock he groaned, he still had eight hours until he could get the devil off his chest.

Chapter Ten

Rawley was sitting in the parking lot of the feed store at seven o'clock the next morning when Ranger and Ryker pulled in. Getting out of his pickup, he took a deep breath and walked towards them.

"Something wrong?" Ryker asked.

"Yeah. I was wondering if I could talk to the two of you." Rawley waited for Ranger to unlock the front door to the building before following his brothers inside. Ryker motioned towards his office.

Rawley took off his hat and had a seat in front of Ryker's desk. "I know you guys have to get started this morning, but I needed to get something off my chest."

"Okay," Ryker said, clearly confused.

Swallowing around the newly formed lump in his throat, Rawley closed his eyes. "I'm gonna say some things and I want you both to know I'm not trying to embarrass you. There are just some things that need saying."

"Okay," Ranger said, looking at Ryker.

"I never understood how you two could be in love with each other. All I saw was the affect it had on everyone

231

around you. I was a selfish bastard and I was angry that, despite the way your relationship tore up daddy, you loved each other anyway. I'm ashamed to say it wasn't until I was making love to Jeb last night that it hit me. That all consuming, overwhelming, feeling of love. The kind of love where you'd gladly die to save the other person. I never had that before. And as I was making love I realised I almost missed out on the best thing to ever happen to me because I was afraid of what people would think." Rawley wiped the tears out of his eyes and took a deep breath.

"Since you were babies, the two of you knew you belonged together. You've taken hell for it, been made to feel like you needed to hide it away. Well I just want you to know, that I'm damn proud to call you both my brothers. And if the two of you want to show affection for each other while we're together, you just do it." Rawley stood and nodded his head. "That's all I came here to say. I'm headed into town to have breakfast before I go see Channing about getting my job back. I decided life was too short to wait for what you want. If you don't have the balls to go for it, then you might as well have stayed in bed."

Rawley walked out of Ryker's office towards the door. "Rawley, wait," Ranger said, coming after him.

With his hand on the doorknob, Rawley looked back at his brother. Ranger walked up and gave Rawley a hug. "Does the affection thing apply to you too? Cuz right now I'd like to hug my big brother."

Rawley grabbed Ranger and hugged him with all his might. He felt his eyes tearing again and quickly blinked them away. "Thank you, I needed that." He looked over Ranger's shoulder to Ryker. He broke his hug with Ranger and pulled Ryker into his arms. "I love you, boys. I always have. I just wanted life to be easier for you than the road you chose. I was wrong. You chose the right path for you."

"I love you," Ryker said, just before releasing his hold on Rawley.

"I'll see ya'll later. I've got blueberry pancakes waiting for me at Belle's." With one last nod, Rawley walked out the door and to his truck. He grinned as he pulled out of the lot. He felt redeemed in the eyes of his brothers. That was worth more to him than becoming Sheriff again, but he wasn't stupid. He was still going to ask for his job back.

* * * *

Rawley wasn't the least surprised when he stepped into the diner to the buzz of Lionel's arrest. He found an empty booth and turned his coffee cup over. Two minutes later, Belle herself, came bustling over to fill his cup.

"Sorry for the wait, Sheriff. It's a mad house today." She popped her gum and winked. "What can I get ya?"

"I think I'll have your blueberry pancakes and a double order of bacon with a tall glass of orange juice."

Belle nodded and put her hand on her hip. "So tell me, what's the real story on Lionel? Does this have something to do with Sonny's shooting?"

Rawley looked up at the grey haired woman he'd known all his life. She was a sweet woman, but she was also one of the biggest gossips in town. Deciding that evasive honesty would be the best approach, Rawley shrugged. "I've no idea what their charging him with," which was the truth, "remember, I'm not the Sheriff anymore. Although I'm fixin' to go see Channing right after I eat my breakfast."

Belle narrowed her eyes, knowing she was being put off. She finally grinned and nodded towards the counter. "I'd start with Chuck Peterson, he's been grumbling since you lost your job. I think he might be willing to go with you to see Channing."

Rawley looked over at the oldest member of the Summerville City Council. He'd always gotten along with Chuck, but he seemed to be rather old-fashioned and Rawley didn't know that he'd like the new relationship Rawley was involved in. "Could you ask him if he'd like to join me for breakfast?"

"Sure thing, honey." Belle walked off, and he watched as she said a few words in Chuck's ear.

Nodding, Chuck rose off his stool and carried his coffee cup over to Rawley's table. As soon as he was seated, Rawley stuck out his hand. "Thank you for joining me."

"No problem. Belle tells me you're going to see about getting your job back."

"Yes, sir. I don't have an appointment, but I'm hoping the Mayor will see me this morning."

"Well, I've made my thoughts known to the Mayor about your dismissal. I'd be more than happy to back you up. You're the best Sheriff this town's seen in decades."

Taking a deep breath, Rawley knew he had to come clean with Chuck before the man stuck his neck out for him. "Thank you for saying that. I've…um…well, you just need to know, I'm in a new relationship since I lost my job."

"You mean with that Greeley fella. Yeah, I heard all about it. It's hard to keep secrets in a small town."

"You know? And you're still willing to talk to Channing?"

"Well hell, son. Is it something that's going to affect the way you do your job?"

"No, sir."

"All right then. Let's eat our breakfasts and head over."

Rawley breathed a sigh of relief. If Chuck Peterson was open enough to accept his homosexuality, maybe he'd been wrong about the town all along.

* * * *

As soon as Rawley got out of his two-hour meeting with Chuck and Mayor Channing, he turned his phone back on. He checked his messages and found one from Jeb. Waving goodbye to Chuck, Rawley got into his truck and called him.

"Hello?"

"Hey, good news. I got my job back. I start on Monday." Rawley put the truck into gear and headed home.

"That's fantastic, I'm so proud of you, Sheriff."

"Thanks. I thought maybe you'd feel like going into Lincoln tonight and doing a little dancing." Rawley turned onto the county road and watched as a dump truck loaded with debris from the Douglas farm went by.

"Yeah, that sounds great. Hey listen, Nate called earlier. He wanted to know if you'd stop by the apartment. I think he's feeling kinda lost without someone to follow."

Slowing down, Rawley executed a U turn and headed to the feedlot. "I'll stop by on my way home. Hey, uh, did Agent Bitterman call by any chance?"

"No, you want me to try him again?"

"If you don't mind. I'd sure like to know what The Sundowner Corporation is doing with the Douglas farm."

"I'll call him as soon as I hang up. If you get home and I'm not around, it's because I'm going to ride fences with Sonny."

Rawley chuckled, "Four months ago, I would've never pictured you working along side of my brother."

"I know, cool isn't it?"

Shaking his head, Rawley pulled into the feedlot. "I love you."

"Good, because I love you back."

Rawley said his goodbyes and hung up. He waved at Ryker through the window as he headed to the back of the building and up the stairs. He knocked and waited for someone to answer. He was just about to give up, when the door opened and a dishevelled Nate stood in front of him. Rawley was shocked. He'd never seen Nate look so unkempt. "You okay?"

"Yeah," Nate said, turning and throwing himself on the couch. "I've been trying to catch up on my sleep, but nothing I do seems to be working." Nate ran his hands through his normally perfectly styled hair.

Rawley took a seat next to the couch and glanced around the small apartment. "I'm taking Jeb into Lincoln tonight to do some dancing. Maybe you should meet us there? Now that Lionel's in the county jail you could take the weekend off and get a hotel room, get caught up on your sleep."

"I might just do that. If I have to listen to Rio and Ryan fuck each other one more time, I'm afraid I'm going to slit my throat."

Oh, now Rawley saw what the problem was. "Having a hard time, huh?"

Nate rubbed his eyes with the heels of his hands. "You have no idea how it feels to be in love with someone you can't have."

That got a bark of laughter out of Rawley. "Well, I kinda do, only in my case, Jeb wasn't with someone else. Nope, my problem was me, and this town." He looked into Nate's eyes. "Just out of curiosity, have you told Rio you love him?"

"No, but you see the problem is, I like Ryan. I didn't want to. I wanted him to be a total asshole so I wouldn't feel bad about trying to steel Rio away. I can't do it though. They're so much in love it's sickening."

Grinning, Rawley rubbed the back of his neck. "Yeah, I know a little something about that kind of love. It's not meant to hurt anyone though."

"I know. It's typical of my life. After searching the entire city of Chicago, I have to fall in love with a committed man in a small town. Shit."

Rawley stood, and thumped Nate on the leg. "Try and get a few more hours of sleep. We should be at The Regency Lounge around eight o'clock. There's a nice hotel just down the block if you're interested."

"Okay, thanks, man."

"I'll let myself out. You try and catch some zzz's." Nate yawned and grinned as Rawley turned and left.

When he passed back by Ryker's office window, he caught a glimpse of his brothers sharing lunch at Ryker's desk. He felt like a voyeur but he stood to the side and watched for several minutes. Ranger was laughing and using hand gestures to tell some story and Ryker was wiping tears from his eyes as he held his side in laughter. Rawley was struck dumb. He hadn't seen his brothers this animated since they were boys. He smiled to himself knowing he'd done the right thing that morning.

Skirting the window, Rawley walked to his truck. He felt better than he had in a while. He had his job back, he'd made peace with his brothers, and he was taking a hot man dancing. Life just didn't get any better.

Chapter Eleven

By the time Jeb came riding in that afternoon, Rawley was asleep on the couch. He knelt beside the sleeping man he loved and just studied him. God he was beautiful, even without those amethyst eyes looking into his soul, Rawley was breathtaking. Reaching out, Jeb ran his fingers through the close cropped black hair as he bent to kiss the long black lashes that rested on Rawley's high cheekbones.

Rawley stirred, "Why don't you move those lips farther south and give me a real kiss."

"My pleasure," Jeb said as he kissed his way down Rawley's perfectly shaped nose to his well defined lips. Covering Rawley's mouth with his own, he was instantly hard. Rawley's tongue twining with his own caused a moan to escape him as he covered Rawley with his body.

Rubbing his erection against the front of Rawley's jeans, Jeb continued the kiss until he felt Rawley's hands between them unfastening and unzipping.

"Need to feel you," Rawley said breaking the kiss.

"Yeah, I'm needin'," Jeb replied undoing Rawley's pants.

"Shit, yeah," Jeb groaned as Rawley took both cocks in his hand. Jeb couldn't stay still and began riding Rawley's fist. "Not gonna last," he panted, feeling his balls draw up close to his body.

"Yeah." Was all Rawley said before Jeb felt warmth shoot over the head of his cock.

"Rawley," Jeb yelled as he came in his lover's fist.

* * * *

After another nap, Jeb pulled his jeans up and tucked himself inside. "I'm gonna feed and water the horses before I get showered."

Rawley pulled him back down for a kiss before he could get too far away. "I told Nate to meet us at the club. I figured he could use a break."

"Good thinking. By the way, Bitterman called me back and said he couldn't tell me anything about The Sundowner Corporation, and you have an email from a Quade Madison."

"Hmm, well if Bitterman can't talk about Sundowner, I think our assumption was right on. I bet Hibbs and England must be behind it."

Jeb played with the magazine on the coffee table. "And Quade? Who's he?"

Rawley grinned, "You feeling a little of that green-eyed monster?"

"No, just wondering."

"Last week I applied for a job I found on the internet. There's a town in Wyoming, Cattle Valley. They're looking for a new Sheriff so I applied." Rawley saw the look on Jeb's face. He stood and pulled him into his arms. "I'm not going anywhere. I'll admit, if I hadn't been able to get my job back, I might have been tempted to beg you to move with me, but we don't have to think about it now. Although I might email Quade back and give him Ryan's number. I think he'd make a damn fine sheriff."

Jeb leaned in for a kiss. "I'm gonna take care of my chores. What time do you want to head to Lincoln?"

Rawley looked over at the clock. "Oh…maybe around six. I'd like to take you out for dinner before meeting Nate."

"I'll be ready," Jeb said, grabbing his cowboy hat off the peg beside the door.

After Jeb left, Rawley read Quade's email. He reached for the phone and dialled Ryan's cell phone.

"Hello?"

"Hey, it's Rawley. Listen, I received an email that I thought you might be interested in." Rawley told Ryan about the sheriff's opening. "So anyway, I thought I'd find out if you were interested before I emailed Quade."

"I don't know. I haven't been involved with law enforcement in years. Where exactly is this place?"

"Wyoming. Seems years ago some rich guy owned a large section of land there. His son was murdered because he was gay and the rich old guy decided since he had no other heirs, he'd form Cattle Valley. So he left the land and all his money to set up a town where gays weren't discriminated against.

"How come I've never heard of this town? Sounds like heaven."

"That's probably why you haven't heard about it. If word got out, the town would be overrun with every gay man and woman in the country. Let alone every religious zealot known to man. Cattle Valley has a population of around twenty-five hundred and I think they like it that way. The question is would you be willing to give up that ranch you're so fond of?"

"For a settled life in a town where I don't need to hide who I am? Are you kidding?"

"Well then, I'll email Quade back and give him your phone number." He admitted to himself that the town of Cattle Valley sounded too good to be true, the only thing missing was Jeb and his brothers.

"Tell him I'll look forward to hearing from him."

"Will do. Hey, tell Nate that we might be a couple minutes because we're going to stop and have dinner before meeting him at the club."

"What club?"

Shit, Rawley didn't realise Nate wouldn't have told Rio and Ryan where he was going. "Nate's decided to spend the weekend in Lincoln. Jeb and I are meeting him at The Regency later."

"Is it a gay bar?"

Rawley grinned at the protective tone Ryan had taken. "Yes."

"And Nate's going by himself?"

"Well no, I told you, Jeb and I will be there."

"You gonna watch out for him?"

"For Christ's sake, he's a grown man who could probably kick both our asses." Damn, Rawley was enjoying this.

"Right, okay. I'll give Nate the message. And thanks for the heads-up about the job."

"No problem. Talk to you later."

Rawley hung up and rubbed his hands together. It seemed Rio wasn't the only one with feelings for Nate. Damn, if the three of them would just get their thoughts out in the open, they could all be happy. "Oh yeah, now you're the voice of authority on love," Rawley snorted as he headed for the shower.

* * * *

Nate studied himself in the bedroom mirror. He had his favourite low-rise jeans on and a white silk-blend T-shirt that fit his leanly muscled frame to perfection. He fussed with his hair for a couple more minutes before getting a strip of condoms out of his drawer. He didn't know if he'd have the nerve to use them, but better safe than sorry.

Sticking the condoms in his front pocket, Nate put on his loafers and left the bedroom…and ran smack dab into Rio. "Hey," he said surprised.

Rio took a step back and looked Nate up and down. "So it's true?"

"I don't know. Tell me what the hell you're talking about and I'll tell you if it's true." Nate took a step to the side and pushed by Rio. He just couldn't trust himself to be that close to the man.

"Rawley told Ryan you were meeting him at a gay club in Lincoln. Said you were going to stay the weekend," Rio turned to face Nate, crossing his massive arms over his chest.

Nate felt his mouth begin to water at the site of all those muscles on display. He also felt his cock lengthen and fill. Turning back around, Nate picked up his cell phone and his keys. He realised he'd forgotten his suitcase in the bedroom and sighed. Shit. He was going to have to squeeze back by Rio.

"Well?"

"Well what? Am I going to a club? Yes. Am I going to spend the weekend in Lincoln? Yes. Am I gonna get fucked? Hopefully." He tried to push past Rio again, but the larger man pinned him up against the door jam.

"Don't do this."

Nate looked into the dark brown eyes of the man he'd fallen in love with. He saw the hurt and it almost made him forget about the whole thing. "Why do you do this to me?" Nate asked. "You have to know how I feel about you. No way can you be blind enough not to see how hard my dick gets when you and Ryan are around. It's killing me, Rio. I need to move on."

Nate thought Rio was going to kiss him, but instead he buried his face in Nate's neck and whispered in his ear. "I don't want to think about you in another man's bed."

"And I don't want to think about you in Ryan's without me. We don't always get what we want in life." He put his hands on Rio's chest and closed his eyes. It took every ounce of his willpower to push him away.

Without looking at him, Nate retrieved his suitcase and walked towards the front door. "I love you," he whispered before walking out.

* * * *

The club was in full swing by the time Rawley and Jeb stepped through the door. Rawley had heard about the place from Sonny but this was his first visit. He was impressed at the classy elegance of the lounge. Creams and browns mixed well with the dark woodwork. The chairs, covered in buttery leather, were grouped together with a low table in the centre.

They immediately spotted Nate, surrounded by a group of what appeared to be business men. Jeb leaned into Rawley. "This is definitely Nate's playing field."

"Yeah, and it looks like the whole team wants a go at the fresh meat." He led Jeb over to a quieter spot, away from the dance floor. "I'll go tell Nate we're here. Order me a beer if the waiter comes."

"Will do."

Rawley weaved his way through the crowd, surprised when more than one man purposely brushed up against him. Damn, these guys were in some kind of feeding frenzy. He thought about Ryan and how he'd be fighting mad if he saw Nate surrounded by all these good-looking men. He even thought about calling him just to push the issue. He felt in his bones that the trio would eventually end up together, but then he remembered how he felt when Sonny tried to push Jeb on him. No, it would be better to let them work it out on their own.

Squeezing his way through the group of men, Rawley finally caught Nate's eye. "Hey, I was beginning to think you guys stood me up." Nate got to his feet and picked up his drink. "Sorry fella's my friends are here. I'll catch up later."

Rawley watched as he winked at several of the men before coming to stand by him. "Ready?"

"Sure, lead the way." Nate followed close behind Rawley as they made it back to Jeb.

Rawley rubbed his ass. "Damn, someone pinched me."

Nate laughed, "You? My poor body's going to be black and blue in the morning." He took a seat with his back towards the crowd and set his drink down. "So what took you so long?"

Rawley watched as Jeb looked at Nate and blushed. "We...um...got a late start."

Nate's brow rose as he grinned. "Decided to ease the tension before grinding against each other on the dance floor?"

"Yeah, something like that," Rawley answered as the waiter brought their drinks. "I got a call on the way over. Garron thinks the judge is going to set Lionel's bail on Monday."

Nate sat up a little straighter. "Why the hell would he do that? What about the attempt to kill Sonny?"

"He's not being charged with that, yet. The DA said he needed more proof than just the say-so of Kyle and so far, his other buddies aren't talking."

"What about the ballistics expert determining the shooting was done from Lionel's father's building?"

Rawley rubbed the back of his neck and took a drink of beer. "I know it's frustrating, but the DA has to make sure he has an airtight case and he doesn't. I'll start back to work on Monday and get involved in the investigation."

"So where does that leave me?" Nate asked, slowly ripping his napkin into shreds.

"That depends on you. If you continue to follow Lionel once he gets out, I think you'll have to do it covertly, which means, no following him into The Zone."

"So this is my last free weekend until he goes to trial," Nate said accepting his new assignment.

"Yep, looks that way. I can have Rio watch him in the bar. I don't think Lionel has a clue that he's working with us. Ryan? I don't know. He's a wildcard. Lionel knows that you know him, so he can't follow openly either. Of course, maybe Ryan'll just end up going back home until the job's done."

Rawley watched several emotions pass over Nate's face, first happiness and then despair. The music started picking up and Jeb grabbed his hand. "I love this song, come on and dance with me."

Rawley looked down at Nate. "You okay by yourself for a dance or two?"

Nate looked around the club. "Who says I'll be sitting them out?"

Shaking his head, Rawley let Jeb lead him through the crowd to the dance floor. Once there, Rawley pulled Jeb into his arms.

"Uh…Sheriff? This is a fast song."

"Yeah? So? I wanna dance like this. Besides, if I let you get too far away, someone will probably grab your ass and that'll just piss me the fuck off."

Jeb batted his long dark lashes, "It's so nice to have a big strong man around to protect me."

Giving Jeb's butt a good swat, Rawley bit his neck, "Smartass."

One dance led to two and by the time the third one was over, both Rawley and Jeb were hard as steel. "Fuck," Rawley said, leading Jeb back to their seats. "As much as I want to take you home, I think we need to keep an eye on Nate for a while longer."

Jeb looked towards the dance floor where Nate was sandwiched between two men. "Looks like he's doing okay on his own."

"Yeah, but I told Ryan I'd keep an eye out for him."

"Or…you could call Ryan and tell him we're leaving and if he wants to watch Nate in the centre of all these men he can damn well do it himself."

Thinking about that phone call, Rawley shook his head. "I don't know that I can do that. Right or wrong, Nate's in love with both Ryan and Rio. If they come up here and get into a fight, I don't want to be the one responsible for breaking up a good thing."

"What good thing? They don't have a good thing. What they have, is a fucked-up mess."

"Yeah, but it's their mess."

"Exactly," Jeb said, grabbing Rawley's phone from his belt. He scanned the phone log for a few seconds before pushing a button and holding the phone to his ear. "Hey, it's Jeb."

Rawley looked back towards Nate. He thought he looked like he was having a damn good time until he caught a glimpse of his face. Although Nate's body might have been interested in the two men on either side of him, his mind definitely wasn't. Nate's eyes looked completely blank. If the eyes were the mirror to the soul, Rawley would guess, Nate left his back at the apartment.

Jeb shoved the phone in his face. "Here, they said they were on their way. Now, can we get out of here? I'm sure Nate can handle himself for the hour it'll take them to arrive."

Clipping the phone back onto his belt, Rawley nodded. "We need to stop by and tell him we're leaving. I wouldn't mention that you called Ryan though."

"Okay, I get ya." Jeb finished off his beer and stood.

Rawley broke into the threesome and leaned in to Nate's ear. "We're gonna take off, are you gonna be okay?"

Nate nodded and winked. "I'm walking to the hotel from here, so I should be fine."

"Give me a call in the morning."

Nate smiled for the first time all night. "Worried about me?"

"Sure, buddy. I worry about everyone who means something to me."

"Thanks, I needed to hear that."

With one last wave, Rawley and Jeb left the club. On the drive home, Rawley squeezed Jeb's thigh. "I hope you did the right thing calling Ryan."

"Yeah, me too."

Chapter Twelve

Ryan gripped the steering wheel a little tighter as he sped towards Lincoln. "What the hell were we thinking?"

"As you pointed out earlier, he's a grown man. It's not like we could have kept him from going." Rio didn't even turn his head away from the passenger side window.

"That's not what I meant. Do you love him?" When Rio didn't say anything, Ryan continued, "Because I think I do."

Rio's head whipped towards him, "What? All this time, you've watched me die a little every day and you didn't say anything?"

"I didn't realise it until today, when Rawley said Nate was going to the club. After I got off the phone, I went outside and puked. That's when I realised it."

"Shit, so where does that leave us?" Rio said, putting his hand on Ryan's thigh.

Taking one hand off the wheel, Ryan covered Rio's hand. "I guess that's what we need to figure out. Do you think he'd be interested in a relationship with both of us?"

"Yeah, he said as much before he left earlier."

Rio scooted closer and kissed Ryan's neck. "What about jealousy? You know you're prone to that."

"I'm not going to lie. I have no idea if it'll make me jealous to see you with him. Shit, I can't believe I fell in love with a guy I haven't even kissed."

Groaning, Rio covered Ryan's hard cock with his hand. "I can't wait to kiss those gorgeous lips of his, and to watch you do the same." He gave Ryan's cock a squeeze. "I can see the idea turns you on."

"Hell yes it does, but if you don't scoot back over, I'm gonna wreck this damn car and we'll never get to Nate."

With one last grope, Rio moved back over and re-fastened his seat belt. "Spoilsport," Ryan heard him mumble.

Ryan smiled, he felt lighter than he had in days. He hadn't realised how much this situation with Nate had weighed on him. Now they just had to convince Nate to give them a chance. He thought of the phone call earlier with Quade Madison. He hadn't told Rio about it because he didn't want to get him all stirred up. Quade told him he'd need to do a little checking into his background before officially offering him the job, but Ryan wasn't worried about that. He'd done his years in the Marine's before eventually going to the police academy. After finding out his kind wasn't treated the same by his fellow officers, Ryan got out and went into the mercenary soldier field with Rio.

Some people thought mercenaries were nothing but paid killers. Ryan had only shot one person in his years in the field and that was in self-defence. What he and Rio did most of the time was to guard medical aide workers as they travelled from village to village. No overthrowing governments, no rescuing kidnapped dignitaries, they were basically well paid bodyguards. So no, he didn't worry about a thorough background check. He'd miss his ranch though if they moved to Wyoming. Of course, there was a lot of land in Wyoming just waiting to be turned into a Cattle Valley for him, Nate and Rio.

"What are you thinking about so hard?" Rio asked.

He turned and gave Rio a wink. "Just the future. Trying to map stuff out in my head." He looked at the scribbled piece of paper on the dash with the directions to the bar. After a few more turns, he parked the car. Turning to Rio, he held out his hand. "Ready to do this?"

"Let's go."

* * * *

Reaching over, Rawley put his hand on Jeb's thigh. "Thanks, I enjoyed dancing with you."

Covering his hand, Jeb moved it towards his erection. "Just get us home so we can dance some more."

"Oh that's what you wanna do? I thought maybe I'd have some of that pretty little ass of yours, but if you'd rather dance…"

Jeb put his feet up on the dash and opened a little for Rawley's wandering hand. "Can I ask you a question?"

"Sure," Rawley replied. He looked over at Jeb and saw the concern on his face in the glow of the oncoming traffic.

"Do you think you'll ever let me make love to you?"

That stilled Rawley's hand. He suddenly felt ashamed that he'd never even considered it. Would it make him less of a man?

"Rawley?"

He looked over at Jeb. "I've never done it before."

"I know, and it's not something I'll ask for all the time, but..."

"Okay. I think," Rawley said taking a deep breath. His hands began to sweat and he felt beads of perspiration pop out on his forehead. He thought he'd come so far, but he realised he still had a long way to go. How could he feel this way? He could tell by the look in Jeb's eyes this was important to him. Why hadn't he ever taken Jeb's needs into consideration? Hell he didn't even know if Jeb was used to being bottom or top in a relationship. With his smaller size he'd just assumed.

He looked around and determined he had about ten more minutes to make up his mind before they arrived home. Jeb had gotten quiet beside him, and Rawley knew his own silence was hurting the man he loved. He needed to work this out though. He had to figure out why, mentally, it made him feel weaker to let another man mount him.

Pondering his options, he ran out of time when they pulled into the ranch yard. He started to open the door, but Jeb stopped him with a hand on his arm. "Rawley?"

"Yeah?" He looked over his shoulder at Jeb.

"Forget I asked, okay? Let's just continue as we have been."

Rawley knew it was the coward's way out, but God help him, he just wasn't ready. "Okay. Thanks." Jeb released him and Rawley got out of the pickup. He waited for Jeb beside the truck and took his hand as they made their way into the house.

Jeb gave him a quick kiss, "I'm going to make myself a sandwich, you want one?"

"No," Rawley shook his head. His stomach was in so many knots, he wasn't sure he could keep down what he'd already eaten. "I'm gonna take a shower." Jeb nodded and Rawley walked into the bathroom.

After undressing, he stood under the hot spray berating himself. He'd screwed up the entire evening and there wasn't a damn thing he could do about it. He glanced down at his flaccid cock. That sure wasn't going to help. Maybe Jeb would be too tired and Rawley could just hold him until they fell asleep?

He stood there until the water went cold, but he still wasn't ready to face Jeb. Climbing out, he left the water running and dried off. Sitting on the closed toilet seat, Rawley put his head in his hands. He was going to lose it all if he didn't get over this.

A knock sounded on the locked door and Rawley knew his time was up. He turned off the shower. "I'll be out in a second," he said through the door.

"Ryan's on the phone. He wants to speak with you," Jeb answered.

Wrapping the towel around his waist, Rawley opened the door, embarrassed that he'd locked it. "Thanks," he said as Jeb handed him the phone and walked towards the bedroom.

"Hey, Ryan."

"You sonofabitch, I can't believe you just left Nate at the bar like that."

"He's a goddamn grown man and you were on the way." It registered that Ryan had to be pissed for a reason. "Why, what happened?"

"Some sick fuck drugged him. Luckily Rio and I got there in time. The asshole was trying to carry him out of the club when we got there."

"Oh shit, oh fuck, man. I'm so sorry. We had no idea something like that would happen. Is he okay?"

"Yeah, now. He had to puke his guts out in the club's bathroom, but I think he'll be fine."

Rawley looked towards the bedroom and watched as Jeb crawled under the covers onto his side facing the wall. Rawley closed his eyes, fuck.

"Anyway, we're at his hotel for the night. We'll probably just stay up here for the weekend."

"Okay, look, I'm really sorry."

"I know, I just needed to get that off my chest. I'll talk to you later."

"Goodnight," Rawley said hanging up the phone. He went through the house to make sure Jeb turned off the lights and locked up before making his way into the bedroom. Dropping his towel he slid under the covers. Jeb didn't move although Rawley knew he wasn't asleep.

Moving to spoon against his back, Rawley wrapped an arm around the man he was so desperately in love with. "Ryan said someone drugged Nate after we left. He and Rio caught the guy before he carried Nate out of the club though. They think he'll be all right."

"That's good," Jeb mumbled.

"I love you," Rawley whispered in Jeb's ear.

"I know," was Jeb's only reply.

Deciding to just let it drop for the night, Rawley tightened his grip on Jeb and drifted off to sleep.

* * * *

The next morning Rawley wasn't surprised to wake up in an empty bed. Looking over at the clock he saw that it was only a little after six. He covered his eyes remembering another morning not too long ago when he'd woke to an empty bed.

Knowing a peace offering wouldn't do any good, Rawley sat on the edge of the bed trying to figure out what to do. He couldn't talk to Jeb about what was bothering him because he didn't really understand it himself. Deciding it would be better to just bypass the whole scene until he worked out his own hang-ups, Rawley got dressed for the day and went into town for breakfast.

He'd just ordered his usual when his cell phone rang. Looking at the caller ID he saw it was Sonny. "Hello."

"Hey, big brother. Is there something going on I should know about?"

"What're you talking about?"

"I just saw Jeb. He seemed pretty messed up."

Rubbing his eyes, Rawley sighed. "We're just working out a few things."

"Do you need to talk about it?"

"No, I need to work it out on my own. Can I ask you a personal question though?"

"Maybe, depends on the question."

He couldn't believe he was about to ask his brother about his sex life while sitting in the middle of the town's diner. "Have you ever topped Garron?"

Sonny started laughing, "When you're in love you don't think of it as topping. You think of it as making love to the person most important to you. And yeah, sure, I've made love to Garron."

"Okay, that's what I needed to know. Would you do me a favour and check on Jeb a little later. I'm going to be out most of the day."

"Coward."

"Yeah, something like that. Talk to you later." Rawley hung up just as his breakfast came, although suddenly he wasn't hungry.

* * * *

Deciding to run by the station, Rawley walked the four block and opened the door to all sorts of chatter. Looking around at the group of secretaries and deputies, Rawley held up his hand. "What the hell is going on here? I leave for a while and the place turns to shit?" They all stopped and looked at him. Rawley grinned letting them know he was just giving them a hard time.

"Sheriff," Verna cried as she waddled over to him. Wrapping her arms around his waist, she gave him a big hug. "We've missed you. We heard you were going to start back on Monday?"

"Yep, just thought I'd stop in and see what was going on." He grinned again. "I can see you've been busy."

Verna slapped his arm and moved back to her dispatch desk. "We were just talking about Lionel. Something new must have happened overnight, but we can't get any more information."

"Oh? Is there anyone using my office?"

"Well no, why would anyone be using it, it's yours."

"Good, I'll go see if I can find anything out. And it's good to be back, I've actually missed all your mugs." Rawley walked down the short hall to his office. After closing the door he sat at his desk and looked around. "Yes, this is where I belong," he said to himself and picked up the phone.

Chapter Thirteen

After getting off the phone with the County Sheriff's office, Rawley placed another call to Garron. "Hey, did you hear?"

"A little, I'm heading into town now, why don't I meet you at the diner and we can compare notes."

"Sounds good, I'll try and get out of the station in one piece and meet you there." Rawley hung up. Walking out of his office, all eyes were on him.

It was Verna who eventually spoke up, "Well?"

Rawley held up his hand. "I've been told not to discuss the recent developments until the official announcement this afternoon. I'm sorry guys. I just can't chance losing my job again."

Although they all nodded, Rawley could tell they were disappointed. "Maybe I'll come back and sneak you all the information just before the word comes down."

Verna winked, "Thanks, Sheriff. What's the use of working here if you don't get inside information, you know what I mean?"

"Yeah, I know. The whole protecting the innocent is just a side detail." Rawley winked back and walked out.

Strolling down the street, Rawley's mind wandered back to Jeb. He wondered what he was doing right now. He longed to call him just to hear his voice but he didn't know what to say. It was quickly becoming evident that he needed to talk to someone. He thought about Sonny, but he was afraid his brother wouldn't understand. Despite what Sonny said, it was clear that Garron was definitely the natural top in that relationship. Maybe talking to another Alpha about his concerns would help?

Finding a booth, Rawley slid in and turned his cup over. Seconds later, Belle appeared with a pot of strong black coffee in her hand. "Hi, Sheriff, back so soon?"

"Yeah, I'm meeting Garron for lunch."

"Speaking of, how's Sonny doing? He doesn't come into town much anymore."

"Well, he's not been cleared to drive yet. He still has seizures once in a while. He drives around the ranch some but he's not supposed to do it at all. I told him if I ever caught him, I'd give him a ticket for sure." Rawley grinned. "Being Sheriff definitely has its advantages."

"So the doctors are worried that he'll have a seizure while driving," it wasn't a question. He could tell Belle was working it out in her mind. "Everyone in town assumes because he survived the shooting and is at home he's back to normal, but that isn't the case is it?"

"No, Ma'am. Sonny will be on seizure medicine for the rest of his life. He has debilitating headaches that cause him to hide in a dark room for hours. His personality has changed a bit as well. His sweet side seems to be more dominant these days."

"Oh heck, Sonny's always been a sweet boy, even when he was getting into trouble." Belle started to turn away and stopped. "I just want you to know. I don't think most people in town blame you for doing everything you could to catch his shooter. Badge or no badge, you're a brother first."

Rawley felt warmed by the statement. "Thank you, Ma'am."

Belle squeezed his arm briefly before turning away to wait on her customers. Rawley looked around the room and realised these people accepted the Good boys because of who they were, not what they were. He was smiling to himself when Garron slid into the seat across from him.

"Something funny?" Garron asked.

"No, just had a chat with Belle about Sonny. She misses him. You need to bring him into town with you more often."

"I think he's a little afraid he'll forget something or have a seizure while in town. He doesn't want people to see him that way."

"You need to talk to him. Explain that the town's people won't like him any less if something happens. They're all aware of what he went through, and believe it or not, the majority of the town cares about him." Rawley took a drink of his coffee.

"Wow, you're good at telling other people what to do, how 'bout cleaning your own house before you start on mine." Garron looked at him, eyebrows raised.

Rawley rolled his eyes. "I take it you've talked to Sonny?"

"Nope, I talked to my brother. Well, I tried to talk to him. He pretty much shut the conversation down when I asked how he was getting along." Garron looked into Rawley's eyes and leaned forward across the table. "I know Jeb's voice when he's been crying. Are you responsible for that?"

"Yeah, but it's not intentional, I swear its not." He leaned forward so no one else could hear their conversation. "Listen. Before we get into my problems can we discuss Lionel?"

"Sure, tell me what you've heard and I'll tell you if I know anything more," Garron said.

"Lionel, the dumbass that he is, tried to hire someone inside the county jail to kill Kyle so he couldn't testify. Not realising of course, that it was a county jail and not a fucking maximum security prison. The guy he tried to hire was in for assault because he got into a bar fight when some other guy tried to muscle in on his lady, a far cry from a hit man."

"Yep, so now the DA has something else to charge him with and Lionel is looking at a very long prison sentence even without Sonny's shooting. Evidently, Kyle called one of his buddies and told him what Lionel had tried to do. I guess the DA's been getting calls all day from Lionel's ex-buddies. They're all ready to testify that Lionel not only bragged about shooting Sonny, but they were there when Lionel ordered them to sweep and clean the roof of the Hibbs' Building. My guess is the delayed announcement has to do with Lionel's buddies trying to work out a deal with the DA. I'm sure they want immunity if they testify against him."

Rawley scratched his jaw. "So either way, Lionel will be looking at more than one trial."

"Yeah, I was just thinking it's time to celebrate. I thought maybe I'd have a barbecue at the house later today. You interested?"

"I'm interested, but I have a few things I need to work out with Jeb first."

"Okay, now that Lionel's out of the way, you feel like talking?"

"Yeah, but not here. Let's walk down to the park." Rawley stood and tossed a couple dollars on the table. He waved to Belle on his way out.

Walking beside Garron, Rawley tried to get his thoughts in order. Garron thankfully must have known because he kept quiet. Reaching the park Rawley gestured to an empty bench off to the side. Settling himself beside Garron, Rawley rubbed his hands together. "Jeb asked me if he could make love to me," Rawley said without any lead in.

"And?"

"What do you mean, and? I've never allowed a man to do that to me. I mean, I thought being a top meant I wouldn't have to do that."

"Who said you were the top? And what exactly does that mean? I don't mean literally, I'm talking about a top in a relationship. What exactly is that?" Garron just looked at Rawley waiting for an answer.

"You know. I'm the guy who does the fucking. The Alpha. What would it make me if I let Jeb mount me?"

"Okay, first, don't ever say Jeb is going to mount you because I'm expecting to see your head on the wall of the living room someday with that term. Now, that said, I gotta tell you, you're starting to piss me off. Do you ever stop to listen to yourself? Alpha? What's that make Jeb? Your beta? I don't think so." Garron ran his fingers through his long hair, "Listen, I know this is all new to you, but you've got some fucked up ideas about relationships. Jeb doesn't need an Alpha, he needs a partner. Can you say partner?"

"Knock it off," Rawley grumbled.

"What I'm trying to get through to you is that a partnership doesn't have an Alpha. You're both equal, and as far as letting Jeb make love to you? Try it before you knock it. You might just surprise yourself."

"But..." Rawley didn't know how to explain his biggest hang-up. "I love Jeb, and only Jeb, but if I allow him to do...that, I'll look at myself as a gay man instead of just a man." There he'd said it. It may not have been pretty but the words were finally out there.

Garron stood and paced around the bench with his hands on his hips. He watched as Garron took several deep breaths before turning back to him. "Do you think I'm less of a man because I love your brother? I'm not talking about who fucks who, I'm talking about love."

"No."

"Do you think Jeb is less of a man because he loves you enough to allow you to make love to him?"

"God no."

"Then what exactly is the difference between a gay male and a hetero male in terms of manliness?"

Rawley didn't have an answer. He felt totally drained by the entire conversation. "I think I have some more thinking to do," he mumbled.

Garron sat back down and thumped Rawley on the back. "Well do it fast, because the next time you pull a stunt like this and make my brother cry I'm gonna tear you apart. Now get your shit together and make up with Jeb. We'll expect you for dinner around seven." Garron stood and walked towards his truck.

Rawley rested his head in his hands. It was bound to be a long day.

Chapter Fourteen

Putting his horse away, Jeb walked towards the house. He looked at his phone to make sure he hadn't missed a call from Rawley. Nope, still nothing. He knew leaving that morning before Rawley woke was a shitty thing to do, but he deserved it. He knew what Rawley's problem was even if Rawley didn't. He'd been through it before, with Caleb most recently. He was an idiot for thinking Rawley would be different. Lord knew he enjoyed a big strong man, but he didn't enjoy all the baggage that came along with them.

Stomping the dust off his boots, Jeb went inside. He had a little over an hour before he was supposed to be over at Garron's, so maybe he'd get ready and sit on the porch and have a beer. Jeb sighed, and waited for his wayward man to come home.

Pulling his dirty T-shirt off, he turned on the shower. Once naked he stepped in and tried to let the hot water melt his tension away. He soaped up and washed his hair, but after ten minutes he still felt as bad as he had before. Deciding to give up, Jeb got out and dried off. After hanging his towel on the back of the door, Jeb made his way to the bedroom. He stopped dead in his tracks and almost swallowed his tongue.

"I've been waiting," Rawley said from his position in the centre of the bed.

"Wow," Jeb said in awe. Rawley laid spread eagle on the bed with what appeared to be Jeb's plug inside him. "Um...did I miss something?"

"Not yet, come over here." Rawley held out his hand. "I'm sorry but I used your toy. I'll buy you another one, I just wanted our first time to be good and I figured this way there wouldn't be any pain. And believe me, when I stuck this bad boy in, there was definitely pain involved."

Jeb tried not to grin as he settled beside Rawley. "There would have been less if I'd helped. It's easier to do when you're aroused." He leaned over and kissed his man. "I appreciate the gesture though." Jeb reached down and wiggled the plug.

Rawley jumped, "Oh, shit." Rawley looked at him wide-eyed. "Do it again," he moaned.

Stretching out beside Rawley, Jeb kissed him. "I love you."

"I know," Rawley smiled. "If you didn't you wouldn't put up with my stupid ass. I'm sorry."

"You don't have to do this. I'll love you anyway," Jeb said circling Rawley's nipple with his finger.

Shaking his head, Rawley pulled Jeb on top of him. "I want you to make love to me."

Jeb looked into his lover's beautiful eyes and smiled. He could see the want there, yes, he saw apprehension but that was totally normal. Reaching over, Jeb took the bottle of lube off the table and sat back on his heals. Applying a liberal amount to his hand he stroked his cock as Rawley watched.

"You're so sexy," Rawley crooned.

"Ha, you should see what I'm lookin' at." Jeb reached down and shifted the plug a few times before sliding it out. Even though it appeared Rawley had used most of the bottle, Jeb decided to add a little more. Slipping his fingers inside, Jeb smoothed a digit over Rawley's prostate.

"Hell, yeah," Rawley howled, arching his back. "Need you, now."

Leaning down, Jeb pressed a kiss to Rawley's lips as he positioned himself. He was surprised at what a good job the plug had done in stretching him. After only one minor wince, Jeb was buried to the hilt. Maintaining eye contact, Jeb slowly began to move.

Rawley hooked his arms under his legs and brought them to his chest. "Feels good," Rawley said, sounding surprised.

"Yes, I know," Jeb replied smiling. When he thought Rawley was ready, he began to thrust harder and faster. The look on Rawley's face was absolutely breathtaking. Jeb felt mesmerised by the light dancing in his lover's eyes as he surged in and out.

When Rawley reached between them to wrap his fingers around his cock, Jeb knew he was doing something right. Moving to another position, Jeb went at Rawley from a different angle. The result was immediate and Rawley cried out his name as cum splashed across his chest.

Relieved he could finally let go, Jeb sunk into Rawley's heat twice more before burying himself as deep as possible. He came growling his love for Rawley, before collapsing onto his man's chest.

Jeb buried his face in Rawley's neck and hummed. "Thank you," he said reaching up to run his hands over Rawley's face. He felt tears and sat up enough to look at him. "Did I hurt you?"

"No, it was beautiful, you're beautiful. I'm just ashamed that I thought I'd be less of a man if I ever experienced it." Rawley went on to tell Jeb about his fears and his conversation with Garron.

"I can't believe you talked to my brother about this. I think I love you even more." God, Rawley must have really been confused if he'd gone to Garron for advice. He had to keep reminding himself that this was Rawley's first relationship.

"Do you love me enough to call us in sick to the barbecue?"

"No, because I need to give my brother a big hug and you need to tell everyone who's helped with Lionel thank you." He licked the side of Rawley's face. "Get up and take a shower with me and I'll let you make love to me tonight when we get home."

"Promise?"

"Definitely," Jeb said, startled when Rawley jumped off the bed and carried him to the shower.

* * * *

After getting another beer out of the cooler, Rawley sat down on the porch steps next to Nate. "I wanted to apologise for leaving you at the club like we did."

Nate waved his concerns away. "If you hadn't left me, Ryan and Rio wouldn't have come to my rescue." He looked at Rawley and tilted his head to the side. "You look different."

Rawley grinned, "It's the look of a completely contented man."

"Oh, well then, in that case, I must be wearing the same look."

"Ryan said you were going back to Texas with them," Rawley said, taking a swig of beer.

"Yeah, I don't really see the two of them fitting into my Chicago life, so I'm gonna become a cowboy." Nate looked down at his expensive loafers. "I might need to invest in some snake-skin boots."

"Real cowboys don't wear fancy boots," Rawley reminded him.

"Look, just because I'm going to live on a ranch doesn't mean I can't look good. I've got two hot men to keep interested."

"Oh, I don't think that's going to be an issue," Ryan said sitting down behind Nate. He wrapped his legs and arms around him and leaned down to kiss his neck.

Rawley tipped his beer towards Ryan. "So, have you heard anything about the Sheriff's job?"

"Not yet, but hopefully in the next week or so. In the meantime," Ryan reached down and pinched Nate's nipple, "if we don't get on the road, we won't make Kansas City tonight like we hoped."

"Well if you don't stop doing stuff like that, we won't make Kansas City at all," Nate replied.

With a grunt, Ryan stood and pulled Nate up beside him. He stuck out his hand, "It was nice to meet you. I hope we'll be living close enough that we can still get down here from time to time."

"I look forward to it. The three of you are always welcome," Rawley said shaking first Ryan's and then Nate's hand. He looked over his shoulder, "Where's Rio?"

"Trying to get that barbecue sauce recipe out of Sonny," Ryan chuckled.

"Good luck. He doesn't share his recipes with anyone."

* * * *

As Jeb and Rawley laid in bed that night, coming down from an explosive bout of love making, Rawley thought about everything his family and loved one's had been through lately. They all came out of it changed. Maybe not physically, like Sonny, but changed none the less. He was so happy. He couldn't imagine anything making him happier. "You know, I don't think I want to be Mayor. I love my job."

"Sure, you say that now, but after the FBI finishes with their investigations, this town's going to need a leader who can pull them through this and get the job done. If that doesn't sound like something you'd love, you're foolin' yourself. And as much as I like the idea of shagging the Sheriff, it would be a real turn on to make love to the Mayor."

Rawley laughed, "Well then, Mayor's office here I come."

TWIN
TEMPTATIONS

Dedication

To my friends, who are supportive
no matter what I write.

Chapter One

Ranger leaned back and put his boots up on the old scarred desk. "I think it's great that you've decided to run for Mayor, but I've no interest in running for the City Council."

"Just give me a chance to talk you into it. You're an excellent businessman, and it's time for a change. The Council has been stagnant for too long," Rawley said, pleading his case.

"Sorry, brother. Still not interested. Running the feed-lot is about as public as I ever care to be." A sudden feeling had him sitting up and looking out the window. "Sorry, but I need to go. I think something's happened to Ryker." Ranger didn't give Rawley a chance to answer before he was heading out the door.

He ran to the northwest lot and scanned the area. "Bub?"

"Over here," Ryker called.

Turning his attention to the large group of cattle, he spotted Ryker limping towards him. Jumping over the fence Ranger ran towards him, pushing cattle out of the way in his haste. "What happened?" he asked, as wrapped an arm around his brother's torso.

"Stupidity is what happened. I knew to be wary of number three-twenty-nine, but I dropped my guard, and the damn cow kicked me." Ryker leaned on him as they walked out of the muddy lot.

As soon as they cleared the fence, Ranger stopped and knelt in front of Ryker. "Where exactly did she get you?"

"Mid-thigh, but if you think I'm gonna pull my jeans down out here where anyone can see you're nuts. Help me get to the office. I'm sure it's probably just a bruise."

Ranger helped him to the office and sat him on the cracked avocado green vinyl couch. It said a lot about their relationship that Ryker hadn't had to ask how Ranger knew he'd been hurt. They'd just always been that way.

Undoing, Bub's jeans, he looked up and winked. "If you really wanted to flash me this morning all you had to do was say so."

"Smart ass," Ryker said lifting enough to push his Wrangler's down to his ankles.

"Woo-wee, that's some bruise you've got started there," Ranger said, as he looked at the swollen area on Bub's upper thigh. "A little higher and you'd have been out of commission for a long time." Despite his humour, Ranger hated to see Bub in pain and leaned over to kiss the hot, raised area. It looked to be about six or seven inch diameter of hurt. He was sure the bruise would spread well beyond that, but this is where the pain would be focused. "Let me get some salve out of the medicine cabinet."

Ranger went to the bathroom nestled between his office and Bub's. Running a washcloth under the cold water he rung it out and grabbed the salve. He caught Bub clenching his jaws when he returned, a sure sign he was in pain but didn't want to show it.

Kneeling, he placed the cool cloth over the angry red welt. "Do you think you should go for an x-ray?"

"Don't be stupid, it's a bruise."

"Yeah, well do you remember Curtis Eben? He got kicked in the shin by that horse and ended up having a stroke when a blood clot made its way to his brain."

Bub rolled his eyes. "I promise not to have a stroke, okay? Just put the damn salve on it. I'll be okay until I can get home and ice it."

"Stubborn mule," Ranger mumbled under his breath. He removed the compress and opened the tin of salve. Dipping his fingers in, he scooped up a generous portion and began lightly rubbing it on the raised area. After wiping his hands, he wrapped his arms around Ryker's waist and just held him. Just the thought of something happening to Bub had him shaking.

"Hey, guys, Momma asked me to drop these…"

Ranger's head whipped around towards the door. Lilly was standing with what appeared to be a box full of yellow sweet corn. "Fuck," he said, going still. "Don't you know how to knock?"

Lilly bit her lip and even from across the room, Ranger could see the tears in her jade green eyes. He hadn't meant to growl so harshly, but shit, it was Lilly.

Dropping the box at her feet, Lilly turned and walked back out the door without a word. Ranger closed his eyes and rested his forehead against Bub's chest. Most people were sickened by any display of physical affection between the brothers and they knew it. It was exactly the reason they'd built a house back in the woods of their family's ranch. There, they could hold each other and kiss on occasion and no one cared.

"I want her," Ryker said, as he closed his eyes and threaded his fingers through Ranger's hair.

Resting his head on Bub's chest he sighed. "I know, Bubba, I want her too, but it's still too soon. She's just not ready for what we have in mind."

"How much longer? We've waited damn near four years for her to grow up. She's twenty-one now, don't you think she's old enough to make up her mind? What if she gets snatched away from us?"

Ranger looked at the spilled box of corn. "You know one of us is gonna have to go talk to her about what she walked in on. I'd say it should be me. You'd just melt at the first sign of tears. Besides, I'm the one who yelled at her. It should be me that apologises."

"When?"

"Tonight, after the lot closes. I'll drop you by home and then come back to town." Ranger released his hold on Ryker and sat back.

"That plan doesn't make sense. Why don't we both go into town and you can drop me off at the diner. I'll get us a couple plates of chicken fried steak to-go while you talk to her." Ryker reached for his jeans.

"How's the leg?" Ranger asked when he saw Ryker flinch.

"Sorer than a motherfucker, but it's my own damn fault."

Helping him stand, Ranger pulled Ryker's jeans up. "We'll get it iced tonight and put some more salve on it."

Slipping on his boots, Ryker sat back on the couch while he tied them for him. "You think we disgusted her?"

"Lilly? Hell no. I think she probably would have joined in if we'd invited her. Naw, I think she was just surprised and got her feelings hurt when I snapped at her. It'll be okay." He stood and kissed Ryker. His brother was the sensitive one of the two of them, and always had been.

Dipping his tongue into the dimple on Ryker's left cheek, he grinned. "Thanks for the mid-morning snuggle, but I think it's time we both got back to work. Why don't you take over manning the phones and I'll go out and make sure everyone's still got some work to do."

* * * *

With his leg propped up on a chair from the entry way, Ryker made a few phone calls. He ordered feed and arranged for some of the cattle to be shipped out to the county auction the following week. Now, with his head rested on the high back of his desk chair he thought of Lilly.

His fascination with her had started the summer before her senior year. He'd felt like a dirty old man, but the look in her eyes when she had caught him and Ranger kissing in the feed barn, had caused an ache that had yet to go away. He wanted to go after her when she'd turned eighteen and graduated from school, but Ranger would have none of it. He'd explained that Lilly was the perfect woman to let into their lives for the long-haul, not just a quick affair. In order to assure she'd be ready to commit, they needed to give her time to grow-up and experience a little bit of life.

"Yeah, right," Ryker said to the empty office. The evening Nate had teased Ranger about Lilly hooking up with one of the bar patrons had almost killed him when Ranger told him about it. Ranger had to talk him out of going to the Dead Zone and carrying that little five foot five woman out over his shoulder. Just the thought of one of those sweaty cowboys putting their hands on Lilly had him seeing red.

By the time Ranger came back in at the end of the day, Ryker had worked himself up pretty good.

"Ready?" Ranger asked, tossing him his black cowboy hat.

"Yep. I think I need to go with you to the Zone." He adjusted his hat and locked the front door.

"What brought this on? I thought you were going to get our dinner?" Ranger got into the quad-cab pickup.

"I've been thinking. I don't like the idea of Lilly working in that place. I think we should talk to her about it." He buckled his seatbelt, refusing to look at his brother. He knew what he'd see anyway. "And stop rolling your eyes at me."

"Geez, Bub, you can't just walk in and start demanding stuff of her. You'll scare her all the way to Kansas City. Why don't you let me handle it?"

"Fine, just make sure she understands that she shouldn't be working in a bar. She's better than that."

Ranger unbuckled and leaned over to give him a kiss on the neck. "You're so damn cute when you get all protective and shit."

"Just drive."

Chapter Two

Lilly was bussing a table when he walked into the dark smoky bar. He waved his hand in front of his face as he passed a table of chain-smoking cowboys. Finding a seat in the back, he watched Lilly work. Damn, she was beautiful. He'd give anything to take those long black curls out of the messy haphazard ponytail.

He watched as she spotted him and chewed on that raspberry coloured lip of hers. It must taste damn good because she seemed to chew it enough.

Straightening her shoulders, Lilly lifted her chin and walked over. "Ranger."

"How come you're the only one outside my brothers that can tell me and Ryker apart?" He asked, giving her his best playboy grin.

"You have two dimples, Ryker only has one. Now, what can I get you?" Lilly asked in a business-like tone.

"I don't suppose you can spare a couple of minutes to talk to me?"

Lilly turned her torso to glance at the clock over her shoulder. The movement accentuated her already large breasts even further and Ranger had to swallow a groan. "I get a break in ten minutes. If you're still here, I'll give you a couple minutes. Can I get you something from the bar?"

"Bottle of Michelob."

He watched the natural sway of her hips as she walked back toward the bar. Ranger caught himself staring and quickly looked around. Good, no one was paying any attention to the queer in the corner. After what happened with Lionel Hibbs, Ranger reckoned any bigots in town had learned their lesson. He didn't care if he disgusted people with his relationship with his twin, but he'd be damned if he'd let people try and intimidate him because of it.

Lilly came back with his beer, she set the bottle on the table and turned without a word. *Oh boy, he had a hell of a lot of climbing to do to get himself out of this hole he'd dug.*

The more he watched her, the more animated she became. He wasn't sure if this was the way she usually was at work or if she was trying to get him riled up. Regardless, Lilly was doing a damn good job of it. Ranger watched as she rested her hand on her cocked hip, laughing at something one of the cowboys at the bar said. When he saw the man smooth a hand across her ass, Ranger stood. Running on pure instinct he stalked toward the bar. He knew Jeff, and he wasn't someone he wanted Lilly around.

Lilly must have seen Ranger coming because she quickly turned to face him and put up her hands. "Stop," she warned. "Just go back to your table and I'll be there in a minute."

Ranger was taken back by the vehemence in her voice. He narrowed his eyes and studied her for a few second. Lilly put her hands on her hips and stared right back. Deciding it wouldn't do much good to apologise for earlier if he was an ass now, he turned on his heel and went back to his table. He couldn't help but to feel like a kid who'd just been sent to his room.

His vibrating cell phone snapped him out of his pout. He looked at the caller ID and saw it was Bub. "Hey, sorry, I'm running a little late."

"You want me to come over? Our dinner's getting cold. Betty put them in one of those nice insulated containers, but sitting here's just making everything soggy."

"Give me ten minutes. Lilly's just walking over to take her break. Boy, Bub, we gotta talk. Lilly actually snapped at me a few minutes ago."

"Damn, what did you do? Lilly's one of the sweetest people I know." Ryker chuckled on the other end of the phone.

"Some asshole was taking liberties with her ass and I guess I took exception to it. Lilly shut me down fast."

"Who was taking liberties with our girl?"

He didn't dare tell Ryker that asshole had been Jeff Brown. "Doesn't much matter whose hand it was. By the way she reacted it wasn't an uncommon occurrence." Lilly was almost to the table, his heart lurched despite himself. "Here she comes, be there as soon as I can."

Ranger drank the rest of his beer as Lilly looked at him with narrowed eyes.

"What do you want, Ranger?" She crossed her arms, accentuating her breasts and stared at him.

"I wanted to apologise for earlier. Ryker was kicked by one of the cows and was...you just surprised me. I didn't mean to snap at you like I did." Ranger watched as Lilly bit down on her plumb bottom lip.

"I shouldn't have just walked in like that, I know, but I can't say it didn't hurt when you yelled. And as far as that..."

Lilly motioned toward the cowboy at the bar, "...that is none of your business."

Ranger felt the hairs on the back of his neck stand on end at the statement. "Do you always let men grope you while you work?"

Lilly sighed and leaned forward, resting her arms on the table. "Listen, Ranger, I've spent a good portion of my adult life mooning after two people who obviously aren't interested. This is my time. I've decided to live life to the fullest and if a pat on the ass from a good-looking cowboy happens, I'll decide what I want to do about it, not you."

"You're wrong about those two guys not being interested, but you're too young for what they have in mind. You need to live a little before you settle down."

"Ha," she said, getting right in Ranger's face. "Either make the offer, or butt out of my business." Lilly stood and bent over, her lips barely touching Ranger ear as she whispered. "I guess the only thing you have to worry about is whether I'm still available once you think I'm old enough." She finished with a lick to the shell of his ear. When she pulled back it was to look directly into his eyes. "You want me to live a little? You just sit back and watch."

Lilly turned and sauntered off, sweet ass just swaying from side to side like she knew she'd drive Ranger crazy. He blew out a long breath and shook his head. Shit, had he just talked to her or issued a challenge? Ryker was going to kill him.

Ranger stood and after giving Lilly one last glance, walked out. Pulling up in front of the diner, he decided not to tell Ryker about everything that had happened. It was bad enough that he'd opened his big mouth about the ass groping incident. He sure didn't need to tell him Lilly was thinking about other men.

Ryker jumped in with the take-out bag. "It's about time you got here. He set the bag in the seat between them before reaching out to squeeze Ranger's thigh. "What's wrong?"

"Nothing, I apologised for being an asshole when she walked into the office. She accepted my apology but said it had hurt her feelings." He pulled out onto Main Street and headed toward home.

"And?" Ryker inquired.

"And nothing. I finished my beer and left." He refused to look at Ryker, afraid he'd give away his deception.

As soon as they pulled off the county road onto their long winding driveway, Ryker moved the bag to the floor and scooted over next to Ranger. He kissed Ranger's neck and moaned. "Why do I smell Lilly back here?"

"She leaned in close to talk so the whole bar wouldn't hear. She must've been wearing perfume." He jumped a little when Ryker grabbed the hardening shaft between his legs.

"Then tell me why you have lipstick on your ear?" Ryker asked.

"I just did," Ranger said in a defensive tone. "She leaned in and whispered in my ear."

Ryker's eyes narrowed at the obvious omission on Ranger's part. When Ranger stopped the truck in front of the garage, Ryker grinned. "You know I'm gonna be smelling on this neck all night."

"Be my guest," he said, and gave Ryker a quick kiss. "First let's eat, I'm starving. After dinner we'll get a nice ice-pack and ice your leg while we watch TV."

"Sounds like a plan."

Ranger grabbed the bag of food before Ryker could. "You're going to have enough problems getting up the steps without carrying something."

"Ahh, you're always thinking of me," Ryker teased and batted his long black lashes.

"Always," Ranger replied with a wink.

* * * *

With a large ice pack and towel in hand, Ranger crawled back in bed. "Let me put this under you so you don't get the bed all wet," he said, carefully lifting Ryker's leg to spread out the towel. He looked down at the still swollen bruise. "Have those pain pills kicked in yet?"

"If they'd kicked in already I'd be asleep." Bub ran his fingers through Ranger's hair as he adjusted the ice pack. "Thanks."

"You're welcome," he said, placing a kiss on the heated skin. "I think you should stay home tomorrow and keep this elevated."

"Stop frettin', it's just a bruise. Besides," Ryker said, pulling him into his arms, "you know I go crazy when I'm here without you."

"I could call Sonny." He kissed Ryker's neck up to his chin, running his tongue over his heavy five-o'clock shadow.

Ryker lifted his chin to give him more room to play. "I love Sonny, but he's not you. He's always so jittery when he's away from the ranch, he makes me nervous."

Ranger continued to distract Ryker with kisses while he thought about Lilly. Her words kept going round and round in his mind. Damn, he sure wished he knew what she had planned.

"What's wrong," Ryker asked.

"Nothing. Go to sleep, Bub."

"Now that's the second time you've lied to me tonight. What happened with Lilly?" Ryker drew lazy circles over Ranger's back.

"I told her we were interested in her, but she needed to live a little first. She just got this really strange look on her face, and then she licked my ear and told me to sit back and watch while she did some living. I guess I'm trying to work out what she meant. I mean, I think I know, but I can't see Lilly getting wild just to prove something to us."

Ryker cleared his throat, and tilted Ranger's head up to look at him. "Why can't we just ask her out on a date? I'm sorry, but I really don't understand why we're waiting. I know I'm not the only one with feelings for her so why wait?"

How could he tell Ryker his greatest fears without sounding like a selfish asshole? He'd fought with himself for four years, ever since that day Lilly had first caught them. The heated look Ryker had given her almost boiled his blood. Was it jealousy or fear?

"Ranger, talk to me."

"We can ask her, I'll call her this week and see when her next day off is," he agreed, not wanting to analyze his feelings.

"Really?" Ryker grabbed Ranger's head and pulled him forward, thrusting his tongue into his mouth. "Turn off the light, I got a man to thank before these pain pills kick in."

Chapter Three

Driving to work the next afternoon, Lilly gripped the wheel so tight her knuckles turned white. "What were you thinking?" She couldn't believe she'd told Jeff she'd go out with him. "Okay, calm down and take a breath," she said out loud. "You're almost twenty-two years old, it's past time you explored the dating scene.

"But Jeff? Of all the men you could have spread your wings with, why'd you have to say yes to him?" Even though she'd asked herself that same question over and over since the previous night, she already knew the answer. Because he would give her the experience Ranger and Ryker seemed to want her to have. Evidently the twins weren't into virgins. A bark of laughter erupted from her throat. "Just my luck. I've saved myself for two men only to find out they want me more experienced."

Pulling into the lot, Lilly parked her fifteen-year old Toyota Corolla beside the light pole. Taking a deep breath, she rested her head on the steering wheel. So many sleepless nights she'd spent since she'd first seen Ranger and Ryker kissing in the feed shed. Watching the two of them felt like looking into the sun, you knew it was dangerous but you couldn't help yourself. Lilly had watched them for several long, passionate minutes before they'd heard her sigh.

They'd jumped apart so quick it made her head spin. While Ranger turned red and told her they'd be out in a minute, Ryker just stared at her, his eyes heavy-lidded with desire. She may have only been seventeen, but she knew what that look meant. From that moment on, she hadn't given other men the time of day. She knew someday, Ryker and hopefully Ranger, too, would follow through on that look.

Well, she knew what they wanted from her, and come hell or high water she would do anything she could to get herself the experience they seemed to require. She'd cut off one her red Dead Zone T-shirts so that it now exposed her belly ring. The shirt along with her short denim skirt and red cowboy boots should attract plenty of attention. Friday nights at the Zone were always packed with the town rowdies, and tonight was hers for the taking.

* * * *

"Ready to go?" Jeff asked, leaning against the bar.

No, she wanted to scream, but instead nodded. Going behind the bar, she picked up her purse and plastered a smile on. "Let's go."

Jeff put his arm around her bare midriff and walked her towards the door. "Where did you say we were going?"

Reaching his truck, Jeff opened the door and pulled Lilly into his arms. "That depends on if I need to buy you a burger before taking you home."

Panic froze her on the spot. No, no, not this fast. She wasn't ready yet. Looking up into Jeff's handsome face she smiled. "A burger would be nice," Lilly said, hoping to stall. God she hoped he was joking.

Jeff lifted her into the passenger seat and shut the door. Lilly fastened her seat belt and tugged her shirt down as far as she could. Why hadn't she thought to bring another shirt?

Starting the truck, Jeff looked over and winked. "Scoot over here, sugar." Jeff ran his hand up her bare thigh and started to dip underneath her skirt.

Without thought, she reached out and shoved his hand away. "I'm sorry, I just can't." She felt the tears welling in her eyes and shook her head. "Please forgive me." She unbuckled her seatbelt and got out of the truck. Digging for her keys, she quickly unlocked her car door as Jeff continued to stare at her.

God, she was embarrassed. This was all Ranger's fault. If he hadn't pressured her she would have never...

Her thoughts were interrupted when Jeff yanked the door handle out of her hand. "What the hell's going on with you? You tease me all night long with that damn outfit, and then the minute I touch you, you act like a scared virgin."

"Please, Jeff, let's forget about it," she pleaded.

He looked at her for several seconds before shaking his head. "You're not worth it," he said, slamming her car door. Jeff stalked back to his truck and roared off, spraying dust and gravel in his wake.

Lilly closed her eyes. She didn't know whether to be pissed or grateful. One thing was for sure though, as much as she desired the touch of a man, she'd found it was only Ranger and Ryker's touch she craved. Why couldn't they be the ones to take her virginity? Deciding she deserved the answer to her question, she started her car and drove towards the twin's place.

When she pulled up to the house it was dark. She looked over and spotted both trucks so she knew they were home. Feeling guilty for coming uninvited, Lilly pulled her cell phone out of her purse and called the house.

"Hello?"

The deep steady voice was all it took to break her down. She started talking without censoring herself. "I'm so sorry, I just can't do it. I tried, I was going to go out with Jeff but I just couldn't go through with it. I've never really dated because I've been saving myself for the two of you, and I'm sorry that you want me to have more experience but I don't. I only want the two of you. Not some other man. Why can't you accept me the way I am?"

"Lilly," Ranger yelled into the phone, "calm down. Where are you, sweetheart? Do you need help?"

Lilly grabbed a tissue from the box between the seats and blew her nose. "I'm out front. I came over here to talk to you, and then the house was dark and I chickened out. I embarrassed myself with Jeff tonight, and now I'm doing the same with you. You must think I'm acting like such a child."

"Hang up the phone and walk towards me. We'll figure this out."

Looking up, Lilly saw Ranger standing on the deep front porch of the log and stone house. He was dressed in a pair of jersey shorts and nothing else and Lilly's breath hitched in her chest. Damn, he was a beautiful man. As if in a trance, she turned off her phone and dropped it back into her purse before opening the door and walking towards the porch.

Ranger stepped back and opened the front door. "Come in," he said, holding out his hand.

Without hesitation, Lilly took the offered hand and followed Ranger inside. "Ryker's still sore. He took a pill earlier and he's out like a light." Ranger turned towards her and started to say something but stopped himself, his gaze raking across her body like a branding iron. He gestured to the couch, "Have a seat, I'll get us a glass of iced tea."

Lilly nodded and sat on the couch. She tried to pull her skirt down as far as she could, aware that she was showing a lot of leg. Maybe that's why Jeff put the moves on her so fast? She suddenly felt like a cheap imitation of her true self. Looking around, she spotted a thin blanket on the back of the old-fashioned rocking chair in the corner. Rising, Lilly quickly walked across the room and picked up the blanket.

"Cold?" Ranger asked, setting two glasses of tea on the coffee table.

Biting her lip, she shook her head. "More like embarrassed." She looked down at her bare midriff and short skirt before unfolding the blanket and draping it across her shoulders.

Ranger smiled and sat on the couch. "You've got a beautiful body. I like looking at it, but unfortunately for me and Ryker so does every other straight man with a pulse."

"Straight man? Do you consider yourself straight?"

"Yeah, why?"

"Well because I've seen the way the two of you kiss and I walked in yesterday to you wrapped around him with no pants on. I wouldn't exactly say those are the actions of a straight man." The look on Ranger's face confused her. Lilly couldn't tell if she'd pissed him off or if he was amused.

"It's hard to explain my relationship with Ryker. No one's ever been able to understand us and what we mean to each other. I can tell you that he is the only man on earth that I find physically attractive. I'm sure being my identical twin that sounds rather vain, but it goes beyond that. To love him is to love myself. One of us cannot function without the other, we've tried."

"But you both like women?" Lilly realised she'd been in love with these two men for years and had never talked to them about their relationship. She just figured they were gay or as she hoped bi-sexual. She was honest with herself enough to admit that she still didn't understand their relationship, but at least Ranger seemed willing to talk to her about it.

"Yeah," he chuckled, "we both like women. Well, we did like women, now we're only interested in one woman, you. Ryker and I haven't taken a woman to our bed for almost four years."

"Since that day…"

"Yes, since that day. I think Bub fell in love with you on the spot. Since then, he's refused to have any other women."

"And you?" She pulled the blanket closer, needing the security.

Ranger looked her in the eye before leaning over to take her hand in his. "Honestly? I don't know. I find you incredibly beautiful and I enjoy your company. I believe I have feelings for you, but I'm not sure how deep they go yet. I know they're nothing like Ryker's. If you can handle dating us, knowing how I feel, then everything should be fine."

Lilly wasn't sure what to think of the rather monotone statement. She saw wariness in Ranger's eyes and wondered just what he was so afraid of. This was her chance though. Despite Ranger's speech, she knew the three of them could make a relationship work. She may be young and inexperienced, but she wasn't stupid. "I'd like that. Uh, to date, I mean."

"I'll ask Ryker to call and ask you out. If he finds out you were here tonight, dressed as you are, he'd never forgive me for not waking him. I'd rather you didn't tell him about our talk."

Hmm, she thought. She'd never known Ranger and Ryker to keep something from the other. Ranger was definitely hiding something. Lilly hoped eventually she'd be able to break through the wall he'd already constructed around his heart where she was concerned. Though his words were definite, his eyes showed her promise. "I'll be waiting for his call." Lilly stood and walked back to the rocker. Taking the blanket from her shoulders, she refolded it and placed it over the back.

When she turned around, Ranger's eyes were glued to the sparkling gem in her belly button. She self consciously crossed her arms over her bare skin. "I promise to dress more appropriately for our date."

Ranger rose and walked towards her. "I told you before that you looked beautiful. As long as you're with Ryker and me, wear what you'd like, no one will bother you. It's you being in a room full of drunken men with neither of us there that's upsetting to think about."

Ranger then surprised her by leaning forward and placing a soft kiss on her lips. "I look forward to our date."

"Me, too," Lilly whispered.

Walking to the door, Ranger walked with his hand on her lower back. "Drive safely."

"I will," she said as she walked down the porch steps.

Watching Lilly drive away, Ranger couldn't decide whether to jump for joy or break down and cry. It was the beginning of something. He just hoped it wasn't the beginning of the end for Ryker and him.

Chapter Four

Ryker and Ranger worked in tandem making breakfast the next morning. They knew each other so well they worked quickly and efficiently. Ryker cracked the eggs into the frying pan and Ranger handed him the salt and pepper. "So, I was thinking maybe you should call Lilly and ask her out."

"Me? I thought you were going to do it later this week." He flipped the hot bacon grease over the top of the eggs, trying to figure out what was going on. It wasn't like Ranger to change his mind so quickly.

He glanced at Ranger and shrugged. "Maybe ask if she'd like to go into Lincoln. We could go out to dinner and a little dancing or something. I know the bar is closed on Sunday and Monday, so it would be a perfect day to call her."

Transferring the eggs to their plates, Ryker eyed his brother. "You're sure?" At Ranger's smile and nod, Ryker felt something in his chest lighten. "I'll call right after we feed the horses."

They carried their plates to the table. He still had a slight limp but his leg felt much better. Easing down into the chair, he leaned over and gave Ranger a kiss. "Thanks."

Ranger grinned. "Don't thank me until she says yes."

"Thanks for agreeing to it in the first place. I know you still have reservations."

Ranger set down his fork and cupped Ryker's cheek. "You know I'd do anything to make you happy."

"I know. You always have. You're the only person I know who's never let me down." He covered Ranger's hand with his and leaned in to the caress. "Love you."

"I know. You're my soul. You know that right?"

"Yeah I do, and you're mine."

* * * *

Wiping his sweaty hands on his jeans, Ryker picked up the phone and called Lilly's cell.

"Hello?"

"Hi, Lilly, um, it's Ryker." He rolled his eyes at his own stammering, knowing he sounded like a sixteen-year-old boy asking a girl out for his first date.

"Hi, Ryker." Well that's good, he thought. At least she seems happy to hear from him.

"How's it going?" He asked, wincing.

"Good."

"Uh, the reason I called was to see if you'd be interested in maybe going to dinner with me and Ranger tomorrow evening? We thought we could go into Lincoln so as not to attract as much attention."

"I'd love to go to dinner with the two of you, but something tells me it wouldn't matter where we went, the two of you together will always attract attention."

Shit, he hadn't really thought of that. "Well, I guess you can come over here and we could cook out. It doesn't matter to us. We'd just like your company."

"I didn't say it would bother me, Ryker, but if the two of you would feel more comfortable at home, that's fine with me. The important thing is we spend some time together."

"Good, great. Uh, how 'bout we pick you up around seven? It should be cool enough by then to sit out on the deck." Ryker thought his face would split with the wide grin he was wearing. He felt lighter than he had in years.

"Seven's good, but wouldn't you rather I just drove myself over?" Lilly asked.

"No. Believe it or not, Ranger's pretty old fashioned about stuff like this. He'd have a fit if we didn't pick you up on our first official date. As a matter of fact, I'm not sure what he'll think about us not taking you for a proper evening out."

"The important thing is that we're all comfortable enough to talk. I think we can accomplish that best where the two of you feel most relaxed. Tell Ranger we can go to Lincoln next week if tomorrow night turns out nicely."

"Okay, I think he might buy that."

Speak of the devil. Ranger came walking in the back door. He tilted his head and gestured to the phone.

"Lilly, Ranger just walked in so I'll let him know about tomorrow night. I, uh, have to say, I'm really looking forward to it."

"So am I."

"Well, I guess I'll let you get back to doing…whatever it was you were doing." He rolled his eyes again and looked at Ranger.

"I'll be ready at seven."

"Okay, 'til then." Ryker hung up the phone. "God that was nerve-racking."

Ranger walked over and wrapped his arms around him. "So?"

He grinned and kissed Ranger. "She said yes, but she thinks the three of us should be comfortable enough to talk so she suggested we just grill out here at home." He waited for Ranger's reaction.

Ranger narrowed his amethyst eyes. "Promise me you won't try to ravish her. We need to take this slow if it's going to work for the long haul. Remember what Momma always said, slow and steady wins the race. It'll be easy to forget that once Lilly's here, but taking it slow is the right thing to do."

Ryker grinned and held up his hand, "I promise." He hugged Ranger and kissed his neck. "I've got a lot of stuff to get done by tomorrow evening."

Ranger looked around the clean kitchen. "Like what?"

He shrugged, "Just because we aren't taking her out doesn't mean we can't make the evening special. I thought maybe I'd do something with the deck to make it seem a little more romantic."

Now it was Ranger who rolled his eyes. "Do what you want, Bub, but don't go overboard. I don't think Lilly will mind a simple barbecue."

"Of course she wouldn't, but that's no reason not to put forth a little effort to make it special for her."

"You're right," Ranger kissed him again. "How's the leg?"

* * * *

Standing beside Ryker at Lilly's apartment door, Ranger had to smile. His brother was so nervous he hadn't sat still all day, which was totally out of character for him. Usually on Sundays, they lounged in bed reading the paper, watching sports and snoozing on the couch, but Ryker had been up since six hanging fairy lights around the deck and picking wildflowers. They didn't have enough vases for all the flowers Ryker brought home so they'd improvised with jars.

When Lilly opened the door with a bright smile on her face and one of the prettiest dresses he'd ever seen, Ranger decided all the hard work was worth it. Ryker had been right. Lilly deserved a special evening.

As Ryker stammered a greeting, Ranger realised it was going to be a full-time job to keep his brother's lust in check. He didn't blame Ryker for his apparent attraction. Lilly looked absolutely edible in the pink and white polka dot halter dress, her sun-bronzed shoulders left bare. "Ready?" he finally asked, trying to save Ryker some embarrassment.

"I'm ready," Lilly held up her purse and keys.

After locking the door, Ranger let Ryker lead her to the truck. As Ranger flipped up the centre console, Ryker lifted Lilly into the seat. It seemed awkward having someone ride between him and Ryker, but the smile on Ryker's face assured him they were doing the right thing.

They made small talk on the way back to the house, Ryker fidgeting with the power button on the window. He'd never seen Bub like this. Usually he was laid back, ready for anything thrown his way. This was a totally different Ryker.

Pulling up to the house, Ranger watched Bub help Lilly out and the three of them walked into the house together. "I'll put the twice baked potatoes in the oven if you'll start the grill," Ranger said, stopping in the kitchen.

"Sounds good," Lilly said.

"Would you like something to drink? We have tea, beer and red wine." Ryker asked as he opened the refrigerator.

"I'll have some tea right now, but maybe a glass of wine with dinner would be nice."

Ryker looked up at Ranger. "Beer for me," Ranger said, getting the potatoes into the oven.

After filling two glasses with tea, Ryker gestured towards the French doors that led out to the deck. "Would you like to sit outside?"

"Yeah, that would be great." Lilly said and looked over at Ranger questioningly.

When Ryker turned his back, Ranger mouthed the words, "He's nervous."

Lilly smiled and took a deep breath. "Me, too," she mouthed back. She let Ryker lead her out to the deck.

Ranger could hear her gasp and utter words of approval at the decorated deck. Shaking his head, Ranger washed up a couple of dishes letting Ryker have a few minutes alone with Lilly. He didn't understand why the two of them were so nervous. It was obvious they all wanted the same things. He didn't think any of them wanted a simple affair, so why were they so skittish around each other?

Deciding to ease the tension, Ranger went out on the deck with a new resolve. Lilly and Ryker were standing beside the grill watching the flames dance over the grate. Walking up to the pair, Ranger put his arm around Ryker and pulled him in for a short kiss. If Lilly was going to get used to the sight of them showing affection, it might as well start now.

He didn't miss the heated look Lilly gave them as she watched the kiss. Well, that went so well, Ranger decided to take it one step further. He broke the kiss with Ryker and leaned over to place a soft kiss on Lilly's plump lips. She surprised him by opening right away for his questing tongue. Groaning, he used his available arm to pull her into an embrace with him and Ryker as he took the kiss even deeper.

A whimpering sound from Ryker had him breaking the kiss. "What?" he asked Bub.

"My turn," Ryker groaned, right before covering Lilly's lips.

Watching the two of them kiss was even more erotic than he'd thought it would be. He was afraid it would seem awkward, but knowing Ryker's feelings, he felt happy for his brother. When their kiss started to become too heated, Ranger figured it was time to break them apart. "Shall we sit?" He asked, breaking into their apparent mouth fuck.

Ryker released Lilly's lips and looked into her eyes for several seconds. "Yeah, that would probably be a good idea." They broke apart and walked over to the outdoor dining table.

Ranger had to readjust his jeans as he noticed the hard points pressing against the thin material of Lilly's dress, it seemed they were all aroused. What he'd intended as a tension breaker had created a whole new set of problems. Even knowing it was too soon, didn't cool his desire for the two people seated across from him. It was going to be a long night.

Chapter Five

After dinner, they felt comfortable enough with each other to settle on the double wide lounge he and Ranger liked so much. Now, with Lilly between them, it quickly became Ryker's favourite piece of outdoor furniture. He was hoping that someday, their big bed became his favourite place to have Lilly, but for now, he was in heaven.

Turning to his side, he draped his arm over Lilly to land on Ranger's hip, who did the same. With the fairy lights glowing in the dark, Ryker watched Lilly's face as Ranger talked about the future.

"We just need to make sure you know what you're getting into. Ryker and I are private people, but we do like to venture out occasionally, and when we do we have to watch ourselves. It's plain to see we're twins, and any show of affection is usually greeted with disgust, so we usually keep that here at home. When we take you out, it would be better for all of us, if you pretend you're with one of us only," Ranger explained.

"Why? I mean, I can understand pretending here in town, although everyone knows the two of you are lovers, but why in Lincoln? Sure there's a time and a place for everything, but there's that gay bar there. I'd think the two of you could dance together or both with me and not draw too many eyes."

Ryker couldn't resist placing a kiss on her neck. "It's a little more acceptable yes, but even in that atmosphere we'd draw attention. Hell, until recently, we even embarrassed Rawley. People just don't understand our relationship. You need to give it a lot of thought. There's your mom, for example. Will she accept us or reject you because of us? What about your friends? We know it's a lot to think about, but we don't want you to be hurt by what people will undoubtedly say."

"Well, my mom already knows I've had a crush on the two of you for years. I'm not sure if she knows that entering into a relationship will mean the three of us, but I'll talk to her. I have a couple of girlfriends, but they also know me well enough that I don't think it will come as a shock to them." Lilly stopped and worried her lip with her teeth. "I think I'd be okay with the odd looks from strangers as long as the two of you are with me, but maybe we should go out in public to test that theory now that we're more comfortable with each other."

"I like that idea," Ryker said, moments before kissing her. Even though it was only the second time they'd kissed, his tongue felt right at home sweeping the depths of Lilly's mouth. He tasted the wine they'd had with dinner and it went straight to his head. The bulge in his jeans let him know just which head, too. As the kiss continued, Ryker couldn't help himself and moved his hand to Lilly's breast. Running his fingertips over the swollen nipple caused the two of them to moan. Slipping underneath the material, he lightly pinched the hard nub unsurprised when he felt Ranger's lips join his fingers in their quest.

Lilly's moan was swallowed by his mouth as she lifted into their touch. Feeling Ranger's hand run up the length of his cock, Ryker thrust his hips. The action seemed to have caused Ranger to come back to his senses because he broke the connection with Lilly's nipple and removed his hand from Ryker's erection. "Stop," he said, tapping Ryker on the arm.

Breaking the kiss, he looked at Ranger. "What's wrong?"

"We need to slow down before things get out of hand."

He looked at Lilly, her exposed breast and bee-stung lips were a testament to how quick things had escalated between the three of them. He noticed the moisture from Ranger's mouth still clinging to the cinnamon coloured nipple and licked his lips. "I'm sorry, Lilly. You're just so beautiful."

Lilly shook her head. "Don't apologise. I've waited years for the two of you to touch me like that."

"Soon," Ranger said. "First we need to get over a few of the hurdles in our path. Namely your mom and going out in public. I don't think we should go any further until we know for sure this is what we all want."

Running her fingers, through Ranger's short black curls, Lilly gave him a chaste kiss. "For the record, I know this is what I want. It feels right. But I can wait until after our next date."

"How about tomorrow?" he asked.

"I'm off, but the two of you have to work," Lilly said, still with her hand in Ranger's hair.

"That's the beauty of owning your own business. We'll just take off early enough to come home, get cleaned up and pick you up, say around six? That'll put us into Lincoln around seven," Ranger said, tucking Lilly's breast back in her dress.

Ryker was sad to see it go, but understood what Ranger was trying to do. Thank God one of them had maintained control. If it had been left up to him, he'd be buried as deep as possible inside Lilly's pussy by now. Condoms, fuck, he hadn't even thought of buying condoms. He mentally added that to his list of things to do tomorrow at lunch.

"I think it would be best if we took you home," Ranger said, looking at Ryker. "I'm not sure I trust the look on Bub's face right now." Ranger grinned and gave Ryker a wink.

"Yeah, that might be best," he agreed, feeling way too horny to trust himself much longer.

* * * *

After they both gave Lilly a good-night kiss at her door, Ranger held Ryker's hand as they walked towards the truck. "It was a good date," Ranger said, breaking away to open his door.

"The best," Ryker grinned, getting in his side.

As soon as they left town, Ryker scooted over next to him. "Thank you," he said, nibbling on Ranger's neck.

Tilting his head to the side, he smiled. "You can thank me when we get home. I'm horny as hell now."

"Why wait," Ryker said, opening Ranger's jeans.

He felt Bub's hand cover his cock, seconds before his thumb pressed against the slit at the top. "Oh, fuck." One more mile and they'd be in their own drive where he could pull over. He didn't dare stop on the side of the road, not with his family living just down the road.

Trying to concentrate on the road, he rested a hand atop Ryker's. "Feels good."

"Mmm hmm," Ryker pumped harder kissing his neck.

Pulling onto their private drive, Ranger waited until they reached the tree-line before stopping the truck. He tilted the steering wheel to give Ryker more room and thrust up into Bub's touch. "Yes," he growled, feeling his sac draw up tight to his body.

Ryker held his hand still while Ranger continued to thrust into it. "Gonna," he panted moments before the first spurt of seed left his cock. He grabbed the back of Ryker's head and pulled him in for a deep kiss. "Oh, oh that was good," he moaned.

After cleaning Ranger's cock, Ryker tucked him back in. Ranger smiled and kissed him once more. "Let's get home so I can take care of you."

"I'm all for that," Ryker said with a smile.

* * * *

Lying in Ranger's arms, Ryker kissed his chest. "Where should we take her tomorrow night?"

"Oh, I don't know. I was thinking of LaMonts." Ranger swirled his fingers around Ryker's short curls.

"Kinda fancy. Lilly doesn't really strike me as the fancy-type. How about we just get a steak at Cattleman's Choice?"

"That sounds fine. You might want to give her a call and let her know. Women like to be prepared so they dress appropriately," Ranger grinned.

"Feels weird, taking a woman's needs into consideration." Ryker bit Ranger's already red nipple. "I like it."

"Rawley called again today. He's still bugging me to run for City Council."

"You thinking about it?"

"Hell no. But the more I think about Rawley running for Mayor, the more I think he's making a mistake. That man was born to be Sheriff, he loves it. Can you honestly see him behind a desk all day dealing with government bureaucrats?"

Ryker shrugged. "He just wants some changes around here. Since Mayor Channing's indictment for bribery and tax evasion, Rawley's been on a mission. So tell me why you don't want to help him?"

"It's not that. It's the fact that I don't want to live my life under a microscope. I enjoy working and then coming home where I don't have to answer to anyone but you."

"And hopefully Lilly," Ryker interjected.

"Yeah, and hopefully Lilly," Ranger whispered before they both drifted off to sleep.

Chapter Six

Pulling up to the small farmhouse, Lilly looked out over grounds knowing her mom would be outside somewhere. The farm had belonged to her grandpa before he'd passed away. Lilly had never known her father, so it had been just the two of them since her grandpa died when she was thirteen.

Spotting her mom's legs sticking out from under the old red tractor, Lilly walked towards the barn. Sitting in the small area of shade given off by the tractor tire, Lilly picked a blade of grass and began shredding it. "Hey, Momma."

"Hey, baby girl, what brings you out here on your day off?" Debbie Turner asked, crawling out from under the broken machinery.

"I need to talk to you." Lilly continued to pick and shred grass, not looking at her mom.

Debbie wiped her hands on a rag and scooted to the shade, shoulder to shoulder with Lilly. "So talk."

When Lilly hesitated, her mom bumped her shoulder. "You know there's nothing you can say to me to make me love you any less, so out with it."

"I want to date Ryker and Ranger Good," Lilly blurted out.

"Oh, Lilly." Her mom shook her head and wrapped her up in a hug. "There's so many things wrong with that idea. First and foremost, those two men are closer to my age than yours."

"Please, Mom, it's not about the age and we both know it."

"It'll be hard on you, but I guess growing up without a father was hard too and you made it through just fine. Do you see this becoming serious or is it just a whim."

"I've loved them for years, and Ranger told me Ryker feels the same way."

"What about Ranger? He's involved isn't he?"

"Ranger's different. I mean, I know he likes me and he's attracted to me, but he seems to be holding himself back."

Resting her head on Lilly's shoulder, Debbie sighed. "Some men are afraid of commitment. I've also never know those brothers to do anything separately. You can't have one without the other."

"I know."

"What happens in the future? I know you're still young, but I hope you talk with them before things get too serious. You love children, always have. Someday soon you need to discuss what you want for the future. Sex and dating is all fine and dandy, but you have to move towards what you want out of life, and I don't see you giving up the idea of having a husband and children. Even for the Good twins."

Lilly couldn't help but giggle as she gave her mom a little shove. "God, we've just started dating. I can't ask them about marriage and babies yet."

"Well you need to do it before you get yourself in too deep. I know from experience."

That snapped Lilly back to reality. Yeah, her mom did know something about that. She'd dated her high school sweetheart, sure he'd want to marry her after they graduated, Debbie Turner let Jes Mackey take her virginity. When she came up pregnant right before graduation, Jes turned his back on her and went off to college. He'd been killed in a drunk driving accident when he was in his junior year. Debbie had never dated another man. To this day she claimed he'd been the love of her life. Lilly always thought her mom was simply too afraid to love again.

"I'll talk to them, soon, but not yet," Lilly finally agreed.

Her mom kissed her forehead. "That's all I can ask. Well, that's not true. I do have one more favour. The three of you get down to the clinic and get yourselves checked out, and you get yourself on the pill."

"Mom," Lilly said, feeling completely embarrassed.

"You want my blessing? That's the price." Debbie winked.

* * * *

Wearing a pink and orange floral skirt and orange tank top, Lilly greeted her dates at the door. "Hey, guys, you're a little early," she said as she gave each of them a kiss. "Just let me get my shoes and purse and I'll be ready."

Ranger and Ryker followed her inside her tiny garage apartment. Ranger jabbed Ryker in the ribs with his elbow. "Someone was a little anxious, sorry."

Waving their concerns away, she sat on the bed to strap on high-heeled white sandals. "It's not a problem." Transferring her wallet and brush to her small white purse she smiled. "I know, women!" She rolled her eyes as Ranger and Ryker chuckled.

Walking towards the door, she leaned in for one more kiss from both of them. "I've been looking forward to this."

Ryker took an extra kiss and patted her ass. "You have no idea how hard it was to concentrate on work today."

"Ready?" Ranger asked, opening the door.

Ryker's brow lifted as he grinned. "Guess that's our cue to break it up."

With Lilly nestled between the two brothers, they made their way out of town to the interstate. "I haven't been to the Cattleman's Choice for years." She rested a hand on Ranger's thigh and was happy to get a grin and a wink. When she put her hand on Ryker's though, he winced. Lilly quickly lifted her hand. "I'm sorry, is that your sore leg?"

Ryker took her hand in his. "Yeah, best either go above or below." He brought Lilly's hand to his upper thigh. "My vote is for above."

Lilly felt herself blush as her fingers grazed the prominent bulge behind the denim fly. "You're trying to get me in trouble."

Grinning, Ryker leaned forward and looked at Ranger. "You planning on yelling at Lilly for trying to grope me on the way to Lincoln?"

"Nope, can't say as I blame her for wanting to do that."

Ryker looked back and Lilly and flashed a big toothy smile. "See? No trouble, amuse yourself."

Lilly knew he was teasing, but the temptation was very strong to do just that. She tried to keep her hand still, but Ryker kept squirming in his seat, causing the back of her hand to continually brush his erection. "Now you're tormenting me and you."

Ranger reached behind Lilly and thumped Ryker's head. "Behave."

"Yes, sir," Ryker said, biting his lip to keep from laughing.

After parking the truck, Ryker wrapped his arm around Lilly and walked her towards the door with Ranger following a few steps behind.

"We decided as far as the public goes, you're my date tonight," Ryker whispered in her ear. "Poor Ranger drew the short straw."

Lilly turned to look back at Ranger. "Well I guess we'll just have to make it up to him later." She turned back around giggling at Ranger's sultry growl. Boy, was she glad she took her vitamins today.

The hostess took them to a booth, and Ryker scooted in next to Lilly with Ranger sitting across from her. Picking up her menu, Lilly eyed the choices, finally deciding on the pot roast. When she set the menu down she noticed both men watching her. "What?"

Ryker wrapped his arms around her shoulders and pulled her in for a kiss. "Do you have any idea how beautiful you are?"

"Stop," she swatted him on the arm. "You'll either get me too embarrassed to eat or too horny, and I'm starving."

Their waitress came over and took their orders, all of them deciding to start off with a glass of red wine. Lilly couldn't help but notice the looks the waitress was aiming Ranger's way. She felt a little of the green-eyed monster rise up, and as soon as the perky blonde left, Lilly cleared her throat. "I'm not sure this is going to work."

"What?" Ryker asked in a panicked voice.

Before he could get himself all worked up, Lilly lifted her hand to his cheek and kissed him. "Stop thinking what you're thinking. That's not what I meant. This, me pretending to date only you or Ranger in public, isn't going to work for me."

Calmer now, Ryker kissed her nose. "What's wrong, sweetheart?"

Crossing her arms under her breasts, Lilly huffed. "I don't like other women thinking one of you is eligible." She pouted and glanced towards the waitress who was still ogling Ranger from across the room. "I was an only child and I'm not used to sharing."

Ranger grinned and leaned across the table. "Then give me a kiss, sweet thing."

With a smile, Lilly leaned over and let Ranger tongue fuck her mouth. She felt Ryker's hand inching up her skirt as he moaned. Breaking the kiss she looked into Ranger's eyes and then over at the waitress who was standing with her mouth open. "Much better." Pleased, she sat back down.

Settling back in his seat, Ranger smiled. "I would've never taken you for the territorial type."

"Well get used to it," she said. "Now, let's eat our dinner, and get out of here." She felt Ryker's hand slip under her skirt and turned towards him. "We're getting enough looks without you trying to make me writhe and moan. As nice as your hand feels, maybe we should save it for dessert."

Ryker grinned and removed his hand. "Wow, you're tough."

"One of us has to keep a level head or we're likely to be thrown out. Since I love this place, I'd like to come back sometime."

"Okay, we'll be good, and anytime you want to come back you just say so. It's nice to get out of Summerville once in a while."

Deciding it was better to talk now rather than later, Lilly took a sip of her wine. "I talked to Mom today about us."

Ranger's eye brows shot up, "Really? What did she say?"

Giving away only part of their conversation, Lilly unwrapped her silverware and put her napkin on her lap. "She made me promise that we'd all go to the clinic and get checked out and that I'd get on the pill."

Ryker grabbed Lilly's hand. "The clinic's not a big deal, we can go this week, but I guess I'm a little surprised you aren't already on the pill."

Lilly felt her face heat and looked down at her lap. "I've been saving myself for the two of you." Looking back up at Ranger she said, "When you told me you wanted me to live a little before you asked me out, I tried to get the courage to allow Jeff to take my virginity, but I couldn't go through with it."

"What? You'd let that womanizer take something as special as that?" Ryker almost shouted.

"It's what I thought the two of you wanted."

"No, God, no. We only wanted you to have fun with your friends and stuff. We both knew once we began dating you it would be for keeps. The last thing we wanted was for you to feel like you'd missed out on a part of your life twenty years from now. That's all, I promise." Ranger took her hand and continued. "And we're honoured that you saved yourself for us. As a matter of fact, Nate was teasing me a couple of months ago about the fact that there was no way you could be a virgin at twenty-one. I wanted to kill him."

"Wait a minute," she narrowed her eyes and looked from Ryker to Ranger. "Why did you discuss my sex life with Nate?"

"Oh, I didn't really. I think Nate said something about Rio not coming home from the bar, and maybe he'd gone home with that pretty waitress." Ranger shrugged. "The thought of you going home with Rio was enough to tear me up. Little did I know, Rio was trying to avoid Nate because he was sweet on him and didn't want to cheat on Ryan."

Lilly grinned, "So it bothered you huh?"

"Hell yeah it bothered me. Believe it or not, it's been hard for me and Ryker to wait for you to get older."

Ranger stopped talking while the waitress brought their food to the table. Lilly was pleased that the sly flirting had stopped but she grinned when the waitress winked at her. Yep, that girl knew a lucky woman when she saw one.

"Mmm," she moaned at the look and smell of her pot roast. Lilly looked up to see both men staring at her. "Sorry, smells good."

"Let's just hurry and eat so we can get out of here," Ryker said, squeezing her leg.

Chapter Seven

The closer they got to the house, the more Ryker wanted to play. He stole brief kisses and rode with his arm stretched behind Lilly, buried in the depths of Ranger's black curls. "Will you stay the night?" he finally asked Lilly.

"Yes," she replied, giving him a kiss.

Ryker could tell she was nervous. Smoothing his palm down her cheek, he kissed her again. "We'll take it slow. If nothing else it would be heaven just to hold you between us while we sleep."

"We'll see how things go. I've waited so long nothing seems real." Lilly worried her lip which Ryker was becoming accustomed to.

He licked the poor offended lip and ran his hand up under her skirt to rest on her thigh. Ryker looked up and caught Ranger watching his every move. He couldn't tell by the look on Ranger's face whether he was getting horny or something else. "Sweetheart, I think Ranger's feeling left out."

"Oh, we can't have that," Lilly said as she turned to kiss Ranger's jaw. He turned his head slightly and tried to kiss her while keeping his eyes on the road. Ryker smiled when Ranger released a soft moan as they broke the kiss. Knowing Ranger was just as nervous as Lilly was somehow very endearing.

With the mood in the truck shifting into playful, Ryker moved his hand higher under Lilly's skirt as he began kissing her neck. He smiled against her soft skin as she shifted enough to let him know his actions were welcome. Running his fingers over the lace of her panties he could already feel moisture soaking his fingers. "Mmm," he moaned.

Ryker looked into her green eyes seeking permission to go even further. Her answer was to open completely for him, hooking one leg over Ranger's thigh and one leg over his. Ryker rewarded her faith with a deep thrusting kiss as his fingers slipped under the leg of her panties to drag across her slit.

Lilly broke the kiss and tilted her head back as the first of his fingers worked its way inside the creamy depths of her pussy. "Oh God."

He watched as Ranger fidgeted in his seat as he tried to keep his eyes on the smooth blacktop. "Come on," he said to Ranger, "you can drive one handed, I know you can."

With a sideways glance, Ranger removed one hand from the wheel. As soon as Ryker felt Ranger's fingers slide in beside his, he withdrew and sucked one digit into his mouth. "Holy fuck, you taste good." He held the other finger in front of Ranger's mouth.

Ranger opened, seemingly eager for his first taste of Lilly. Ranger sucked his finger like he wanted to take the skin off. "Hey, I didn't expect to draw back a stub," Ryker joked.

"Sorry," Ranger mumbled, releasing Ryker. Ranger looked down at the speedometer, "Ten more miles," he said, pressing a little harder on the gas.

Whatever Ranger was doing with his hidden hand, seemed to be doing the trick for Lilly as she began to squirm in her seat, panting. Ranger looked over at Ryker. "Rub her clit."

Unbuckling his seat belt, Ryker grinned. "I can do better than that." He flipped Lilly's skirt up as he buried his face against her partially exposed pussy. Running his tongue over the small triangle of closely cropped hair about her slit, he inhaled. "You smell good, sweetheart."

Lilly answered by reaching down and trying to pull her panties off. Her actions were so frantic and mindless she wasn't getting anywhere. "Off," she cried.

Chuckling, Ryker slid her wet panties down her legs and off. He handed the garment to Ranger. "Smell."

As Ranger inhaled the scent of Lilly's desire, Ryker went back to her pussy. With his tongue poised at her channel, he thrust deeply into her core.

"Uhh," Lilly stiffened and grabbed Ryker's hair.

With his nose pressed against her clit, Ryker began torturing her pussy with his tongue, lapping every ounce of cream her body produced. When her grip tightened even more he slid his tongue up and covered her clit with his lips, sucking and biting down gently.

"Ryker," she screamed as she came.

Moving back down, Ryker scooped cum from her body with his tongue as he unzipped his jeans. Taking his throbbing cock in hand it only took two strokes for his own orgasm to overtake him.

"Fuck," Ranger howled.

Ryker looked up in time to see Ranger's cock empty its seed onto the steering wheel with Lilly's hand wrapped firmly around it. The smell of sex was so strong inside the truck cab, Ryker's cock continued to twitch in his fist.

By the time they pulled in front of the house, and Ranger put the truck into park, the three of them were exhausted. Ranger, resting his head against the back of the seat, turned to Ryker and Lilly. "Don't ever do that again. I could have easily wrecked and killed us all."

Ryker leaned up across Lilly to give Ranger a kiss, sharing Lilly's essence. "For that? I'll take my chances." He used the tails of his shirt to clean himself up before crawling back onto the seat and opening the door. "How about we take this inside?"

As Ranger tucked himself back in and fastened his jeans, Ryker got out of the truck. He turned back towards Lilly and scooped her out of the seat.

"I can walk," she whined.

"Yeah, but I'd rather carry you. Ranger's too damn big for me to carry around or else I'd carry him too."

Ranger had the door unlocked and opened by the time Ryker made it to the top of the steps. Walking straight to the bedroom he lowered Lilly to the side of the bed. "Would you like some wine while we recuperate?"

"That sounds good." Lilly started to undress right before his eyes.

Instead of running off to get the wine, Ryker stared in awe. As the tight tank top lifted over her breasts, his mouth began to water. "So pretty," he groaned, falling to his knees in front of her. Just before burying his face in her cleavage, he turned to Ranger. "Would you get us some wine, please?" he asked with a boyish grin.

Ranger rolled his eyes and walked off muttering under his breath. Lilly tossed the shirt to the floor, and Ryker captured both breasts in his hands. Bringing the generous mounds together he sucked on one nipple before moving to the next, happy when they pebbled immediately. He was sure her chest would probably be dotted with hickeys the next day, but he liked the thought of marking her.

A throat clearing behind him drew his attention. He pulled off one of the generous nipples with a pop and looked behind him. Ranger was standing with a bottle of wine and three glasses. "Why don't you give Lilly a break long enough to get undress and have a glass of wine, Mr. Greedy."

Ryker released Lilly's breast as she sighed. "Sorry," he said feeling like a lecher. Standing, he walked to the bathroom and cleaned himself up from his earlier orgasm. Running a soft washcloth under the hot water, he carried it back to the bedside table, hoping they'd need it later.

Lilly was already under the covers, nestled in the centre of the bed. She looked perfect there, Ryker thought. Although he did acknowledge it would be strange not to sleep next to Ranger. They'd slept spooned together since they were babies. In the past, they'd shared women, but none of them had been invited to spend the night, this would be the first.

As he undressed he looked over at Ranger. Seeing the stunned look on Ranger's face as he poured the wine, Ryker guessed he was thinking the same thing. Lilly must have noticed the sudden tension in the room. "Is something wrong?"

Tossing his clothes aside, Ryker got in bed and pulled Lilly into his arms. He decided to be honest with her. If this relationship would work honesty needed to come before shame. "Ranger and I have never been separated in sleep. It just hit us both, I think."

"Well, that's easily fixed," she smiled and scooted over to the far side of the bed. "The two of you will just have to take turns sleeping in the middle."

Ryker loved her more at that moment than he ever thought possible. She hadn't questioned or made them feel ashamed.

Lilly had simply come up with the perfect solution. Ryker pressed his lips to hers. "God, you're perfect for us."

Ranger stood over them, handing them each a glass of red wine. Ryker looked up to take his glass and met Ranger's gaze. He knew Lilly had jumped her first hurdle in gaining Ranger's love as well.

Getting in bed, Ranger quickly finished his glass of wine, and set it on the table. He motioned for Ryker to look at Lilly and grinned. Glancing over, Ryker saw Lilly trying her best to stay awake. Seems her orgasm combined with the nerves of their first date had worn her out. Finishing off his wine, Ryker took Lilly's glass out of her hand and passed them both to Ranger. "Poor baby," he crooned, pulling Lilly against his chest.

They both watched as she yawned and promptly fell asleep. "She's just so damn cute," Ryker said, putting his other arm around Ranger, who cuddled up against him.

"She is," Ranger agreed. He brushed the hair away from her face. "You think it's going to work?" Ranger asked, lips barely touching Ryker's.

"Yeah, I really do." Ryker opened his mouth and kissed Ranger. After several minutes they broke apart and settled in for the night, Ranger's head resting on Ryker's chest next to Lilly's beautiful face.

Chapter Eight

Waking up before dawn, surrounded by the people he loved put an immediate smile on Ryker's face. He could feel Lilly's soft curves against his morning erection as well as Ranger's half-hard cock tucked against the cheeks of his ass. "Life just doesn't get any better," he whispered to the morning sunrise.

The need to explore was strong, but his conscience kept telling him to wait, Lilly deserved more than a quick, before-work, kind of loving. It would be her first time, and Ryker wanted it to be memorable for all of them. Still, a little groping couldn't hurt, as long as they didn't do too much.

Working his way up from her stomach, Ryker brushed his palms across her warm breasts, happy when they immediately pebbled for him. His fingertips explored the raised bumps and ridges surrounding her tight buds as he kissed her bare shoulder.

Lilly arched her back, pushing her sweet ass against his aching cock. "Morning," she said, reaching behind her to hold on to his hip as she continued to grind herself against him.

He felt Ranger's cock stiffen the second his eyes opened. "Having fun without me?" Ranger asked in his rough morning voice.

"Just starting," Ryker said. He reached back and pulled Ranger closer.

"What about my morning hand job?" Ranger chuckled.

"You'll have to make do rubbing against me this morning because I've got my hands full at the moment." Ryker looked over his shoulder and kissed Ranger.

Ranger looked at Ryker before glancing towards Lilly. Ryker could tell what he was worried about, but they all needed to get used to each other. Nibbling on Lilly's neck, he whispered in her ear. "You don't mind if Ranger rubs off on me this morning do you?"

Lilly took his hand off her breast and drew it down to her pussy. "Not as long as you take care of me, too."

"Hot damn, pass me some lube, brother."

"Uh...I thought we agreed..." Ranger stammered.

"Right, I need to talk to Lilly about that." Ryker kissed Lilly's shoulder again. "Sweetheart, Ranger and I think it would be better to wait a little longer to make love to you. Lord knows it's not because we don't want to, but you deserve something special. And we aim to give it to you."

Lilly turned her head and kissed him.

"That said, I thought we could do a little playing this morning before Ranger and I have to get you home."

"I like to play, but just so you know, any time would be special to me as long as it was with one of you." Lilly turned in his arms to face him.

"You do say the sweetest things," Ryker grinned. With his hand to the back of her head, Ryker pulled her in and licked her lips. When she opened, he delved in deep, tasting her passion just bursting to be set free.

The ringing phone and a nudge from Ranger finally broke them apart. "What?" Ryker asked looking over his shoulder.

"There's a call for Lilly. Its Rawley," Ranger said, passing the phone to her.

Ryker looked at Ranger and he shrugged. "He wouldn't tell me anything. Only that he couldn't find Lilly so he called Debbie, and she told him to phone here."

Turning his attention back to Lilly he listened to her side of the conversation as Ranger's hand wrapped around his cock. He thrust his hips back against Ranger's erection as he tried to concentrate on what Lilly was saying to Rawley.

"Okay, yeah, I'll have the guys drop me by the station. Thanks for calling, Sheriff." Lilly disconnected and handed the phone back to Ranger. "My landlord called the police this morning. She went out to get her paper and saw my car had been vandalised. Rawley wants me to come by the Sheriff's office and file a report." She bit her lip, "I know you guys need to get to work, but could you wait after you drop me off so I can make sure my car will run?"

Ranger released Ryker's cock and crawled over the top of both of them to sandwich Lilly in between their warm bodies. "Of course we will. If you want, you can borrow one of our trucks until you get your car fixed."

"Thanks, but depending on the damage, it's probably not worth fixing. My poor baby was on her last leg anyway."

"We'll figure it out. The most important thing is to find out who would do something like that. Did Rawley say if he suspects kids or a different type of threat?"

"He didn't say. It's only me and Mrs. Clemens, and she doesn't even hear her own phone half the time. Rawley doesn't even know when it was vandalised, could've been any time after you two picked me up yesterday evening."

Brushing the hair off her face, Ryker kissed her. "I don't like the thought of you there alone if someone's trying to start trouble."

"It's probably just kids. I'll be fine, besides I can't leave Mrs. Clemens there to deal with it, she's darn near eighty."

"As much as I'd like to stay right where we are, we need to get going. Ryker, why don't you go hop into the shower while Lilly and I make breakfast?"

Sticking his bottom lip out, Ryker sat up. "You've always been a party pooper."

"No, I've always been the one who gets your ass to work on time," Ranger grinned, swatting Ryker's ass as he walked by on the way to the bathroom.

* * * *

As soon as Ryker shut the door, Ranger looked back at Lilly. "Do you think it could have anything to do with your failed date with Jeff the other night?"

Sitting up, Lilly swung her legs over the side of the bed. "I can't see Jeff doing something like that. He was a real jerk Saturday night at work, but I've never heard of him having a violent streak." Lilly looked towards the bathroom.

"Maybe you should come back and stay the night tonight after you get off work." Ranger slipped on his jeans and watched as Lilly put on her clothes. Damn she sure was a beauty.

She seemed to be thinking about his invitation as she slipped her skirt on. Lilly paused and slapped her forehead. "Oh, no, I can't. Dang you two have completely fried my brain for anything but the two of you. I forgot tonight's

Bunco night at Jeanette's house, and I promised Mom I'd go. I even scheduled an evening off."

"How long does it usually last? You can always come by after." Ranger hated to beg, but he really didn't like the sound of someone destroying her car. He tried not to make a fuss, not wanting to worry either of them, but he planned on making a phone call to Rawley later.

Lilly was back to biting her lip as she slipped the shirt over her head. He sighed as her perfect breasts were once again covered. She seemed to know what he was thinking and gave him a wink. "Later," she teased.

Hearing the water shut off, Ranger grabbed her hand and led her to the kitchen. "Quick, let's get breakfast going. Do you need a shower?"

Lilly shook her head and retrieved a carton of eggs from the fridge. "I'll just put my hair in a ponytail until I get back from filing the report." Pulling down a bowl, she began cracking eggs. "I hope you both like scrambled. Sorry to say, I'm not much of a cook."

Ranger hugged her from behind, "Scrambled's my favourite." He ran his tongue around the shell of her ear as he slipped his hands under the thin tank top and up to cover her breasts. Lilly rested her head back on his shoulder as she arched into his touch.

"Oh, now I know why you wanted me to shower first, you pig," Ryker said, still drying his hair with a towel.

"I couldn't help myself," Ranger said, squeezing her nipples.

He felt the snap of the towel on his ass and turned his head towards Ryker. "You're asking for it, Bub."

Ryker smiled and pressed against Ranger's back. "Yeah? What am I asking for?" Ryker used the position to stretch his arms out around Ranger and onto Lilly's breasts.

With two sets of hands on her, Lilly moaned. "Well unless you both stop, it sure ain't breakfast."

Ranger and Ryker both laughed and released their hold on her. "Okay, I'll get in the shower," Ranger said, placing one more kiss on Lilly's neck. He turned towards Ryker and kissed him. "You be good and let the woman feed us before we're late for work."

"Yes, sir, boss." Ryker saluted.

* * * *

Pulling up in front of her tiny apartment over Mrs. Clemens garage, Lilly gasped. "Oh, no." As soon as she saw the busted out windows, she was glad Ryker had insisted she borrow one of their trucks. They'd still followed her home, but at least now she had a way to get to the Sheriff's station. She felt Ryker's arm wrap around her waist as Ranger parked and got out of his truck.

"Holy shit," Ranger said, as he walked towards her destroyed Toyota. He narrowed his eyes and looked around the street and yard. "This wasn't done by kids." He looked right at her. They both knew who'd done it.

"Excuse me, but is there something you all want to let me in on?" Ryker asked.

Lilly looked up at Ranger, who closed his eyes and nodded. She turned back to Ryker. "It's just a guess, but Jeff wasn't very happy with me the other night. When we got into his truck, he immediately started putting his hand up my skirt and I kinda freaked out. I apologised and told him I couldn't go through with it. Needless to say, Jeff's not used to being shut down. I don't know how we'd prove it though."

"I'll kill him," Ryker said, jaw tensing.

"No, you won't, Bub. It's Rawley's job, let him do it."
Ranger put a hand on Ryker's shoulder. "Our job is to protect
Lilly, not play cops."

Lilly looked at her battered car again. Every window was
either cracked or busted along with her tail lights and
headlights. She decided to take Ranger up on his offer for a
place to stay. "I'll talk to Mrs. Clemens and tell her I'll be
gone for a few days until they find out who did this. I'd like
to try and convince her to go stay with her sister in Lincoln. If
she agrees, I'll probably drive her up this afternoon, if it's
okay that I use your truck?"

Ryker hugged her. "You can use anything of mine you
want," he gave her a grin and a wink. "Just make sure when
you come back to pack, you have one of us or Rawley with
you."

"Will do," she said standing on her tiptoes to give him a
quick kiss. "And I'll be by after Bunco tonight."

With one last look at Lilly's car, Ryker shook his head.
"Let's get out of here."

Chapter Nine

By mid-morning, Ryker was back in the office. He looked at the clock and picked up the phone. Surely Lilly had had time to fill out her police report by now. Dialling Rawley's number he waited. When he got a recording he hung up and tried his cell phone.

"Sheriff Good," Rawley answered.

"Hey, did Lilly come by?" Ryker leaned back in his chair and put his muddy boots on the edge of the desk.

"Yeah, I'm over at her place right now. She's upstairs getting some things together while I take some fingerprints off the car." Rawley paused, "Lilly's staying with you for a couple of days I take it?"

He could almost hear the censure in his big brother's voice. "Yes, something wrong with that?"

"Nope, not as long as you're sure of what you're doing. And before you get all defensive, it's not because of her age, even though I know that's a sore spot with you and Ranger. I just need you to be sure this is what you want, because it might not go over very well in town. You need to think a little about what's good for Lilly and the consequences of your actions."

"Rawley, we know all of this. Ranger and I have talked about it for years. What it would all mean to our personal and professional lives, and we decided that Lilly had a right to choose for herself. We had a nice talk last night and the night before. I think she knows what she's getting into. She talked to her momma, so we're not sneaking around behind anyone's backs. Just let us deal with it."

"Deal, huh? What about Lilly's car?"

Worrying his fingers through his hair, Ryker closed his eyes. "I don't think that had anything to do with me and Ranger. I'm sure she told you about her almost-date with Jeff."

"Yeah, she told me. If you're going to continue this with her it will be your responsibility to make sure she stays safe."

"Yes, Sheriff, we realise that. Why do you think we're insisting she come stay with us until this whole vandalism thing is settled?"

Rawley sighed on the other end of the phone. Ryker could just picture him taking off his hat and wiping his brow. "On a brotherly note, if this is what you all want, I'm happy for you."

Ryker knew his brother meant it. Ranger told him about the talk Ranger and Rawley had a couple of months ago, and it meant the world to them to have his blessing. "Thanks."

"Be careful, that's all I ask. Not everyone's going to be as accepting of this new relationship."

"We know. Call us if you find out anything about Lilly's car. Do you think it'll be totalled out by the insurance company?"

"Yeah, I'd say so. The whole car's not worth more than a thousand bucks. I hope she has full coverage."

"Doesn't matter. We'll figure something out."

"Here she comes, do you want to talk to her?"

"If you don't mind," Ryker grinned. He heard Rawley hold out the phone and tell Lilly it was Ryker.

"Hi," Lilly answered.

"Hi, sweetheart. Did you get Mrs. Clemens to agree to go to her sister's?"

"Finally," she chuckled. "I'm taking her up to Lincoln in a few minutes."

Ryker's body began to stir from the sound of Lilly's voice. "Make sure you drive safe, and keep a watchful eye out for anything suspicious. I don't think anyone would be foolish enough to bother you in broad daylight, but it doesn't hurt to keep your eyes open."

Lilly laughed. "I care about you, too. I need to go. Mrs. Clemens is standing on her porch with suitcase in hand. I'll call you before I go to Bunco."

"Bye, sweetheart. I'll see you later." Ryker hung up the phone and closed his eyes. "Life is good," he whispered to himself.

* * * *

Lilly went straight to her mom's after dropping Mrs. Clemens at her sister's retirement apartment. She pulled up to the old farmhouse with just enough time to take a quick shower and get ready.

After her shower, she dressed in a pair of navy shorts and a floral button-up camp shirt. Pulling the sides of her hair back into a large barrette, she went into the kitchen to find her mom.

"Hey, baby girl," Debbie said.

"Hey, Mom," Lilly answered, giving her mom a kiss on the cheek.

"What did Rawley tell you about your car?" Debbie asked, putting plastic wrap over the top of a plate of brownies.

Lilly snuck a brownie off the plate before her mom had it completely covered. "That he'd send a report to my insurance company. He went over with me earlier to take fingerprints and wait for me to pack a bag. Ranger and Ryker think I should stay with them until we know whoever did this has got it out of their system." Lilly pinched off a piece of the dessert and stuck it into her mouth.

Debbie's eyebrow lifted as she looked at Lilly. "You know you could've just come home for awhile. Are you sure staying with them is a good idea?"

Lilly looked at her mom for several seconds. She'd thought about the implications all the way home from Lincoln. "Yeah, Mom, it's what I want. If people are going to have a problem with it, it won't matter if it happens now or two months from now, because I feel that this thing between the three of us is right."

Debbie walked over and kissed the top of her head. "Okay." She looked up at the clock. "You ready?"

Lilly picked up the plate of devilled eggs on the counter while her mom carried the brownies. "Let's go play."

* * * *

Getting out of Ryker's truck, Lilly grabbed her purse and a plate of food. She looked around at the cars lining the street. "Pretty good turn out it seems."

"It's usually a good crowd when we play in town." Debbie came around the truck to meet Lilly on the sidewalk.

"Maybe I'll get lucky, and you won't need me to play after all," Lilly grinned. She'd much rather be playing with her men than a bunch of old women.

They headed towards the big front porch when a voice like nails on a chalkboard spoke up. "Isn't that Ryker Good's truck?" Mary Waters asked. Mary was several years older than Lilly and liked to think of herself as the town beauty.

"Yes, it is. What gave you your first clue? Could it be the Good's Feedlot sign on the side?" Lilly knew she was being snide, but dammit, she wasn't in the mood for this holier than thou bitch today.

"Why are you driving Ryker's truck? I thought you were going out with Jeff?" Mary inquired with her hands on her bony hips.

Lilly really didn't want to get into this before she even stepped foot in the door. "No, I'm not dating Jeff. Someone vandalised my car last night so Ryker said I could borrow his truck. Is that okay with you? Or should I have phoned first?"

Mary narrowed her eyes. "What, you going out with Ryker Good now? I thought he was in that perverted relationship with his own twin."

Lilly took a deep breath. Her mom tried to pull her into the house, but instead, Lilly handed Debbie the plate of food. "You go on in. There's something I need to clear up with Mary."

Debbie looked at her and finally sighed. "I imagine this means you won't be staying?"

"Sorry, Mom. I'll set the bitch straight then I'm outta here."

Her mom gave her a kiss on the cheek, "You don't need to run away just because one person doesn't understand."

"No, you're right, I don't. But I'm also not going to spend my free time around people who think like Mary does. Life's too short to put up with the bitches of the world just to be polite."

Debbie nodded and went inside. Lilly turned towards Mary and started walking. She had no plans of hitting the woman, but that didn't mean she couldn't scare her a little. Mary took a step back for every one Lilly took towards her. When she was finally backed against the porch railing, Lilly leaned in, her face inches away from Mary's. "Now you listen here. If I ever hear you say another bad word about Ranger and Ryker, I'll kick your scrawny ass from one end of Main Street to the other. They're very private people and you need to learn to respect that. Whether I'm dating Ryker or Ranger or both of them, it's no business of yours. Now get your own life and leave the people I care about alone."

Mary looked shocked. "So, you're just as perverted as they are?"

"Look, Little Mary Sunshine, if I were you, I wouldn't talk about perversions. Not with all the talk I've heard around town about you. I've never mentioned what I've heard because it's usually just a bunch of drunk guys talking at the bar, but if you push me, believe me, I've got enough ammunition on you to make both your folks disown you. Now, back the hell off." Lilly didn't wait for Mary to reply. She turned on her heel and walked back to the truck. At least she knew of two sexy men who'd be happy to see her.

Chapter Ten

Ready for their usual evening ride, Ranger finished cinching Pete's saddle and looked over at Ryker. "You about done?"

Hoisting his long frame into the saddle, Ryker reached down and pet Magic. "We're ready."

Their attention went to the front of the house when they heard a vehicle pull up. Ranger groaned, "Sounds like company." He mounted Pete and they rode towards the front of the house. Ranger was surprised to see Lilly still sitting in Ryker's black pickup with her head on the steering wheel.

Riding over to the window he knocked. Lilly's head sprang up and she smiled. The window rolled down and Lilly leaned her arm on the door. "What are you two cowboys up to?"

"Just going for our usual evening ride. What happened?" He could tell by the look on her face she wasn't happy, though he didn't see tears so at least he knew she hadn't been crying.

Lilly smiled and waved away his concerns. "I just realised that I'd rather spend my evening with the two of you."

Ranger knew she wasn't telling them the whole truth. He suspected she'd had her first brush with the ladies of the town and their attitudes towards him and Ryker. "Well, lucky you caught us. Care to slip up behind me and go for a ride?"

"I'd love that." Ranger moved Pete back and Lilly opened the door.

Looking over his shoulder, he could see Ryker and Magic waiting patiently by the corner of the house. Evidently Ryker was giving him a few moments alone with Lilly. It said more than words could have about Ryker's hopes the two of them would fall in love as well.

It wasn't until Lilly climbed out of the truck that he saw her white shorts. Smiling, he pointed towards them. "You might want to change into some blue jeans. If you don't those pretty shorts will be brown by the time we get back."

Lilly looked down and blushed. "Yeah, I guess you're right. Give me a second?"

"Sure, let me just get your bag for you," Ranger said. He dismounted and reached in the truck bed to heft out the large suitcase. Walking towards the house, he gave Ryker a wink. "I won't be but a minute." Without the actual words, he was assuring his brother he wouldn't take liberties with Lilly while in the house.

Ryker surprised him with a wide grin. "Take your time. Magic and I will graze the lawn."

He narrowed his eyes at Ryker. "Keep Magic away from my grass." He'd worked for years to try and get a nice lawn to grown in the thick shade of trees that surrounded their house, and Ryker knew damn well he didn't want Magic grazing.

Following Lilly into the house they walked through to the bedroom. Ranger sat the suitcase on the end of the bed and turned towards the closet. "We emptied out half this dresser and a good amount of closet space."

Unzipping her suitcase, Lilly rifled around for a pair of jeans. "The dresser space I can definitely use, but I didn't bring many hanging up things. I'm a pretty casual girl."

Ranger couldn't resist and stepped up behind her. Pressing himself against Lilly's back, he kissed her neck. "My kind of woman. Although, I'll admit, I sure did enjoy that pretty dress you wore the other day." He reached down and unbuttoned her shorts. Sliding the zipper down, he let the white cotton shorts fall to the floor as he ran his hands over the pretty white lace of her underwear.

"I brought a few. I wish I had something sexy to wear for the two of you, but I've never really had a need for such clothes." Lilly dropped the jeans in her hand and reached back to place them on the back of Ranger's neck.

Subtly shifting one of her legs up onto the bed, Ranger slipped his fingers under the waistband of her panties. "Mmm, you're always so wet," he groaned against her neck.

"Only when I'm around the two of you," Lilly replied.

A sudden attack of the guilts stilled his hand as it rubbed against her clit. "How 'bout we take a blanket on our ride with us. You, me and Ryker, under the stars for your first time?"

"Yes," she whispered, turning her head to get a kiss.

Ranger removed his hand and spun her around into his arms. "I can't think of anything more beautiful than the sight of you spread out naked on a blanket by the pond." He kissed her, delving his tongue deep, sweeping inside her mouth with a passion that was quickly becoming unmanageable.

Lilly was the first to pull back. "If you don't stop kissing me like that, I'll tell you to forget the ride and take me right here," she winked.

"Can't have that. Ryker and I promised each other we'd make it special for you. Why don't you get changed and I'll hunt up a blanket and some supplies." Ranger turned from her, and dug through the bedside table for several condoms and a tube of lube. Stuffing the supplies in his shirt pocket, he went to the kitchen and found a large freezer bag and added a wet dishtowel.

Lilly came into the kitchen smiling, "Anything I can help you with?"

He turned around and shook his head. "Nope, just need to get a blanket and we're all set. Why don't you go out and make sure Ryker's horse isn't destroying my lawn."

By the time he had everything together and went outside, Ryker and Lilly were already kissing, Lilly leaning over the porch rail and Ryker still on Magic's back. He cleared his throat, breaking the two of them apart and handed the blanket and baggie to Ryker. "You carry these. I already called dibs on riding with Lilly."

"Oh, you so did not call dibs, but I'll give you this round because you went in and did all the work."

Ranger knew Ryker was still in matchmaking mode because he could argue with the best of them and if he'd really wanted Lilly to ride with him, he'd have gotten his way. Ranger gave Ryker a look that told him he knew exactly what he was doing. Ryker flashed his stunning toothy grin and looked up at the sky.

"Clouds are moving in. If we don't get to riding, we'll all get wet."

Ranger took Lilly's hand and muttered, "Some of us are already wet."

Ryker did a double take, looking from Ranger to Lilly. "Well let's get a move on."

Ranger let her saddle up first before seating himself behind her. He kissed Lilly's neck and whispered in her ear, "You'll be safer in the saddle and I can play." He handed the reins to Lilly, knowing she was an excellent rider. "We'll have to bring your horse over from your mom's."

"I'd like that, being able to ride along side the two of you in the evenings." She moaned as Ranger cupped her bouncing breasts. "Although this way definitely has advantages."

As they neared the pond, the sky started to rumble. Looking up Ranger could smell the rain in the air. As long as the lightening didn't get too close, let it rain, he thought. His cock was so hard he thought he might be putting dents into the back of the saddle as he continued to rock against it, fondling Lilly's breasts through her open shirt. By the time they arrived at the pond, Lilly's back was arched as she leaned into his ministrations.

Ryker was the first off his horse. He didn't bother tying Magic, instead dropping her reins to the ground. This was her home and she felt as comfortable by the pond as anywhere. Spreading the blanket in a soft patch of grass, he undressed in no time, never taking his eyes off Ranger and Lilly. Stalking towards them, Ryker eyed Ranger's hands still fondling Lilly's breasts. "My turn," he said, pulling Lilly off Pete and into his arm.

Ryker carried Lilly to the blanket and eased her out of the remainder of her clothes. When they were both naked, Ryker wrapped himself around Lilly. "I love you," he whispered, looking into the green depths of her eyes. "I'm nervous. I want this to be special for you."

Lilly cupped his cheek, "It's already perfect."

Ranger knelt beside them and dropped the lube and condoms on the blanket. Ryker looked over and watched as his brother fisted his hard cock, pumping it slowly. As the first raindrop fell, he began licking his way down Lilly's body, squeezing and nipping at her engorged nipples before moving on. He got a sigh as he sucked the skin at the top of her pelvis. He needed to mark this woman, the need was undeniably caveman mentality, but as he brought the blood to the top of the skin, he felt satisfied. Swirling his tongue through the small patch of closely cropped curls, Ryker glanced over at Ranger. Although he was still stroking himself, he had a look on his face Ryker had never seen before. Lilly thrust her hips, and wrapped her fingers in his hair, pushing him lower. Well if that wasn't a hint, he smiled. Separating the lips of her pussy, Ryker inhaled. Damn, her scent was forever imprinted in his soul. He licked the soft folds, scraping his teeth lightly across the tender flesh, before sliding his tongue through her channel and up to her clit. Taking the swollen flesh in his mouth, he bit down gently. Lilly moaned and gripped his hair in a tighter fist. Releasing his hold on her clit, he moved down to delve his tongue deep into her core. Ryker moaned as Lilly's taste exploded across his tongue. He felt his pre-cum dripping down onto the blanket and knew if he didn't bury himself in her depths he would die.

Ryker looked up from his position between Lilly's thighs and looked at Ranger. "You plan on joining us?"

"Yeah," Ranger said looking up into the rain. "I'm trying to figure out what area to delve into first."

Ryker saw that look pass over Ranger's face again as he stretched out beside Lilly and took her mouth in an erotic, tongue lashing kiss. Ryker watched them for a few seconds making sure Ranger was indeed okay with this, before reaching for a condom. Tearing the foil package open he looked to Ranger. The question of who would make love to Lilly first had never really been discussed, and Ryker wanted to make sure before taking the lead.

Ranger gave him a solemn look and nodded. Ryker assumed the look had to do with the fact that Ranger wanted a turn. Well, he'd have to just wait. As Ryker rolled the condom down his length, the sky opened up. "Would you rather take this back to the house?" he asked Ranger and Lilly.

Lilly shook her head. "Not until I'm officially yours."

Deciding they needed to get Lilly into the house as soon as possible, Ryker reached down and checked to make sure Lilly was wet enough. He knew the first time would be a little painful, but at least he could make sure she was well lubed. Smiling, he buried two fingers in her drenched pussy. Pulling them back out, he held his fingers to Ranger's lips. "Our lady's ready."

Ryker moaned as Ranger took the offered gift, licking Ryker's fingers clean before releasing them. Leaning over her, Ryker held his cock by the root and positioned it at her wet pussy. As he slowly, inched his way inside her tight sheath, he watched her face for any sign of discomfort. What he saw, was the face of a woman in transformation. When his cock came to the barrier of her virginity, Ryker kissed her. "This might hurt for a second."

Lilly's answer was to thrust up, impaling herself on his cock. Her face showed nothing of pain, only joy as she tossed her head from side to side. Confident that Lilly could handle him, Ryker began a slow rhythm in and out of her wonderfully tight pussy. "So good," he moaned, as her body tightened around his cock every time he withdrew. He saw Ranger sit up out of his peripheral vision and figured Ranger was stepping back to give Ryker and Lilly this special time together. God he loved that man.

As Ranger watched Ryker and Lilly he felt something shift inside him. This was as big a step for Ranger as it was for Lilly. He'd seen Ryker have sex with women before, just as Ryker had seen him, but this was different. This was Ryker declaring his love for Lilly. Though their relationship was admittedly odd, he and Ryker had never had intercourse with each other. They allowed themselves to express their love through kisses and hand jobs. Hell, once or twice they'd even gotten drunk and given each other head, but they'd always drawn the line at penetration. Now, looking at the love in Ryker's eyes, a wave of jealousy clouded his vision. They'd always loved each other, been connected in a way no one else had understood, but until this moment he'd never known the true depths of those feelings. Now watching Ryker making love to Lilly, Ranger was suddenly terrified Lilly would somehow take his place in Ryker's heart. That she would have a piece of Ryker he'd never have.

Ranger pulled back a little and watched as Ryker and Lilly writhed on the blanket as one. They were so beautiful together. Suddenly, Ranger was glad it was raining so neither of them would notice the tears that began running down his face. This was the reason he'd put Ryker off from Lilly for so long. He'd made excuses about her age for years, but he knew in his heart, this was what he hadn't been prepared for.

As he watched Ryker kiss her, Ranger felt cut-off. He felt his breath hitch as the two of them began to pick up speed. It looked like they'd been doing this for years, both of them looking at each other with love in their eyes. It was suddenly too much and Ranger started to stand, to run back to the safety of his home. What kind of freak was he that he suddenly wished with all his heart that he was Lilly. That Ryker was making love to him. He could never let Ryker know, the thought of seeing disgust aimed towards him from Ryker was enough to keep him silenced forever.

A hand shot out and wrapped around his wrist before he even had time to move. Ranger looked up into Ryker's amethyst eyes. "Don't," was all Ryker said.

Ranger flashed a glance down at Lilly who apparently was in another world. Her neck arched, eyes closed. The knowing look Ryker gave him made him feel ashamed. This was a beautiful moment for Ryker, and Ranger knew he was ruining it. Shame filled him as Ryker drew him in for a kiss, his knowing eyes never breaking contact with Ranger's.

Lilly yelled as she climaxed. They broke their kiss and looked down at her. She was staring at the two of them, watching them kiss. Ranger just hoped like hell she couldn't read his thoughts as well as Bub could. At least he knew he still held his secret.

Ranger watched as the veins in Ryker's neck stood prominently as he emptied his seed into the condom. Several seconds later, he was pulled down with Ryker to help shield Lilly's body from the pounding rain. He watched Ryker give Lilly a tender kiss before turning back to him. He knew what Ryker wanted.

Swallowing his hurt, Ranger placed a tender kiss on Lilly's lips, knowing things may never be the same between him and his brother.

Chapter Eleven

Ranger insisted Ryker cradle Lilly in his arms on the ride home. He was afraid she'd be sore after her first time and didn't want to take chances with her riding on the hard saddle. Now, cradling Lilly's small body against his chest he watched Ranger's back as he rode in front of them.

"What's wrong?" Lilly asked, her head resting on his chest.

"Nothing," Ryker said, holding her a little tighter.

Lilly looked up at him before turning her head to look at Ranger. "Have I done something wrong?"

"No, sweetheart, you haven't done anything wrong." He looked down and gave her a tentative smile. "Ranger's hurting. I'm not sure why, but I can feel it, I always could."

"Do you want me to leave?"

"No, but I need a little time alone with him to try and find out what's going on. I'll draw you a nice hot bath when we get home and while you're soaking and getting warm, I'll talk to him." He just hoped Ranger would let him. Ryker knew the second Ranger started to pull away. It was almost like a physical sensation going off in his brain. He wished he knew the reason. The only thing he could come up with was that Ranger had figured out he'd never be able to fall in love with Lilly. The thought broke his heart. Loving her was as natural as breathing to him, and he wouldn't give her up without a fight.

He thought about what it had felt like to finally sink his cock into Lilly, knowing no one had been there before. She was tight and hot, and goddamn he loved her.

As Ryker rode up to the barn, Ranger was there to take Lilly into his arms. He waited until Ryker dismounted and passed her back. "I'll take care of the horses while you get Lilly warm and dry."

Ryker felt like a lead weight had landed in his stomach. Taking a deep breath he nodded and carried Lilly inside. He felt like he was outside his body, unable to reconcile his feeling between his brother and the woman he loved. Drawing a warm bath, he used his favourite bath salts and lit Lilly a few candles. It was bad enough he was going to leave her after making love for the first time to talk to Ranger. He didn't want her to think she was unloved.

Slipping under the water, Lilly cupped his cheek. "Go to him, I'll be fine."

Ryker leaned over the edge of the tub and kissed her, trying to put all the love he felt into this one awkward moment. "Hopefully I won't be long."

Lilly gave him a slight smile and nodded. He could tell by the strained look on her face that she was hurting as well. Dammit, this was supposed to be the answer to all his prayers, so why did everyone he loved feel sad?

Ryker closed his eyes and stood. Walking out to the great room, he spotted Ranger making a fire even though it was barely October. Sitting on the floor in front of the large river stone hearth, he stared at the flames. "Talk to me."

"Huh?" Ranger looked over seemingly unaware that Ryker had even entered the room. "Where's Lilly?"

"Taking a bath. I came to talk to you." He reached out and ran his fingers through Ranger's wet curls. "What happened back there?"

"What do you mean? I think you were pretty much involved in the whole process," Ranger tried to pass Ryker's comments off as a joke.

Ryker put a hand to either side of Ranger's head and made him look him in the eyes. "What happened to you while I was making love to Lilly? Don't tell me nothing because I could feel it—feel you—pulling away from us."

Ranger shut his eyes. Ryker watched as his Adams apple bobbed up and down in the firelight. He could tell Ranger was trying not to cry. He'd only seen him cry twice before. The day their Dad died and the night Sonny was shot. Ranger was tough, always had been. He was the one who'd held Ryker together when they'd been forced to leave their home at the age of eighteen. It had always been Ranger.

Now his brother clung to him fighting to keep the tears at bay. "I'm scared," Ranger finally whispered in a guttural voice.

He pulled Ranger into his arms and buried his face in his neck. "I love you. You're part of me, I can't live unless I know you're beside me, but I love Lilly, too. Please don't ask me to give her up."

Ranger shook his head, "Never. I'd never ask you to do that. I'm not sure how I'll fit in with the two of you though. I like Lilly, a lot, but it doesn't feel right making love to her knowing I don't love her like you do, and I'm not sure I ever will. She's yours and she always will be. So where does that leave me?"

Fuck! He'd never even thought of a scenario like this happening between them. "Are you saying I can't have you both? That I have to somehow choose?"

"No, my mind's just all screwed up right now." Ranger said.

Feeling a warm hand on his back, Ryker turned to see Lilly, wrapped in the large blue terry robe he'd laid out for her. "Can I say something?" Lilly asked chewing on her lip.

Nodding, Ryker released one of his arms that held Ranger and pulled Lilly into a hug. The feel of both of them against him was right, dammit.

"I know I shouldn't have heard what I did, but I'm glad I took the chance." Lilly kissed Ranger's cheek. "I don't want to take Ryker away from you. And I was wondering if you could give us a chance. I don't expect you to vow your undying love for me right away, but I already love you, I have for years. Just give me the opportunity to show you I'm not trying to come between the two of you? I wanna make a life here, with Ryker and you. I can be patient, give you time, hell, I'll give you whatever you need. But please, don't give up on me. I'm not sure how you feel about sharing his love and attention, but I'd rather have part of him than none of him."

"How does that work?" Ranger asked, his voice hoarse with emotion.

"I'm not sure. This is all new to me. Maybe we could both try loving Ryker and maybe someday soon you'll grow to love me, too."

Lilly didn't have to spell it out. He knew she was talking about intimacy between her and Ryker and between him and Ranger. She seemed to know his brother pretty well. Ranger didn't want to make love to Lilly with his feelings still up in the air and Lilly was saying she understood that. She was also telling Ranger he could still be intimate with him and she'd give them the space to do that. He shook his head, finding it hard to believe he'd found a woman who understood what Ranger meant to him.

Time seemed to stand still as Ranger and Lilly looked at each other. Ryker finally released the breath he'd been holding when Ranger kissed the tip of Lilly's nose. "We'll see how it goes. Who knows, maybe it's my own confusion about what comes next that's getting in the way." He cupped Lilly's cheek. "I do care for you, no matter what, I need you to understand that. I'm just confused right now. Who knows, I may wake up tomorrow and realise I'm madly in love with you and this whole conversation will have been wasted."

"Never wasted," Lilly kissed Ranger's forehead. "Your feelings are as important to me as Ryker's, and if something's bothering you, we need to work it out together."

"Deal," Ranger agreed.

* * * *

The alarm woke them the next morning. Ryker was in his usual spot sandwiched between Ranger and Lilly. Stretching, he wrapped himself around Lilly as Ranger snuggled up to his back. "I don't want to go to work," he groaned, burying his head against Lilly's warm neck.

"Sorry, Bub, but we've got a hundred head being loaded this morning for auction." Ranger kissed his shoulder.

"What's your day like, sweetheart?" he asked as he kissed his way around Lilly's shoulder and neck.

"I need to call the insurance company and see what they're going to do about my car. I have to be at work at three, but I'll get off around eleven-thirty if we aren't too busy." She groaned as he slid his fingers between her pussy lips to the core of her.

"You sore?" Ryker asked, nipping her shoulder.

"No, make love to me," she said, turning her head for a kiss.

Ryker looked over his shoulder at Ranger. "We have time for some love?"

"Yeah," Ranger said, "I'll just go get in the shower."

"I really wish you wouldn't try to run away every time I wanna make love to Lilly." He pulled Ranger's head down for a kiss.

Wide-eyed, Ranger looked over at Lilly. "Is that okay with you?"

"Of course," she smiled at Ranger.

Rummaging in the drawer, Ranger came back with a condom and lube.

Ryker watched as a spark of desire flashed across Ranger's face as he threw back the covers. With the three of them nude, it was easy to see Ranger's need in the erection bobbing against his stomach. He is scared, Ryker thought. It wasn't that he didn't desire the two of them together, it went deeper. Ryker was determined to root out the problem, and soon.

Sitting back on his heels, he looked at the condom in Ranger's hand. "Care to put it on me?"

Looking nervous, Ranger tore open the package and scooted closer. Ryker pulled him into a kiss as Ranger slid the latex down his aching cock. His hands felt natural on Ryker's shaft as they continued to kiss, Ranger reaching down to run his fingers over Ryker's heavy sac.

A physical shiver from him and a moan from Lilly broke their kiss. "Thank you," he whispered against Ranger's lips.

He hoped Ranger understood he was thanking him for everything, not just the sexy two-minute hand job.

"Stretch out beside Lilly, I'd like to look into the eyes of the two people I love." He smiled as Ranger did as he asked. "Feel free to play if the mood strikes," he teased as he placed the head of his cock to Lilly's core.

As his cock slid into the tight channel, Ryker leaned over and kissed her, pushing his tongue in as deep as his shaft. "Oh, sweetheart." He felt Lilly's body tighten around him as he pulled out only to fill her again.

The harder he thrust into her, the more she appeared to like it. He smiled when he watched as Ranger put a hand on her lower stomach, stroking her soft skin. Ryker didn't think Ranger was even aware he was doing it. His smile grew wider. That was a very good sign.

Lilly's gaze connected with his, yep, Lilly was thinking the same thing. Hooking one of her legs over his shoulder, he looked down at Ranger. "Help a brother out?"

Ranger grinned and held Lilly's other leg up against his body. As his hips pistoned faster, driving his cock deep into her depths, Lilly's breathing changed, going from panting to stuttering. He knew she was close. Reaching out, he held his finger in front of Ranger's mouth who automatically opened and laved Ryker's digit thoroughly.

Withdrawing his finger he positioned it at Lilly's back puckered hole and slowly inserted it. If she was going to eventually make love to both of them at the same time, she'd need to get used to having both holes filled.

Lilly, it seemed, was more than ready. As soon as he breached her tight ring of muscles her back bowed, body tightening around his cock. Her cry of release was like music to his ears. Removing his finger he buried himself and pumped his seed into the condom. Falling forward, he caught himself with his arms and loomed over her. Sealing their passionate session with a kiss, he moaned as he felt Ranger's hand skim down his back to land on his ass.

Turning his head, he kissed Ranger. Ryker was surprised when a finger ran down the crack of his ass to tap against his hole. He opened his eyes, still kissing Ranger's soft lips. The small touch was beginning to wake his cock, still buried inside Lilly.

Ranger seemed to realise what he'd done and his eyes flew open. For a split second, the need was apparent. Could it be? His train of thought was interrupted as Ranger leapt off the bed. "I'm going to grab a shower," he mumbled walking away.

Ryker closed his eyes. A soft hand to the side of his face had him smiling. Opening his eyes he stared down into Lilly's jade green jewels. "I'm in love with you."

"I know. I can feel it when you look at me," Lilly replied, bringing his head down for another kiss. Their tongues lapped at each other's mouths as his hands buried themselves in Lilly's long black curls.

"We have a lot of head of cattle to get loaded this morning, but maybe I can talk Ranger into taking the afternoon off. I thought we could go to the walk-in clinic in Lincoln."

Lilly smiled and wrapped her legs around him. "I like that idea. As long as I can be at work by three-thirty, I'm game."

Ryker licked a path from her ear down to the hollow of her neck. Swirling his tongue in the divot of skin, he moaned. "I want to bury myself deep inside your sweet pussy without anything between us."

"Mmm hmm," Lilly sighed as he worked his way down to her pebbled nipple. Nipping at the turgid flesh with his teeth, he laved the sting with his tongue. "Did you like when I filled your ass with my finger?"

"Yes," she whispered.

"I want the three of us to make love. That'll mean either Ranger or me taking you there. Are you okay with that?"

"Yes," she grinned. "Actually I look forward to it." Lilly looked towards the bathroom door. "Maybe we should get Ranger drunk and seduce him."

"I thought about asking Sonny to talk to him. Whatever's really wrong with him, he won't tell me, but maybe he'll open up to Sonny."

Lilly shook her head. "You know he won't. If he eventually opens up to anyone it'll be you. I think the two of you need to go out drinking. It's been my experience that more things are said with liquor on the breath."

"Maybe we'll just get drunk here. Ranger likes to dance when he drinks and I'd rather be home for that." Ryker heard the water shut off in the bathroom. "Don't be surprised if you come home tonight to two sloppy drunks. Ranger can usually drink me under the table so it'll take a lot to get him loose lipped."

"I'll happily pour you both into bed."

Chapter Twelve

By lunch-time the three of them were on their way to Lincoln. On orders from Ranger, Ryker drove this time. It appeared Ranger didn't want a replay of their last trip. The highway thrummed under the tires as they travelled up the interstate. "So what did the insurance company say about your car?"

"That they were totalling it, and the check should be to me by the end of the week. It won't be much, but maybe I can use it, with some of my savings on a down payment for another one."

Ranger who'd been looking out the passenger window turned towards Lilly. "What are ya looking for?"

She shrugged and turned the stereo down. "Don't really care. Something cheap and reliable."

"Oh, that mystery dream car that every used car buyer searches for," Ryker joked. He reached down and squeezed Lilly's thigh. "We'll find something."

"Yeah, I was going to ask if we could go into the city this weekend."

"Sure," Ranger said, placing a kiss on Lilly's forehead.

Ryker almost drove out of his lane at the unsolicited gesture.

Ranger must have caught the look on his face because he cleared his throat and looked back out the window. He knew Ranger wasn't as unaffected by Lilly as he let on. Now he just needed to find a way to get Ranger to see it.

"I thought maybe Bub and I would come into the Zone for dinner later. Check to make sure Jeff isn't anywhere around."

He'd said it so casually. Ryker knew Lilly wouldn't think anything about it, but he could tell by the tick of his jaw that this thing with Jeff had been on his mind. Ryker'd heard Ranger talking to Rawley on the phone earlier in the day. He knew they hadn't found any evidence to link Jeff with the vandalism, but Rawley had promised to have a Sheriff's department vehicle out in the parking lot when Lilly got off shift.

"Oh, it's a good night too. Kathy's making pot roast." Lilly gave Ryker a look, eyebrow raised.

"We'll probably just stay for dinner and a couple beers before heading home." He looked over at the back of Ranger's head before giving Lilly a wink.

* * * *

The clinic was a busy, but they'd promised to give the three of them a call the next day with their test results. "One more day," Ryker sighed as he tilted the icy mug of beer to his lips.

"Yep," Ranger said absently. His mood brightened when he spotted Garron and Sonny coming through the door. Ranger stood and waved them over. "Hey, guys, what brings you to the Zone?"

Sonny and Garron looked at each other and said at the same time, "Pot roast."

Smiling, he sat back down. "Pull up a chair." He saw Lilly making her way over to them. There didn't seem to be as many drinkers here tonight as there were roast eaters.

Lilly kissed Sonny's forehead. "It's good to see you in here again. You two looking to eat the special?"

"You know it," Garron said, rubbing his palms together in anticipation.

Lilly grinned and turned towards him and Ryker. "Another round of beer?"

Ranger nodded and finished off his mug. "Thanks, sweetheart."

Lilly picked up the two empty glasses and raised her brows at Garron and Sonny. "Beer or whiskey?"

Garron spoke up, "Beer for me and a Coke for Sonny."

As soon as Lilly walked off, Ranger turned to his brother. "You been having headaches again?" He knew Sonny didn't drink when he was taking pain medication for his headaches.

"A few," Sonny shrugged.

Ranger reached across the table and covered Sonny's hand. "You call if you need anything."

Sonny chuckled and rolled his eyes. "I think you've got your hands pretty full right now, but it's nice to know."

A picture of having his hands full of Ryker and Lilly flashed through Ranger's mind. He immediately felt his cock harden behind the fly of his jeans as he pictured the three of them making love, only instead of them both inside Lilly he was buried deep inside Ryker. A beer being set in front of him snapped him back to the present. He felt his face heat at the thoughts that had swirled around his head all day. What the hell was going on with him? He shook his head in disgust.

Carol Lynne

And just like that his mood turned. Needing to get away, he drank his beer as fast as his throat would allow. When he set the empty mug on the scarred table top, he looked over at Lilly. "I'd like my food to-go." Ranger said, his voice deep and rough.

"Sure, I'll go tell Kathy to put it in a container." Lilly looked at him for another second or two before turning and walking towards the kitchen.

"Something wrong?" Ryker asked.

"Need to leave." He looked at Ryker, the image of being buried inside him still fresh in his mind. "You stay. Have Garron and Sonny drop you off on their way by."

Without waiting for a reply he stood and walked towards the bar, Lilly was just coming out of the kitchen with his dinner. Digging in his pocket, he hoped Lilly wouldn't notice his rock hard erection. He pulled out a twenty and handed it to her. "Good-bye."

Turning on his heel, he left the bar and drove straight to the liquor store.

* * * *

By the time he was dropped off, Ryker had worked himself up pretty good. He'd wanted to leave with Ranger earlier, but the stubborn ass hadn't even given him a chance. He'd been forced to try and explain Ranger's actions to not only Lilly but Sonny and Garron as well.

Needing time alone before he confronted Ranger, Ryker had Garron drop him at the end of the drive. Now, as he walked the long gravel drive, he started to feel strange. At first he thought maybe it was the beer and food combined with the worry that was upsetting him, but as the ache became more severe he knew it was more, it was Ranger. Something was wrong.

Despite the ache in his gut, Ryker took off running through the trees towards home. As soon as he broke through to the clearing he noticed Ranger's truck wasn't parked in its usual spot. "Fuck," he screamed to the singing birds as he ran up the steps and into the house.

The first place he went was to the bedroom. Seeing the closet door ajar, Ryker swallowed the bile rising in his throat. He knew what he'd find before he even opened it. The ache in his gut telling him Ranger had gone.

After checking out the closet, Ryker picked up the phone in a daze.

"Dead Zone."

"I need to talk to Lilly," he managed to rasp out.

After a few long minutes, Lilly got on the phone. "Hello?"

"He's gone."

"What?"

"Ranger's gone. I came home and most of his clothes are missing. He's left me." He felt the sting of tears seconds before they began to fall. "I'm gonna have Garron bring me back to the bar to pick up my truck. I gotta go find him."

"No. I'll be home as soon as I can. I love you," she said before hanging up.

He fell back onto the bed and covered his eyes with his arm. "Where are you?" he whispered to the quiet room. Replaying the scene in the bar once again, Ryker tried to figure out what had set Ranger off. No matter how many times he went through the conversations, nothing odd stuck out in his mind.

The pillow under his head was Ranger's and when he turned he could smell his familiar scent. As he buried his face in Ranger's pillow, a thought occurred to him. "Shit," he said picking up the phone. He hit speed-dial and waited for Ranger to answer. Why hadn't he thought of it before? His hopes were soon dashed when Ranger's voice mail answered telling him to leave a message.

"I need you. Why'd you leave me? You've never done that before and I don't even know what I did wrong. Please, love, please call me."

* * * *

Fumbling with the phone, Ranger was barely able to figure out how to retrieve his message. Hearing Bub's voice asking what he'd done wrong was like someone taking their finger out of the hole in the dam. A rush of regret and self loathing washed over him in a wave of pain. Throwing the phone down, he picked up his second bottle of Jack, sloshing a good amount down his chin as he drank.

Looking around, he sighed. Sonny, he thought. Maybe I need to call Sonny. Although he was the youngest of the Good boys, Sonny seemed to be the glue that kept them all together lately. Since his injury, Sonny had changed, and in Ranger's opinion, for the better. He couldn't just leave town without telling someone where he was going and he knew if he tried to tell Ryker, his Bub would say anything he thought he wanted to hear to make him stay.

Falling off the couch in his attempt to retrieve his phone, he shook his head. "Damn, who moved the couch on me?" Blinking his eyes several times, he studied the display on the tiny phone before remembering Sonny's number.

"Hello?"

Ranger opened his mouth to talk and a sob erupted instead.

"Where are you? Ryker called here frantic. He's got Lilly on the way to pick him up so they can look for you."

"Don't tell." Ranger fell back to the floor and rubbed his eyes.

"Okay I won't. Just tell me and we'll figure this out together."

"The apartment. I can't go back there, Sonny. I can't. I'm...there's something wrong with me."

"You just stay where you are and I'll come over. Don't you move."

"Gotta throw up," he said getting to his knees. He tried to stand and fell back again. He heaved what little contents his stomach held and fell back to the floor.

Chapter Thirteen

Running towards Ryker's truck, Lilly was so busy digging the keys out that she didn't notice Jeff pull up. Opening the door, a hand reached out and grabbed her arm.

"I heard you was messing with them Good twins. I was right about you. You're nothing but a filthy slut." Jeff pressed her against the side of the truck flinging the door the rest of the way open. With a hand around her throat, he pushed her down onto the seat. With her legs still on the ground, Lilly's back felt like it would break in her present position.

"I don't have time for this," she tried to get up, scratching at Jeff's face, hoping to get free.

A jarring slap to the side of her face stopped her. "Listen to me, bitch, if you can spread your legs for those queer perverts, you can spread for me. Nobody teases me and gets away with it." He started unfastening her jeans, the smell of his breath a testament to how much he'd already drank before coming to the bar.

Looking around, Lilly spotted the keys on the floorboard where Jeff had tossed them in his haste to get her into the truck. Taking a deep breath, she managed to get a hold on his hair with one hand. She pulled and kicked while stretching out to grab the keys. Another blow to her cheek came seconds before she swiped a key across his smarmy face.

"Fuck," Jeff screamed, releasing her and bringing his hands to his face. Blood ran between his fingers as she kicked him out of the way. Jeff seemed to be so shocked that she'd hurt him he let his guard down long enough for her to scramble and get the door closed and locked.

As soon as he heard the snick of the lock, he charged the truck, his face red from both blood and fury. Lilly's hands were shaking as she worked the key into the ignition. A loud crack sounded and she looked over just in time to see Jeff's foot come flying once again towards the driver's side window. Putting the truck in reverse, she hit the gas, not caring whether she ran him over or not.

Pulling out of the lot at a high rate of speed, she looked around the truck for her purse. "Dammit," she screamed when she realised it must still be in the parking lot. Lilly didn't know if Jeff would follow her or not, but she didn't have time for this shit. She knew if she went to the Sheriff's station they'd make her stay until they tracked Jeff down. Unwilling to waste the time, she decided to go straight to Rawley's house.

Lilly honked her horn as she pulled up at Jeb and Rawley's ranch road. Both men came flying out of the house, running towards the truck. She tried to get the window down but the damn thing wouldn't budge. Finally opening the door, Rawley pulled her out of the truck. He took one look at her face and cussed as he held her in a tight embrace.

Shaking off his hold, she tried to calm down enough to tell him what happened. "I can't stay, Ryker needs me."

"He didn't?" Rawley's face went white.

"No, it was Jeff. He attacked me, tried to get my pants off in the parking lot. I hurt him. You'll see the evidence on his face. He's probably half-way to Lincoln by now. Arrest him, do whatever you have to do, but I have to get home to Ryker. Ranger's gone. We don't know where but we're going to find him."

"What?" Rawley gave Lilly a gentle shake. "Slow down, where's Ranger?"

Exasperated, Lilly huffed. "I don't know. Ryker got home and his clothes were gone. I need to go," she tried to pull away. "They need me." The words stopped her. "Or maybe they don't," she said in a small voice. "Maybe I'm the problem." It was suddenly too much and she started to sink to her knees. "Oh God, this can't be happening." Her dreams were crashing down around her as Rawley did his best to hold her upright.

Turning his head, Rawley yelled for Jeb. "Get my truck."

The next thing she knew she was being cradled in Jeb's arms as Rawley drove towards Ryker and Ranger's house. Jeb dabbed at the tears on her cheek with a bandana. "I called the station. They'll find Jeff. It'll be okay, Lilly. We'll get you to Ryker and help you find Ranger." He continued to talk to her until, in her exhaustion she drifted off.

* * * *

Ryker heard the sound of a vehicle pull up and ran to the front door. Opening it, he was surprised to see Rawley running towards him through the dark yard. "What're you doing here?"

Rawley ran up the steps and blocked his view of the truck. "There's been a situation."

"Yeah, I know, I'm waiting for Lilly to get home so we can find him."

"No. Yes. Oh fuck." Rawley ran his fingers through his hair. "I know Ranger's gone, and we'll help you find him, but right now Lilly needs you."

"Lilly?" He tried to look around Rawley's bigger body. "Where is she?"

Rawley grabbed his shoulders to keep him still. "She's in the truck with Jeb. Jeff attacked her in the parking lot of the Zone."

"What," Ryker fought the restraining hands trying to hold him back. "Let me go," he growled taking a swing at Rawley.

"You need to calm down before you upset her even more. Jeb called the station and we've got people out looking for Jeff. He'll be charged, but Lilly's the one I'm most concerned with. She seems to think Ranger left because of her."

"No! It's because of me." He struggled again. "So help me God, if you don't let go of me I'm gonna kill you." He narrowed his eyes at Rawley who released him, holding his hands up and backing off.

Running to the truck, Ryker swung open Jeb's door. Lilly was cradled in his arms with her head buried in his neck. "She's asleep," Jeb whispered.

"Get in," Rawley said, getting behind the wheel. "We'll drive around and see if we can't find Ranger."

Jeb scooted over as much as he could while still holding Lilly. Ryker climbed in and immediately took her into his arms. When she was transferred, Ryker got his first look at her face. Two big bruises were blossoming on her otherwise perfect skin. "Oh, sweetheart," he said, cupping her face in his hand.

Lilly opened her eyes and looked up at him. "I'm sorry."

"Shhh, just rest while we look for Ranger," he soothed. He looked down and noticed her unbuttoned jeans, the zipper half down. "Sweetheart? Did he touch you?" He asked, pulling up her zipper. He flashed a scowl at Rawley and Jeb who shook their heads like they hadn't noticed.

"N-No, he tried, but I cut his face with the keys."

Bending down, he tilted her chin and kissed her. The overwhelming relief that that animal hadn't raped her had him squeezing her to his chest. "He'll pay for this, sweetheart. Ranger will make sure of it." The thought of Ranger finding out what Jeff had done seemed to galvanize his strength. Ranger may be able to just walk out on him, but he'd never let someone hurt Lilly and get away with it.

* * * *

Sonny let himself in to the apartment above the feedlot offices. "Ranger," he called as he entered the dark living room. Stumbling around, he finally found the light switch and flipped it on. "Oh shit," he said as he saw Ranger face down on the carpet beside a pile of vomit.

Squatting beside his brother, he rolled him over. "Ranger," he said, slapping his cheeks. Sonny couldn't tell if Ranger was just passed out or if he needed an ambulance. He started to worry when he couldn't rouse him. Ranger was a lot bigger than he was, so he knew he couldn't carry him into the bathroom.

Rubbing his chin, he looked around the apartment. With a grin on his face, he walked into the kitchen and dug around until he came up with a large stew pot. Filling the pan with ice cold water, Sonny carried it back to Ranger. "Forgive me, brother." He poured the contents of the pot in Ranger's face, after making sure it was at least turned to the side. The last thing he needed was to drown him while trying to help.

Ranger coughed and swatted at the water pouring down on him. "What the hell?" Ranger tried to sit up but fell back to the carpet.

After setting down the pan, Sonny helped Ranger to the sofa, away from the mess. "You called me over here and then passed out." He took the blanket off the back of the couch and dried Ranger's face and hair. Ranger was still swaying until his head fell onto the back of the old sofa.

Sonny had never seen Ranger like this. He wasn't sure that he'd even seen him tipsy more than a couple times in his life, but this? Something was seriously wrong. While he waited for Ranger to wake up a bit, he pulled out his cell and called Garron.

"Sonny?" Garron asked as soon as he picked up the phone.

"Yeah, it's me. I found him passed out next to a pile of puke. I got him onto the couch but I still don't know what the problem is."

"Rawley came by looking for him. He had Ryker and Lilly in the truck with him and Jeb. Babe, Jeff attacked Lilly tonight when she left the bar to go home."

"Shit, is she okay?" He looked over at a still dazed Ranger.

"Physically she seems okay. She's got a couple bruises on her face where he hit her. Damn, babe, I guess he tried to rape her."

"What!"

"He didn't get further than undoing her jeans before she slashed him across the face with the keys and managed to get away, but emotionally she's not doing well. Rawley said on top of everything else she's been through this evening, she's blaming herself for Ranger."

"What the hell is going on?" Sonny shook his head. "Okay, give me fifteen minutes then call Rawley and let him know where we are."

"Sure thing, you doing all right? Getting a headache or anything?"

Sonny smiled at the concern in Garron's voice. "I'm fine. Just need to put my family back together."

"Well if anyone can do it, it's you. Love you."

"Love you. I'll call when they get here." Sonny hung up and looked at Ranger. "Come on, wake up. We need to talk, and there are some things you need to hear."

Chapter Fourteen

Giving Ranger another cup of coffee, Sonny stepped into the bathroom and called Ryker.

"Hello?"

"Did Garron call?"

"Just a few minutes ago. We're on our way."

"Well, I'd like you to stay outside 'til I come get you. I'm not trying to piss you off, but he asked me here to talk, and I'm just now getting him sober enough to form sentences."

"Sober?"

"He was passed out when I got here." Sonny went on to tell Ryker what he'd found. He heard Ryker's broken sigh on the other end. "Please, let me talk to him. I don't know what's going on with the three of you, but I've never seen him like this."

"I'll be waiting at the bottom of the steps."

Sonny hung up and flushed the toilet, hiding the phone away in his pocket. "You ready for another cup?" he asked walking back into the living room.

Ranger turned his head and looked at him through half-closed eyes. "Doesn't matter," he sighed, "nothing does."

Stopping by the kitchen Sonny filled a cup for himself before carrying the pot to the living room. He topped-off Ranger's and set the pot down on the table. "Drink," he pointed towards the cup. "Then you can tell me why nothing matters."

Taking a sip of the hot brew, Ranger stared into the black depths. Sonny thought he was about to drop off again when he finally spoke. "I can't do it anymore."

"What can't you do? Are you talking about your new relationship with Lilly? I thought you really like her."

"I did. I do. But…I'm jealous."

"Jealous?" Sonny didn't understand. Ranger and Ryker had bedded several women in the past, why was this one making him feel this way? Setting his cup down, he scooted closer to Ranger, who it seemed had curled in on himself. "You're jealous when you see Ryker making love to her?"

"Yeah."

"And she doesn't let you make love to her?" Hell, maybe Ranger wanted Lilly all to himself.

"I haven't really tried."

Sonny rubbed his eyes. It was like trying to get a piece of candy out of a child's hand. "I'm sorry, but I still don't understand. Why are you jealous?"

In a moment of sudden rage, Ranger threw his cup across the room. "Because she gets to make love to Ryker."

Trying to calm his brother, Sonny cupped his face. "I love you so much and I really am trying to understand…"

Before he could get any further, Ranger broke down, tears pooling in his eyes. "I'm sick. That's why I have to go away. I love him so much, and I want to make love to him. And I know that's dirty and wrong, but I can't help myself." The tears began running down his chiselled cheeks as Sonny pulled him into his arms.

"Are you telling me the two of you have never had sex?" That was totally unbelievable to him. He'd never known two closer people in his life. The love they had for each other was completely pure, whether the rest of the population felt so or not. The idea that Ranger had never allowed himself to physically demonstrate that love with Ryker broke his heart.

He hugged Ranger tighter, rocking him back and forth. "I had no idea. We all just assumed…"

"We kiss, we jack each other off, but there's a line we promised we wouldn't cross. It never hurt like this until I watched Lilly and Ryker make love for the first time. They love each other so much that it wasn't just about sex. It was like, while I watched, their souls joined."

Ranger pulled back and buried his face in his hands. "I've thought of nothing since but making love to him."

"Tell him."

"No, I'd rather just leave than to have him look at me with disgust."

"Ranger, forget about what society thinks for a minute. Who told you not to make love to the person you love most in the world?" He already had a good idea, but he needed to hear it.

"Dad. He came into our room one night after we thought everyone was asleep. We were almost eighteen, but we still couldn't sleep apart. So after everyone else was down for the night, Ryker would crawl into bed with me. We didn't do anything then, not even kissing. We just needed to hold each other. But one night Dad came in and caught us. He screamed at us and told us we were disgusting. That we were too old for that kind of thing and it would only lead to us fucking each other like a couple of sick perverts. We promised him we'd never do something like that. Then we begged him to allow us to sleep together at night."

Ranger looked into his eyes. "We both know how that ended. We tried for two nights to sleep apart. Ryker would try and hold my hand from his bed. Dad came in almost every hour to make sure we were separated. Finally it was too much, so we moved out." He looked around the apartment. "We were damn lucky Mr. Zook let us live up here and finish high school."

Running his hand over Ranger's wet curls, Sonny sighed. "I won't begin to understand the bond the two of you have. I don't think anyone could understand unless they had the same thing." Sonny stood and walked over to the front window. He saw Ryker and Lilly sitting on the bottom step.

"Society thinks it's morally wrong to want what you want, but it used to be acceptable. Just look at all the old Royal families. They married within their own family quite often. Over time, people decided it was wrong. I think a lot of it has to do with inbreeding, but hell, you and Ryker don't have to worry about that." He tried to chuckle but it stuck in his throat.

"My point is we think it's wrong because someone told us it was. You're two grown men, and as private as the two of you already are, I see absolutely nothing wrong with expressing your love the way the two of you want."

He looked back towards the couch. Ranger was looking at him in awe. "You mean you wouldn't be grossed out?"

"Ranger, everyone already thinks the two of you are making love. And I mean everyone. The people who still love you and talk to you are the ones who've looked beyond society's code of morals to their own set. And what they see is two people very much in love." Sonny walked over to the door. "There are a couple of people sitting out here that would like to talk to you. Just be honest with them."

Sonny opened the door. Ryker and Lilly were already standing, looking up expectantly. Turning back once more, he smiled at Ranger. "I love you, brother, I'll always love you." He turned and walked down the stairs to stand in front of Ryker and Lilly. Seeing Lilly's face he placed a kiss on her nose. "He's coming down from a pretty good drunk. He was lucky he emptied his stomach of a lot of the whiskey but be warned, it smells like the inside of a Jack Daniels bottle in there."

Ryker grabbed him up in a hug. "Thank you." He looked at him for a few seconds. "Can you tell me what it was that set him off?"

"Shame." Sonny kissed Ryker's cheek. "Talk to him." Sonny looked at Lilly. "If you'd sit down here with me for a few minutes, I'd appreciate it."

Seeming to understand, Lilly turned to Ryker and kissed him. "Go get him and talk him into coming home."

* * * *

As he walked up the stairs, Ryker's mind played through a dozen different scenarios of why Ranger would feel so ashamed he'd leave him. Didn't he understand nothing would ever make him want Ranger gone?

With a twist of the knob, he was standing inside the apartment that held so many memories. Damn, Sonny hadn't been kidding about the smell of the place. He shook his head and walked towards the couch. Holding out a hand, he gestured towards the back of the apartment. "Let's go talk."

After a few seconds hesitation, Ranger took his hand and managed to stand. Leading him to the bedroom, Ryker put his arm around Ranger's waist. They'd always had their most serious discussions spooned back to front in bed. It only seemed right that they do that now.

Not bothering to take off their shoes, both men stretched out on the small twin-sized bed that had been Ranger's growing up. The only difference was now, Ranger needed to be held. He spooned his body to the back of Ranger's and wrapped him in his arms. "Don't ever do that to me again," he whispered, kissing Ranger's neck.

"Hold judgement until I tell you why I left," Ranger said. As he told him his reasons, Ryker began to hold him even tighter. He wasn't sure what would explode first, his head or his cock. Over the years he'd tried giving Ranger hints while they were in bed together, but Ranger had been so adamant forever about never crossing that line, Ryker had finally given up.

It wasn't until Ranger mentioned the promise they'd made to their father that he understood. To Ranger, a promise was set in stone as soon as the words left his lips. To know a single sentence uttered thirteen years ago had kept them apart angered him. Ryker wasn't mad at Ranger, but at wasted time. He'd always known Ranger would be his life-time love, partner, whatever title a person wanted to attach, but the thought that they could have gone without expressing that love fully because of one stupid promise...

"So, what do you think?" Ranger asked. "I can move back in here if it'll make you uncomfortable to have me living at home."

Ryker smoothed his hand down Ranger's chest to the semi-hard cock trapped in his jeans. He applied a good bit of pressure and kissed his neck. "I've wanted to make love to you since I was fifteen. I know that comes as a shock because we never really talked about it back then, but that doesn't mean I didn't dream about it almost every night."

Ranger stilled a few seconds before turning in his arms. "I love you," Ranger said, taking his mouth in a heated mating of tongues and teeth.

As much as Ryker wanted to strip off Ranger's clothes and make love to him right there, he wanted Lilly with them when it happened. She'd earned the right to be part of this beautiful occasion. Breaking the kiss he cupped Ranger's cheek. "Let's go home. I'd like Lilly to be part of this."

"Do you think she'll be grossed out by us?"

"Lilly? Are you kidding? She loves it when we touch each other. Just think what it'll do to her when she watches us make love." Speaking of Lilly, he knew he needed to tell Ranger about Lilly's attack this evening before he saw her. Ranger's emotions were so close to the surface he wasn't sure how he'd react to the news that Jeff had dared hit their woman. He was grateful that Jeff was right now sitting in a cell at the Sheriff's station. Rawley told him he'd let Jeff sit there overnight until Lilly went in and formally identified him as her attacker.

"Love, before we go, I need to tell you something. It's going to piss you off and you're gonna feel like killing someone, but it's already being taken care of."

"What?" Ranger sat up and looked down at Ryker.

"When Lilly left the bar..." Ryker went on to tell Ranger everything he knew, not wanting to keep anything from him ever again. He banded his arms around Ranger's to help control his instant desire to rush out of the room.

"She's calm now. It took a while, and I don't want you to go running out there and dredge it all back up again. Just love her, please."

"You know I think I can let myself do that now. Love her, I mean. Before there was just too much…"

"Shhh," he whispered kissing Ranger. "Come on, let's go home." Ryker got off the bed and pulled Ranger to his feet. Funny how a good cry and an emotional breakthrough could sober a person. As they walked through the living room arm in arm, he looked at Ranger. "No more Jack for you."

"Don't worry. Jack and I are no longer friends."

Chapter Fifteen

Ranger cradled a still slightly shaken Lilly in his lap the entire ride home. Ryker put his foot down, however, when he attempted to carry her into the house. "You're still too shaky to take chances like that with her," Ryker said, taking Lilly from his arms.

"I can walk," Lilly reminded the pair.

"Yes, you certainly can, but not tonight." Ryker gave her a quick kiss and carried her into the house.

Getting his suitcase out of the truck, he carried it back into the house. He must have known deep down that he wouldn't be able to leave Ryker because he'd never bothered taking the bag up to the apartment.

Setting it in front of the closet, he turned towards Ryker and Lilly. They were both sitting on the end of the bed looking at him. "What?"

Ryker grinned, "We're just waiting for the okay to attack you."

Ranger laughed and spread his arms out to the side. "Attack away."

Before he could take another breath, Lilly was pulling his T-shirt over his head as Ryker fumbled with his jeans. When he started to sway, Ryker stopped and pulled him towards the bed.

"Let's get you horizontal first."

Ranger sat on the bed while Lilly unlaced his work boots and pulled them off. He looked at a still dressed Lilly, her smiling face marred by the puffy looking blue and purple bruises. His insides still seethed with the thought of Jeff touching her. He'd better hope they put him away for a while. Otherwise he'd have to deal with the Good brothers. "Hey," he looked up at Lilly. "Am I the only one getting nekkid around here?"

Lilly grinned and pulled her T-shirt over her head. "I should probably shower. I probably smell like beer and pot roast."

"Two of my favourite things," Ryker said, taking a nip of her exposed breast. He bent back down to pull Ranger's jeans and underwear down and off, before wrapping his arms around Ranger's mid-section.

Threading his fingers through Ryker's curls, he sighed. "Your turn, Bub."

Ryker nodded but didn't remove his head from Ranger's chest. "I just want to hold you for a second."

Now naked, Lilly climbed onto the bed. With her knees planted on either side of Ranger's hips, she pressed herself against Ranger's back. Ranger looked over his shoulder at the plump breast resting there. With one hand buried in Ryker's hair, Ranger used the other to trace the dark areola with his fingertips. "You're so beautiful."

Lilly tilted his head up and ran her tongue over his lips before delving inside for a long, slow kiss. She glanced down at Ryker before meeting Ranger's eyes. "This is a very special night for the two of you."

Ranger glanced down at the top of Ryker's head. "Yes."

"Would you like some time alone?" she asked.

Ranger thought about it for a second. The fact that Lilly even asked warmed his heart. She was a good addition to their family, and for the first time, he honestly felt they all had a future together. "No." When Lilly continued to question him with her eyes, he continued. "After Ryker makes love to me, I'd like to make love to you."

Lilly's brows shot up. "You feel like making love to me?" Lilly asked, her voice coloured by a hint of disbelief.

"It was never that I didn't want to before. It was just that I felt a certain amount of jealousy." He paused and bent to kiss Ryker's head. "It was like being consumed by guilt. I knew I'd never be complete without making love to both of you. I didn't think it would ever be an option, so I figured it was better to not have it than to have half of what I really wanted."

Ryker lifted his head. "Well then, let us give you the whole enchilada." Ryker placed a kiss on his bare chest before standing. He quickly stripped out of his clothes as Lilly folded down the covers as far as she could.

"Snugglefest with you in the middle this time." Lilly pulled him into the centre of the big bed. The sheets were cool against his heated skin as he was surrounded by two beautiful, naked people.

Ryker started by running his hand across Ranger's chest, stopping to pinch and tease at his nipples, before moving to his corrugated abdomen. He traced each ridge and indentation like he was a blind man trying desperately to memorise every detail. Ranger felt his cock drip pre-cum onto his stomach at the loving caresses.

Not wanting to miss out, Lilly quickly moved between Ranger's spread thighs. As she swirled her tongue around his balls, stopping to suck them one at a time, Ranger let himself go. No longer would he think about anything but these two people loving him. He spread further when Ryker joined Lilly at his groin. His cock began to twitch and bob, desperately asking for attention, but both his loves ignored its silent pleas.

"Hold your legs up for me," Ryker moaned, trying to lick a path under his balls to the crease of his ass.

Lilly backed off enough for Ranger to hook his forearms under his knees and pull them to his chest, leaving himself open for Ryker's questing tongue. Lilly, bless her heart, moved around on the bed to straddle his face. Lifting his head, he took his first real taste of Lilly directly from the source. Her cream was sweet and thick and Ranger began eagerly lapping all the essence he could reach.

The first contact Lilly gave his cock was with her tongue, drilling the tip into the dripping slit at the top. "Uhh," he moaned, face buried in her sweet tasting pussy. The combination of Lilly's lips wrapped around the wide girth of his cock, Ryker's tongue lapping against his puckered hole and the taste of Lilly's cream had him on edge. Damn, he didn't want to come. This moment was too perfect to shoot like a teenager.

Blowing a puff of air across Lilly's swollen clit, he gritted his teeth as she moaned, sending a vibration down the length of his cock. The introduction of Ryker's finger into his virgin ass had him crying out as he thrust deeper into Lilly's mouth. "More," he groaned. Taking Lilly's clit into his mouth, Ranger sucked greedily.

Another finger soon followed and a zing of pleasure ran up his body as Ryker found his prostate. Unable to help himself,

Ranger's cock shot burst after burst of pearly white seed down Lilly's throat. He should have felt guilty for not warning her, but right then he didn't even remember his own name. Apologies were the furthest thing from his mind. Lilly evidently had the same problem because within seconds, she began bucking against his face, signalling her own release.

As he tried to catch his breath, Ryker licked a path up his crack, across his sac and spent cock and up the ridges of his torso to land on his mouth. Every inch Ryker licked tingled. Ranger didn't think he'd ever been this sensitive or stimulated in his life. He ate at Ryker's mouth like a starving man, tasting his own earthy essence on Ryker's tongue. "Fuck me," he whispered, when they broke their kiss.

Ryker grinned and nodded. Reaching over to the bedside table, he pulled out the lube and a couple of condoms. As Ryker rolled the latex down his shaft, he seemed to be studying Ranger. "I don't want to hurt you. Like you, I've never done this before."

Reaching up, he grabbed the back of Ryker's neck and pulled him down for another kiss. "It'll hurt more if you don't do this."

Stretching out beside him, Lilly smoothed her hand over his flaccid cock as she rested her head on the pillow beside him. He looked into her jade green eyes, seeing his own love reflected back at him.

A slick finger snapped his head towards Ryker. Kneeling between his spread legs, Ryker's face was one of concentration as he continued to ready Ranger's body for his possession. "You know," Ryker said, "it will be easier on both of us if you got on all fours."

Ranger thought about it for a split second before shaking his head. "I want to look at you, please," he pleaded.

With a hand to his cheek, Ryker nodded. "Any way you want, love."

Lining up his sheathed cock, Ryker took an extra second to apply more lube around Ranger's hole. "Just breathe and let me in," Ryker whispered.

The initial stretch of his outer muscles took Ranger's breath, the burning pinch of pain causing sweat to break out on his forehead. Trying to ease the process, Lilly began kissing his neck as she wrapped her fingers around his burgeoning erection. "It's okay, breathe, baby," she continually crooned in his ear.

Ranger looked down to where Ryker's body was joining with his. It was finally happening. Meeting Ryker's eyes, he saw the worry and the love his brother felt. With a deep breath, Ranger's body automatically bore down allowing Ryker's cock to slowly slide in to the hilt. Once totally inside him, they both felt it, the connection that they'd both longed for. It was evident in Ryker's face that he wasn't alone in his feeling of euphoria.

Ranger felt tears drip down the sides of his face only to be quickly licked away by Lilly. "Love you," he silently mouthed to Ryker. The moment was too perfect to break the silence with words. He felt his body lighten and relax as Ryker began a slow slide out, only to push back in again.

"More," he moaned a few minutes later as both Ryker and Lilly picked up their pace. The feel of Ryker's heavy sac slapping against his sensitized skin on every thrust, had him out of his head with pleasure in no time.

Lilly's hand around his cock slid back and forth as she continued to whisper in his ear. She spoke of how much he was loved and how right this was. Ranger knew he only caught about half of what she was saying, his climax building to a level that had a roar sounding in his ears. "Close," he grunted, as Ryker changed angles just enough to peg his gland on every thrust.

"Bub..." he howled as he came, jets of fluid coating his own chest as well as Lilly's hand. His mind took flight, lost in a sea of colours as his body continued to tremble with the last of his orgasm.

When he opened his eyes again it was to see Ryker looking down at him, while continuing to piston his hips, driving his cock again and again into Ranger's body. He could tell Ryker had waited for him to come down from his climax before slipping over the edge himself. After two more hard thrusts, Ryker yelled his name and buried himself as deep as possible. Ranger would swear he felt the force of Ryker's cum even though securely encased within the condom.

He pulled Ryker's sweaty body down on top of him and tilted his chin up for a kiss. Even the feel of Ryker's tongue tangled with his seemed different now, deeper, closer. Breaking the kiss, Ranger pulled Lilly in for a kiss which soon evolved into a three way mating of mouths.

No words were needed between him and Ryker about what they'd experienced, they both knew. Ryker finally pulled back and smiled. "Sorry to interrupt this Lovefest, but I need to go take care of something." He reached down and held onto the condom as he slipped from Ranger's body.

He watched him disappear into the bathroom as he continued to stroke the soft skin of Lilly's lower back. "It's been one hell of a night." Suddenly remembering everything Lilly had been through, he felt ashamed. "Are you sure you're okay?"

"I'm more than okay, I'm feeling fabulous." Her face became serious and she kissed his chin. "Jeff can't touch me, not where it matters. My heart is so full it can't be tainted by what anyone else says or does. I have you and Ryker to thank for that."

Before he could say anything, Ryker was standing over him with a warm washcloth. He tenderly cleaned Lilly's hand and his stomach before moving down to clean his tender ass. Ryker tossed the rag and climbed back into bed.

Pulling the covers up around them, Ryker yawned. "Let's take a little power nap."

It had been a long hard day on all of them and the bliss of sleep overtook them in minutes.

* * * *

The alarm woke them the next morning. Ranger reached over and slapped at the clock until it finally shut off. He looked at the two people in his arms and smiled. He couldn't believe they were all still in the same position. They must've been dead to the world all night long.

Without opening his eyes, Ryker grumbled, "How long before we have to get up?"

"Well, eventually we're going to have to get up for food and water, but I don't see that happening for several hours."

That had Ryker's head popping up off his chest. "What? We're playing hooky?"

"Yep. I've got a woman to make love to this morning and I have a feeling I won't be satisfied with just one round." Ranger grinned as Lilly perked up.

"Cool," she said with a grin.

Ryker released his hold on Ranger to retrieve a condom from the floor where'd they dropped it the previous night. As Ryker handed it to him he got the cutest little boy grin on his face. "Can I ride when Lilly's done?"

Ranger smacked him on the ass with one hand as he took the foil packet with the other. "I'm not a damn horse."

Laughing, Ryker looked down at Ranger's hard shaft. "I'm not so sure."

Shaking his head, Ranger rolled the condom on before he stretched out over Lilly. Starting with her lips he licked and teased his way to her swollen nipples. Latching on, Ranger suckled as he reached out and pulled Ryker against them. He glanced up and released the nipple to join the twosome in a three-way kiss. "You love these beautiful breasts while I explore."

Nodding, Ryker broke the kiss and replaced Ranger's mouth on the still wet nipple. Hearing Lilly's moan, Ranger moved down between her legs. He ran his tongue over the soft, hairless lips before parting them with his fingers. Now open to his gaze and mouth, Ranger licked his lips. So perfect, every inch of Lilly was like an artist's rendition of the perfect woman.

With temptation this close, it didn't take him long to stop admiring and start loving. He ran his tongue around the delicate fleshy folds of her pussy, grunting when a drop of cream dripped down the crack of her ass. Not wanting anything to go to waste, Ranger ran his tongue up the tight crevice catching the river of essence now streaming towards his open mouth. With a lick up to her clit he took the tiny swollen bundle of nerves between his teeth and bit down enough to drive Lilly crazy. Her hips bucked towards his face as she begged him to fuck her.

"Please," she moaned.

With one last pull to the sensitive clit, he worked his way back up her body. Using his upper body strength, he pushed up over Ryker's head to kiss her. "I love you," he said, sinking into her hot depths. The tightening of her inner muscles squeezed his cock like a vice. "Damn you feel good."

Ryker popped off her nipple and looked at Ranger. "Told ya," he chuckled, moving his head out of Ranger's way. Ranger saw him reach for the tube of lube and squirt some in his hand. He knew exactly what Ryker had planned.

Hooking Lilly's legs over his shoulders, Ranger picked up his rhythm. The harder he pounded into her, the more Lilly begged for it. He felt Ryker's hand brush his sac as he rimmed Lilly's ass with his lubricated fingers.

"Like that?" Ryker asked Lilly after inserting a finger.

Ranger could've told Ryker how much Lilly enjoyed it just by the tight squeeze on his cock at the insertion.

"In me," Lilly yelled. "Please."

Ryker looked at Ranger. "How do you want to do this?"

"Me on bottom," Ranger said as Ryker removed his fingers. Without losing contact, Ranger flipped them so Lilly was now riding him. He pulled her head down for a kiss which left her ass at the perfect level for Ryker.

"You sure you're ready for this, sweetheart?"

"Yessss," she hissed as Ryker's latex-covered cock inched its way inside.

Ranger stilled his movements until Ryker was fully seated. "Tell us when you're ready, sweetheart."

"Kiss me and then move," she said, kissing him passionately.

She seemed to be setting a rhythm with her tongue that Ranger decided to follow. As he thrust into her, he felt the slide of Ryker's cock through the thin membrane. "Oh fuck," he cried, breaking the kiss. He looked up at Ryker. "I can feel you."

"Uh huh," Ryker grunted trying to match his rhythm.

Lilly's nails dug into his chest as she rocked back and forth between them. "Yes," she screamed throwing back her head as she came.

The continued friction against his cock from Ryker, combined with Lilly's tight heat had him growling his release next. He watched Ryker through spotted vision as he buried himself and shook with the force of his orgasm.

Pulling both of them down, Ranger attacked their mouths and necks with his teeth and tongue. His world was at peace for the first time in his life and he would allow no one to tear them apart.

Epilogue

Two Years Later

Answering the knock at the door, Lilly smiled and stepped back. "It's about time you got here," she scolded, as Garron grabbed her up in a hug, Sonny spinning her around to hug her next.

"Sorry, we had to wait for Mr. Mayor to get off the phone," Garron said, looking over his shoulder at Rawley.

"Hey, you could've driven separately. It's not like you were chained to my truck." Rawley nudged Sonny out of the way to place a kiss on Lilly's cheek. "How does it feel to no longer be a newlywed?" Rawley asked, holding up a decorated bottle of bubbly.

"With those two men? I'll always feel like a newlywed." She grinned. Lilly thought back to her wedding with Ryker a year ago and then the ceremony directly after where she committed herself to Ranger in front of their friends and family.

"Speaking of...where are they?"

"In the barn, feeding the horses," Lilly winked. "I think they just wanted to get out of party preparations."

"Sounds like them." Rawley handed her the bottle of champagne and headed towards the back door.

Jeb swept her up in a big hug. "So, please tell me you're making ice cream?"

Lilly kissed Jeb on the cheek. "Don't I always. I know it's your favourite."

"Well," Sonny said, "if we're going to be fair, I like it as much as he does."

Lilly held up her hands and walked towards the kitchen. "Sorry, fellas, you'll have to fight that one out on your own. I have enough trouble refereeing two men, I'm not about to start with you two."

"Spoilsport," Sonny said, sticking his tongue out.

* * * *

Ranger and Ryker were both sitting on the floor of the barn, playing with the new puppy they'd gotten for Lilly. "Ow," Ranger cried when the dog's tiny white teeth sank into his finger.

"What the hell's going on in here?" Rawley asked, coming into the barn.

"He bit me," Ranger said in return.

Rawley put his hands on his hips and looked down at Ryker. "Didn't your momma teach you better than that?" He asked with a laugh.

"Ha ha, very funny," Ryker grinned and held up the puppy. "This little guy has good taste in chew toys."

Bending down, Rawley scooped up the puppy. "Lilly know about this?"

"No," Ranger narrowed his eyes, "and don't you go spoiling the surprise. We're going to give this little guy to her in the morning." Ranger grinned and looked at Ryker. "We're both in agreement that if we give it to her tonight, she'll insist on having it in bed with us. And Ryker and I have too many plans for that."

Rawley held the puppy in the crook of his arm and rubbed its tiny belly. "Hi, little guy. I'm going to be your favourite Uncle." Rawley lifted the chubby puppy and rubbed noses with it.

Ryker hooked an arm around Ranger's waist and rolled his eyes. Who'd have thought the biggest, toughest member of the Good family would have the biggest soft spot for dogs. "How ya doin'?" he asked thumping Rawley on the back.

"Okay, don't seem to have enough time in the day, but I'm happy."

"How could you? Working as part-time Sheriff while running the Mayor's office."

"Well if Garron would stop being an ass and take over as Sheriff, I wouldn't have to do two jobs." Rawley continued to scratch the puppy behind the ears.

"He might be more inclined to consider it if you didn't make him cut his hair." Ryker took the dog from Rawley and put him back in the kennel before leading the group towards the back deck.

"Sorry, but you can't have a small-town Sheriff with long hair, it's just un-American."

Ryker stopped and turned around. "Seems to me you're holding a few prejudices you need to let go of."

That had Rawley spitting and sputtering just like Ryker knew it would. Ryker used the opportunity to climb the deck steps. "Where's my wife?" he asked looking around.

"She's in the kitchen showing Jeb how to mix up homemade ice cream." Sonny said, from atop Garron's lap. "She looks good by the way. I was worried about how she'd hold up with Jeff's trial, but she's come through it just fine."

"Yep," Ranger said, wrapping his arms around Ryker. Ryker leaned back against the solid wall of muscle. Two years ago they would have never shown this type of affection around people, even their family, but everything was different now.

"We'll see in another couple of years how she does. I imagine Jeff will get out on parole by then," Ranger said, squeezing him tight.

"Well, even if he does get out early, he'd be a damn fool to come back here with a Sheriff like Garron in charge." Rawley looked at Ryker and winked.

"Dammit, I told you, I'm not cutting my hair," Garron fumed.

"Well I've been thinking about that, we may be able to negotiate the hair thing."

Chuckling, Ryker pulled Ranger towards the kitchen as soon as he saw Jeb come out the door. Spotting Lilly washing a few dishes, they both pressed against her. "Forget the dishes, it's a party."

Lilly turned and gave them each a kiss. "If I don't wash them now, I'll have to stay up late after everyone leaves and we won't have time to celebrate before we all fall asleep. I was hoping we could take a ride out to the pond. I have a Lady Godiva impression I want to do for you both," she said, blowing them kisses.

Ranger poked Ryker in the stomach. "Pass me a dishtowel, brother."

About the Author

An avid reader for years, one day Carol Lynne decided to write her own brand of erotic romance. Carol juggles between being a full-time mother and a full-time writer. These days, you can usually find Carol either cleaning jelly out of the carpet or nestled in her favourite chair writing steamy love scenes.

Carol loves to hear from readers. You can find her contact information, website details and author profile page at http://www.total-e-bound.com

Total-E-Bound Publishing

www.total-e-bound.com

Take a look at our exciting range of literagasmic™
erotic romance titles and discover pure quality
at Total-E-Bound.

2957489

Made in the USA